COMPOSING LANEY

THE SWEET VALLEY SERIES

BOOK THREE

S.E. REICHERT

5 PRINCE PUBLISHING

Published by 5 PRINCE PUBLISHING & BOOKS, LLC

PO Box 865, Arvada, CO 80001

www.5PrinceBooks.com

ISBN digital: 978-1-63112–344-3

ISBN print: 978-1-63112-345-0

Cover Credit: Marianne Nowicki

F10132023

Writing this series has been, in the words of Gran, a long and winding set of tracks. The place where I grew up, the small town that raised me, and the wild and open space that I was blessed to have been born into, shaped who I am. A lot can be said about rural communities, and just like any dynamic, both positive and negative ideals can exist in them. I hope it is always the kindness, community, and selflessness that wins the day. Thanks Wyoming, you big, beautiful, ruggedly independent conundrum.

A huge thank you to my family, my daughters and husband. Their support and love mean the world to me, and I couldn't have the space and time to do what I do without their help.

Acknowledgments

Thanks to Writing Heights Writers Association and your supportive and inspiring members. You are the resource that made me a better writer and gave me the courage, confidence and skill to make it this far.

To Rebecca Cuthbert, my favorite writing buddy and soon to be NYT bestselling writer. You've encouraged me through some of the darkest nights of my soul. You are bright and funny and patient, and not at all like the agent I gave your name to. I wouldn't be able to do this writing thing, or this living thing, without you on my side.

To my beta readers, Misty, Kristine, Heather, Lucinda, Jean, Heidi, and Jessie; thank you for taking the time to read and give me feedback. You make a better book and you help make me a better writer.

To Lauren Newman-Lipp, who has encouraged my folly, uplifted my self-worth, and supported me through many hard times. Your enthusiasm for my work makes me want to keep writing steamy, wonderful stuff. Someday when I'm rich and famous I'll treat you to a live Denis Morton ride. Pinkie promise.

Thank you to the fantastic team at 5 Prince Publishing. To Bernadette Soehner who has given me warmth, laughter, opportunities and encouragement since the first day I met her. To Cate Byers who takes my rough work and makes it so much better, with a level of talent and kindness that is unparalleled. I am so grateful for your support and help.

I'm sure he'll never read this, but thanks Kenny Chesney.

To Jamie Blaha, now you're kinda, semi-famous.

To Jeremy Williams—your middle name, did in fact, end up in a book.

To all my readers, thanks for continually picking up these books. Thank you for sticking with the characters and for believing in their happily ever afters. May we all find a little of the same for ourselves.

ALSO BY S.E. REICHERT

Composing Laney

ONE

IT WASN'T SO MUCH THAT HER PIECE-OF-SHIT CAR WAS stalled out again, or that it gave its last death rattle in the middle of the busy intersection. It wasn't that it was snowing heavily with twenty-mile-an-hour winds gusting up the back of her shirt because she'd given her coat to a forgetful daughter before school. It wasn't the blinding white and freezing cold while she tried pushing the car out of the way. It wasn't the muffled honks and flashing headlights from impatient drivers behind her. It wasn't that her socks were wet or that she'd finalized her divorce the week before. It wasn't that she couldn't afford repairs, and certainly not a new car. It wasn't that her next book was two weeks overdue, or that she had no ideas for how to begin it. It wasn't the million and one reasons that would justify her just laying down in the middle of the road and trusting that the conditions and college-student drivers would take care of her misery.

It was that she was tired.

Tired of doing it alone. Tired of slogging through the muck of life, while trying to paint beautiful landscapes on the page for other people to daydream about.

"Jesus Christ," she grunted as her boot slipped and she fell to her knee in the dirty slush, "a little help?" She looked skyward and gave the car a useless and final shove before falling to her ass in the cold and wet street. Flinging two unapologetic fingers up at the sky she shouted, "You're an asshole!"

"Uh—ma'am?"

Laney looked past her wet hair, now plastered to her face, to the young officer standing beside the car door.

"What seems to be the problem, officer? Was I speeding?" she said morosely.

Then—as the icy slush melted into her shirt and through to her skin, she laughed wholeheartedly, unable to contain the crying hoots that wracked her body. The officer offered her his hand.

"You really shouldn't talk to God that way." He cleared his throat.

"Ah, young man, God and I have a special kind of relationship. She knows I'm a disastrous example and I know she's a cosmically heinous bitch. It's a mutual distrust kind of thing." She groaned as she got to her feet.

"Uh," the officer stammered as snow fell into his confused face.

"Never mind. Let's see if we can get this piece of sh—" The officer cleared his throat, and Laney scowled. "Metal off the road."

Just a typical glamorous start to another glamorous day in the life of a divorced and bitter, soon-to-be-washed-up romance novelist, Laney thought as she waited beside the road for a tow truck and dialed Marc, her best and nearest friend.

"I don't want to hear any 'I told you so's," she said.

"Fine, because I'm your friend, I won't. But, because I'm also a bitch who tells it like it is, you should have gotten rid of that piece of crap car three years ago."

"Right? While I was still married and I could have infidelity-guilted him into a fancy little sports car—oh wait. That's right, he had already spent most of our money on her by that time."

"I'll come get you," Marc sighed. "Which intersection?"

"Uh, Grand and Fifteenth."

"My word, Laney! How are you still alive?"

"I don't know. I've been trying for weeks. Nothing's working."
Marc rolled his eyes so hard Laney could see it from across town.

"I'll be there in five. Do you need anything else?"

"Dry underwear?"

"I'm not even gonna ask," he sighed.

"Thanks, Marc." Laney leaned into the phone with delicate
humility.

"No problem, funny face, I'll see you soon," he said and
hung up.

Laney waited and thought about school getting out in a week.
She thought of her ex, David, taking her kids to France with his
new girlfriend over the holidays. She could have kept them from
going, just to spite him, but she didn't want to hurt her kids by
taking away their opportunity to see the world beyond the square
borders of their state. She didn't know what she'd do with herself
for a month without them. She could go back home to Sweet
Valley. Be with her family, hang out in the small downtown and
ache for a better cup of coffee. Wallow in misery and drag down
the rest of her family in the process. She thought of her sisters'
newfound happiness. Elle, who'd suffered an abusive marriage and
escaped to come home and find herself and her strength again.
Katelyn, who'd fallen in love last summer with a man in need of a
new start himself. They were all still glowing with the light of new
love. Laney's stomach turned. She couldn't imagine being happy
for them, presently.

"Be an asshole to yourself, but don't be an asshole to the few
people left who love you," she grumbled and resolved to stay in
Laramie, in her small apartment, and finish her damn book. At
least maybe then she could afford the payment on a new car. Marc
pulled up, in the middle of her resolution, and she smiled at him
before making a gun with her finger. She pointed it at the car,
pulled the trigger and then pointed her finger at her own temple.

"Don't be dramatic, nobody makes a death pact with an Isuzu.

Get in," he said as he opened her door. Laney nodded in agreement and slid into the seat. Marc had had the foresight to put a towel down.

"Lord, Pigpen, what the actual fuck happened to you?" Marc asked.

"Darling, it's been a rough day."

"Daaaarling," he corrected, "it's been a rough year."

"Or ten."

"You need a break, Laney. A bonafide vacation."

"Uh, okay? Shall I just, camp out in front of the Loaf 'N Jug for a month? Because that's about where the budget stands."

"Let me consider our options. You just sit back and relax. And by sit back I mean try not to touch anything."

"Okay." She scowled and folded her arms across her chest as they rambled to her small apartment, close to campus.

Two

The statuesque woman came straight off the beach. The glistening, crystalline sand still speckled her blonde locks and the Caribbean breezes tousled them into golden waves around her face.

Luke had been away for most of the season. He spent summers racing in the French Riviera, and wintered in the islands. The patrons of his favorite beach-side club were ever-changing. But she shone, brilliant and angelic, among them in the early evening light. The wispy linen wrap dipped low to reveal the Brazilian bikini and a hard, young body beneath. His fingers trailed down the glass of beer sweating in the heat. His eyes drank her in as she strode up to the bar, woven satchel in one hand and sunglasses in the other. He had to meet her. He couldn't not...Why not...why did he have to meet her?

Because of her stupid hot body? Or her obviously stunning personality... because he needs another object to own? ...

"SHIT." LANEY TORE THE PAGE OUT, CRUMPLED IT ferociously, and sent it across the room into the pile of its fallen brethren. The unforgiving pad of paper sat, wordless again, angry pointed lines, and empty... so empty. Her brain was a massive jumble of words and thoughts that wouldn't fall into place. She let out a frustrated growl and pulled at her dark blonde hair. Dirty dishwater blonde, they called it. Not stunning platinum or honey gold.

Dirty. Dishwater. Everything about Laney was a shade plainer than the rest of the world, especially the worlds she built on the page. She closed her eyes and thought about the book she'd already gotten an advance on, and how it faltered at every step. When she tried to pep talk herself, it only got worse.

"This is bullshit. Hard young body? Who the hell has that? And what in the hell do I know about the French Riviera? What in the hell do I know about any of it anymore?" She spun in angry half arcs in the old office chair as she looked out of the window.

Snow had started. Fresh white stuff to cover the graying brown and speckled layer. The wind blew it around, dry as sand and pelting. Eight weeks into the heart of winter in southern Wyoming felt like six months. She sat dazed, her brain fogged over with the numbness of a life half-lived. She tried to picture a different world. A brighter, more romantic place, with brighter, more romantic people, but the same picture she'd been staring at, day after day, remained. She couldn't escape into her mind, because it had become just as barren as the landscape outside.

She only had an hour until her last class of the semester. She looked back down to the page and tried to refocus. But the truth was staring at her undeniably in those blank lines.

She had nowhere to go.

She was dead-ended in her life and in her writing. With only three books out and the deadline at her door for a new series, she was floundering, empty, and lost. The everyday stresses of being a single mom and working two jobs to make ends meet while her family back home struggled, keeping up with a ranch that was in peril every season from being bought out by encroaching conglomerate ranches, had worn her to the bone.

Laney sighed and knocked her forehead against the desk.

"Cursing at your imaginary friends and committing self-harm? What are you? One of those after-school specials on mental illness?" Marc's voice broke through the stillness. Laney kept her head down on the desk in pathetic surrender.

"Yes," she sighed. "I'm the poster child for 'don't let this happen to you, get a good engineering job'." Her mumbled words drew the large, goateed man inside with what she could only guess was an eye-rolling head shake.

"Girl, you're going to knock yourself unconscious."

"I'm all right with that," she mumbled into the worn wood.

"Laney!" Marc yelled, and she sat up and looked at him like a child in the throes of a tantrum.

"What?" she grouched.

"About that vacation we were discussing—"

"Even if I had the money, honey, I don't have time. The deadline is in four weeks. And plus, where would I go? The mountain and interstate are both snowed out. One sister is building up her therapy business, one is busy making biscuits for half the Rocky Mountain region. Plus, and this is the truth of the matter, there's no place I can go where I'll actually be a better writer." She barely breathed as she continued. "Marc, my friend, you are witnessing the death throes of my short-lived career. I've no romance left in me. I don't even think I believe in romance." She slumped back into her chair. Marc crossed his arms.

"God, you're dramatic. Honestly, I don't remember your first books being so wordy," he laughed. "You just need a change of perspective. You need to *rediscover the romance*." Laney snorted unattractively and threw her head back.

"Um ... let's just file that under 'not a damn chance'. Have you seen me lately? I'm Plain Lane, remember? I'm un-romanceable." Marc leaned against the doorjamb and sighed.

"Oh, God, not Plain Lane. You can't fall back on your high school nickname every time you want to justify the shitty way your ex treated you. That had nothing to do with you—he was just a bonafide douche."

"Well, I won't argue with that," she whispered. Marc stared past her, out the window, looking across the street to the south side of the campus.

"Alan and I have to visit his parents in Florida over the break." He said it like a man naming the date of his own execution.

"I'm sorry?" Laney said.

"Which means we won't get to use our cottage in St. Croix like we had hoped."

"Oh, poor you?" She frowned up at him and he returned it with a smile.

"Aren't the girls going with their loser dad all month?"

"Yeah, so?" Laney stopped and stared out the window while an invisible fist clenched her heart and she swallowed down the pressure it caused.

"So?" he led.

"So?" she retorted angrily. "What? Am I supposed to talk more about that?" Marc made an impatient sound in his throat and rolled his eyes skyward.

"So, you should take the cottage on St. Croix."

Laney looked up at him as if he'd grown another head. "What? Me?"

"Uh, do you see another starving writer with a deadline in this office?" Laney looked over her shoulder and then stared down at her baggy sweater and tattered jeans.

"Marc, I don't think that—"

"For the gods' sakes don't think," Marc slapped her shoulder. "The cottage means four weeks of uninterrupted, inspirational time."

She stared at him blankly. "Marc, I can't do that."

"Yes, you can."

"Of course I can't!"

"Because?" he led. Laney stopped to think about what he was saying. When had she last taken a vacation? She'd gone to Colorado to promote her last book for a couple of days, but with both of the kids, she'd been on mommy-duty the whole time. She hadn't traveled alone in twelve years. She shuddered with an introverted calamity of fear.

"But I don't even have a bathing suit."

"So, get one. In fact, let's go shopping Thursday, after you throw some more paper around and call your characters worthless pieces of shit." Laney sputtered, but he interrupted. "And," he said in a hushed voice while looking over his thick-rimmed glasses at her, "you'll need to get waxed too. I'm sure that's long overdue."

She scowled at him. "I beg your pardon?"

"Don't feign offense, you know what I'm talking about. Probably looks like you got a tumbleweed in a headlock down there."

Laney tried not to laugh. "Marc, no way."

"Laney, yes way!"

Laney growled under her breath as he whistled his way out of her office and across the hall to his own. Later, while she finished up a short outline and gathered up her papers for class, she tried to decide how she would graciously decline. Perhaps she could fake a kidney stone. He yelled across the hall as if sensing her gathering excuses.

"Friday flight okay?"

"Fine?" The word slipped out between her lips in an exhausted sigh. She wound her hair into a bun and secured it with a teeth-marked pencil as she made a quick jaunt to his office. She peeked in. He sat in the sleek, modern furnished space, severely contrasting the old, worn, hand-me-down relics she'd scraped together. She felt like she was infecting his clean lines with her frump.

"Uh, Friday is only three days away."

"Yep."

"That's too soon. I mean, isn't it? Sudden?"

Marc looked up from typing. "Sudden? Laney? At our age we have to take all the sudden we can get." He looked back to his computer screen with a smile. She sighed and slumped against his door.

"You are going to let me pay you, right?"

He didn't look up. "No."

"Marc, really."

"Pay me back by writing a glowing dedication to me in your next masterpiece."

"Masterpiece? Really? Have you seen my numbers? You'll never get paid back." She smirked and kicked a wayward ball of yellow paper back into her office.

"I think you are going to surprise yourself. And don't underestimate how much women will pay for a good romance."

"Lies," she argued.

Laney's phone called her back before she could argue. It was David. He and Tasha would pick up the kids Thursday afternoon from school. She remained calm and light-toned, all the while her heart fizzled and faded in her chest. David hung up, satisfied long before she was. Such was the story of their relationship. She roused herself enough to get out the door and into the cold wind.

Four weeks without them. Four weeks that would either be spent snowed into the small town, or off in some exotic locale. The choice shouldn't have been difficult to make, but she wasn't a person who readily left her cozy comfort zone. The trek across the street gave her a few moments of alone time to think. She stopped in the main library and reached for the well-worn phone book, just to spite the tech-savvy student behind the desk. It was archaic, but she liked the weight of it and the particular smell of the newsprint-thin paper. Her short nail skimmed down the left side column.

The Screaming Peach. For all your waxing needs.

Well, if anyone needed a change, she smirked, it was her. And if she had to be alone, it might as well be some place different.

THREE

JAMESON CLARK WAS DRUNK AGAIN. THE REVELERS around him moved through a hazy fog that threatened at the edges of his consciousness, promising a hangover tomorrow. He watched the beautiful women laugh, swaying their long legs and narrow hips to Lynyrd Skynyrd while their drinks sloshed over and splattered on the concrete edge of his pool. Hell, he didn't even know ten of the hundred that were at this party.

He stood up in a spinning world and staggered, unnoticed, off the deck and down the private walkway. When he'd gotten far enough, his bare feet pressed into the sand and the music was only a distant wave behind him, he plopped down. His hand still clung to the half-empty bottle of rum. He crossed his arms over his knees and stared out into the horizon. His eyes were heavy, but he knew what he'd see if he closed them. He did it anyway.

There was Dad. Steel worker, blue collar, and beaming with pride. A pride that fell from his face when his one and only son started trashing tour buses and hotel rooms. When the music became a money-making machine, cranked out yearly for the hungry crowd of beach cowboys and bikini-clad country girls. His dad's eyes crinkled just like his own, when he smiled or squinted into the hard truth of something he didn't like.

Jamie's head pounded. What he'd give to have his dad look at him again. What he'd give up to take back the cutting words and their last devastating fight. He took a long pull, straight from the bottle. He couldn't even remember the last song he'd written himself. Hell, it had been three years since the last album; the last tour. He didn't want to remember the last time he'd sang.

The cool, coastal breeze blew past his face, and he sat up to inhale. Something strange filtered through his senses, something cold and fresh. He opened one eye and, even in his drunken state, could tell that the wind had shifted from the north. His father's words echoed in his mind. He was a man without direction. A boat out to sea.

What he wouldn't give to walk off this beach, and into obscurity. To change his name and disappear. He'd spent the better part of the last twenty-five years beneath the stage lights, the noise of crowds thrumming to music that he wasn't even sure he believed in anymore. A boat out to sea, indeed. He was a lost man. His father's last words came back to him with harsh and piercing clarity, and he drank until the bottle fell into the sand, shortly followed by his body.

Clothing haphazardly spilled from all sides of the open suitcase with no discernable order. Laney hobbled around the room, and angrily tossed in an array of clothes, as if she'd never actually been on vacation. The delicate skin of her bikini line might never be the same. Who knew so much hair could grow in such a small space? Other women did things like this all the time, but even as the oldest of three girls, she'd never been caught up in typical standards of beauty. She had always been a t-shirt and jeans girl.

Marc had specifically forbidden her from wearing t-shirts and jeans on the island. When they'd gone shopping, she'd protested, especially when he'd bought over half of the purchases.

"You can't—"

"Think of it as my holiday contribution to charity." He chuckled and held a bikini up to her sweatshirt.

"Oh, so now I'm a charity case?"

"Oh, darling, don't think of it like that. You're more like my own personal Make-a-Wish kid."

"What if my wish is to stay in sweatpants for the rest of my life and die alone surrounded by Twinkie wrappers and ten cats?"

"Don't slouch, go try this on." Marc refused to be baited.

Laney looked through her new collection of clothes. She had to admit, Marc had made it fun. They'd even met up with his husband afterwards, and he'd let Laney buy them dinner. She'd ended up with flowy and light sundresses, and tank-tops that hugged her curves rather than hid them. Marc had even thrown in a pair of cut-off jean shorts.

But then came her appointment at the waxing studio, and the fun stopped.

Her hand gripped her phone while she steadied herself on the bedframe. The line clicked as he answered.

"Marc. Did you know they go all the way up the crack of your—"

"Yes."

"And you couldn't have maybe warned me about that?"

"Why don't you cry me a river? Beauty is pain."

"Why does it matter if I don't wear a bathing suit!"

"You'd better wear those bathing suits, Laney Sullivan! It's an island!" he yelled. "Besides, you've got that cute heart-shape bottom, and I hear that's what guys are into."

"Like you would even know! What was I thinking?" she seethed and adjusted her underwear, but nothing brought comfort. "Who's going to see a hair-do down there anyway?" she snapped.

"Well, we must prepare as if someone might," he prayed resolutely. Laney snorted. "It's time to dust it off and put it out there."

"Well, at least it will make a well-groomed, cobweb-free entrance now," she snickered.

"Please bring that laugh with you," he said softly. "You're so beautiful, Laney, so deserving and I—I hope you have a fabulous time. Take lots of pictures so I can continue to be jealous long after you're back." He sniffed. Laney's heart grew two sizes. How lucky was she to have such a dear and true friend?

"Thanks," she said quietly. "Thanks, Marc. Even if I get malaria or become a drug mule for some cocaine cartel. Thanks for trying."

Marc's bursting laugh made her smile.

"You're so creative!" He snapped his fingers. "Maybe you should try and write a book."

"Ha ha," she said. "I should wish you a merry Christmas before I go. You know, in case I'm the first person to ever be eaten by a whale shark."

"You're not going to die!"

"You know I love you."

"Back at you, funny face. Now, go pack. And none of your ugly sweaters. I know that you have cute things, now wear them." He hung up.

Laney dialed David again, left another message with her departure time, arrival time, and the phone number of the cottage in case there wasn't cell service. He'd been shocked when she'd told him earlier that day about the spur-of-the-moment trip to St. Croix.

"Really?" he'd said, as if she'd just told him she was going to join the Russian circus and live like a gypsy. "Are you sure, Laney? You hate the ocean."

"I don't hate the ocean."

"You're scared to death of it." he laughed. Anger rose in her chest and she straightened her spine.

"I am not! There's a lot that doesn't scare me anymore." She'd hung up on him, and now he wasn't answering her calls. They probably were in-flight anyway. She'd try again when it was morning there. She tossed herself on the bed with a deflated sigh. What in the hell was she thinking?

The phone rang in answer.

"Laney June Sullivan," came her mother's stern voice and all three names.

"Mom."

"Is it true? Dad said you were going off to some island in the middle of nowhere by yourself. Is that safe? I mean do you really think that's wise in your state?"

"My what? What state am I—" Laney began, but her mother was already plodding ahead.

"Crime sprees, unchecked police, drug cartels, all that pot—" her mom went on while something sparked in Laney's chest. Like a kid taking off their helmet in the hot summer sun and continuing, free to the wind and the road. "You've never been anywhere on your own like that! What if you get mixed up with bad people?"

"I'm nearly forty, Mom!"

"Exactly my point. You've never done anything like this before."

"Yeah, Mom. I'm going on a four-week *bender*. I have a ten-thirty appointment with the head of the drug cartel and we're going to smoke a lot of pot and then I'll probably sleep with every drunk stranger I can find below the twenty-fifth parallel."

"Please be serious. I just don't want you to start living dangerously."

Laney threw her hand over her eyes and snorted.

"And don't snort at me. I'm just worried. Maybe this isn't the best time. I know the divorce was just finalized and you're probably dealing with a lot of emotions. I've never known you to do something like this. I think you may be depressed." Laney thought about her mom's words. That she was predictable was a given; depressed, a very real possibility. She didn't know what to say. "I'm just worried," her mom reiterated.

"I know," Laney sighed. An uncharacteristic silence sat on the other end and Laney thought about her own daughters. She'd never stop worrying about them either.

"I know this has been a strange few years, and sometimes, when everybody in the family is going through things I forget to check in on you, because you're always so strong and handle things. I should check in on you more too."

"Mom," Laney halted the guilt trip before it was fully formed. "You're a good momma hen. I'll be fine. Thank you for being concerned. I just need 'me' time."

"Well, all right," Melissa sighed in a resigned way that meant she knew she wasn't going to get through to her headstrong daughter. "Your father says to enjoy yourself. He says the fishing is supposed to be great down—oh, for Heaven's sakes, Warren, she's not going fishing!"

"Love you guys. I'll call you when I get settled."

"All right. Be careful. We can wire you money if you get stuck in one of those horrible prisons—"

"And now I know where I get it from," Laney whispered.

"What's that?"

"Nothing, it's nothing. I love you, Mom."

She hung up and peeled herself off the bed and tumbled, clumsily along the short hall and into the kitchen. A glass of wine was just the thing to work up the nerve to pack the skimpy swimsuits, short shorts, and sundresses that Marc had insisted she 'rocked.' Four weeks. She didn't have enough clothes for four weeks. Maybe she wouldn't need clothes for the whole trip—

Her skin flushed, she snorted loudly in veiled hope before throwing in the bright blue bikini.

To hell with it. Her mother was right. She didn't do things like this. She was the stable one. No one knew her down there. She could storm in, live as she pleased, dangerously or hermit-like, and leave without further ado.

Though she had published a few books, a dozen articles, done a few signings, and gotten a couple of interviews, she was far from recognizable. The limited fame of a writer was nothing like the fame of actors or musicians. Books were something people had to take an intimate interest in. It couldn't be passively absorbed over streaming music services in rush hour traffic, or played over and over in preview. So, there'd be very little fear of anyone even knowing who she was.

She could be anyone there. Maybe she could take a break from the single mom, divorced and weighed down with guilt part of herself. Maybe she could just be Laney. She repacked neatly and made sure she had her running gear and some comfy sweats, despite Marc's advice. If she was holed up in the cottage, there was no point in 'rocking' anything uncomfortable. Before closing the lid, she picked up her grandfather's old compass, which had been her college graduation gift, from the nightstand and threw it in.

She called and left a message for her girls. She told them she missed them, and wished them a good night and a safe trip. She gave them all of her undying love, told them to have fun and enjoy their trip.

She would try to do the same.

FOUR

JAMIE WOKE UP WHEN THE TIDE REACHED HIS FACE. HE sat up sputtering and gasping for breath in the new dawn. The bottle beside him had washed out ten feet, and he stared at it with confused anger before wading out to catch it and bring it back to shore. When he fell back to face the open blue of the sky, the water rushed into his shorts and up his shirt.

"Jamie?" he heard a gravelly voice from above ask. He opened one eye and turned his head to see a tall, bearded man walking up the beach towards him. "What are you doing out here, man?"

"Dyin'," Jamie responded, half joking, and half not. "When'd the sun get so bright?" Brody laughed and offered him a hand.

"Somewhere between the Cuervo and the Cruzan, I imagine. Hell of a party!"

"Was it?" Jamie scowled. He sat up and tried to wipe the sand from his lips. "I can't seem to remember it being much different from the one before."

Brody gave him a quizzical look. "Come on. Let's get you a hot shower and some coffee."

Jamie didn't budge. He stared out at the ocean while something tickled his memory. He'd been dreaming when that water hit him. Dreaming of somebody. Somebody far from this twisted road of purposeful forgetting that he was driving himself down.

"No," he said lowly. "What am I doing, Brody?"

Brody only stared back in response. "I don't know what you mean."

"Never mind." Jamie shook his aching head and sighed. "Doesn't matter." He lifted the dead weight of his legs through the sand and up towards the house.

Laramie's airport was a three-runway pit-stop in the wide-open space between town and the Snowy Range. Deep rolling hills to the west undulated until they met with the high plains forest and granite peaks some 12,000 feet up. The open prairie was framed with the blue mountains beyond. Laney tried to focus on the view instead of the old, haggard blue and gray Beechcraft 1900 slumping on the tarmac like an old man waiting for bingo to start. Way past its prime and kept together with what Katelyn would have said was "duct tape, spit, and the grace of God."

Laney wondered if the spit or the grace would fail, knowing duct tape rarely did. She smirked; some things were built to last. Her left thumb absent-mindedly rubbed against her ring finger to spin the band around, but it wasn't there anymore. The smooth skin it found drew her gaze down.

Nothing lasts forever, no matter what it feels like today.

Laney felt oddly calm all the way to Denver International Airport, despite the rattling death trap that flew her there in bumping arcs of sheer terror. She was on her way now, and with her frugal nature there was no way she was cancelling the ticket and losing Marc's money. Being published didn't make her rich. Neither did teaching. If it had, she could have afforded to take the girls on a European tour over Christmas vacation. If it had, she wouldn't be flying economy on the way to a borrowed beach shack. If it had, she could quit her teaching job, move back to the quiet introvert-haven of Sweet Valley, and spend her days writing and riding horses with her girls. If it had, she could help her parents keep her family's ranch safe and protect the way of life that had raised her.

"If the world was built on if's we'd all ride unicorns and shit rainbows," she muttered to herself as she walked the long archway from the farthest terminal to the main hub of the airport. Laney made her gate in plenty of time and texted Marc before getting on the nearly-full flight.

> Hey, I know I just met you, and this is crazy, but I'll see you in four weeks…maybe.

A few minutes later her phone sang happily.

> You're so weird.

> Cute weird or scary weird?

There was a pause as she scooted into her crammed middle seat and shoved her run-down leather satchel under the seat in front of her. Fate always put her in the middle seat. Where Plain Lane belonged. Her phone pinged.

> Frighteningly cute. Go get laid!

Isn't pity-fuck the actual term kids use these days?

Stop compromising the safety of the flight and turn off your phone.

OK, OK. Thanks again. Love you and Alan.

Back at you, funny face.

She shut off the phone after sending Sylvia and Charlotte a text to their dad's phone. Then, she missed them. In the heart-aching aloneness, she missed their fighting and their loud and crazy singing. She missed their constant questions and their fairy daydreams. Even though she and David shared custody, he rarely had time for them, so being away from them seemed a deeper hole in her heart.

The row filled, and rather than trying to maneuver enough elbowroom to break out her laptop, and risk some stranger's eyes on her work, she sat back and waited for the plane to take off. Maybe it would lose an engine somewhere over the Gulf of Mexico and she'd never have to find out if the bikini wax was worth it. The larger woman to her right spilled over ungraciously into her space. Laney felt claustrophobic. She closed her eyes and began to breathe, slow and deep.

"Charlene!" the woman called over her shoulder, startling Laney from her quiet meditation. "Says here that he lives in Palamo Bay! We should stop there first. If we get in at night, maybe we can crash a party!" Laney was in the middle of her inhale, trying to picture her crisp autumn lake in the mountains, a chair on the edge of a dock, hot coffee in hand. Palamo Bay. She opened an annoyed eye towards the woman.

Marc's cottage was in Palamo Bay.

"Shoot, girl! I'm sure the place is crawlin' with security. Maybe we'll see him around the town though. I read he doesn't go home for the holidays since his daddy passed three years ago, and the whole breakdown happened."

One, breathe in. Two, breathe out. Three, breathe years. Three years? Laney's internal meditative voice sounded perturbed. Whose daddy passed? She had been able to block out their words, but not the insistent twang of their excited voices. Only when the plane began to move did they quiet and she was able to let go... sitting alone on her dock, watching the cool fall descend on the lake in her mind's eye.

Six hours and very little rest later, the plane touched down in St. Croix. Charlene and Darla, having been in opposite rows, had managed to talk over Laney's head for the last two hours of the trip. She'd had her earphones on with Jimmy Page's voice, raspy and loud, drowning them out. Still suffering the debilitating writer's block, she'd settled for getting her papers graded, sifting through the pile with an ever-present sense that she had failed over half of her students. Some of the essays she slogged through made her wonder if they'd even attended class. As she was stowing her belongings for landing, she tugged out her earbuds to the ongoing conversation of Darla and Charlene.

"Girl! I don't know if he'll ever settle down after what that witch of an ex-wife put him through. What was her name? Annie? He needs a good, solid woman like me!" Darla sloshed her overpriced house wine onto Laney's arm. "Sorry, sweetie," she said, and tried to wipe it off with her shirttail.

"Between the two of us, we could help him forget her. I bet together we could break that ol' wild stallion!" Charlene's wheezing laugh put a crooked smile on Laney's face.

"Killing by tag-team sex?" Laney blurted out. Darla exploded in an approving laugh.

"Tag team! I love that! Didja hear that, Charlene?" They both cackled. Laney wondered if she could crawl into the overhead compartment, unnoticed. "Did you know Jameson Clark lives in St. Croix part of the year? We hear he'll be around this Christmas, so me and my friend booked this trip to try and catch him at one of the local bars. I heard he likes to do surprise concerts every now and again." Laney stared blankly at them. Her brain was fried from grading; no neurons left to even start a novel, let alone finish one. Darla nudged her out of her zombie like stare.

"You know? Jameson Clark? Country music's most eligible, sexy-assed bachelor?" Laney knew the name. She'd even attended one or two of his concerts when she had been younger and slightly more carefree. She tried to recall the cowboy-hat-wearing Tennessean, but the image blurred with all the other thoughts in her head.

"Oh? I'm not sure I know him," she lied.

"Girl, you should stick with us! We're going to be hitting all the clubs, out all night until we find him!" Darla was five sheets to the wind and stood up to raise her glass to the idea.

"That sounds like a heap of fun, girls." Laney smiled. "But I came here to do some work."

"Work? In St. Croix? Girl, please!" Charlene scoffed. "That's like doing homework on spring break. Don't be a nerd!"

Laney blushed. She had never gone anywhere for spring break. If she had though, she probably would have done homework. She had always been, through college, through high school, probably since kindergarten, a nerd. She looked up at Charlene and thought about who she could be in a world of strangers.

"Well, maybe I can catch up with you sometime on the island."

"Attagirl!" Charlene slapped her thigh and, in sloppy drunk writing, scrawled out a number where they could be reached. Laney smiled and, in turn, made no mention of her cottage on Palamo Bay.

It was early evening when she arrived at the gates of the cottage. The taxi sped off without any further instruction, and she was left wondering if she had copied down the right address. The affluent houses, each cocooned in the safety of vegetation, seemed far too dreamlike.

"Full of surprises, Marc," she breathed as she reached into her bag for the keycard he had given her. It unlocked the heavy iron gate, and a cobbled path, surrounded by lush tropical plants, led her to a small blue cottage. Beautiful blooms outside of every window greeted her, and she had to pause to take in the picture it made with its wide windows and secluded front porch.

It wasn't the largest house in Palamo Bay. In fact, it may have been the smallest. But it was perfect, and she ran to the front door with a giddiness she'd misplaced in recent years. Stepping into the tiled living room was like coming home. The comfortable color schemes of white and blue drew her eyes outside to the ocean view. The left wall was made of bookshelves, full of seashells and old favorite tomes, including, she smiled with a shake of her head, her own trilogy.

In front of the ocean-side windows was a small desk, and the living room was filled with comfortable, laid-back furniture and plenty of throws and pillows. In the middle of the library wall was a doorway that led to the small kitchen. To the right was a bedroom and bath. The bookcase wall, closest to the desk, hid a narrow staircase, barely noticeable in the cozy space. She dropped her belongings and clambered up it.

At the top she found a sleeping loft, outfitted with a fluffy bed covered in comfortable white linen. Despite Marc's insistence that she make use of the master suite, she felt much more at home in this space. In the quiet, alone with herself at the end of an emotional day, she took a deep breath in and smiled. This might not be so bad after all.

FIVE

JAMIE HAD TAKEN A WEEK OFF FROM DRINKING. HE'D called in his nutritionist, gotten a cleanse started, and tried to shoo the young coeds from his property. But the problem was that when he was alone, the creeping pain and sense of failure found him and hit him hard. Soon he was craving company. Uncomplicated company. Company that could distract him and make him still feel like somebody worthwhile. He texted Brody, who was always good about knowing of distractions in various sizes.

Jamie took his disappointing breakfast replacement out onto the deck and wished it was a cup of coffee. Over Christmas break, the island had a small influx of tourists. He'd even seen a girl running out on the sand earlier when he hadn't been able to sleep. She had one of those short and strong figures, and her strides were steady.

He hadn't run since high school football practice, and even then, it was a punishment. He watched her for twenty minutes from his mansion on the hilltop. She came to the roped-off section of his beach, looked around with a scowl, ducked under the rope and just kept on going. At first, he was mad she'd trespassed, but watching her move, the way the sunrise lit her light brown hair, and the pale perfection of those strong legs pumping, he felt calm and happy. If she wasn't going to let a little obstacle interrupt her morning, he wasn't going to let her determined set of footprints on his beach ruin the day either.

By day two on the island, Laney was already getting used to sleeping in. Without the kids' school schedules to keep, errands to run, and her own classes to teach, she was finding a rhythm to herself. Today she wanted to get out of the house, away from the paperwork that she was finally caught up on, and the seven failed attempts at her first chapters.

She took her phone and left her shoes when she went out for an early morning jog on the beach. The weather was perfect, and the light came earlier, so close to the equator. She ran up the beach until she was stopped by privacy fencing by one of the larger homes. Annoyed, but not put out, she ducked under the fence and continued on. Chances were they wouldn't care. She was just passing through. With bare toes hugging the sand, she carved an even path of prints into the snowy white sand. Her calves felt the burn in no way the icy sidewalks of Laramie could have prepared her for. On the way home, she stopped to watch the waves tumble in and out, with a gentle and chaotic beauty.

Still sweaty, she sat in front of her computer and beat out an outline to a story that had been dancing around her brain. A woman in need of a fresh start. She thought of herself. She thought of her sister, Elle. She thought of all the women out in the world who'd been stuck in a rut for too long. It was sketchy at best, but more promising than anything else she'd tried so far. There still weren't any messages on her phone.

She stared out at the foamy line of the morning tide and sighed. Though the scenery was nice, and the weather divine, she was having a hard time finding romance, even away from her normal life. She needed to go people-watch and see if it would spark her creativity.

Her stomach rumbled. She'd exhausted the cottage's small store of canned goods, so it was time to go out anyway. Marc had sent her with a list of the best and least touristy places to eat, nearby shopping, neighbor's phone numbers, and the caretaker's information. If she was truly on vacation, then the last thing she wanted to do was cook. Especially if it was just for one.

After a shower, she dried off, tied up her hair in a bun and threw on a tank top and shorts. Her cheeks were pink from the hot water and the morning run, and she'd begun to look less drawn. More like the girl she used to be, so many years ago.

She took Marc's directions and her beat-up leather satchel, overstuffed with notebooks, pens and her laptop, and headed down to The Salty Claw, a nearby dive frequented by locals, that was only a quarter of a mile from the cottage. The walk down the dirt road, mangroves hugging either side, was peaceful, and Laney tried to turn off the dark thoughts of what might be lurking in the bushes beyond her sight.

When she arrived, she sat on the porch, ordered a coffee from the young man at the bar, and got out the newspaper to unwind her mind with a crossword. She didn't bother to look around, as the teak-walled restaurant was uninhabited. She put on her glasses and smiled at the bartender who brought her pastries and coffee.

Halfway through breakfast, he came into the bar sporting a young girl on each of his well-toned arms. She wouldn't have looked up from the five-letter word for *Montana motto metal*, but the giggling voices broke her concentration and drew her ire. Peering over the frames of her thick-rimmed glasses, Laney's gaze fell on the smiling face of a man who seemed familiar. When he tossed his head back and laughed, revealing perfect white teeth below his straw cowboy hat, Laney froze with the recognition. The pencil between her teeth sunk as she bit down.

Darla and Charlene would have shit themselves.

Jameson Clark laughed; his eyes lit with joy and mischief, and the un-retouched crinkles around his eyes captivated Laney. He was, unfortunately, more handsome in person. Her chest felt warm. The girls fawned under his attention and his hands seemed too comfortable in their caresses. Laney snapped out of her shock. She rolled her eyes at herself and his teasing laughter.

She could only imagine how he would handle Charlene and Darla had they been in The Salty Claw. For a moment, Laney thought to call them. Wouldn't that serve his skirt-chasing ass right? Being mauled by some enthusiastic and sturdy fans? The Clark trio ordered bloody mary's and Laney checked her watch disapprovingly. She knew it wasn't the early drinking that bothered her. It was the sight of an older man with two younger women that hit too close to home. She clanked her cup down irritably.

Jameson swiveled on his bar stool towards her.

What had surely been meant as a short glance towards her turned into a curious study. The two young ladies giggled and chatted about their exploits from the night before beside him, but Jameson Clark's attention was uncomfortably kept on Laney. The way his blue eyes melted over her body made her feel strange and warm, and she wanted to bite her lip and come all undone. Her rational brain gave her romance novelist brain a good hearty shake. *Skirt chaser. Cad.*

She quirked one eyebrow over her glasses and stared back at him fiercely.

"What?" she growled, barely registering that she'd said the word out loud. His brow rose in surprise and he turned back around to the more friendly conversation beside him.

Laney's cheeks felt hot. She didn't expect him to even notice her, especially with the distractions on either side of him. She abandoned the crossword, paid, and swept past the inebriated group, out the door into the sunlight. She should head back into town for groceries so she didn't have to risk running into that whole mess again. But his smiling and crinkled eyes on her felt like the first heat of sunburn. Men didn't look at Laney. She hung her head and walked along the widening road into the small marketplace.

The people were friendly and at ease, speaking in Spanish, English and French Creole. It was a beautiful and melodic mix, and she found herself relaxing into the low-key culture surrounding her. Her arms were heavy, laden with fruits, bread, cheeses, and tea. While she struggled with the load, a rickshaw stopped to offer her a ride. She hefted the bags in her arms and considered. There was no reason to be tough. When she agreed, the young man smiled brilliantly, and took her hand to help her up.

The ride took much less time and he smiled and talked about the island and asked how long she would be staying. She answered shyly, feeling odd that so much attention should be given to her. When they got to her gate, he nearly passed by it. She sat up and stopped him.

"Oh, this is it! This is me." She started to gather her things.

"Here? I thought that a pretty lady like you would be staying at Mr. Clark's." He skidded to a halt. Laney's gut tightened. Why would he think she was anything near Jameson Clark's type? That also meant he lived close by. Maybe just down the road.

"Nope, just here," she said. He helped her out with her things and she paid him the rest of the cash in her wallet. "Sorry, I don't have much. I'm sort of bumming off friends."

The young man smiled at her. "A person giving you the last dollar in their wallet means more than some rich guy throwing hundreds."

"Yeah well, it would still be nice to have the hundreds though," Laney laughed with a shrug.

"You need another ride, you call me. I'm Ricardo." Laney, accustomed to handshakes, held hers out. He returned it warmly.

"Laney. I will, thank you so much."

She swiped the key card and went in. Ricardo sped off and left her with odd thoughts in her head. Apparently, Mr. Clark had women hand-delivered by rickshaw to him. She gritted her teeth. The rest of the day filled up with finishing her outline and calling her girls. They were in southern France today, exploring wineries with their father and his former student, turned mistress, turned girlfriend.

"Sounds lovely," Laney said. She paced over the cool tiles and stared up at the large leaf ceiling fan. When she hung up, she called Marc.

"It's so ugly here," she began. "You should be happy you aren't suffering through all of this sunshine and boat drinks."

Marc laughed. "Oh, I hardly think Laney Sullivan is drinking at noon."

"You never know, I may start."

"Inspired yet?"

"Inspired to hate men more. Did you know Jameson Clark is your neighbor?"

"Oh, that's right! He's just up the road. Jamie's a great guy. Did you meet him?"

"Uh huh. Sort of."

"Oh, tell me he made a pass at you!" Marc's gleeful tone made her bristle.

"Why in the hell would he make a pass at me, Marc? I'm his age."

"You're gorgeous."

"You're delusional. How's Alan?" She changed the topic immediately.

Marc sighed. "You may want to try stepping out, Laney. You are on your own down there, no responsibility to anyone else. You don't even have to tell me."

"Marc, I haven't had sex in three years, of course I'd tell you. Hell, I'd take out an ad in the *New Yorker*. Unfortunately for newspaper sales, that ship has sailed. And even if it hadn't, it's not like that skirt-chasing Casanova would be the one. Besides, I have enough work that I shouldn't leave the cottage until the morning of my flight."

"Ugh, you're such a nerd! Live a little, Laney. Promise me that you won't waste moments down there. Take those moments by the balls."

"You should needlepoint that on a pillow."

"Laney, I mean it!"

"I'll do my best."

"Best? Pish posh! Balls, Laney. Grab those moments!"

She giggled and shook her head. "Good night, Marc."

"Goodnight, funny face."

Laney's dreams were laced with foreboding. She found herself on a boat in the middle of the sea. A man, his back to her, shared the boat and wouldn't turn her way. His strong shoulders worked tirelessly, adjusting the rigging, fighting against the undulant waves and the rising winds as the tiny vessel was tossed in the current. She clung to the sides, her white knuckles slick with salt water and her hair plastered to the sides of her face. Her heart pounded with fear as the man struggled, and his frustrated cries filled her ears.

"It's okay," she shouted, more concerned with his despair than the storm that swirled around them. "It's all right!" She let go of the edge of the boat to hold on to his shoulder. His muscles were tense beneath her fingers, and rock hard. Just as he was turning back around, dark eyes lit with the fire of fear, she woke, sweaty, her heart pounding. The dawn hadn't broken yet, and the quiet sounds of the house filtered into her awareness.

She couldn't reason why she knew him, but she did. Or maybe her heart did, as odd and romantic as that sounded. She wanted to touch him again. She wanted to find him and pull him into her arms; keep him safe from that storm. Wrap her legs around his waist and her fingers through his hair. She felt her breasts tighten. She'd forgotten how desire felt, but it coursed through her, warming her skin and causing her to writhe under the covers. When her phone rang, it startled her into sitting. On the other end of the line was her mother.

"Oh, thank god, you still have your phone!"

"Yeah, my kidnappers let me keep it if I promised not to chew through my restraints again."

"Good Lord, Laney, that's not funny."

"Is everything okay?" Laney ran her hands through her knotted hair.

"It's all good here. Your father is a little sore after taking a tumble off a horse he had no damn business being on in the first place."

"That rebel," Laney said with a smile, thankful that her mother couldn't see her eye roll from across the miles.

"I was just checking in to see how you were."

Laney looked around at the softly lit room, took a minute to think about it. Except for wanting to go back to bed and dream of the muscle-bound stranger in more and intimate detail, she was actually feeling well.

"Mom, I've never been better. The weather is beautiful and I'm hoping to go write on the beach today." Her mother sighed with relief.

"I'm so glad, Laney. I hope you have a wonderful day of writing. And the beach. Watch out for jellyfish, their sting is wicked. If you get stung, I think I heard urine neutralizes the poison."

"Uh, okay. Thanks, Mom. I'll keep my eyes open." Laney got out of bed and shimmied down the ladder on the way to her coffee pot. They said their goodbyes and Laney found a light throw to put over her shoulders as she stepped out the back door towards the tiny beach. The weather was warm and pleasant, and the sun was just starting to peek above the horizon. While the coffee brewed, she plopped down on the white sand and watched the waves tumble over each other in their search for shore.

She couldn't get the man out of her head. She wanted so much to help him. She wanted so much to get him to shore. She wanted...her hand paused, gently running over her bare knee, and thought of the way his muscles had felt under her fingertips... Something she hadn't wanted in a long time.

Laney spent the morning banging her head on the keys. Nothing was coming, nothing would. She wrote a short poem about boats, and storms, and mysterious men caught in the desperation of life. It wasn't bad. Poetry wasn't her strong suit, but at least it was writing, so she'd take it. Every word, no matter how disjointed from her current work in progress, was a word that would, hopefully, unlock more.

Halfway through her frustrating morning, her agent called.

"I hear you're on an island."

"Uh, it was coerced?" Laney said, in defense against Rebecca's tight tone.

"That might be the most desperate excuse for not meeting a deadline that I've ever heard," Rebecca said. "They have internet there you know. You can email me those chapters whenever you want."

Laney sighed into the dregs of her fifth cup of coffee. "I know, I just—"

"God, Laney, tell me you have something, please."

"Of course, I do!" she protested in what she hoped was a convincing lie. "I have lots of chapters. Loads of them. Tons. Like a literal shit-ton of chapters."

"Literally? A shit-ton, Laney? Really?" Rebecca called her bluff.

"Sure. Just, you know. They're a little rough."

"Laney—"

"I'll have them to you in a week," Laney said quickly and hung up before Rebecca could press further. "Shit," Laney said to herself and stared at the flashing cursor, keeping time on an empty document.

"You know what?" she said to no one in particular. "I need a drink."

She didn't bother to look at the clock, because she knew if she saw it was only three in the afternoon, she'd talk herself out of such an asinine idea. Normal, non-alcoholic people didn't drink in the middle of the day by themselves. Surely it was a sign of a problem. Laney sighed when the thoughts came through with her mother's voice attached to them.

"Fuck that, I'm an adult. On an island. I can have a beer. I deserve a beer," she grumbled to herself, grabbing her purse and the crossword, and heading out the door into the hot afternoon sun.

She enjoyed the walk down to The Salty Claw, despite the sweat that dripped between her shoulder blades and made the hair around her face curl into waves. She was done thinking about writing for the day. She was done thinking about her agent, and David, and her daughters she couldn't talk to, and storm-drenched strangers she would never meet. She wanted an afternoon off.

Six

Laney walked into The Salty Claw, vaguely remembering that Jameson Clark had ruined her last experience there. It was probably not his time of day. It was nap time for night owls like him. She picked a seat at the end of the bar, then took out her glasses and the crossword.

"Coffee? Tea?" the wide-smiled young man asked. He must have remembered her from the other morning. His smile contrasted with his beautiful, dark skin, and long dreads framed his high cheekbones. Laney stared at him for a moment. He was too young for her, but she couldn't help the softening attraction she felt. She blushed. What was up with her libido lately? She cleared her throat and smiled.

"I'd like a beer, please."

"Oh? Look at you, coming around to the island way! I will take care of you." He winked.

Laney flushed deeper. Did he just flirt? How long had it been since she'd been flirted with? She smiled.

"Well then, I'll put myself in your capable hands," she said.

He raised his eyebrows and laughed, deep and full, and Laney liked the way it made her toes curl. He set the cold beer on the bar, and she watched the water condense and slide down its sides in the heat. Just like her failed story start, less than a week ago. She sighed and took a long pull from the bottle. She started the crossword and pushed away thoughts of romantic novels, agents, and the uncomfortable feeling of coming alive to the world of men again.

Halfway into her second beer, and feeling the effects of not having had lunch beforehand, she was closing one eye to focus on the crossword and counting the letters one more time when Jameson Clark and one of the young women from the previous day sauntered in. He must be narrowing down his options, Laney thought crossly. The woman ordered a sugary-sweet pink drink and swayed into Jameson's hand at her back. Laney watched, part in fascination, but part in the study of the interplay between the younger woman and Clark. She'd always been a good reader of body language and all the ways humans spoke without words.

She could tell the young lady was trying to delve deeper. The seriousness of her tone told Laney she wanted more than just the obvious one-night fling he'd had in mind. His laughing smile and deflecting answers were like a brick wall building up right in front of her eyes. When he shook his head and laughed at her, as if to call out the ridiculous idea, the younger woman's tone wavered, and she stepped away from his hands.

Laney's brow rose over her glasses as the argument escalated and the young woman launched into a tirade, including some very unladylike name calling. She picked up her belongings and splashed the rest of her drink into his chest before storming out. He held up his hands as it dribbled down the front of his shirt and soaked into his jeans.

"Well, there's a surprise," Laney snorted, ungoverned by her brain on sabbatical. She quickly put the bottle to her lips. Maybe he hadn't heard. The scowl on his face said otherwise. When he frowned like that, it hid his dimples and made his lips thinner. He reached over the bar and took a towel to wipe the front of his shirt.

"Oh? And *you* know so much about dating, sitting at a bar, all by yourself? Alone?" His tone was mean, and Laney could tell he was pride-stung.

That kind of accusation would have normally made Laney cringe, gather her things and leave the bar. But she wasn't normal on the island. She was something else. She didn't know this man, beyond his famous persona. What was more, they would never meet again. She was off-path; she wasn't known. No one expected her. She was Laney Sullivan, the girl who used to shine. Whip-smart and full of sensual energy. And now, an opportunity to speak her mind stood in front of her, to take back something she'd lost.

"It doesn't take an expert to understand your problem," she said bluntly.

"Oh? And what's *my* problem?" The smile on Jameson's lips was wolfish and cruel; not at all the easygoing man he so often portrayed. Laney rolled her eyes, exasperated.

"She's too young for you!" He stopped patting at his shirt and threw the towel into the sink behind the bar. He leaned over and poured himself a double whiskey from a bottle. "They're all too young for you," she added.

"On my tab, Noah?" he yelled, and the bartender waved him off dismissively.

Laney took another swig of her beer and looked back down at her crossword. It had felt good to say it to him. As if she was saying it to all of the men in the world with that particular habit. Jameson took his drink, and to Laney's horror, sat down on the stool next to her.

"I suppose I should be dating women *your* age?" he answered snidely.

"Women *our* age," she corrected. "But we both know that women *our* age wouldn't date you. We've already been through the bullshit your type carries." The spar shot back and he raised his eyebrows in surprise.

"My type?"

"Men easily distracted by shiny things." She looked up from the page and then filled in the fourteenth word across for *Coleridge storyteller*.

"Sounds like someone's jaded."

"And how do you think women get that way, genius? You're just the latest in a long line of good reasons to be." She pushed her glasses to the top of her head. They both stopped talking and stared at each other. Laney lost herself in the twinkle of his eyes, and the way his crow's feet deepened in a smile. A real, brilliant, melting smile.

"Bitter hag," he chuckled.

"Useless playboy," she countered with a tight smile.

Jameson Clark burst out laughing, and she sat back, perplexed, with her hackles raised. He leaned in closer, and Laney's skin tingled at the warmth of it. She stared back down at her paper and feigned disinterest, only the words were blurry and she squinted.

"Maybe you should try these." He plucked the glasses from the top of her head and handed them to her. She glared and snatched them away, flicking her pen angrily through her fingers. Jameson shrugged. "Just looking out for the elderly." He smiled as he waited for her reaction. She looked over her frames at him and smiled ferociously.

"Working on a Boy Scout badge, are you? Since you failed in getting your underage-coed-notch-in-the-bedpost-certification?"

He coughed when his drink went down the wrong way.

"She's not underage—probably?"

"You sure about that, grandpa?" she drawled in a way that sounded like her father was speaking through her.

"Nope," he drawled back. The devil-may-care smile was back, and he winked at her. She flicked her pen, twirling it over her knuckles in the odd, ingrained habit. He watched her hand in fascination.

"You know, she's a human being, right? Not just some object to chase? Some conquest." Jameson stopped smiling. "And even despite the fact that she's somebody's sister, somebody's daughter...she's somebody. A whole world in herself, and all you see and treat her like is a pair of tits to be grabbed at." Laney spoke lowly. The way his eyes fell to the bar and his neck flushed told her she had struck a nerve.

"And what do you know about my life?"

"I know I've only been here a few days, and every time I see you, there's a new something pretty on your arm." The muscle in his jaw twitched, and he took a drink. "Most of them wet behind the ears and no smarter than a two-day-old foal. Certainly, none of them old enough to know better as to what kind of man you are."

"You seem to know an awful lot about me. Are you a reporter or something?" He said it darkly and rounded to face her. "The story's been done, redone...done to death."

Laney had no idea what he was talking about, and her scowl told him as much.

"I'm a teacher. I don't care about your story." The half-truth was good enough for her, and as he stared into her eyes, his shoulders relaxed. She studied his face, the wide-spaced eyes, lightly tanned skin and soft stubble beginning to grow in on his chin. Lord, he was nice to look at. She felt her cheeks get warm, and she dropped her gaze back to her crossword. He broke the silence.

"But you *do* know who I am?" Jameson asked, his voice suspicious. She didn't look up.

She didn't know him. Any more than anyone who'd ever seen him on TV or heard his songs on the radio *really* knew him.

"Someone who's in need of an ego check?" She glanced up, disinterested. "Satisfied," she said huskily and smiled as she filled in the word for twenty-two down.

"Which clue did they give you, *what buttoned-up schoolmarms rarely are*?"

Laney laughed out loud, and the sound made his smile deepen. "Who says 'schoolmarm?' You're so old!" He laughed with her and nodded to Noah to refresh both of their drinks. "I don't need another. And especially not from you."

"Come on, have one more with me? I need the ego check." He smiled to the bartender. Laney paused. Wasn't this part of getting the most out of life? Accepting something you wanted, despite all the conformities that said you shouldn't?

"All right. A little ego therapy for you," she said and raised her bottle. He clinked his glass to it.

"Yeah," he laughed. "I need ego therapy, and you need hormone therapy."

"Easy," she growled in mock insult. "I'm just hitting my peak." She quickly put the bottle to her lips to silence herself. He glanced over and raised his eyebrows suggestively.

"Is that so?"

Laney cleared her throat and turned back to the black and white squares, half-wishing she were still in the cottage, holed up with the cold comfort of her computer. Jameson seemed to sense her discomfort, the wall she was trying to retreat behind, and he scooted in closer to her.

"Is that really a crossword...on paper?"

"I realize there are apps. I just like paper."

"God, you're dull," he said and leaned in closer still. The smell of whiskey on his breath was woody and smoky, and oddly alluring. His skin smelled like sunshine and the slightly dark smell of a man, which had been long absent in her life. He whispered in her ear softly, "Cunnilingus."

"What?" Her breath caught in her throat and she looked into his eyes. He sat back into his space.

"Number thirty-two across."

"I highly doubt that." She glared and searched the list to read the clue out loud. *Clever speaker*. She paused, her finger counting the number of spaces out fifteen. "Cunning linguist—" Laney cleared her throat. "That's not at all what I thought you said."

"Really? What did you think I said?" He grinned and rolled his tongue over an ice cube.

Laney watched him and felt her whole body burn from her belly down. Her body simmered with heat. Her eyes fell to his lips, his mouth, the way his teeth grazed the cube. She drew in a quick breath.

"My, my, I didn't know a woman your age could still blush."

"Probably just a hot flash," she squeaked.

"Is it? I think it may be something else. I think maybe you've been a button-upped schoolmarm for too long."

Three years was an awfully long time. Laney shifted in her chair.

"Well, not all of us are so worldly as you."

"Worldly?"

"Diseased? Is that the better word?" He snorted, and she found the familiar sound a little too cute.

"I'm Jamie," he said and held out his hand. She stared at it and stopped wondering if she should touch him. She wasn't going to overthink this. She shook it firmly and his smile warmed.

"Laney. Laney Sullivan."

"So, tell me, Laney Sullivan, why haven't I ever seen you on the island before? Did you just move in?"

"No, I'm just borrowing a cottage."

"Borrowing?"

"More like a coerced vacation," she grumbled.

"Yeah, it must have been a real fight to try and stay away from this shithole," he chuckled.

She laughed and took another drink. The warm haze took over, and she studied his face. He looked back at her with equal curiosity, an action she wasn't expecting from a superstar who could have been with any woman he wanted.

"It has been pretty torturous."

"How long do you have to suffer?"

"A little over three more weeks."

He whistled as if disappointed. "That's too bad. Think you'll make it?" he asked.

"I don't know," she said and pushed her glasses back on top of her head. He smiled goofily. "All of these gold-diggers and trophy-wife-hunters are not my crowd."

He looked down to his drink. "What do you teach?"

"I'm an adjunct English professor at the University of Wyoming."

"Oh yeah? A real professor? Wyoming's a beautiful state." She scowled at him in disbelief. "No really! All that—space."

She snorted and nodded her head, putting her arms behind her on the chair back to stretch the tension from her shoulders. Jamie's eyes fell to the fabric stretched over her breasts. His eyebrows rose, smile quirked, pupils dilated. Laney watched his body even as her own read the chemistry between them.

"Hey, asshole, my eyes are up here. Besides, aren't these a little too real for your tastes?" she said, as if privy to his thoughts.

"I'd say that I'm sorry, but you know I'm not."

"What do you do? I mean besides pick up young women and whisk them off to the island for debaucherous trysts?"

"Lot of big words in there for me." He took another drink and weariness took over his features. A cloud covered the lightness he'd playfully bantered with moments before. "I used to be somebody." When he turned back to her, her hard feelings softened. She gave him an understanding smile.

"Didn't we all?" she said. "As far as I can tell—" she sat forward, "you must still be someone." He looked at her quizzically.

"Oh? I thought you didn't know me."

"I don't, but I'm sure there's a syphilis clinic somewhere that's just dying to get ahold of your records."

Jamie laughed so hard that tears formed on the corners of his eyes. The dark moment had passed and Laney smiled to see him come out of it.

"I'll say one thing, Laney, you do have a pretty smile, but the things that come out of your mouth—not ladylike." His eyes dropped to her lips, and he studied them just as hungrily as he had her breasts. Laney was suddenly self-conscious of the laugh lines around her mouth.

"I've never been accused of being much of a lady." She nodded and took another drink.

"What are you doing tomorrow?"

She sat back and tried to swallow her beer without spit-taking in his face.

"Uh—"

"Go kayaking with me."

"You should save the kinky stuff for girls with younger hips."

He chuckled. "Come on. You're alone, right?"

It stung, and she screwed up her lips in a frown. He glanced at the pale line around her left ring finger. She put her hands in her lap.

"I have a lot of work to catch up on."

"On the island? Work? You realize that's sacrilegious."

"Sacrilegious? Did you get new word-of-the day toilet paper or something?"

"Maybe you're rubbing off on me." He smiled.

"There won't be any rubbing off of anything."

"Well, now, don't count it out just yet." He smiled wickedly. Her phone pinged, and she took the distraction with relief.

"Excuse me." She flicked across the screen and opened the newly sent picture, in front of the sprawling vineyards and surreal, soft light. Her two beautiful girls, now eight and six, in the arms of David and Tasha. Tasha, with her perfect, always-coiffed hair, her perfect Vanna White smile, perfect long and tanned legs; perfect everything. Laney wanted to cry. She tossed the phone on the bar and signaled to Noah.

"Darlin', can I have seven of what he's having, please?"

"Whoa, professor! You okay?" Jamie asked. Noah looked to them both, then poured Laney a single with a wary eye.

"Not really." Laney refused to look up, all of the playfulness from moments before drained away. A breeze blew in from the beach, cooling her neck and playing the loose strands of hair against her cheek. She sipped the whiskey and coughed.

"Laney?"

"Let's just do it," she said with eyes tearing up from the burn in her throat.

"What?"

"Tomorrow, Kayaking. Whatever. Let's do it. Grab life by the balls and all that nonsense."

"All—all right," Jamie stammered.

"Hell, maybe I'll get lucky and drown. Or get knocked out of the boat and killed by a frenzy of sharks." Her eyes went distant as her brain ran through the far-fetched scenarios of her tragic demise.

Jamie reached over and grabbed her phone before she could stop him.

"Hey!" she shouted.

"I gotta see what would make you want to commit suicide by shark." He looked at the antiquated phone, grabbed her hand in his warm fingers and put her thumb on the button. The picture was still there. She sat back, her fingers tingling from the brief warmth of his. She picked at the corner of a napkin while Jamie's eyes looked over her girls, light eyes and smiles like their momma. It burned a hole of embarrassment in her belly to have him see her ex, with his shiny new model.

"Oh, man," Jamie said. He slid her phone back towards her.

"Yep," she said and leaned away. "Welcome to my bitter, schoolmarm life."

"Didn't I see that on MTV once?"

Laney laughed despite the hard moment. "My episode airs in June sometime." He snorted into his drink. "When's that documentary about over-the-hill playboys who look for their glory days in between the legs of girls named Bambi coming out?" she asked.

Jamie nearly fell off his chair laughing. "Holy shit, you're something!"

"Sorry, that was mean."

He paused and clinked her glass to his.

"It's on in February," he said.

"I'll have to record it. I can't stay up too late."

"See that you do, Ms. Sullivan. It's 'must-see' TV." They smiled at each other and then looked away quickly.

"What time in the morning?"

"You have too many more drinks, and it won't be until afternoon."

"I can handle my liquor, thank you very much."

"I really don't think you can," he said, shaking his head.

"Said as if you know me."

"Well, after two and a half beers and one failed attempt at a sip of whiskey, you're listing starboard and your cheeks and lips are all pink and—" He stopped and sat back. "How about I pick you up at eight?"

"Pink and what?" she asked.

"Wear your shark attractant," he said and rose out of his seat.

"Thank God I brought some."

Jamie smiled, winked, and reached over to finish her whiskey for her. He unfolded a stack of bills from his pocket and tossed them on the bar next to Noah before leaning in close to her.

"Make sure you eat something and if you need a ride back to your cottage, you call this guy." He slid a card in front of her with a plain black number in bold face typed across the front. She opened her mouth to protest his patronizing order but couldn't find words. There was too much tenderness behind them.

"Okay." She watched his near-perfect ass, hugged in ratty jeans, leave. What in the hell had just happened? And what the hell was wrong with her? There was a whole morning of writing she wouldn't get to. She stared at her empty glass, traces of his lips on the edge.

She was going kayaking with Jameson Clark at eight tomorrow morning.

"Holy shit," she said and buried her head in her hands.

"Must have gotten to him." Noah's voice startled her as he wiped down the bar and threw the towel over his shoulder. "Usually when women leave him like that, he spends the rest of the afternoon burying himself in a bottle."

"Good to know he's getting better at his rebound," she grumbled.

Noah smiled and looked at her admiringly. "I don't think that's it." He came closer and took her empty beer bottles. "He's had a rough few years. This is the first time I've heard him laugh, for real, the way he did with you."

Laney blushed. She didn't want to start thinking she was special to a man like Jameson Clark. But her mind did stow away what Noah had said about Jamie's last few years being rough. She didn't know much about him, only that it had been a few years since his last album. And the thus-far-proven rumors of his alcohol consumption and carousing. She scowled at the door where he'd left; she didn't like the way her heart worried even a little over him. She felt the world spin and looked up to Noah.

"Could I trouble you for something to eat?" she asked.

Noah winked and nodded.

"No trouble at all, *mon petite*."

SEVEN

JAMIE RODE HIS OLD BROWN CRUISER BACK DOWN THE road. Sure was easier without Meghan perched on the handlebars, squealing giddily. He passed by what he thought would be Laney's cottage. The place was owned by those nice fellas who were usually here at Christmas time. They weren't here this year. He wondered if they knew her or if she was just renting it from them. A teacher probably couldn't afford that kind of place for weeks in any season. She could have been a reporter...though they didn't usually make much more. Despite the possibility, he really didn't think she was. She didn't seem manipulative enough. If anything, she might have been the most straightforward woman he'd ever met. He felt the unfamiliar mix of being charmed and confused at once.

The feeling was probably what had driven him to invite her on the kayak trip he and Meghan had booked. Long-legged, strawberry blonde Meghan, a nutritionist turned lover who came in heavy with questions. Who wanted to know why he didn't go home at Christmas. Who wanted to know why she couldn't sleep in his bed. Who wanted him to write her a song. Who wanted to know why he wasn't making plans for New Year's with her. She would be on the next flight off the island and back to L.A. by the weekend.

Maybe it would be a good change to hang around someone like Laney. Someone he wasn't trying to bed, someone who wasn't looking to be the next Mrs. Jameson Clark. She took him down a notch, and maybe, like she'd suggested, he could use a break from trying to find his glory days between the legs of girls named Bambi. He smiled and continued down the road to his own house.

He punched in the code after skidding to a halt at the large iron gates and parked his bike against the fence. He whistled a tune, that seemed to rise up from somewhere in his chest. Despite returning with his arms empty, he didn't feel lonely. Once inside the cool, marble-tiled foyer, he grabbed his phone, which was ringing insistently from the side table. Thankfully, it wasn't his mom.

"Hey, Leonard! How's things?" His voice fell back into a familiar twang when he talked to a fellow Tennessean. The moment of silence after Leonard asked him sheepishly about his next record was tense.

"Ya know man, I just haven't had a lot of time down here... been real busy working on some other things." Jamie paused to listen to Leonard's disbelieving and sarcastic response. "Look man, soon. Sooner than you know. Just getting all the lyrics on paper now," he lied. "Listen, I got a lot of things going on at the moment, I'll be sure to tell you when it's all Jake with Jesus. Yep. Yeah, you bet. See ya man, take care." He hung up.

He sighed and slipped his phone into his back pocket, and thought about the problem of not having any new material for the next album. It had been too long. He could have just sifted through the piles of demo tapes and sheet music that his agents had been shot-gunning his way for the last few years. But he knew what he would find. The same things he always sang about. Beaches and girls, drinks and escaping to someplace warm.

He'd built his empire on the beach party life, only his heart wasn't in it anymore. He was scared no one out there, none of his fans at least, would want to hear anything else from him. He'd never been good at opening up, not even to his two ex-wives, let alone the massive and faceless crowds that surrounded his spotlight. It had been three years since he'd toured officially. He'd done a couple of Christmas specials, a tour in Vegas for a week, a couple of charity concerts. But his voice wasn't what it had been. The loneliness of the last few years held him down, and the happy memories of home and people who genuinely loved him only made it worse. He couldn't write, couldn't find inspiration anywhere. And three years was an eternity in the business.

Laney's words came back and, this time, stung him like a slap to the face: *washed up has-been.* He felt his stomach tumble and wondered if the best years of his career, his life, were behind him. It was easier to forget when he was throwing parties, entertaining coeds, and living up to his easygoing party boy image. It was easier to relive his glory between the legs of younger women. It was easier to forget.

It was easier, but it wasn't real.

He stared at the ocean view and took his phone out again, and stared at the small red reminders before tossing the phone on the couch. He had ignored the two missed calls from his mother. He knew why she was calling. She'd done it every holiday for the last three years. She was wondering if he was coming home. Maybe this year, she would say, *you could come back. Your sisters and I miss you awful.*

It broke his heart, but he couldn't. He hadn't been back since the falling-out with his dad. Not even for the funeral. He opened up the accordion doors to let the sound of the waves and cool breeze into the house. The whole wall opened, allowing the large entertaining space to become one with the coast and beach outside. He walked past his infinity pool and smirked at the extravagance that he no longer felt at home with.

He'd spent so long surrounding himself with the comforts that only money could buy, that he'd stopped trying to fix the actual uncomfortable emptiness inside of his chest. As he sat there, beside the sleek stone architecture that protected his grounds from nosy neighbors, her voice sounded in his mind.

Someone's in need of an ego check.

He smiled. Tomorrow might be just what he needed. Jamie took to the old beach chair at the edge of the sand, and watched the ocean rolling slowly in and slowly back out, tumbling over itself. He closed his eyes to the rush and whisper of it until the sun sank lower, giving the night away to darkness. Five days until Christmas on the island.

He should call his mom.

He felt his eyelids grow heavy, and he closed them, falling asleep in his old blue chair again. The night cooled around him. In the soft stillness, something danced around the edges of his brain. Words. Notes.

> That's somebody's little girl,
> She's somebody's great big world.
> Tiny hand wrapped around his finger, big blue
>   eyes always gonna linger
> 'Fore you take her for a ride,
> Remember her daddy's always on her side.
> Remember her momma's heart'll break
> If her little girl comes home too late.
> She's everything to someone's heart,
> So think where you're taking her before you
>   start...
>
> You're staring at her lips, those knock-me-down
>   hips,
> You're thinking of all the ways, you'd like to have
>   her tonight.

But before you undo that dress, before you leave
    her an easy mess
That's somebody's little girl,
That's somebody's great big world.
She's got her momma's eyes and her daddy's hair
And all their love and hope to spare.
She's the jewel in their crown
Think of how you're thinking of letting her
    down.

The words played and tumbled through his mind, like dexterous and strong fingers through his hair, until he drifted to sleep and felt a woman just on the outside of his mind. He moaned a little and felt the pull of something deep inside when she laughed. She was leading him gently by the hand, sunlight sparkling through her hair, and he followed, without hesitation.

When Laney finally made it back to the cottage, stomach full of fish tacos and feeling much less woozy, it was night, nearly her normal bedtime. But her mind was too busy to settle. Why in the hell had she ever agreed to go out with Jameson Clark? For years, she hadn't been on a date. She just didn't see the reason or purpose, especially when she'd suffered such a burn from her ex-husband. She had been determined not to go down that road again and let another man pick her apart, settle on her imperfections, and find someone younger. So, what was so special about Jameson Clark? If anything, he was exactly the kind of man she shouldn't be dating.

"Maybe he's not special. Maybe this is okay because it's not a date," she reprimanded herself. "It's just an opportunity to avoid writing, and possibly drown in the process. The ultimate procrastination," she grumbled to the empty cottage.

She didn't know the first thing about kayaking or the ocean. In fact, the idea of being out there scared her shitless, just like David had said it would. She thought of writing her children a letter explaining everything before she died tomorrow. After all, they should know the odd circumstances that had led her to meet her demise with the most eligible, self-described playboy in the world of country music.

At least her death would be highly publicized. Maybe it would bump her book sales posthumously and she could contribute to her kids' college fund, and finally keep her parents' ranch safe from being bought out. She wondered, with dark amusement, if that could really work.

Laney sat down at the desk and looked over at the window facing the ocean. The whitecaps crested on black waves, and the palm trees rustled back and forth in the night breeze. At least she could end it in paradise. She set about writing the letter. If nothing else, she needed to leave some sort of will.

Who would she leave her crappy office furniture to? Her incredible 1980s Isuzu? Could she put in a clause that Tasha would never be allowed to adopt her children? Would that be catty? Certainly not uphold-able in court, but what the hell? She might as well tell her what she thought of her, beyond the grave.

Laney wrote through four bitter-laced, humorous pages. Then, she settled down and wrote more for her girls. Her hopes for them, and how much she loved them. What she knew about being ten, twelve, sixteen, twenty, twenty-five. What she knew about love, about men, and her hope that whoever they fell in love with would appreciate their worth. That no matter how many Tashas their father went through, all women deserved better treatment. Equal and loving partners who respected their ability to do things themselves. Treated them not like some delicate glass dolls, but humans. All the things she wanted for herself. Respect, honest affection, passion. Love. Real, true love. Not the kind that was played in the alternate realities of social media, or the false pretenses that the world pushed on people. But just love.

When she was done, she went back to her four-page will and wrote in at the very bottom;

> *I leave to Jameson Clark, the ability to find something greater in life than beer and boobs. I will him the ability to open up, scratch the deep itches and find someone who can handle whatever it is he's hiding in there. May he discover optimism for the future in his life and look beyond the superficial to find a friend in the woman he loves.*

She smiled.

It had been a long time since she had written anything in the magical flow of getting caught up in the moment. The book was a stumbling, self-doubting mess that stalled and started with every setback and frustration in her life. This—she thought and traced Jamie's name with her fingers—was art. She looked up at the clock. It was midnight and way past her bedtime, and it left little time to sleep before her death march into the ocean tomorrow. She sighed, stretched her arms high above her head, and switched off the light. Laney climbed the steep stairs and fell into bed, still in her clothes.

Eight

THE MORNING SUN WAS SOFT, COMING FROM THE OTHER side of the island. Despite its gray and pink ease, it was not kind to Laney, who woke with a headache and the run-down feeling of someone who needed at least two cups of coffee to just reach normal. She glanced with a blurry eye at the clock. She had half an hour. She rolled out of the bed with a groan. Her left knee twinged. Age was sneaking up on her from every facet of her life. She should shower. It wasn't as if she cared what he thought, but maybe it would help wake her up.

While the coffee pot began its glacial-paced brewing, she jumped under the cool spray of the shower and let it spring her awake. She didn't bother washing her hair. He wasn't *that* important. When she stepped out, the coffee was done, and she took a cup of it upstairs while she dressed.

She tied her hair up in a bun and, with a nervous breath, slid into the blue bikini. Its supportive cups helped boost her breasts, and the bottom managed to cover most of hers. She looked in the mirror. Marc had said "classically hour-glassed." Laney scowled. While her waist had recovered from her pregnancies, there was a curve of flesh to her hips that rounded her bottom out. She wasn't stick-thin like the women he'd dated before. She stuck out her tongue and frowned at the idea she had anything to prove.

"It's not a date, and it's not like you're going to see him ever again." She threw on a white button-down shirt and linen shorts. She grabbed her beach bag and packed the essentials. Phone, sunblock, pen and notebook. She left her glasses behind but wondered briefly if she should pack snacks.

"God, Laney. He's a grown man, you're a grown woman. You don't need to prepare for it as if you were taking the kids. You can survive a few hours without crackers."

She had a big bowl of fruit with her coffee and got out the door at 8:01. She was at the gate as he drove up, not expecting him to be on time. She figured he'd left the bar and gone on to party the night away, getting even less sleep than she had. She watched as he parked the jacked-up old pickup truck right in front of her. It was far too high off the ground to be practical. Too beat up and rusty to not have been used. It reminded her of her Isuzu in an odd way, but his piece-of-shit car still ran.

"Well, would you look at that! I didn't even have to honk the horn to have you come a-runnin'!" he teased from the open window. She frowned below her sunglasses. *Pompous, egotistical...* she fumed and thought of going back inside.

"What can I say, my dementia is kicking in. I've actually been wandering around all night, looking for who it was stole my ketchup." She said it without smiling but he laughed as he put it in neutral, pulled the brake and jumped out.

She opened the gate, stepped through with a shaky breath, and locked it behind her. Laney met him on the passenger side, where he held the door open for her and studied the baggy shirt and crumpled shorts. His eyes traveled down her legs. He winked and smiled at her.

"Are you ready, Ms. Sullivan, for quite possibly the most exciting morning of your schoolmarm life? Does your pacemaker have new batteries?" She came close enough that she could tell he'd showered too. The smell of clean man hit her nostrils, and she swayed towards him, her well-wired brain tripping over the thought of him in a shower. To counter the effect, she pushed her sunglasses up on her head with a smile.

"I'd like to say I'm on the edge of my seat with anticipation, but a has-been playboy isn't quite enough to get me excited." He smiled and stepped even closer. His hand traced the outside of her wrist, and a ripple of excitement ran through her body.

"What would excite you? I wonder." His voice was husky, flirtatious. Her smile faded into a frown and she backed away.

"At my age? Bingo and re-runs of the Dick Van Dyke show, probably. Nap time and Jell-O salad, for sure."

He laughed and motioned to the open door with a flourish.

"Well—I'll see what I can do about the Jell-O."

Laney snorted and looked at the large step-up into the cab crossly.

"What in the hell did you do to this poor truck?"

"Do you like it?"

"No."

He laughed and offered her a hand up but she knocked it away. Jamie made a small grunt as she brushed past him.

"You smell good. Like fresh peaches," he said.

She looked down at him from the step and decided to ignore the compliment.

"The fact that I have to vault into this truck makes me wonder if you aren't compensating for something," she said. He smiled and glared up at her. "Thankfully, I won't live long enough to find out what that something is."

"Well, I'm not compensating. But if you're looking for one last thrill before you die by shark, I think I can oblige. Though, I'm not sure an old biddy like you could handle a man like me." He stared up at her as she scooted into the seat. When she turned to look down at him, he smiled, his fingers brushed her bare leg.

"Narcissistic of you to offer, but I want to die by shark, not a venereal disease." She closed the door in his face even as he grinned. He must have seen the way her eyes grew soft at his touch. Despite trying to raise her prickly guard against him, her body and long-term loneliness were working against her.

Jamie climbed into the driver's seat.

"I'll have you know the last test was clean."

She looked at him with her full lips smiling. "Really? Huh. Groupies must be taking better care of themselves these days."

"All right, all right. Enough about my sex life."

"Oh, is it ever enough?" she teased and looked for a seatbelt but found none. Dangerous. He laughed deeply and his hand slipped off the shifter to her knee.

"Whoops," he said with a wink and put it back. She crossed her legs and scooted farther away. Dangerous times two.

"What do you know about kayaking?" he said, pulling out of her drive.

She was silent for a moment as they bumped down the two-track dirt road.

"Well, there's a boat of some sort. I believe the native word is 'kayak.' And then you put it on a large body of water, say, for example, an ocean. And then...um...you float on it? Push it around with some sort of paddle?"

He stared at the road ahead and grinned.

"Whoa! Easy there professor, you're getting way ahead of my skill level! Shoot, I didn't know I was taking out an expert. Now I feel self-conscious."

"Okay, settle down."

"I'm sure that's a first for you...not knowing what you're getting yourself into?"

"Happens more than you know," she grumbled, clinging to the open window as they bumped along. "Wait, are you insinuating that I'm a know-it-all?" She looked over at his profile, studying the curve of his strong jaw and the fresh-shaven cheek with its dimple.

"Yes. I am."

Laney leaned her elbow on the open window, letting her hand fly into the breeze. It felt strange, without a seat belt, in a vehicle with a barely-known man, in a land she was unfamiliar with. She was open and exposed, and his words were too telling. She didn't like doing things she didn't know anything about. She didn't like jumping in unprepared. She was a planner, a thinker, a by-the-booker. She was smart and stuck to things she could control. Despite that, she'd never been told she was too smart.

She thought about how often her hawk-like ex-husband had stared down at her liberal arts degree from his lawyer's perch. Her face fell—she'd never been enough. Not in her career path, not in their marriage. She felt a sob forming in her chest. Jamie cleared his throat next to her.

"Might come as a surprise to you, but smart women scare the pants off an old backwoods kid like me." He turned his eyes from the road to look at her. In his eyes she saw something new. Honesty. It startled her, and she felt like maybe she wasn't the only one feeling out of their element. She smiled unexpectedly.

"You and I might just get along," she said, a hint of surprise in her voice.

"Now, don't go gettin' my hopes up."

As they continued down the bumpy dirt road, past his villa, Jamie hummed a few notes quietly. But the words he occasionally whispered became jumbled, and he faltered back into the melody; lost in the dirt blowing up through the window and in the gentle stutter of an engine long overdue for a tune-up. They fell into an easy silence. Laney felt relaxed. So relaxed and not thinking about much of anything, she got a flash of something, a woman, a man. There was a story there...somewhere. She smiled to the warm breeze in her face and let them play in her mind, her brain gently adding details to them like colors to a black and white drawing.

Two more miles down the dirt road, Jamie made a sharp right into a barely visible drive. The turn startled her out of her meditative thoughts, and she clung to the dash. The mangrove trees were so thick that Laney couldn't see around the curve in the road to where they were headed. He slowed down, and the truck bumped along the heavily pitted drive. The last hard left brought them to a small lot in front of a white shack. "Brody's Boats" was painted red on a yellow sign above the door. Various small watercraft, surfboards, and paddleboards leaned up against the outside of the building. On the beach, lined up haphazardly, were kayaks and two-person catamarans. The beach, like all the ones she'd seen on the island, was beautiful, but unlike the more populated places, there were no other tourists around. Seemed he knew how to stay away from the Charlenes and Darlas of the world.

The beach was white crystalline, and framed out the blue-green hues of a small cove. She stared out the truck's window at the peaceful water. Her brain was still busy with the faint lines of her characters.

"Ugly, huh? Perfect deathbed." He startled her with the comment before jumping down from the truck.

She yanked at the handle and jumped down before he could come to help her.

"Well, let's get this over with," she sighed. The calm of the drive had vanished and now she was terrified. She felt her insides squirm at the thought of launching out into the wide and open ocean in a tiny piece of plastic.

"Wow, you're really eager to end it all, huh?"

"Why delay the inevitable?" she shrugged and looked up at him. Her bottom lip trembled.

He stared at it and his eyes and voice went soft.

"Well, nothing's inevitable. Follow me." He led the way up the steps to the shack.

A man met them at the open door. He was tall and thin, with dark hair that curled around his ears, and an unshaven face. His bright brown eyes smiled when he did. He wore an old Hooters shirt with his board shorts and had the easy grace of a man used to balancing.

"Hello there!" he said with obvious interest as he looked over Laney. Her heart skipped.

"Hey, Brody! How's it?" Jamie shook Brody's hand while Laney shuffled behind them.

She pushed her glasses up onto her head and thrust her hand out.

"Laney Sullivan."

Brody took her hand in both of his and squeezed it warmly. "Ms. Sullivan, I'm Brody Stevens. Completely enchanted to meet you and at your absolute beck and call." Laney squeezed his hand back with invented confidence and smiled.

"Well, there's a thought to keep a girl up at night, thinking of ways to 'beck and call' you." The flirtatious words popped out before she could check them and she blushed. Brody laughed and Jamie stepped between them.

"All right, all right. Beck and call, Brody? Really? Watch this guy, he's 'beck and called' half the island." Jamie sounded light-hearted, but Laney felt a tickle of jealousy in his words.

"Oh yeah? Pot meet kettle," she said snidely back at Jamie. "Seems I'm surrounded by shady men, hellbent on impugning my honor, yet here I stand, completely un-impugned. You boys are all talk."

Brody laughed so hard at this that he doubled over. "I like her. Thank god she's not your type!" he said to Jamie, who scowled back.

"That is true. But to be fair, we're not a couple." She gestured vaguely between herself and Jamie, before moving inside to look at the shop's equipment. "He found me in a roadside bar, separated from my family, and felt sorry for me. I'm more of a rescue-turned-contingency plan." She smiled and leaned in to whisper, "the original model dumped her drink on him and left in a huff." She turned and winked at Jamie before meandering through the small shop, her hands lifting a paddle off the shelf and gauging its weight.

"So, you're not dating?" Brody asked.

"She said it best." Jamie sighed. "We're just—" He looked at Laney who waited with raised eyebrows at him. "Just friends."

"Jameson Clark has a female friend?" Brody said, disbelieving.

"I believe that was one of the seven signs of the apocalypse," Laney laughed. "Are we going to get this party started? How many life vests can I wear at once?"

Brody walked over to her with a smile. "Can't you swim?"

"No. But I do a lovely flail."

Brody laughed and got them set up with their equipment for the day. He gathered snorkeling gear, two coolers, a couple of fishing rods and some emergency supplies. Laney carried all of her own gear, balking at them when they offered to help.

"Neither of you have ever had to take two screaming toddlers and all their shit through an airport, have you?" She set it all down on the worn-soft dock and looked back, expecting the familiar flinch of their features when her children were mentioned. But neither budged. Probably because Jamie already knew, and Brody didn't seem to be shaken by anything. "All right, so—" She gestured to the large orange craft and Brody began.

"Right, so this is the front." He pointed to the front.

"Great! Making this the back?" She pointed to the other end.

"Fast learner!" He pointed to her. "You sit in this roundish part."

"And paddle with this long do-hickey?"

"Careful, you'll be taking my job soon. If you like, you can leave your bag here, including your clothes." He flashed her a smile. Laney laughed lightly; Jamie glared. "I mean, so you have something dry to change into."

"It's been a while since I've been told to undress by someone who wasn't a doctor."

Jamie cleared his throat. "We'd better get going."

Laney turned to the sound of his growly voice.

"Alright, calm down." Laney stepped out of her sandals and sighed. She didn't care anymore what Jamie or Brody would think. As far as Laney was concerned, she'd probably never see either of them again after today. She started to undress, down to her bathing suit.

In the heat of the mid-morning, freed from the confines of her self-shame, Laney unbuttoned her shirt. She shimmied out of her shorts and put the clothes in the pack to stay behind. When she looked up, into Jamie's hungry eyes, slowly caressing her skin in an unguarded moment, she blushed brightly.

"Stop it." She threw a life vest at him. He caught it distractedly without taking his eyes off of her.

Brody came up to her and helped adjust her life vest.

"Sure you'll be okay?" He smiled as he tightened the strap. His fingers grazed the delicate skin between her breasts. Laney shivered. "Sorry," he muttered without remorse. She stepped away.

"Well, I think so. But if you hear Jamie yelling for help, don't come too quickly. I've decided to die by throwing myself into a shark frenzy today."

"Oh? Is it choose-your-own-death Saturday?" He checked his watch. "All right, but for the record I hope you come back."

"Sure. I'd hate for you to lose your kayak," she said and saw Jamie give Brody a scowl before pushing out his boat beside hers. She teetered but found balance as they practiced in the small cove.

"How are you doing there, professor?" he asked after watching her wobble once or twice with a grimace.

"Don't talk to me, I'm trying to concentrate."

"Oh, do I distract you? Would you like me to adjust your life vest?" he said grimly.

"Speaking of distracting." She turned back to look at him and her kayak shifted. A heart-stopping moment later she continued. "What was that ogling you did on the dock back there? Aren't I too old for you?"

Jamie glided up next to her. "Well, you failed to mention how well you filled out a bikini."

"I didn't realize that was need-to-know information," she snorted, and turned away to stare at the horizon line.

"Well, I sure as hell know it now." He bumped her kayak from behind. Her brows turned down into a scowl. "Though I always did learn better with a hands-on approach." Laney looked back at him and turned away just as quickly. Now she couldn't help the vision of his strong hands, calloused fingertips from years of playing his beloved guitar, on her breasts, caressing, playing, pinching. Laney clenched her knees together suddenly and cleared her throat.

"Where are we headed? Just in circles?" She put space between them.

"We could go all the way." He caught up and bumped her again and she let out a shriek as her boat tipped dangerously. Clinging to the edges with white knuckles, she looked at him.

"All the way?"

"Out the cove and down the coast, I mean."

Laney looked out at the evenly spaced ocean waves, rolling in swells outside the safety of the cove.

"Hmm."

"Chicken?"

"I do not respond to immature dares from grown men." She lifted her chin even as she stared out at the open ocean, so big, so powerful, and her, admittedly not a good swimmer.

"I won't let anything happen to you, Laney." Jamie's soft voice broke into her fear. She looked back at him. "I'll take care of you out there."

"I don't—"

"Bwaaack! Bwaack...bwaaack!" he clucked. She glared.

"Fine, hotshot. Let's head out. This water is much too shark-free anyway." She took the bait and crossed through the small inlet into the ocean. Her annoyance with him superseded her fear and once they were out, riding the waves up and over until they merely rocked the steady crafts, she felt a calmness take over. Her fright turned into excitement, and the sudden beauty of it made the moment all the more amazing.

"See, it's not so bad," Jamie said. "Stepping out of that comfort zone." She smiled over at him and, for once, had nothing barbed to say back.

The day was beautifully sunny, and she enjoyed the calm and easy rhythm of paddling next to him. They skirted the coast, racing each other. Her shoulders began to ache, and she watched the muscles of Jamie's back pull with taut and well-toned strength. The man in her dream came back to her. The strong back, the desperate way he had fought against the storm. The way he needed help but was too lost in his fear to let her in. She shivered in the warm sunlight.

Laney had no business having such deep thoughts about Jameson Clark. Nothing would ever come from this afternoon, and she was better off just nipping the feeling in the bud. She stared at the tan, sleek skin of his back, and thought that she would at least enjoy the view while she had it. She let her eyes wander over him and wondered what he would feel like, taste like, smell like. Her cheeks grew warm. Her whole body grew warm. When he turned back to check on her, his brow dropped.

"Are you okay? You're turning red. Are you getting burned? That pale skin of yours—"

"I'm fine," she said, shaking herself out of the enamored thoughts.

"Let's head in for lunch," he said and pulled alongside her. "Little beach picnic? Or, is that too romantic for you?"

"Romantic?" she said incredulously. If he only knew the hopeless romantic in her, and the thoughts that had just barely vacated her lonely brain. "You won't think it's romantic when you see how an actual woman eats."

"Women eat?" he teased. She snorted and followed his lead as he paddled at an angle into the shore. She was focusing on how she'd survive sitting next to him on a blanket on a secluded beach when she heard him shout. A split-second later the wave hit her kayak at an off angle and the craft tipped up and over. She didn't even have time to cry out before she plunged, weightless, into the ocean.

Salt water filled her mouth, and she choked. The life vest bobbed her up briefly, but another wave washed over her head. She barely had enough time to gather another breath before the water forced its way up her nose and down her throat. She came up sputtering and coughing, her hands flailed uselessly until they came into contact with something hard.

"Settle down! I've got you." Jamie said gruffly, his arm coming around her waist. His chest was at her back and she felt his stubbly cheek pressing into her temple. "Stop fighting me, so I can get us to shore."

Laney couldn't speak; the fear that had gripped her only moments before was replaced with a feeling of safety and relief. Things she hadn't felt in a while. She continued to cough as he pulled them through the water with an easy grace, and she turned in the bobbing waves to put her face against his cheek. She shook, and he gripped her waist tighter.

"Hey, it's all right." He smiled against her skin. "I'm impressed, I didn't think that you *actually* wanted to die today."

"I don't—" She coughed, and her hands clung to his shoulders. Her legs found their way around his waist. "I don't want to die," she said breathlessly and held on to him, letting her tough façade drop.

Jamie's breaths came in gasps as he swam the short distance. She felt him shift under her, and they stopped their progress. She looked up at him. He was standing on the sand now, but not moving, as if bracing himself. She loosened her grip but he held her closer.

"Hang on." He lifted her up against him as a wave hit them

from behind, taking the brunt of it with his back. Her legs were still tightly wrapped around him. She stared into his chest, her fingers still gripping his steel-like shoulders after the wave passed them and rushed to the shore. Heat blossomed between them, and Laney moved one hand to his chest and closed her eyes. She could feel his heartbeat under the pads of her fingers, steady and fast.

Jamie looked down at her, and she looked at him. Her body shook against his skin, and his hands trailed up her back to hold her tightly as another wave rushed them. If she tilted her head up, could she kiss him? The thought made her whole body tighten. His lips would be salty, warm. A droplet fell from his lashes to his cheek and she sighed.

"Are we going to stand here all day and get beat up?" she whispered huskily. He smiled and used the next wave to glide up and closer to the beach, and he stopped.

"Think you can reach now, shorty," he whispered. She clung a moment longer, liking the warmth and security of him between her legs. She nodded and unlatched herself, feeling the sand beneath her feet even as the waves kept their relentless pace. She looked back and saw that he'd tied the kayaks to himself and was towing them behind them. He wasn't a young man, but he was strong as hell. Jamie suddenly crumpled beside her with a yell.

"Son of a bitch!"

"What? What is it?" He limped quickly now towards the shore, cursing with every step on his left side.

"Ah, damn it! Ouch! J-J-Jellyfish!" he stammered as they came out of the water. He barely made it to the cover of the mangroves before falling over and grabbing his foot in pain. Laney ran up beside him, beneath the canopied shade of the trees and knelt at his side.

"What do I do?" she said, her hand going to the injured foot and trying to still him. He writhed under her hands. "Wait! I've heard if you—" She stopped. The idea was too much. She couldn't, possibly.

"Jesus, please—" he seized and yelled out again, part laughing part crying. "Whatever it is, do it!"

"I think I've heard urine can neutralize the venom? But I'm sure that's probably a myth—" She bit her lip and blushed. Jameson's breath was coming quickly now, and he looked pale.

"Do it!"

"Jamie, I don't think that's really a thing—" He clawed at his foot and she saw angry red welts already starting to appear.

"Laney, please!" His handsome features drew up in pain. She clenched her teeth.

"Goddamn it, Clark, this is the weirdest fucking day," she said and stood up over his leg. "Close your eyes." He started laughing with tears pouring down his cheeks. It took a few moments but the immediate relief that it brought made him sigh.

"Oh, god, Laney," he groaned. "Thank you. Thank you..." Laney pulled her swimsuit back up and turned back to him.

"I didn't think that would work—"

He laid back down in the sand, beneath the shady mangroves and put his hands to his eyes.

"Well, it still stings but not nearly as bad." Then, he laughed, uncontrollably. Laney sat next to him and shook her head before burying it behind her hands. "I can't believe you just peed on me."

"You told me to!" she yelled and started laughing too when he reached out and pushed at her thigh. For a moment they were quiet, and he looked up at her. When his eyes dropped to her lips, she felt the world spin.

"I think my pacemaker needs new batteries," she said.

Jamie chuckled and sat up, his hand brushing the small of her back, just as Brody came through the bushes, with a med kit, alerted by the yells.

NINE

LANEY STOOD AT JAMESON CLARK'S FRONT DOOR, wondering what madness had overtaken her. It wasn't fair that he'd used the afternoon's incident to guilt her into coming to the party.

"I did save your life after all," he had said. "And you repaid me by pissin' on me." It was bad enough how vividly she remembered the way he had rescued her in fumbling steps through the water until her feet touched the ground, and the way his skin had felt against hers. How her thighs had pressed into his waist, and the warmth of the ocean around them pulsed in a rhythm that made her weak all over again. Those moments before the sting, when her eyes and body had told him everything that was on her mind.

She should thank the universe for sending the jellyfish when it had. She blushed and died inside when she thought of what she had done to him on the deserted beach. He had taken it in stride, laughing with tears in his eyes from the pain of the sting. She wanted the earth to swallow her whole and have Jameson Clark forget she'd ever existed.

Brody opened the door and smiled when he saw her.

"Hey! You made it! Recovered from the jellyfish attack?"

"I don't think I'll ever recover."

"You can't imagine how many women would have loved to do what you did."

"Ew! That might be the weirdest thing I've heard—"

"Hey! I make no judgments...just maybe draw the line at a number two." Brody shrugged and looked at her with a flirtatious glint in his eyes.

"That's gross, Brody." She smiled, and he put his arm around her to draw her inside. "I think I'd rather curl up in a closet somewhere and die of embarrassment than be here. Why am I here, again?"

"What, and miss out on a Jameson Clark party? Trust me, you'll want to be here for this." She looked at the swarm of attractive young people, enjoying the music, drinks and food in his ostentatious house.

"I don't think I do." Just as she'd decided to leave, Jamie came through the crowd, limping on the left side. The smile on his face was almost too priceless to miss. Goddamn him.

"Hey! There's my favorite introvert."

"Probably the *only* introvert at this thing," she said, and tried to look anywhere but his face. Her eyes fell to his bare foot, and the red welts from the sting.

"Oh God, is it okay?" Laney's face turned pale.

"No! It's fine, don't worry about it," he brushed her off and handed Brody a beer. "Doc says it took just the right combination of minerals to work. You have magical pee." Laney blushed and put her hand to her forehead. "Of course, next time, she said to dislodge the stingers with sand and save ourselves the hassle. But that wouldn't have been as fun."

"Could we please talk about anything else?" she said and walked past him. "Like, where's the booze?" He followed her through the crowd. The women were leggy and towered over her.

As she looked up around her to the blonde and beautiful throng, she felt self-doubt creep in. "Why is everyone here so goddamn pretty?" she grumbled. Jamie laughed.

"Well, you're in good company—"

"Don't sweet-talk me, Clark."

"Come on, you'll have a great time, it'll be fun!" She was unconvinced as he took her by the hand into the kitchen. Two young women with Florida State T-shirts smiled, and waved, and oozed fawning adoration at him over the counter. Jamie smiled their way and then looked back to Laney.

"Fun for who exactly?" Laney said as he looked from her to them, trying to decide. She let go of his hand and pushed him. "Go on then, your adoring fans are beckoning." His brow furrowed as Laney turned away and went to the keg. "Worst. Day. Ever," she muttered as she poured a Solo cup of beer and situated herself in the corner and watched people start the karaoke machine in the main room. He was ignoring her now, giving the girls his best smiles and putting an arm around each of them. The afternoon hadn't changed anything, and she didn't know why she'd thought it would. She rolled her eyes at her own stupid hopefulness. She'd just finish her beer and leave quietly.

But then Jamie looked at her, with that damn smile, and yelled, "Laney Sullivan! It's time to get this party started! Kaylee and Jessica say you look like a karaoke kind of girl!"

Laney scowled. Kaylee and Jessica could kiss her lily-white ass. She strode over to them, took Jamie's hand, and pulled him away from the younger women's clutches.

"What? Hey!" He laughed and joined her. She flipped through the booklet briefly and punched in a number. "What are you doing?"

"Getting the party started! We wouldn't want to disappoint Kaylee and Jessica, now would we?" She bared her teeth sharply and handed him the microphone. He stared down at it as the familiar melody of one of his first party ballads started. Jamie's eyes fell, anger set his jaw.

"Come on, isn't this your thing?" she pushed him. He shot her a warning look, but Laney saw a past the anger to his fear. As the opening strains of the mega-million dollar hit began to play, she could see the pangs of something heart-wrenching and destructive pass over him. He looked like he couldn't breathe. He looked to the gathering crowd of partygoers as though they were a pitch-fork wielding pack of angry villagers.

Jamie shoved the microphone back at her and muttered an apology to the swarm of people, now rapt with attention. His face was white as a sheet as he stormed away. Laney heard a tall blonde whispering to the fake beach cowboy beside her.

"No wonder he hasn't toured since his breakdown."

"Maybe he *is* finished."

Laney's stomach fell, and she stared at Jamie's retreating back. His story of plummeting into obscurity had barely registered with her until that moment. She knew he hadn't had an album in a while. She didn't know how deep the problem rooted in him. From his happy-go-lucky lifestyle and easygoing disposition in the last few days, she'd had no reason to think he was affected.

She'd only wanted to distract him; to get his attention off of her and back to his party-hard lifestyle where it belonged. She hadn't seen the wound until she'd torn off the bandage, and now she was forced to step back and see Jameson Clark as someone much more complicated than she'd first thought. He was moving through the crowd now, towards the north side of the house. The eyes of the party turned to her, and she felt heat flood her cheeks. Brody came in from the sidelines and got up on stage next to her. He leaned down and changed the music selection.

"All right!" he shouted and turned the crowd's attention to himself. "I have a sudden urge to ABBA myself into disgrace tonight. There's a queen inside me in need of dancing. Who's with me?" The crowd erupted with applause, and a young co-ed joined him on the makeshift stage.

Laney looked at Brody, thankful for the distraction. He smiled softly at her and nodded towards where Jamie had stormed away. She made a quiet exit and breathed shallowly on her way through the long, dark hallway of open doors. What one man needed with so many rooms, she didn't know. But all of them were empty of character; bedrooms, formal dining, meeting rooms...none of them truly feeling like home. Finally, she caught sight of his silhouette in the last room on the right.

He stared out the window of a small den, standing motionless with his arms crossed in front of his chest. She could hear him taking deep breaths and blowing them out slowly. Maybe she ought to just leave him alone to compose himself. To hide. To escape. But she couldn't leave him, not when she'd been the one to stir up the traumatic memories. She stepped into the room.

The cozy space, easily her favorite so far in the oversized house, was painted a rich gray-blue, and bookshelves lined the lower half of three walls. A small fireplace took up the beachside corner beside the windows. She allowed her gaze to sweep hungrily over the books before skirting between an overstuffed chaise and a leather loveseat. She'd never figured on him being much of a reader, but she'd never would have guessed he was deeper than his surface playfulness indicated either.

Jamie turned around, and she knocked her shin on the beechwood coffee table with a curse. When their eyes met, she swallowed a lump of nerves in her throat. His eyes never faltered from hers. Laney bit her lip while her big brain tried to find the right words. His scowling eyes dropped to her bottom lip in between her teeth. He turned quickly back to the ocean view.

"What do you want, Sullivan? Come to kick me while I'm down? I have a couple tragedies that haven't been rubbed in my face still. Maybe you'd like to talk about the time I broke my leg and missed the state championship game, or hey! How about we go all the way back to my childhood pets dying?" he growled. Laney sighed and closed her eyes.

"Look, I'm sorry. I just got defensive. Those girls—"

"This isn't about the girls, Laney." His voice faltered. Laney took a step closer. She watched as he tried to focus on breathing in time to the waves. She felt his tension and unbalance, as if he were teetering on the edge of falling too hard to survive. His cheek muscles twitched and his steely eyes bored out the window. It didn't suit him. Jamie should always be smiling.

"You're right." She paused and moved another tentative step in his direction while she gathered her thoughts. "It isn't about them. It's about you."

"I don't want to talk about this with you."

"Well, I'm the one here, now." He grunted his dissent. "Jamie, look, if you were a pro quarterback coming off a bad injury, you wouldn't put yourself in the first play of the Super Bowl, would you?"

His head snapped around. "What?" he barked.

"Right?" she prompted again.

"What in the hell are you talking about?"

"Oh, I'm sorry, the answer we're looking for is, 'no,' Mr. Clark," she said in her best game-show-host voice. He scowled and stayed silent. She rolled her eyes with a sigh. "Work with me. I'm about to get into a really awesome pep talk." He glowered at her and turned away.

"You'd do a little rehab. You'd do physical therapy; you'd get your bearings. Then, maybe after a little while, you'd sit in on a practice, or head to the park to catch a game of flag with some buddies. Just you, and the ball, and people who care about you. And that's how you recapture what you loved about it. That's how you conquer being afraid of it. If I had to guess, I'd wager your problem is a matter of heart more than anything else." She waited for him to give her a stout 'go to hell.' But instead, he turned back to stare at her in the soft light of the room.

"A matter of heart? What does Laney Sullivan possibly know about matters of the heart?"

She swallowed hard. Had she not mentioned she wrote about them, dreamed them, studied them, perfected them in every novel she wrote?

"Jamie—"

"Look, nobody knows what happened—why I—I broke down."

"Because you didn't talk about it—"

"It's nobody's business!"

"Okay!" she yelled back. "I just think when you hide shit like that to protect yourself, then it festers!"

"Now festering *is* something you would know about." he countered.

"Well, what does that mean?"

"You're so good at being mad at the man who hurt you, you've convinced yourself that all men are like that." The truth stung like a slap to her face.

"Said the man with the world's worst speed-dating record," she yelled. Jamie's jaw clenched.

"Fair—fair point."

She didn't like the way he cowed. Or how her heart rate climbed and her skin warmed at their argument.

"Look, this isn't about me." Tears threatened and she turned away. "I've got plenty of problems that aren't yours to shoulder."

"Laney—"

"I don't want you to stop being who you're meant to be. I don't want you to stop doing what you love." It was a strange thing to say to a practical stranger, and they both leaned away from the intimacy. "Nobody should. I know," she paused to sigh. "I know what it is to be stuck, and unable to do what you used to love."

"I just—I can't get up there right now. And speaking of

shouldering other people's problems, it's not your place to try to save me or change what happened."

"I don't want to save you. And I don't want to take away a single thing you've lived through. Because then you wouldn't be you and I—I like you just as you are. Even when you're being a moody prick." She stumbled backwards as the outpouring of truth revealed things she hadn't even thought of herself. He snorted out a pained breath and hung his head.

"People use things, Laney. This whole goddamn industry will use your pain just to sell another song. I couldn't bear it if they used this one against me."

Laney wanted to reach out, to hold him close, to keep him safe from the deluge like he'd saved her from the waves. But they didn't know each other that well, and he wasn't in a place that seemed to invite affection. She wavered in closer to him and bit at her bottom lip in nervous frustration. He looked down and watched her. Distracted, his scowl fell away.

"And I could be mistaken, but I swear I heard you say that you liked me." He smiled, not leaving his study of her lips, and her thoughts converged into what it would feel like if it were him biting her instead. How would he taste? How cool would his lips feel on the nervous heat of her neck? She took a breath.

"We can get around to that later," she said. He moved closer in the dark and quiet room.

"Why not now?" he said, his breath heavy.

"I'm still pep-talking." Her voice shook. He leaned back, not quite a smile on his lips.

"Oh, yeah? Well, go on—I've got things to do."

Laney let out a nervous giggle and cleared her throat, angry at herself. "I've been knocked off a horse a time or two, or twelve. Not exactly when the whole world was watching, of course, but it still hurts. It wounds your pride and your sense of self-worth. God, it can make you feel an inch tall. But you still have to keep getting back on that horse." He looked away and sighed out the window as if she were an idiot.

"Why?" His tone was dark and raspy. "Why even bother getting back on that horse?"

She swayed towards him, straightening her spine. "Because that's what life is. A series of lessons, of knock-downs, and get-ups. A string of fights. The minute you stop learning, stop fighting, stop getting back up, you just—well, you just fade away." Her advice settled into her own heart.

"And why shouldn't I just fade away?" His tone maintained its hopeless, dark tenor. The lighthearted, easygoing man she'd come to know stared at her now through shadowy eyes, his jaw clenched. It made her heart race. It made her hands itch to touch his cheek, to bring back the light. She balled up her fists to resist the urge. She wasn't his love interest in some novel. She couldn't be more than a voice of reason in his world of yes-men and what-ever-you-want women. She glared back and took a deep breath.

"Because you're no quitter, Jameson Clark," she said.

Jamie's brows rose, and he snorted.

"You don't know me."

"I know enough! If you were a quitter, I wouldn't be suffering through this party, unfairly judging myself against supermodels." There was a momentary pause and then, quite unexpectedly, a small smile tugged at his lips. His eyes looked slowly over her petite frame.

"You're right. It wouldn't be fair to them to try to live up to you."

"What kind of smooth, bullshit line is that?" She tried to not smile.

"I guess I didn't quit on you. I did get you here, despite the day you had. Most ninety-year-olds would be asleep or in a self-induced coma by now." His smile broke through his sealed lips. The sight of it unclenched the invisible hand on her heart, and she felt so relieved that she pressed a soft kiss to his stubbled cheek. It was spontaneous, and she stepped away from the warmth of his sun-kissed skin quickly.

"Come on, let's go back to the party. You can tell everyone how I pissed on your leg."

The deep pit he was stuck in opened into the light of her laughing eyes, and he found Laney's smile like a lifeline. Jamie gave a small nod and followed her from the room. Her lips had been warm on his skin, and she smelled like peaches. He wished he could have more time in the dark room with her to explore what simmered just beneath her buttoned-up façade. He wanted to bite her lip. He wanted to feel her body shiver next to his like he had on the beach.

Before she led him back into the noise of the party, she stopped in the kitchen to get them each a shot of tequila. Jamie watched her. Then, with a quick look over her shoulder to see that he was still following, she led them to the back of Brody's audience. The crowd was hot and the lights and noise rose up around them. Jamie's heart hammered in his chest, as anxiety reared its ugly head. She saw the misgiving in his eyes and clinked the small glass of poison to his. She threw back her own and coughed, catching a drip of the tequila with the back of her hand. He smiled despite his worry, and he watched in fascination as she smiled back at him.

"Wanna go toss it around?" she asked and nodded up to the stage. He sipped his drink and shook his head. She nodded. "It's okay, but you know, often the best things in our lives come when we aren't ready," she said huskily in his ear and interlaced his clammy fingers with hers. He tried to hang on to her, but she was already walking up to the stage, taking the offered microphone and conversing closely with Brody.

"You sure?" Brody said after she whispered in his ear.

"Yep," she said. The mic picked up her voice, more loudly than she had intended. Her terrified eyes met the crowd. Then, as Jamie watched, she took in a deep breath and smiled to light the night.

"Hey, y'all. I'm Laney. And the first thing you should know about me, is that I can't sing for shit," she announced. The crowd quieted and stared at her. Kaylee snorted with judgmental laughter and Jamie felt the pang of his own failure.

"In fact, I'm pretty sure that what I'm about to do up here is going to be burned into your memory as one of the *absolute* worst karaoke experiences you've ever witnessed." Jamie covered over Kaylee's laugh with a loud whoop. Laney looked at him as his cheer brought about more.

"There's gonna be crying," she nodded. "My own, actually... later, alone in my room, curled up in the fetal position." More trickles of laughter came and more cheers as the crowd warmed. "But someone I know, somebody I care about—" she paused to clear her throat. "Well, he lost something and I want to help him find that again. Whatta y'all say? Help me out?" The crowd clapped and hollered and Brody gave her a thumbs-up as the song began playing.

She caught Jamie's eyes, where he watched from the back of the crowd and felt her cheeks burn as the sweet sound of a fiddle began to play and *Callin' Baton Rouge* fired up its catchy beat. She watched Jamie move closer and stand in front of the young and judgmental girls. She wasn't here for a long time, and she wasn't singing for herself. She was singing for him.

Laney began fearlessly and, to her surprise, on key. The crowd clapped along to the beat and danced to the catchy refrain. Jamie looked up at her, enjoying such a strange situation, and he smiled. She suddenly wasn't afraid. She winked at him, opened her arms and nodded him towards the stage. Showing him the way to his horse.

Jamie shook his head and shrugged and stepped up beside her.

Laney moved aside to give him the center, but he pulled her back and put the microphone between them.

"Where in the hell do you think you're going, Laney? We're riding this thing together," his said and quirked a sassy, tequila-kissed smile at her. The crowd fell away.

"A replay of last night's events roll through my mind—" His voice came out smooth and melodic. Laney faded back, but he nudged her into finishing the line.

"Except a scene or two erased by sweet red wine—"

They sang the refrain together, and the sound of his voice reverberated through the room. He stared into her eyes, and Laney watched the beautiful and strange light of rediscovery shine through them. She took his hand and her fingers lightly laced into his. She watched him take a deep breath as something broke loose inside of him and he hit the refrain.

Laney could feel the moment that the brilliance and magic lit Jamie up. It left her just as breathless as the rest of the room. There was that guy; the one she'd known only from a distance. It was a shadow of his peak, but he was still in there. He captivated the room. His smile gave way to dimpled cheeks that made him even more handsome.

He smiled down at her and she looked away when he sang to her, "Hello, Laney dear, I hope you're feeling fine—"

She did feel fine. Too fine. Too heart-racing and hopeful. Too good. He nudged her out of the frown that started to form and they sang the last few lines together. Laney was in a daze of pride and embarrassment. The crowd disappeared, and it was just him and her, and she had to remind herself that this moment was for him.

Her jaded heart tied reins around the joy. She didn't really matter in the grand scheme of Jameson Clark's life. He would have found this place, eventually. She looked out at the crowd and the jealous stare of the leggy Kaylee, and felt suddenly crumpled inside; she wasn't part of this world. She could pretend for tonight, especially since she'd never see any of these people again. But this was a once-in-a-lifetime Cinderella moment. In the end, her voice wavered, and she pulled away.

He finished strong to an eruption of applause and whistles. People rushed the front of the room, hugging and cheering. Laney was pushed aside by Kaylee, and further back by Jessica. The swelling crowd made her dizzy and nauseous and she crept away, holding her stomach.

Laney made her way out the large doors to the pool. Good for him. At least he looked like he enjoyed it. She sighed as the cool breeze coming off the water helped her heated skin. Her body was wobbly as she crossed the back patio to the deck overlooking the water. She took the moments away from the crowd with relief.

"You okay out here?" came Brody's voice from behind. She turned, thankful it wasn't Jamie.

"Yeah." She breathed out a sigh. The music rose again this time to Jimmy Buffett's *Fins*. Jamie's voice cut through the night. Brody stood next to her, overlooking the view from the balcony.

"Well, I believe congratulations are in order."

"For what?" she said distractedly.

"Jamie," he said.

"What about Jamie?"

Brody smiled and nudged her. "You did something that voice coaches, agents, fans, and even his own family couldn't do. In fact, I haven't seen him do that in years."

She blushed and looked down the beach.

"Aw, shucks, 'tweren't nothin'," she drawled. "He had it in him all along. He just needed a little foot to the ass."

"Your modesty is becoming, Laney," Brody said and Laney blushed. He stepped closer. "You certainly have something that touches the right nerves."

"I do get on nerves. It's a talent." Laney scoffed, nudged him with her shoulder and looked at the starry sky. They stayed in the silence for a while.

"*Are* you two dating?" Brody asked quietly.

"No!" The word shot out of her mouth "Heck no! No. No?" she said one more time to remind herself. "Nope."

Brody laughed. "Me thinks the lady is protesting too much."

Laney smiled up at him. "I think I run a little old for his tastes."

"At the risk of asking, how old are you, Laney?" Wind blew a strand of hair over her cheek and Brody brushed it away with a calloused finger.

"Thirty-seven," she whispered. Brody's finger stayed on her cheek longer than was just friendly, his thumb gently traced the line of her jaw.

"Perfect. I think that's perfect," he whispered. Laney's breath caught, and she felt dizzy. What was happening? She was nervous and shaky and wanted to get back inside. The crowd went wild behind them, and they could hear Jamie laughing and inviting someone else to take the mic. "I hear you're here alone. It's a damn shame, a muse as beautiful as you being alone."

"I'm—I'm not beaut...a muse?" she said breathlessly as he pressed closer to her.

"You inspired one of the most downtrodden men I know, to sing again."

"I doubt I inspire men to do much of anything." Laney shook her head.

"I don't know. You're inspiring some ideas in me." Laney swallowed and a nervous flutter sprung up in her chest. She couldn't think of the last time a man had come on to her, and none of them had ever done it this strongly. She backed up against the railing. Brody stepped closer.

"Hey, you two!" came Jamie's voice from behind. Brody stopped his prowl-like advance and turned. Jamie walked up closer and studied the way Laney's hands were gripping the balcony. She saw him glare towards Brody, and Brody glare back at him.

"Am I interrupting something?"

"No," Brody said, rubbing his neck and glancing back at her, hunger and disappointment on his face.

"Wow, it's getting late. I have to go," Laney said and scrambled around them both.

"What? We're just getting started." Jamie said. She smiled over her shoulder at him.

"Well, go on then! Don't let me hold you back." She waved him towards the house.

"Laney, wait!" Jamie and Brody both called, then looked at each other with a scowl.

She turned their way with a smile, but didn't stop her determined march to the exit. "You boys go play. Us adults have deadlines to meet and papers to grade." She collected her purse and jacket from the couch and went through the door as quickly as she could.

Outside, the night was melodic with the sounds of crickets and tree frogs as Laney breathed deeply with every shaky step home. She didn't know what had undone her more, the intense and emotional hour where Jamie had swung from light to dark and back to a vibrant, shining star, or the way Brody had come onto her like he meant to eat her alive.

She was probably overthinking it, like most things. Aiming her writer's eye to a simple and non-dramatic situation. Still, Jamie hadn't seemed happy about finding them that way, and he had said something as she was leaving. *Laney, wait.* His words, the sweetness of his drawl, sunk into her brain like a warm hug.

She shook rationality into her head. If they were anything, it was surely only friends. A bird sang loudly beside her from the darkness of the bushes, and she jumped. Her mind returned to Jamie and a sneering inner voice reared its ugly head.

You can't have feelings for Jameson Clark, and you know it.

"I know, I know," she said aloud, but her voice was broken.

The last man she'd had feelings for was David. He'd never had a knack for romance, but Laney had liked him because he was practical and smart. Ambitious in the academic world and brooding. He'd had a false idea that a rural upbringing made one simple, and found Laney curious because she was well-read, intelligent and clever. Even though Laney was bright, their marriage worked only as long as she stayed dimmer than David. When she finally found the courage to send in her manuscripts, showed an agent the talent she'd denied for the sake of David's ego, she was surprised at her own success. So was he, and not pleasantly.

When he couldn't feel superior to her anymore, he'd found someone else to take the job. One of his college students, who'd tripped all over herself to give him the praise he needed. Laney found out after the affair had been going on for two years. Two years! She shivered and hugged her shoulders. Being rejected for finally living her dream, cast aside for a younger, more moldable woman, cut deep. Talk about falling off a horse. She thought about Jamie, the resilience he had shown stepping up to the stage tonight.

And soon her blossoming romantic brain was back to reliving the way he watched her when he sang, changed the words to serenade her. The dark library. The desire. A small fire sparked in her belly.

"Ugh!" she said, trying to not get caught up.

But it was too late. Jamie wasn't infallible or perfect. Jamie wasn't broody or emotionless. If anything, he wasn't afraid to be the things that David never was. Vulnerable. Silly. Playful. Naughty.

Jamie had cracked open a door, and now Laney's flood of want seemed to rush out, uncontainable. His voice like velvet, his lips delectable. His hard shoulders beneath her fingers, wet, as he'd picked her up out of the water. The heat of his waist between her thighs as he had held her close and carried her to shore. The inspiration overwhelmed her like wildfire, and she couldn't stop the visions that played over and over, staggering her breath and making her body ache for attention.

Her fingers itched. Her mind ran and tumbled all over itself. She needed to get to her computer. By the time she had climbed the few short steps up to the cottage, she had worked and reworked several ideas and had the opening lines perfectly scripted in her mind.

She pounced on her keyboard without a hitch in her brain and typed like mad; flying through the first chapter in an hour. She felt determined and sure-minded as the characters came to life before her. Maybe it was the night, maybe it was the freedom of being alone, or the lack of writing for days, the sultry sway of waves and moonlight that had snapped open her mind. Maybe it was the warm feeling of Jamie's cheek beneath her lips. Whatever it was, it was working, and she wrote until the dark hours just before dawn.

———

"Laney, wait," Jamie said as he tried to follow her out the door. Kaylee pulled him back by the hand and coerced him up on stage. Laney walked out without so much as a backwards glance. He looked at Brody, who walked past him, his eyes on the same fixed mark before he sighed and went about finding a replacement.

Something reared up inside of Jamie, something that made him angry about the way Brody watched her. The way he'd found them on the balcony ate at his gut. She'd looked like a deer in the headlights of a Mack truck. Was she mad that he'd interrupted Brody? Or was she scared of Brody and relieved to get out of there?

He wasn't sure but the worst of it was having to wonder; to be met with her leaving instead of her honesty. To not have her talk to him. Along with that was the worry that when she walked out of his door, she might never come back again. Suddenly, a world without Laney seemed like a world he didn't want to live in.

"Shit," he whispered to himself. They were both adults, and she was just a friend. He nodded, agreeing to whatever song had been chosen. He felt like he could sing anything, write anything...

Watching her walk away, a rush of ideas came at him, clamoring just behind the veil of his mind. The same way it used to when he was writing three or four songs a week, and his mind was on fire with ideas. Even when she was gone, she was affecting him.

"Jamie!" Brody said. He looked at his equally flustered friend, confused. Brody nodded towards the karaoke machine.

"Yeah, sorry." Jamie shook his head and then read the words on the large screen behind them with dismay. "Ugh. Really?"

It's Raining Men began to play and just like that Jamie was swept up into the evening of revelry.

Jamie went to bed by himself, turning down offers from both Kaylee and Jessica. He was too excited to sleep, but in no mood to share the feelings rushing inside of his chest with anyone. Anyone but Laney at least, and she'd left. Singing with her had felt good, and when she'd grabbed his hand on stage, it seemed to come even easier, as if he'd never left. The crowd became less a scary wave, and more a dull lull when he focused on her eyes locked into his. The fears, the insecurities, the expectations of his career and fame didn't belong on stage with her and the young and expectant crowd hadn't held a candle to Laney.

In her pleased and I-told-you-so smile, he found a new reason to love it. He was sixteen again belting out the lyrics in his favorite old, beater car. He was twenty-one, hanging out with the boys in the garage. Before he'd signed his first contract, or stepped out in front of his first 50,000-person crowd. It was just her. And it was just him. When she'd snuck offstage, he wasn't sure if he was Jameson Clark, honey-voiced superstar, or just Jamie, a humble Tennessean songwriter. He was confused and high, and spent the night elated and mired in thought.

He thought of Laney. And all the pain and rejection she'd been through herself. How could he ever help her the way she'd helped him? Jamie tossed in his empty bed, stared at the fan, and thought of how good and awful Laney could make him feel all at once. Helping him back up on his horse, then leaving him there to ride it alone. She was like a ghost or a muse; whip-smart and jaded, with a soft underbelly that made him want to work for the chance just to get closer to her. A chance to help her. He smiled as the jellyfish sting on his foot itched again.

He couldn't be sure, and he partly hoped it wasn't true, but it seemed Laney Sullivan had officially broken down his wall.

TEN

LANEY HAD FALLEN ASLEEP ON THE COUCH AND WAS roused by the loud buzz of the outside gate's intercom.

"Hmph," she muttered and rolled off the couch and onto the floor. She lay there, still half-stuck in dreams, hoping whoever was buzzing at her gate would give up. When silence fell again, she drifted off, face planted into the rug beneath the couch. A loud and repetitive knock sounded at her door. She sat up quickly and knocked her head on the coffee table.

"What 'n the hell?" Laney muttered a curse and stumbled to standing. She tore open the front door to find Jamie, rocking on his heels impatiently. He smiled beneath his tattered ball cap and lit up her world. She scowled.

"Seems you had a good night. College girls happy about your comeback?" she grumbled, holding the door with one hand and her head with the other. "How the hell did you get past my fence?" She yawned.

"I climbed it."

"Pretty spry for an old fella. Especially after exploiting all night." He chuckled and studied her wayward hair. She touched the fresh bump on her forehead and her eyes were tender from the late night of writing.

"I didn't 'exploit' anyone last night. I did, however, have an interesting epiphany."

"Big word, Clark. What were you, up all night studying the dictionary?"

"Man, you're mean this morning!" He laughed and pushed his way past her. She sighed and turned towards him as he wandered the room, looking through the bookshelves with his hands tucked in his pockets. "Is that because of *your* rough night?"

"I didn't have a rough night," she argued, though her head throbbed.

"Really? 'Cause when *I* wake up without pants—I figure something good musta happened." He smiled. Laney glanced down at her underwear and her face turned pink. She ducked behind the couch and reached over the side of it for the throw. "Well, don't bother covering up, I've seen them before. The panties are nice though," he chuckled and tried to peer around the blanket at her backside, snug in soft blue cotton, trimmed with lace.

"Flashing men my underwear isn't something I'm as comfortable with as some of your 'friends' are," she grumbled, and held the blanket up in front of her. He smiled mischievously.

"I wouldn't be embarrassed if I were you, that sweet little backside of yours—mmm—it's like a soft heart." His eyes found hers and her scowl softened. Maybe Marc was right—maybe men were into that. "And of course, I've been a fan of your legs since at least yesterday. They sure felt nice when you wrapped them around me when you thought you were dyin'." His smile and teasing tone were too much.

"Ugh! What do you want?" She hid her smile behind feigned disgust while she wrapped the throw securely around her.

"Well, Laney Sullivan, your pep talk last night helped me. A lot. It helped me start to get over something that's been hurting for a long time." The humbled change softened her. "I want to return the favor."

She swallowed and clutched the blanket. "What kind of favor?"

"Sort of a surprise."

"You don't have to do that," she said and looked away. "I didn't do anything." He stepped towards her and she backed away. He smiled and kept coming.

"But you believed. You—" He paused and studied her cheeks and lips. "You really *are* something special, Laney Sullivan." Laney's eyes fell away. She didn't want to believe him. Jamie sighed and shook his head, almost like he could read her self-deprecation. "Say, my little, pant-less 'something special', can you ride a horse?" The odd request took her back, and she lifted an eyebrow.

"Yes," she said tentatively. "Why?"

"Well, and I *really* hate to say this, go put on some pants. I've got coffee in the truck," he said.

"I'm just supposed to jump when you say? What if I don't want to go? What if I have work I need to get done? What if I don't like horses?"

He smiled at her protests and stepped forward.

"I have the sneaking suspicion, Laney darlin', that you won't do anything you don't want to. Call it my intuition, or the fact that you seem to be a woman coming into her own, but I think that you *want* to get out. I think that you're tired of being trapped in the same old cycle. I think you're ready to get back on your own horse, so to speak." His quiet words needled their way into her heart. She sighed and looked at his chin, stubbled and square. That bottom lip, just slightly fuller. The way she wanted to kiss him last night in the library and more so this morning. How good would it feel, to break out of her self-inflicted doldrums by kissing Jameson Clark?

"Okay," she whispered. "But I am not getting into a kayak today."

"Fair enough." He smiled. When he didn't budge from his spot, she scowled.

"Well? Are you going to leave so I can get dressed?"

"What are we, twelve?"

"I'm modest. It's a dying quality in this world. At least avert your eyes while I shimmy up the stairs," she said, backing towards the loft.

"Aren't you sleeping in the bedroom?" He turned away from her to check out the rest of the cottage.

"No. I like the loft. It's like a—" she stopped.

"Like a what?"

Laney reached the top and found her cargo capris and bra. She faced away and pulled her shirt off, and the morning sunlight was warm on her naked back. She tried to hurry, as she put on her bra and pulled on a t-shirt.

"It's like a treehouse. I always wanted to live in a treehouse," she finished, and turned to find him watching her change. "Were you watching me? Didn't you get enough half-naked women at the party last night?" Jamie stood still, staring up at her.

"I told you, I didn't get any naked women last night. Your friend Brody had no trouble finding somebody to keep his bed warm though," Jamie said, the last bit coming out as quite a surprise to both of them. He cleared his throat. Laney wondered why he'd thrown Brody under the bus.

"My friend?"

"Yeah, sorry. He's kind of the island's main attraction for girls," Jamie said.

"Ooo, I bet that hurts your ego, huh?" she smirked.

"I just don't want you to think he's a one-woman kind of guy."

"Why would I care how many women Brody has?"

"Well, I thought after he'd kissed you last night—"

"We didn't kiss! There was no kissing." She turned to get her sunglasses and took a deep breath. "I'm more surprised that you spent the night alone. I mean you really didn't have anyone stay over?" she asked. He stared at her curiously.

"No," he whispered and stepped closer. "My mind was someplace else." His eyes searched hers. Laney blushed and tried to remember all of the sensible things she'd told herself the night before. They seem to fade with the soft look in his eyes.

Last night she had been inspired. But that was night, and magic, and full of promise. Today it was a bright morning, and the world was the same one with a crappy car, failed marriage, and a family in trouble. Jamie was magic and promise. Laney was not. Her stomach dropped, her heart ached, and she looked down at her bitten nails and old shoes.

"We ought to get going," she said and headed for the door. Jamie followed, and he didn't say anything else, the whole way across the island.

———

Jamie pulled into a small stable on the northern side. Laney followed him to the office and smiled politely while Carlos, an older man who'd relocated from Colombia some years before and now owned the small stable, went over the paperwork. The horses were already saddled when they went out to the corral. Jamie watched her, the way her body moved, the way she relaxed the minute she saw the horse.

She took a moment to look over her mare. A beautiful Arabian bay, with a shiny red coat. She spoke softly to her, gently scratching her neck and inspecting the tack to make sure nothing was too tight or rubbing her.

"Do you ride? Or am I popping your cherry?" Laney smirked over the horse's back. Jamie's eyebrows rose.

"I've had some experience."

"Wait, are we talking horses or..."

"Both," he said lowly and walked up to the roan gelding that he favored.

"Heya, Ernest," he said and patted him. The horse nickered and nudged Jamie's shoulder. "That's Maria," he nodded to Laney's mare.

"Hello, Maria." Laney's voice was soft and happy. He liked the way she caressed the thick neck of the horse. He liked the softness in her when the horse snuffled her hand, looking for treats.

"Did you grow up around horses?" he asked.

"My grandparents had a small ranch in Sweet Valley until they passed. My dad and sisters took it over. I grew up there—used to spend every summer helping run it when I was in college. After Dav—" She paused, before launching into her marital woes. "After kids and life, I fell away from it. My younger sisters both live there now, and they're working to help my parents. It hasn't been easy, keeping the land from getting bought out."

"Bought out?" Jamie asked. Laney looked at him and shrugged.

"Sweet Valley is a beautiful, little, unknown place. Protected from the worst of winter, close to the mountains with a nice river, and good fields. Lot of rich people buy up the land for second homes or big dude ranches. People don't actually ranch land much, it's too hard of work and too expensive. The Sullivan homestead must get ten offers a year to sell. Some of them...pretty high pressure." Her voice turned sad, and she caressed Maria's long nose.

"Why don't they sell?" Jamie asked. Laney looked at him and smiled sentimentally.

"It's our home. It's the only way of life we've known and—well, some things just shouldn't be for sale. Somethings are bigger than a payout."

· · ·

Jamie stared at her, his gears turning again. Only last night he'd told her how the industry would sell your soul to earn a paycheck. He nodded in understanding.

"My dad's the town veterinarian, and my mom assists him and runs the ranch. My sister Elle has a catering business, and her husband Blake is a vet and may take over for Dad, though I don't think Dad would know what to do with himself if he ever retired." Jamie's heart clenched hard and his eyes filled with tears. Neither had his dad. Laney met his gaze and shifted her tone. "Listen to me chattering! Sorry, I...I don't talk much about myself. Sometimes I don't know when to shut up," she finished awkwardly.

"I don't mind—I like listening to you," Jamie said and sniffed. "What's your youngest sister do?" Laney sighed.

"She and her boyfriend are trying to get a rehabilitation center started. Not just for injured horses but also for people in need of equine therapy. Veterans, kids on the spectrum, that kind of thing. Katelyn—she's a firecracker. You'd like her. She's young and blonde."

"I think I prefer jaded girls with honey-brown hair." He scowled at her self-depreciation. She snorted, blushed and looked away.

"Probably for the best, Grant would probably kill you. All six feet two of him." She sighed. "So that's my family, in a nutshell. Oh—and then there's me, who barely ekes out a living teaching entitled kids how to map out sentences, and tries to support two girls while their dad takes his mistress to France. I do contribute a fair amount of snark and dark humor to save the Sullivan ranch though." She paused and plastered on a fake smile. "Good talk— we should get going."

"Laney Sullivan," He paused and shook his head. "You've got a lot of layers." She looked up to Jamie watching her, mesmerized.

"Like an ogre?"

"Ten points for the *Shrek* reference."

"My kids are obsessed."

He smiled at this and his eyes went soft. "I don't mind learning about you, Laney. It's like reading a really good book."

"The book of me is boring."

"The book of you is underrated and needs to be in the right hands to be appreciated," he said.

Laney crinkled her nose as her body warmed.

"That was pretty damn smooth."

"I know, right? I'm trying," he laughed. She took Maria by the halter. After leading the pair out of the corral in the warm afternoon sunshine, they found the trailhead just south of the stables. Laney took a deep breath, put her foot into the stirrup, and gave her body a couple of quick bounces before pulling herself up into the saddle. He laughed when she grunted with the struggle.

"Nice old lady noise."

"You try hoisting this ass up five feet," she grumbled.

"Well, next time ask me! I'd be happy to hoist your ass." He said and took an appreciative glance.

She stuck out her tongue before he nudged Ernest into an easy trot. For a moment they just enjoyed the ride, the mangroves and sandy path, the deep blue sky above them and the sound of the horses' hoofs against the ground in their patient and steady rhythm.

Laney's eyes fell from the scenery to Jamie, so at ease in his saddle, the way his Wrangler-clad backside fit into it like a glove. The way his legs cradled Ernest's sides and his shoulders stretched the t-shirt tight. He had his cowboy hat on today, made of well-loved and ratty straw, turned up at the edges. Watching him set her at ease. He might have been the most athletic, but relaxed man she'd ever met. They rode this way, easy and slow, for over an hour before he turned back.

"You didn't have plans tonight, did you?" he said as he pulled

Ernest to a stop. The horse danced in place, unused to changing the well-worn path.

"Well, I need to write a syllabus—"

"Psh, nerd! We're gonna play hooky, instead." He charged his horse into a barely noticeable break in the trees.

"Jamie, I—damn it," she sighed, tightened her grip on the reins and turned Maria in pursuit. The path was dappled in the fading afternoon light. She could see Ernest's flank disappear around another small curve just ahead of her. She followed, ducking so low in places that she had to lay against the warm strength of Maria's neck to keep from getting knocked off. "Where are we going?"

"Someplace special." He looked back at her as she sat up in the saddle. Her body adjusting to the shift of the horse like a well ingrained memory. "You've sure been quiet on the ride," he said, breaking their silence.

"Didn't you get enough of my tale of woe earlier?"

"No," Jamie said, so soft she almost didn't hear. "It's good to get lost in thought sometimes." Laney agreed. That was how her best ideas came to her, when she wasn't busy with other things. In the quiet.

"Maybe I'm contemplating snake-bite death, since the sharks were a bust."

"Gonna make me carry you out of the jungle?" he laughed.

"No. I don't think your back could take it. You should just leave me to writhe in venom-induced agony."

"Jesus, Laney. I thought we already discussed how you don't really want to die." He looked back at her. "You do remember that conversation, yeah? When your legs were all wrapped around me?"

She smiled slowly. "I wasn't thinking of anything in particular before, but now I'm thinking about that, thanks." He smiled over his shoulder and looked straight ahead. Laney ducked under a branch and adjusted her reins through her sweaty palms.

· · ·

The truth was that Jamie's brain had been busy since the gentle cadence of the horse had put him on the path. He was thinking. He was wondering. He was daydreaming. Things he hadn't given himself much occasion to do in the last few years. Especially in the company of a woman. There was always a need to impress, to hide the anxiety over his past, and usually to satiate some amount of sexual tension.

But with Laney he could relax; he could just be. She didn't need impressing. The sexual tension though... he looked back over his shoulder and watched the way her strong thighs gripped Maria's back. He thought of her, of the Book of Laney, and how many lyrics came sudden and fast in his mind following that lead. Suddenly, they broke through the vegetation and into a small crescent bay. The water was calm. The sands mired with palm leaves and small black rocky outcroppings. An old boat sat, unassuming, against one of the rocky piles. The sun was starting its slow descent.

"Shouldn't we head back? It's going to get dark soon." Laney's voice was small.

"Is Laney Sullivan scared?" He smiled as she came up beside him. Maria nudged Ernest, and he nipped at her cheek. Laney frowned.

"No. It just doesn't seem like a good idea to take them back through that maze in the middle of the night."

"I love having a mom along to worry for me."

Laney made a disgusted sound and Maria knocked into Ernest's flank when she felt Laney's legs tighten.

"Don't worry, I've done it before."

"I bet you have. Was Bambi nervous when you took her to a secluded beach, or did she sprawl out and thank her lucky stars?" Laney nudged her mare into a trot along the water. Jamie chuckled before following in pursuit. Free from the usual tourist path, the horses frolicked in the waves, happy to let loose and run. Laney smiled as the wind whipped through her hair. She kept just ahead of him. When he did catch her, he grabbed on to her saddle and she slowed. He was close now, and staring at her lips. The sun was setting, the coastal breeze cooling their skin. He brushed her hair back, his fingers lingered on her neck.

"Hungry?" he asked lowly. She wet her lips.

"Yes," she said softly. He wanted so much to kiss her senseless. He felt unbalanced. He felt...the urge to be better. Jamie leaned back and redirected Ernest. Laney turned Maria to follow. They dismounted, tethered the horses to a large log of driftwood, and offered them fresh water from their own packs. Jamie took his backpack towards the boat.

"Ah, hell no! The deal was no boats. That's a boat," Laney said.

He turned and smiled. "The deal was no kayaks. That isn't a kayak. It's just a regular old dinghy."

She sauntered up as he put the pack in the boat and he pushed it into the water. He turned back and offered her his hand. He waited.

"Come on, you can trust me."

"I think we've proven that I can't," she said

"I didn't let you drown before and I won't now. It'll be worth it. You'll have something to tell the old biddies at the nursing home when you get back."

"Better than Thelma's gallbladder stories?" she retorted.

"Way better. Get on in." He leaned over, closed the space between them, and grabbed her hand. He pulled her close. The boat shifted and rocked as he got in and they set out into the bay. The stars were beginning their slow, easy glow in the sky as the night turned darker. When they were in the middle of the cove, he reached into the bag and started spreading out crackers, fruit, and smoked fish on the middle seat between them.

"I was half-expecting bologna and Kraft cheese," she said. He smiled and popped open a bottle of wine. "It's kind of annoying how cool you are." He laughed at this and handed her a plastic cup of wine.

"My sole aim is to annoy you."

"You do it well." She smiled and sipped her wine. "This is an amazing view." Laney looked up at the stars. "There are so many. It's like being at home on the ranch, only warmer." The quiet hush of the waves lapping against the sides of the boat was the only sound between them.

Jamie shoved a bite of cheese in his mouth as he watched her. She looked like a kid, gathered up at the other end of the boat, knees pressed together and watching the stars, like she was getting to stay up late for the first time. He pulled out a jacket from his bag and threw it over her shoulders. Leaned in close like that, he could smell her and the warmth of her body caused his to respond.

"Thanks," she said. "I had no idea you could be such a gentleman."

"At your age, pneumonia is no laughing matter," he said and bit into an apple. She quirked her lips.

"At your age, I'm surprised you're awake past four."

He laughed. "I'm only forty-six."

"I'm only thirty-seven." They looked at each other. He smiled.

"I guess I *am* older than you."

"Only in years. Mental maturity is a whole different matter." They resumed their silence for a moment. Then, when it had gotten truly dark, he put a small lantern between them.

"Well, it's about time, I reckon," he said.

"For what? We're not heading back in already, are we?" she asked.

"Now, I thought you didn't want to be out here," he smiled.

She tossed a cracker at him.

"What's it time for then?"

"The show." Jamie leaned over and took her hand from her knee. She didn't shy away. He pulled it over the edge of the boat in his own. His fingers wove with hers, and when they touched the surface of the ocean, it exploded in brilliant blues and greens. Laney watched in complete wonderment as the trail of their hands in the water was lit by the bioluminescent particles surrounding them. She gasped and laughed, and Jamie's heart went wild in his chest. Her face, lit from underneath, was alive with excitement and joy.

"Damn it, Laney Sullivan, you're about the prettiest thing I've ever seen," he whispered. Laney blushed and tried to pull her hand away. He held it tighter. She put her other hand in and watched the swirling patterns. They both laughed. As they sat back, he grabbed up the oars and paddled them around the cove, lighting up the water in trails behind them.

When she yawned through her smiles, he took them back to shore. He didn't want to leave, but her eyes were heavy and he was having warm and sensual thoughts every time she looked across the boat at him. They landed and gathered up their gear. She helped him drag the boat to its spot. When they went to untether the horses, Maria nervously pranced in place.

"Easy, girl. Easy." Laney tried to calm the mare, stroking her neck and holding her still.

"Maria doesn't like the dark. She can't see as well as Ernest," he said and took the reins, tying them to Ernest's saddle. "Probably for your safety, we should double up on the way back."

"What?"

"Don't worry, Ernest is a tough old bastard. He can carry us both."

"Can't you just lead me out on her?"

"If she bucks or startles and dumps you off in those mangroves, you could really get hurt," Jamie said with concern.

"I'm starting to think you knew this all along."

"I did know it; I just didn't think it would be a big deal."

"It's just that I—" Laney stuttered.

"You?" he led.

"Fine. It's fine," she frowned and bit her lip.

"Great." He growled and let her mount first. "Scoot up," he demanded. She frowned down at him, but did as she was told. He mounted behind her, felt Laney shiver as the warm pressure of their bodies came together. They started off through the dark path. Laney was stiff at first, as if she was trying to not get too close to him.

"It's alright, professor. You can relax, I ain't gonna hurt ya." Jamie soothed.

Laney took a deep breath in and sighed. Her body eased, warm against him. His arms relaxed around her shoulders. The quiet cadence of the horses, the sounds of the mangroves at night, and their steady even breathing matched put Jamie at ease.

"So, how many girls have you conned into sharing your saddle?" She yawned.

He chuckled and pressed his nose into her hair.

"None. I've only been to the bay two other times. Once by myself. Once with Carlos. I can tell you this, it's much more pleasant sharing a saddle with you than him."

A slow and low giggle started in her chest and grew.

"I mean, he's got amazing thighs, but roving hands," Jamie said. She fell into a fit of laughter and pressed back against him. He chuckled into her hair. The crickets chirped and the soft, even canter of the horse beneath them seemed to lull both into a sleepy state. Her hand fell to his thigh. Her body shifted closer. Jamie's body responded quickly, and they were too close for him to even try to hide it.

"Um—did I do that?" she whispered, looking over her shoulder. He sighed into her ear.

"Not my fault that heart bottom of yours is the perfect fit. Fella can't help some things, Laney." His lips brushed her temple. She put her head back against his shoulder and made a small sigh as her backside moved closer against him.

"Sorry I don't have a bonier ass." He laughed and one of his arms sneaked around her waist. "Uh oh, he's making a move," she teased.

"I'm trying to keep you on this horse. Seems like you're about to melt."

"Well, you did stop my world." She smiled into the dark night.

"Eighties song lyrics? Are you trying to seduce me?" he nuzzled her ear and guided Ernest with one hand. She pressed into the warmth of his arms, like a woman who hadn't been held in far too long. Jamie felt her temperature rise, her breathing quicken, her fingers ran down the length of his thigh and he held her closer to him. His lips found the skin of her neck and when he kissed her, she gasped and arched into it. Her hips pressed back against him. Jamie tensed as his arm brushed her breasts, his teeth grazed her neck. The trail widened into Carlos' property.

"Lord, Laney," he whispered softly in her hair. Her hands stayed on his thighs and her nails dug in. "We need to stop," he pulled Ernest up to a halt. "We're here," he gasped and tried to catch his breath.

She sat up as he swung down. He looked up at her flushed cheeks and wanted to drag her off the horse and straight into bed with him. But the vulnerability in her eyes made him realize that this wasn't something Laney did. Let men get close to her. Men that had a reputation especially. He offered her his hand. She bit her lip and shook her head.

"I got it." She got down and faltered on wobbly knees. Jamie itched to take her in his arms, tell her all the weird and wonderful things she did to him. Carlos came from the stables and offered to take the horses. He cast a knowing wink Jamie's way. He shook his head.

He knew Laney wasn't ready, and he didn't want to be just some player to her. She didn't speak to him as they got into his truck and he drove, without saying anything, down the empty dirt roads and back to Palamo Bay's gated community. He stopped in front of Marc's cottage and cleared his throat.

"Laney, I don't—"

"Thanks, Jamie," she interrupted. She yanked open her door,

got out and slammed it without saying anything else. He watched her run to the cottage.

Jamie hated how she'd closed down. Maybe she was right, and he wasn't the kind of guy she deserved to have. The forever kind. For reasons unknown, his stomach dropped. He thought of his own mom, of his dad. The family back home that loved him. He was overcome with harsh homesickness.

"Laney!" he shouted from the open window. He saw her shoulders fall in a sigh and she turned around, hand on the door.

"Yeah?"

"Thanks for going with me. For putting up with my fly-by-the-seat-of-my-pants-ness." He smiled, but she looked down at her feet.

"It was—so beautiful, Jamie. I'm glad you shared that place with me. It meant a lot. So, thanks." Her voice shook before she cleared her throat. His heart broke to hear her normal strength waver.

"I don't think I could have shared it with anyone else." The words fell out of his mouth. He wished she'd take him inside, but instead she turned and went through the door alone. He drove off before he could jump out and chase after her, pull her into his arms, and make love to her all night. Lord, but she had him all turned around.

When he got home, he listened to his mother on the machine. In two days, it would be Christmas. His mom wondered if maybe, this year, he could make it home. He thought of all of the reasons he had not to. He thought of all the ways he'd let his family down. He got a drink of water and went upstairs. Stripping down, he started the shower.

When Jamie stood under the hot spray, he thought of Laney. Of her warm body pressed tightly to his. The way she'd sighed and reached back to touch him. The soft curve of her ass against his thighs. He looked down and saw how she affected him still. He remembered the smell of her hair, the feeling of her skin beneath his hands. He wished she was here now. What would he do with her? His mind played over the scenarios, and his hands followed his thoughts. He leaned against the cool tiles of the shower while his soap-slicked hands slid effortlessly over his skin. Within minutes he'd relieved the pressure, but felt no better for it. He still wanted her. He went to bed naked and sighed into his pillow with confusion and lust in equal parts.

He tossed and turned, eyes open to the ceiling, unsettled in heart and mind. He looked at the clock. Something in his heart had changed, since talking to her in the bar, confessing things in the study, being on that stage the other night. Listening to her talk about her own family, and rowing in the darkness of a magical bay with her. Feeling her body against his. Every memory she was making was better than the last. Jamie groaned into his pillow.

If he could take someone like her with him when he went home; someone who he felt comfortable and stable around, he wondered if it might take the pressure off. He felt his priorities and plans shift. He pictured a green valley and a warm fireplace. Family and home. His heartbeat slowed, his body relaxed into the sheets, he closed his eyes and let the wave of peace roll over him, until he fell asleep soundly.

By five in the morning, he was up and making phone calls.

Eleven

Laney was in The Salty Claw. She couldn't stay in the cottage, not after last night. She'd tossed and turned and tried to relieve the pressure and what he'd left her with, but even when her body was satiated her heart still felt lonely. She continued her writing and tried to put her own wants into the hearts of her characters. There was no stopping the flow of words and her coffee went cold beside her.

Jamie came in, this time alone, and sat down at her table.

"Mornin' starshine," he whispered and his hand found her bare knee under the table. Laney jumped and shrieked before composing herself. "Man, you are wound up," he chuckled. She went back to her work, but stole glances over her laptop and blushed when he wiggled his eyebrows at her.

"Have you no respect for my personal space?" she said and pulled her leg back when he bumped her knee with his. Her fingers continued to type madly. He watched her for several minutes, nodding to Noah for a cup of coffee.

"Seems like you were more than fine with me in your personal space last night."

She looked over her glasses and back down without saying

anything. She was more than fine. But she wanted more than that. Needed more than that. Didn't she? She continued typing even after he'd placed the thought of his body against hers in her mind and finished the chapter. That would make five in this week alone. She smiled as she started the next one almost instantly, as though her words and heart were on fire.

"You just going to sit and stare at me all day?" She paused to sip her coffee and made a face.

"I could, I think." His tone was soft. Her fingers trembled and paused over the keys. "I'm thinking about the first time I saw you, Laney." She stopped typing, closed the screen and looked at him.

"Oh? And you thought, 'does the Claw offer a senior discount day?'"

Jamie smiled. "More along the lines of, 'who let that sexy professor into a dive like this?'"

Laney looked down at her lap. She hadn't thought nearly so nice a thing about him. Noah refilled her coffee and brough Jamie his own cup.

"You shouldn't make fun of the elderly." She bit her lip. He leaned in to watch.

"I'm not making fun."

"I'm past sexy and we both know it."

"I didn't come here to fight with you over how unaware you are of your own sexiness."

"Why are you here?" She stared at him over her steaming cup's rim.

"I came here to offer you a distraction for Christmas."

"Like an unplanned pregnancy?"

He laughed. "Haven't you hit menopause yet?"

She coughed on her coffee. "No."

"As fun as it would be to try, that's not really my style." She opened her mouth to respond, but he spoke first. "So, my driver is going to be out in front of your cottage later, say noon, to take us on a little ride."

"And if I say no?"

Jamie blanched; his forehead crinkled. He looked like a disappointed eight-year-old.

"Well, of course you can say no—just—I thought maybe—"

"I had nothing better to do?"

Jamie squirmed. "Well, no—"

"Oh my god. You don't like being told no, do you?"

"Well, I'm not used to it, but I'm—I'd never make you do anything." He huffed in frustration and a smile broke out on her lips.

"Does it involve a saddle?" she asked. "Because, that's a hard pass."

"It certainly was hard—" he said. Laney's cheeks grew warm.

"Yeah, it was. I'm not sure...I don't think my heart could take it." The words were too close to a deeper truth, and she looked away.

He smiled. "You can bring your work along, if it would persuade you."

Laney sighed, she sorted through her planner took a pencil from her bun and started flipping through pages, ticking off imaginary boxes.

"Well, well. Look at that. Just so happens, I have an opening." She bit her lip and looked over the edge of the book. Jamie's breath came out in a pleased sigh.

"A Jamie-sized opening?" His eyebrows raised.

"I think it'll be a tight fit, but I bet we can make it work," she said seriously at him.

Jamie buried his head in his hands with a groan and laughed.

"You're tryin' to kill me, aren't you?"

"Worse ways to go—where are we going? All the way?" She mocked his drawl.

"Don't toy with my emotions. Just pack a bag." He reached over and pushed a loose strand of hair away from her face and his finger grazed her cheek. Laney froze and her heart stopped. His eyes were on her lips and she wished he would... But he stood up instead and walked away. He looked back over his shoulder.

"'Round noon. Bring your sass."

"Oh, I never leave home without it."

He smiled before strolling out.

Laney tried to keep the delighted surprise from her face as she walked through the airport doors and onto the tarmac. When Jamie's driver had come to get her and dropped her off at the airfield, she had expected a small, sure-to-make-you-vomit plane, typical of the island. Instead, a mid-sized jet sat patiently waiting for her. The afternoon sun lit the clean white lines as its engines began to whine. Jamie was coming down the stairs and laughing with the pilot.

"Where'd you dig up this piece of shit?" She looked up at him as they met on the stairs.

"Junkyard, $3.50."

"What did you say you do? Drug cartel?"

"Investment fraud." He smiled down at her and eyed her summery dress and the way it swished above her knees. Her ponytail hung down her back.

"I'm still not exactly sure why I'm here."

"Laney, I... I need your help."

"Is that so? And what exactly am I helping you with?"

Jamie looked at her hands for a moment and his eyes turned dark.

"It's more of a therapy kind of help."

"Ego therapy or serious-you-should-talk-to-a-real-therapist therapy?" Her tone was suddenly stern. "Jamie, if you need help, real help, I'm here to support that but I'm not qualified—"

"I could just really use a friend," he rushed nervously. Laney looked at him, the night of her journal outpouring. *May he find a friend in a woman.* She sighed. He shook his head. "I'm just, about to do something really hard and I need some solid ground."

Laney cocked her head at his humility. "Come on now, surely this can't be the first STD test you've gone in for."

"I swear to God, professor—" he growled but when her blue eyes twinkled up at him, he lost his mad. "The swab really hurt last time." He stuck his bottom lip out and Laney laughed.

"I'll hold your hand—or—wait, am I doing the swab?"

"While I've fantasized about those strong hands of yours, that's not what I want them doing." He turned to go inside but looked back when she wasn't following his eager climb. She blushed at his words and what he fantasized about. She kept still, her bag on her shoulder. He came back down a few steps.

"What? Look, if you're mad about not getting to swab my—"

"That's not—" she interrupted quickly, "not the problem."

"Well, what is then, Laney?" They stared at one another. Silence hung between them. The pilot peeked out to see their progress and noticed the tension. He went quietly back inside.

"Jamie, I—what if I'm not the right person to be there for you?"

He cocked his head. "Who do you think would be the right person?"

She stared sadly back into the face that had graced a million magazines, websites, and billboards.

"Someone better?" She wanted to say someone from his 'world,' who understood his lifestyle.

"Laney—" He paused when the frustrated sigh fell off her name. "I can't make you come with me. But I can't go with anyone else. I need *you*. Please." Humble and calm. Part of the dark she'd seen in his study, begged from his eyes.

"I don't know if I can." Her words came out desperate.

"Why not?"

"Because I didn't bring clothes. This is just all my work stuff."

The strange confession blurted out and Jamie's mouth turned into a slow, sexy smile.

"I think you work too much, but if that's all you brought, I'm okay with you working naked." He came down the stairs to her. She looked down. He smiled lazily, with a reassuring sigh. "Don't worry about clothes. We'll take care of it." He tucked a wisp of her hair behind her ear. He swayed closer to her lips.

"Well, what in the hell does that mean? Who's 'we'?" she whispered when her heart leapt into her throat.

"The women we'll be with have things you can borrow."

"Women, as in the plural? Your kind of women? The tall, thin model types? What's gonna fit me? Their socks?" She scowled, and he laughed.

"Settle down, you'll have to take an aspirin or something for your heart." He took her bag and climbed up the stairs. Where work went, she would follow. He tossed it into an empty leather seat. He turned back and smiled. "Look at my little recluse. Gettin' on a big scary jet, with a big, scary man—"

"You're barely five-seven."

"Ouch!" he laughed. "Still taller than you." He flashed her a smile so beguiling that her breath stopped. The dimples in his cheek were deep, and she wanted to kiss them, feel his skin beneath her lips.

"I don't know what's wrong with me that I become so unhinged from reality around you." She plopped down on the leather chair and closed the shade of her window.

"Nervous flier?"

"No, not—" she crossed her legs and arms, shutting herself off, "really."

"If it's more comfortable, you can snuggle up on the sofa with me." He sat on the long and cozy couch and patted the spot next to him. "I'll keep you safe."

"You are the farthest thing from safe." She threw a pillow at him playfully, and the co-pilot came back to give them the safety briefing and direct them to the cocktails in the kitchenette.

"My Jamie tells me you're an English teacher?" began the genteel older woman as she sat Laney's tea in front of her.

"Yes, ma'am. Thank you." Desdemona sat gracefully next to her.

"How do you like it?"

"Well, it pays some bills." Laney shrugged. Jamie's mom's bright eyes were just like his. Their smiles were the same too. It had been completely unexpected when Jamie had taken her from the Knoxville airport to an ostentatious house on the outskirts of town. Then, when his mother answered the door, tearfully grabbing him into a hug, followed by his two sisters cuddling and fawning over him, Laney nearly called a Lyft. The laughing, overjoyed women ushered them both inside, and she shot Jamie a disbelieving look.

"You took me to meet *your mom*? Are you crazy?" she whispered when Desdemona had gone to get refreshments.

"It's Christmas." He shrugged, as if it were no big deal as his mom and sisters flurried around her. Now here she was, sitting with Jameson Clark's mother on the couch, discussing pleasantries. His sisters sat, poised on the edges of the chairs, giving their best smiles to her. Smiles that looked like his.

"I'm just so thrilled that you got him to come home for Christmas." Desdemona leaned in and whispered, "And frankly so happy that he's finally met a nice girl."

"Oh! We're not—"

"Nice?" Jamie guffawed as he nudged her to scoot so he could sit next to her, a freshly baked cinnamon roll in hand. "Laney swears like a sailor, and you should have seen what she did to me on the beach two days ago. Hell, she didn't even pack clothes for the trip." He shook his head and tsked his tongue. Laney's cheeks lit up like the red bulbs on the tree and she buried her forehead in her hand.

"It's like a nightmare that I can't wake up from," she grumbled. Desdemona cackled mischievously.

"It's all right, darlin'. If I know Jameson, he didn't give you a chance to pack. Just spirited you away! Cassie, could you get Laney a cinnamon roll? Would you like one? They're fresh. Oh, just bring her one anyway. Hell, bring me one too," Desdemona asked. Cassie and Jill laughed.

"You should definitely have one before he eats them all. You're going to get fat at your age, Jameson," Jill teased on their way out. Cassie ruffled his hair. Laney watched, it dawning on her that Jamie hadn't been home in a long while, and that this was harder for him than he was letting on. Laney turned to Desdemona.

"Just so you're clear, I'm glad that Jamie's home but I can't take credit for that idea. He wanted to come. I just tagged along."

"Well, no matter," she said, squeezing Laney's knee. "I'm happy you're here, just the same." Laney smiled and when she did, Desdemona's features changed.

"You know, you look familiar. Where is it you say you're from?"

Laney didn't answer.

"Laramie, Momma. Well, raised in Sweet Valley, Wyoming. On a ranch. Her dad's a vet," Jamie said and got up to rummage through the drawer, still licking icing from his fingers. "Do you have any extra comp sheets?"

Laney watched his graceful movements around the room as he gathered up a pen and put it behind his ear. He'd remembered. He had listened to her.

"Laramie? And you teach English there?"

"Yes." Laney said.

Desdemona studied her face again." Jamie, don't you think she looks familiar?"

Jamie looked up from his search for the paper.

"Um? She looks—" he stared at her as she nervously perched on his mother's couch, teeth pulling at her bottom lip. "She looks like Laney." Their eyes met, and a spark snapped between them.

"Laney...Laney Sullivan, from Laramie." Desdemona's face lit up. A squeal pealed out of her lips. "Landry! Landry Sultan! You're Landry Sultan! Oh my God! I can't believe I didn't recognize you right away from your cover photo."

"Who?" Jamie looked at his mom. Jill and Cassie ran in from the kitchen.

"Momma? Are you okay?" Jill asked.

"Jilly, Cas! It's her! Laney is Landry Sultan!" She clasped her hands over Laney's in excitement. Jamie dropped his pen.

"Who in the hell is Landry Sultan?" Jamie's voice was thick. They all turned and looked at him as if he'd been born in a barn, a century ago.

"Only our favorite author! The greatest romance novelist since, I don't know when. Come on now Jamie, you really mean to tell me that you didn't know she was a novelist?" Jamie's brow creased, and he turned to Laney with fire in his curious eyes.

"No. I guess she failed to mention it."

"Oh! *The Plains* was my favorite of your series!" Jill said.

Jamie moved, slowly, predatorily towards her. His gaze was like molten heat, undressing her and scrutinizing all at once.

"I love *The Mountains*, but let's face it they're all so good! Tell me what gives you the ideas you have? The women you write are so spirited."

"Well—I, uh, I like to write from women I know," Laney's face erupted with heat and she couldn't look away from Jamie.

"Well, I love the men," laughed Jill. "Jackson, and Daughtry, and Antonio, oh my!" The girls fell into a fit of giggles, and Laney felt flushed. She was never recognized. She hadn't thought she'd sold many books. Desdemona quieted her girls when she saw Laney shrink.

"Oh, honey! Look at us! Why, we're behaving like a pack of rabid wolves, and you look like a little deer caught between us. Please don't be upset."

Laney swallowed and shook her head, her eyes always keeping Jamie and his changed demeanor in view. "It's okay, I'm just not used to meeting a fan. S—so many fans. I appreciate it, I really do."

"Oh, Laney, please tell us, when are the next books coming out?"

Laney swallowed and thought of the countless attempts that sat crumpled in her trash can at home. And the new, fragile start she'd just gotten.

"Soon. I'm working on them, right now." She looked up as Jamie studied her, as if was he was remembering every keystroke she'd made over coffee that morning.

"Would you sign our copies?" Jill asked.

"Please?" Cassie begged.

"Of course." Laney nodded. Her tongue felt heavy in her mouth and she could feel her heart banging inside of her chest. They went to get their books and left Jamie and Laney alone. Jamie leaned over her.

"World-famous novelist, huh?" he growled suspiciously.

"Well, hardly *world* famous," she snorted and bit her lip to stop the sound.

"And why wouldn't you tell me about that?" he fumed.

She sunk into the couch.

The girls rushed into the room.

"She probably didn't have a chance with you carrying on about yourself like you do," Jill said with an eye roll.

"I do not!" he countered.

"Do so!" Cassie jumped in.

"Kids," Desdemona put a reassuring hand on Jamie's shoulder. She handed him his composition paper and a pencil. "Your studio is just the way you left it. If you want a quiet moment." Laney looked up at him. He gave her a glance over his shoulder on his way out.

"What's his deal?" Cassie asked.

Laney shook her head. "He's broody," she said softly, mirroring the word Gran used to use.

"Well, you are right about that. For too many years now." Desdemona nodded and handed Laney a pen. "But I think he may be coming around." She smiled at Laney.

"Well, I hope I didn't make him mad."

"Oh, honey, don't you worry. That boy needs his feathers ruffled," Desdemona said and Cassie laughed.

"He's been unruffled for too long." she said.

Laney looked back to the basement door, where he'd disappeared. She was sure he'd been 'ruffled' recently. Why would he care what she did for a very unprofitable side gig?

After signing the books, Laney excused herself to her room. She was going to take a nice hot bath before dinner and try to forget the way his eyes had turned angry towards her. Surely, he hadn't expected her to tell him everything about her life? They weren't dating. They were barely friends. She'd just undressed when two quick knocks sounded at her door and Jamie strode in without pause. Laney squealed and scrambled for something to cover herself. Jamie looked up just before she grabbed an overstuffed sham from the bed and used it as a shield.

"Jesus, Jamie!"

"Sorry," he said but didn't turn away. He gave her a long and slow glance that made Laney's heart rate climb. When his eyes finally found hers, she saw the fire threatening to burn her alive.

"Well? Turn around!" She waved at him. He clenched his teeth.

"Why are you always covering up in front of me? I have seen a naked woman before," he growled.

"There's no doubt in my mind that you've probably seen hundreds of women sans their clothes, but I am not one of those women. Why are *you* always barging in on me when I'm nearly naked?" she said with a tremor in her voice.

Jamie turned away. "Maybe I'm just *nearly* lucky."

"Pushy, egotistical—" She threw the sham at him, connecting with the side of his head, as she dove for a towel.

"It's not a big deal." He laughed as the pillow hit him.

"It is to me," she said, and turned her back to him to tighten the towel across her chest. He turned back around.

"I'm sorry," he said more sincerely. She shrugged and tried to seem unbothered, as he came nearer.

"What do you want?" she asked. Jamie shook his head.

"Thought I knew but then when I walked in and saw all of that creamy skin, I sort of forgot," he continued.

"You seemed angry, does that help to jar your aging memory?" she said and backed away. He paused.

"Why did you lie to me?" His tone darkened. She stepped forward defensively.

"I didn't lie."

"What is it? Some exposé? Some tell-all? Is that why you came to my island?"

"First of all, it's not 'your island', you don't own it. Second, *you* invited me! Everywhere! *You* asked *me* to go kayaking, to the party, the bay... to come here with you. I would have been happy to stay holed up in front of my dying career for four weeks. Third, I'm not that kind of writer. I write women's fiction, not TMZ-style star-struck bullshit," she said it as if he'd insulted her.

"Why didn't you tell me you were a writer?"

Her eyes fell to the floor. "Because," she paused and sighed. "I don't feel good enough to call it my real profession. Hell, your family must have gotten three of the twelve copies I've sold."

"Twelve? Come on, Laney, I looked you up."

"You did?" she said, embarrassed. "I don't feel like I've earned it, okay? What I write isn't," she bit her lip in frustration. "It isn't great American fiction or anything. None of my colleagues consider it credible work. It's just a way to help pay the bills." When he only stared at her in response, she held her towel tighter. "I mean, I love it. I love writing romance. I wish I could pay all my bills with it, but it's a hard field to make a living in and I don't have the time to devote to it, with being a parent, and all the work my classes take..." Her voice drifted off. Jamie's eyes softened, as he stared at her lips. He took a step towards her. She stepped back.

"Jamie," she said. The lowlight of the sun, coming in from the half-cracked blinds, lit his eyes, determined and caressing her skin.

"What?"

"Don't."

"Don't what?" He shook his head and stared at her lips.

"Don't look at me like that." He was less than a hand's width away now.

"Like what, Laney?" His breath was in her face, and he smelled like cinnamon and sticky sweetness. He leaned closer, and she swayed in.

"Like you want to eat me alive," she whispered, and his lips curved into a slow smile. She may have told him not to, but she wanted more than anything to feel his biting kisses along her skin. He reached above her to lean on the wall.

"I bet you taste like peaches," he said in a sexy, unapologetic growl. His eyes were deep and heavy lidded as he stared at her lips. She leaned against the wall and sighed. Her hands reached up, fingers trailing over his chest. Her heart pounded and her knees felt weak.

"Peaches?" she breathed and pulled him in closer by his shoulders. His chest was warm and hard and pressed into the knot of her towel.

"Uh huh, warmed by the sun. Sweet and tender." He leaned in and his lips touched hers. She wanted to tear into him; wanted his kiss more than she knew how to control, and it scared her, feeling so much for a man after so long without. Being desired, after thinking she couldn't be, was an ocean wave broadsiding her. She pressed closer, opened her lips with a gasp and his hands threaded into her hair.

"Jamie!" came the loud drawl of his mom from the base of the stairs. Jamie pulled away quickly, closed his eyes. The spell broke between them. "Jameson George Clark!" Desdemona tried his full name. He buried his face in the naked skin of Laney's neck and growled in frustration.

"I don't suppose we'd have time?" he gasped. Her fingernails scratched over his chest and she nudged his forehead with her chin.

"I'm afraid they'd hear it all."

"Well, then you should use your inside, librarian voice." He inhaled her scent. His hand fell to her waist, his lips touched her collarbone. She arched into the warm wetness of them.

His mother yelled his full name again followed by; "Jameson! George! Clark! I know you heard me!"

"Goddamn it," he whispered. "I'm coming!" he yelled at the door.

"Really? I'm just breathing hard." Laney sighed to the ceiling and rested her head on the wall behind her. He laughed and nuzzled into her hair and pushed himself away before storming back to the door.

"George?" she said just before he left.

He turned back with a mock glare. "That better not end up in a book." He slammed the door. Laney slumped down against the wall. Maybe a cold shower would do her more good than a hot bath at this point.

All through dinner they laughed and joked, and told stories of Jamie in his youth. He tried to hide beneath his cap, but his mother insisted that he remove it at the table. Laney drank her wine, trying to quench the fire that erupted in her belly every time he looked across the table at her.

"Remember when he drove his truck through the front window of the AutoZone on Third Street?" Jill howled.

Cassie, cheeks pink with wine, laughed with tears in her eyes.

"Then he strolls in, just as calm as you please, over the broken glass and tipped over shelves and says to the clerk, 'Do you guys sell brake fluid?'" Laney roared with laughter; she couldn't help herself. Her guard had been lowered by the wine and the good company. When the room quieted, Cassie cleared her throat.

"That was Daddy's favorite story."

The table turned somber, and Laney remembered the brief conversation between the women on the plane to St. Croix. His daddy was gone. She looked up at him and put the puzzle together that his breakdown had come not long after. He stared at her. The desire turning to something else... something deeper, darker. More painful.

"Tell me about your family, Laney," Desdemona said, trying to break up the moment, and pouring another glass for everyone. Laney's head felt woozy, and she tried to slow the spin of the room. She smiled graciously and cleared her throat.

"My parents are semi-retired. My dad's a veterinarian and boards and breaks horses. My mom just retired as a high school teacher. They have a small ranch outside of Sweet Valley, Wyoming."

"And you teach English at the university? They must be so proud!" Desdemona said.

Laney thought of how disheartened she often felt as a teacher. She smirked and tried to take the compliment in stride.

"And brothers and sisters?"

"Two sisters. Eleanor and Katelyn." Saying their names made her miss them, especially seeing Jamie surrounded by his. It had been a while since she'd been home. They both were busy with new loves and new lives. Both were thriving. While she'd stayed stagnant. She and Jamie shared more than she liked to admit.

"Your family must miss you over the holiday, I'm sure."

Desdemona said. Laney looked down and thought about how this Christmas was worlds away from any other she'd spent. The idea of David and Tasha snuggling up to the kids in some French chalet tonight, waiting for Santa, made her stomach turn. All of her family were with loved ones.

"I miss them. Especially my daughters." She looked at Jamie. He looked back, unfazed.

"You have daughters? How wonderful!" Desdemona said and leaned in. "What are their names? Where are they at?"

"Charlotte and Sylvia. It's their father's turn to have them for Christmas, so he's taken them to Europe with his shiny new girlfriend." Laney took a huge swig of wine and stared down at her hands. Jamie's mouth turned up on one side. "Sorry, that sounded —" she paused to choke back a pitiful laugh, "kind of bitter. I'm not." She stopped and shook her head at the phrase *bitter old schoolmarm*, running through her thoughts.

"Momma, they're the prettiest little girls I've ever seen. Must be, what—eight and six?" Laney looked back at him, dumbfounded. "Smart like their momma too. It's too bad they had to waste the holiday with that useless arm candy."

Laney couldn't answer.

"You must miss them something awful," Desdemona said and squeezed Laney's hand.

"I do." Her eyes grew moist. Jill and Cassie looked at her with sympathetic frowns. "But," she sighed, "at least I'm not alone. And I'm happy that Jamie gets to be with his family, finally." She looked at him and he shifted his gaze down to his lap.

"Well, I for one am glad that you are here. Daddy always used to say, here's to being with the family we make!" said Jill. The table raised their glasses. Except for Jamie. He downed his wine without raising it.

"We should probably call and get the plane warmed up." He avoided looking at Laney. "If we're going to leave tonight."

"Jamie—" his mother began.

"We're not leaving," Laney said with a scowl. "Why would we come all this way and not stay for Christmas morning?"

"Well, you probably have things to get back to. Books to write. And, I have things..." His voice faded.

"Oh, horse shit," Laney said unexpectedly and crossed her arms to lean in. "You don't have anything back there that can't wait a day. You've got everything here." Laney reprimanded. Maybe this was the part he'd brought her for; to give him an excuse, to help him run away again. If that was the case, she wasn't playing along.

Plus—Laney kept the hard stare-down going—she trusted him enough that she wasn't afraid to make him angry. She liked him enough to stop him from making a mistake that could hurt his happiness. She was angry that he was pushing away the warmth and family that had missed him for so long. The exact thing he needed. She was going to be his solid ground.

"Besides, what about dishes? It's your turn!" said Jill, interrupting their stare-down indignantly, ignoring his brooding and taking Laney's side. Jamie growled and put his hands to his eyes.

"I'll help," Laney said with a shrug. "Four hands are better than two." He took his hands away to look at her. His eyes were moist, but the scowl was gone. The lights of the holiday around them, haloed him in a soft glow and she smiled.

"Okay," he said.

Jamie cleared the table and carried the load of plates and forks into the kitchen while Laney filled the sink. She pulled up the sleeves of her borrowed white sweater. When she looked back he was studying her bare calves in the soft, twill skirt she wore. She smiled. The steam rose from the sink. She shifted onto one foot, balancing on it while she waited and relaxed into the quiet.

If there was something that dishes were good for, was getting lost in thought while you washed them. She missed her children and missed her own family. She worried for them all. How bad was the tumble off the horse her father had taken? Why hadn't she asked her mom more about that? What happened if he couldn't work? What if they had to sell? Laney sighed. She fought a losing game between finding herself again and feeling guilty over not being there. Then there was Jamie. She looked casually over her shoulder as he was brought in dishes to put next to the sink and kissed the top of his mother's head when she swept through to deliver more.

He confused her, the supposed big-time country star, looking more and more like a homebody introvert. The sadness and his desire to run away from his loss seemed too familiar to her own. While she loved his pain-in-the-ass demeanor, she felt his darkness. Laney looked back down to the soapy water, bubbles building up from the surface. She was in no position to help him.

"Are you all right?" he said as he took up the rinsing side beside her.

"I was going to ask the same of you," she redirected.

"Oh, you care or you need another chapter?" He smiled cruelly.

She looked up at him with a scowl.

"Even though I could fill a few volumes with your sexual exploits alone, I'm not interested in writing about you." She realized it was a lie the minute she'd said it. She'd written pages and pages inspired by him and her own sex-deprived imagination.

"So, what is on your mind then?" he asked. Laney didn't know how to answer. She didn't want to fill the space with her own worries, either about her family or about him. She didn't want to admit to how much she cared for him. She didn't want to admit how he affected her. She wanted to put up a wall against the warm need that settled in her chest even in the innocence of standing next to him.

"You don't have to stand up for me against Tasha—"

"Was that all?" he led.

"And it was nice, what you said, about my girls," she stuttered unexpectedly.

Jamie handed her the dish rag with a pensive nod. "Yeah—I think you like to bring them up when you feel anyone's getting too close. Like men will be put off or threatened by you being a mom. I guess it's worked so far though, huh?"

Laney avoided looking at him and didn't reply to the confrontational call-out, but instead added soap to the rag. He scratched deeper.

"I don't know why you think that having kids makes you unwanted," he grumbled. "Any reasonable, caring man would be lucky to have a part in their lives, and yours. But maybe you don't think a reasonable, caring man exists. Maybe you just don't recognize them when they do show up." Her heart stopped and the wall inside her chest crumbled a bit more. Jamie continued, "You don't do your girls any favors when you act like love is off-limits for you because of them."

"I don't—" she raised her voice.

"Tell me how many men you've dated, Laney? Since you've been separated?" he interrupted. "Tell me how many times you've brought the girls up, to put distance between you and another person?"

"I don't use them! And you're a fine one to talk about not letting anyone close."

"Just answer the question," he argued with quiet intensity.

She'd been all about breaking down his walls, but now he'd upended her by attacking her own.

"It's not that simple! I have to be responsible for them first." He shook his head and looked out the window. "I can't just date anyone. My standards have to be higher now that I have to look out for their future too. If he isn't good enough for them, then he's not good enough for me."

"Do you even get to know them before you decide that? Or do

you just do it based on how many drinks get thrown in their faces at the bar?"

"I—" she sputtered. "Well, that's not fair." She felt her cheeks go red. "I have two full-time jobs, seven if you count single-parenting. Even if I had the time, I don't have anything of value to offer anyone." She turned away from her own self-doubt.

"There you go again, misjudging yourself," he said. Laney felt her eyes fill with tears. Jamie nudged her hip with his. "Don't cry, Laney. Listen, if your standards are so high, then why are you hanging out with me?"

"Maybe because you won't leave me alone!" she said, putting the attention back on him. He dropped a plate in the sink with a clang. She looked up at him and he studied her eyes. She didn't know what to say, so she let her heart speak. "Because you're more worthy than you give yourself credit for. And I don't feel like I have to pretend to be perfect to get your attention, because I never expected it in the first place. And maybe because it's easy to be around you. And maybe because I...I just genuinely just like you." He opened his mouth, but she quickly spoke, "Do you want to tell me about your dad?"

He shook his head and closed his mouth in a frown. "Not tonight."

"Okay."

"Anything else on your mind? Want to tell me about *your* dad?" he asked as they passed dishes to one another, working seamlessly, as though they'd done it a hundred times before. She saw the doorway into his trust.

"My dad?" She handed him a plate, trying to not let it slip through her soapy fingers. "He's uh—good?"

"How about I get real TMZ journalist on you." He smiled and took the plate. "What's your dad like?" he prompted.

"My dad is tall—"

"Obviously you missed those genes," he snorted, and she bumped him with her hip.

"And thin as a post—don't you fucking say it."

"I wouldn't dare."

"And he's quiet and patient. Steady-handed and mischievous. He's always thinking more than he's speaking and he loves to read. He sneaks into the closet every Christmas and birthday and peeks at his presents." She stopped to smile. "But my mom keeps hiding them in the same place because she loves to see him tiptoe in there, like she won't know." Jamie smiled.

"He's—he's worried about losing the ranch. He's always worried about it," she stopped and tried to not let her mind worry about things she couldn't control. "Anyway, I always had this huge dream that I'd make it big one day, with my writing. And I could support them, help take their worry away, you know?" She looked up at Jamie. His eyes rose to the big kitchen and smiled.

"Yeah, I know. I know, exactly."

"So far, all I can do is come up to help with irrigating and haying. I can't really be there all the time, with work, and the girls. I can't do enough." She shook her head.

"Laney, you could be a millionaire and secure every part of their future, so they'd never have to worry about another single cent. But at the end of it all, they just want you to be happy. They just want you to stay in their lives." The simplicity of his words was swallowed in his regretful tone. Laney's story-brain painted a picture of what must have happened.

"Well, that's pretty insightful for you." He looked away. "Are you sure you don't want to talk—"

"No. Let's just wash," he said softly and didn't meet her eyes.

"Okay."

They worked alongside one another, cleaning the plates and filling the drying rack. She stole glances his way and saw the serious twitch in his jaw. He was sullen and she could tell his thoughts were perpetuating themselves into painful memories. She scooped up a handful of bubbles and flicked them into his face. They landed with a soft plop on his cheek and nose.

"Oops!" She giggled. At first, when he went quiet, she wondered if he was mad. Then, with eyes closed, he smiled.

"S'at really how you want to play? I do have two sisters' worth of experience." He took a handful of the bubbles. Laney ducked away and gave a squeal before he got her squarely in the face. She coughed out the taste of soap.

"Children, children!" Desdemona laughed from behind. "The sooner you finish, the sooner we can open the Christmas Eve gift and another bottle of wine." They both looked back to her and then to each other. The warm ease of the moment made her smile. She turned back to the task and handed him a hot, soapy plate.

They continued the familiar rhythm in silence. Their fingers grazed. The warmth of the water and the gentle clink of china were comforting. She watched from the corner of her eye as his shoulders relaxed. Two dishes from the end, he stopped rinsing.

"What in the hell are we doing, Laney? Mom has a dishwasher," he said. She looked up at him; a cluster of fine white bubbles still on her cheek.

"I know." She handed him a plate. "But I like this better." His fingers touched hers, soapy and slick. Her heart fell and leapt back up in her chest.

"Me too," he whispered and kissed her, quickly before anything else could steal the moment from them. It was sweet and warm and he took her breath with it. When he pulled away, she smiled at the bubbles on his cheek.

"Presents!" Cassie yelled from behind. Jamie touched Laney's chin.

"Think I already got what I wanted." He smiled. They finished up and dried their hands. He handed her the glass that his mother had refilled and his warm hand found her low back. Laney stepped into the inviting living room. His sisters were sitting beside the Christmas tree. They had come later in life to Desdemona and James Clark, so Jamie had had a part in raising them. It was no wonder that they were hellions.

Desdemona and Laney sat on the couch, wine in hand. Laney smiled to see the happy family scene and cuddled into the corner, folding her legs in as Jamie sat between her and his mom.

"I feel bad," she whispered. "I didn't bring anyone anything." Jamie shook his head.

"Their favorite author just autographed their books; I think they'll survive."

"Or you *could* write us into your next novel!" said Jill, overhearing. "Make sure to mention my sparkling blue eyes." She batted her lashes.

"And my long golden tresses!" Cassie flicked her hair over her shoulder. Laney laughed sweetly.

"You've got it."

Jamie stood up and rifled through the gifts under the tree. He handed out one for each person to open on Christmas Eve. Desdemona rose and snuck beneath the tree. She came back to the couch with a small box in her hand. She nudged it into Laney's hand.

"Ms. Clark, I really can't—"

"Oh, yes, you can." She waved Laney off and kept her eyes on Jamie. "You got him here and kept him from running away again. That's not easy when he starts thinking about the past." Laney watched Jamie open a fly-fishing rod from his sister. His eyes lit up like a little kid.

Laney blushed. "I'm sorry I didn't get you anything."

Desdemona wove her hand in the crook of Laney's arm.

"You know what you can do? Keep an eye on him, will you? He's about to come alive, I can feel it. It's that look in his eye. It's that sparkle. He's about to do something amazing."

Jamie looked up at the women conspiring on the couch.

"Well? Go on, and open it." Desdemona nudged Laney again. Laney's fingers shook as she untied the tiny golden ribbon that kept the box closed. When she popped off the top, there was a beautiful set of pearl earrings in a vintage silver setting. Laney gasped and looked at Desdemona. They were the most stunning things that Laney had ever been given. Even her ex-husband had thought jewelry was frivolous, unless it was garnishing one of his mistresses.

"Ms. Clark, I can't take these!"

"No! Nonsense. They are just old jewelry from my grandma. They just sit up in my jewelry box, never seeing the light of day, so somebody should wear them. They would complement your complexion. Plus, I will have the gift of knowing that one of my favorite authors is wearing them."

Laney blushed and smiled. "They're beautiful. I will wear them, thank you."

Jamie got up from the floor, nudged his sisters lovingly on the heads, and walked back to her.

"More wine?" he said and filled her glass where it sat on the side table. She felt lightheaded and warm. The laughter and soft sounds around her were comforting. When he sat back down, she sighed and snuggled into him, the box still pressed into her hand.

"Whoa! Where's my aloof professor?" he said, throwing up his hand. She nuzzled into his chest; her head heavy. Jamie curved his arm around her back, his fingers delicately caressing her shoulder, down her arm.

"I gave her the night off. I'm gonna be a soft-hearted romance novelist tonight. Thank you, Jamie," she said. "Thanks for Christmas. Thanks for staying." She kissed his cheek. He turned to try and catch her lips with his, but her head settled under his chin and she drifted off.

His mother and sisters chatted about the knitting needles she'd gotten them each and Laney started softly snoring into his chest. He couldn't have had a heart fuller than in that moment. He kissed her hair.

"Did we lose a soldier?" whispered his mother.

"I think so," he whispered back. "Big, badass writer can't handle her booze." He smiled as he gently ran his hand over Laney's hair, his other hand caressed her back. He felt like a man who had found an unexpected gift in his arms, and was just now realizing how deep a feeling could run.

"You should take her up to bed," his mother said with a wink.

Jamie shook his head. "Man, she'd be so mad if she woke up in the same bed with me."

"Oh come on! You mean to tell me, that you two aren't sleeping together?"

"No, Mom," he whispered and looked around to make sure his sisters hadn't heard. "She and I—we haven't."

"Well, why not?" his mother raised her eyebrow.

"I'm not sure. It's just different with her. She—she deserves so much, Momma. I guess I'm just waiting for her to realize that herself," he said and stroked Laney's back. He thought of the kiss. He thought of the days they'd spent laughing and gouging each other. About the hard things she'd made him face and the way she had of rousing him from his self-pity, but still stayed stuck in her own self-depreciation. She sighed and snorted, and he hugged her tighter. Laney Sullivan was not like any woman he'd known. She was real and brought him back to his own reality. It was uncomfortable and painful, but it opened up feelings that made him want to write again, to create, to put something out into the world that was true.

He kissed her head again, cuddled her even closer; she scared the hell out of him, excited him, made him angry and protective. He leaned back on the couch and closed his eyes. Her warmth and softness brought comfort to even the stormiest of his thoughts. He listened to the sound of her breathing and his family's soft voices and drifted contentedly in between dreams and reality.

TWELVE

LANEY WOKE TO BELLS RINGING INSIDE OF HER throbbing head. She mumbled, rolled over, and tried to burrow away from it. The phone rang again. Who in the hell was calling her so early? She opened one eye to the blurred morning light. Christmas morning. She scrambled for the phone and answered it.

"Mom?" asked Charlotte.

"Hey, baby. Merry Christmas!" She cleared her throat. "I was just getting ready to call you." She looked around, confused. This wasn't the room she'd fallen asleep in; it wasn't even the guest room. The walls were covered in old autographed guitars, signed posters, state football championship trophies...pictures of a young Jameson Clark. She looked at the empty side of the bed. The blankets were undisturbed, but the pillow was sunken in the middle. The sound of Sylvia's voice cut into the background of Charlotte's chatter, and Laney returned to the conversation. They talked for a few minutes before Charlotte gave the phone over to her sister.

"What are you doing for Christmas?" asked Sylvia. Laney sat back against the headboard and looked down. She puzzled over the

Jameson Clark Summer Son Tour shirt she was wearing. What had she done?

"Uh—you know, I'm just hanging out with some friends. Mostly I'm missing you," she said.

"We miss you too, Momma," Sylvia said. "I wish you could have come with us."

"Oh, well, I think that'd be—" She stopped before she could utter *awful*, "a lot of people. I'm just excited that you girls got to go." Laney tried not to think about how many times she'd talked about going to Paris, but David had refused.

"I can't believe we only have a couple more weeks before we have to come home. It doesn't seem fair," Sylvia said. Before it could twist in her gut that Sylvia would rather be in Paris than at home (who could blame her?), Laney thought about the bed she was in.

Two weeks and she would be back to her old life. The cold, snowy winter. The lonely day-to-day. Out of the warmth of the island, away from the radiance of Jameson Clark's smile. She swallowed a small lump in her throat. It *didn't* seem fair.

"It doesn't seem like enough time, does it?" she swallowed. The jealousy over her ex's vacation drained from Laney's chest. The bitterness couldn't stay in a heart moving on. "I can't wait to see you both. I love you so much, I hope you have the best time," Laney said.

"Did you want to talk to Dad?" asked Sylvia.

"No, honey, that's okay. Tell them happy Christmas for me," she said.

"Tasha too?" Sylvia asked. "Really?"

"Really, really," Laney said.

Regardless of Jamie's feelings for her, just the thought that she'd slept in a country superstar's bed made her feel slightly better about her ex-husband dating a Kohl's model. She told them she loved them and hung up. A knock came from the door before Jamie stepped in, carrying a cup of coffee.

"Wanted to wait until you were done."

"Were you lurking?" she asked. He shrugged and handed her the warm cup. She sighed with pleasure and inhaled its steam. "Oh God, who let me drink all that wine last night?"

He smiled and sat beside her feet. "I think it was Landry Sultan," he said with a wink.

"That lady doesn't get out enough."

"She's fun at a party."

"Like falls asleep on you two minutes into the party fun?"

"I followed shortly after so—we're a matched set."

Laney blushed and looked down.

"How did I end up in this?" she asked with a raised eyebrow to the t-shirt.

"I didn't want you to sleep in that skirt and sweater. You'd have gotten hot."

"So, you undressed me?" she said, cringing inwardly and wished that she hadn't been in the sexy underwear Marc made her buy.

Jamie snorted into his cup. "No, my mom wouldn't let me. My sisters helped you. Interesting thing about that—" He paused and gave her a raised eyebrow. "It seems you told them all about how you'd seen the Summer Son Tour when it had hit Cheyenne Frontier Days. That it was one of the most fun times you'd had." He grinned at her with his sexy smile. "Now, I swear you told me you didn't know me." She sipped her coffee and smiled behind her cup.

"I knew *of* you. I didn't *know* you."

"And now?" His eyes searched hers.

"I think I'm getting there." She set the cup between her knees. "Is there a reason I ended up in your bedroom?" she asked quietly. Jamie leaned back with a confused look on his face.

"Wait! You mean you don't remember *anything* from last night? So—uh, where to begin—" He stopped, rolled his eyes backwards. "You were so rough," he said with mock hurt. "I've never been spanked with a book before, but, Lord, Laney, if you don't have a strong hand!"

"What?" She broke into a fit of giggles.

"I don't think we'll be able to get the banister fixed until after Christmas, but maybe we can hold it together with all those whips you brought along."

"Shut up!" she hooted and nearly spilled her coffee.

"God, Laney, the things you do with your mouth!" He fell back into bed and covered his face.

"Stop—" She giggled and punched him in the arm.

"Like when you smile?" he said softly and peeked out of his hands at her. "That's what really makes me weak."

Her brain melted; her heart threatened to follow. She took another sip and shook her head.

"I'm pretty sure I wouldn't forget a wild night of spanking you."

"Oh? You'd like it?" He leaned in.

Hell yes she would. She looked at his lips.

"Probably." Her voice was husky. "Why am I in your bed?"

"Because I didn't want to wake up without you next to me," he confessed. Laney looked down and blushed. Jamie's fingers trailed up her bare leg, he sat up, moved closer, his warm hand on the soft flesh of her inside thigh. Laney's breath quickened. Desdemona's voice floated up the stairs, calling them down to breakfast. He reached out and pushed her hair away from her face and stared at her lips, leaned in for a kiss. Desdemona called again. He sighed.

"I don't know how my mom knows," he sighed with a mock sob.

"Moms know." Laney smiled.

Jamie kissed her quickly, as if lingering on her lips for too long would lead to Desdemona walking through the door on their heated lovemaking. He left her to get dressed; she leaned over and touched the pillow where he'd slept and wished she'd woken up to him lying beside her. Preferably naked.

Jamie fought with himself the whole flight home while Laney snuggled up on the couch with a book she'd borrowed from his mom. He was across the aisle from her, working in his lyric notebook and stealing glances. She bit her lip and flipped pages faster during the exciting parts. She'd smile sweetly and clutched at her heart. Once he watched her legs draw up seductively and wondered what was going on in the pages. She looked up to see him watching her, and everything about her body said he should cross the aisle and break their sexual tension.

But he didn't want her thinking about two other people falling in love. He wanted her to think about him. To think about herself for once. When he didn't make a move, she cleared her throat and went back to the book. When the wheels of the plane touched down, Jamie put away his things. She gathered her bag. He rubbed his hands nervously against his thighs. She cracked her knuckles and stretched. Jamie's mind was full of song lyrics and notes, but he hadn't had the equipment he needed at his mom's house. He was torn between the pull to put his thoughts and music into motion, or follow her up to her treehouse bedroom and lose himself in her body. At the bottom of the plane's steps, she turned.

"Thank you for the surprise." She cleared her throat. "I should head back to the cottage."

"Oh, yeah?" he said, part disappointed, part relieved.

"My deadline is due two days from now and I need at least three more chapters." He could see the blush in her cheeks and how she was fighting the same dilemma. Her determination to commit to her art inspired him. And made him love her all the more.

He loved Laney. The idea didn't scare him as much as he thought it would.

"The creative process doesn't do well with distraction, no matter how—" he paused, caressed her cheek with a warm finger, "delicious that distraction is. Can I stop by tomorrow or the day after? At least before you leave? I have something I'd like to give you."

"Is it the clap?"

He laughed. "No. But it's a nice itchy rash that you can remember me by for the next two to six weeks."

"How can a girl resist?" The car pulled up and Jamie let her get in first. She stole glances at him, across the wide seat, deep in thought. "I smell smoke. You must be thinking."

"Just planning."

"Planning what? How to fit more groupies into a hot tub?" Jamie turned toward her with a scowl.

"Planning to do some recording. It's good we'll have time apart."

"I'm sorry if I wasted your time by making you stay—"

"You didn't. And it was good to stay. I'm glad we did. It's just what I needed. And by the way, you could never be a waste of time. Time's wasted when I'm not with you. You've inspired me to write some pretty good stuff, but I can't be with you while I record it."

"Jamie, I—" her cheeks were pink, her eyes filled. Finally he felt like he was getting beneath her skin; so he went deeper.

"Because you distract me, Laney Sullivan. Hell, if I had my way, I'd keep you happy and satisfied in my bed for at least a good month. But the inspiration is there and I need to strike while it's hard."

"Hard?"

"Hot—I meant hot." He laughed. "See? That's why I need a day away from you."

"Happy and satisfied for a...a good month?" Laney stuttered through his words and it made him want to affect her even more.

"Probably longer, if I thought it wouldn't lead to my complete and utter ruin." He shook his head and looked out the window.

"Well, I don't want to be the woman who ruins Jameson Clark. Think of the co-eds rioting in the streets."

He glowered at her. "Don't make me take you over my knee. I'll borrow that book, then neither of us will be able to work, and we'll embarrass my driver."

Laney blushed, and he saw her press both thighs together seductively. She cleared her throat, leaned away and took a deep breath. "I'm glad that you're going back to the studio, Jamie, really. I want to see you do what you love."

Jamie stared quietly at her, wanting so much to pull her into his arms, and show her exactly what he loved. The car stopped at her gate and she got out. He leaned out the window.

"Thanks for being there for me, Laney."

She nodded. "Thanks for taking me. And...and for trusting me," she choked.

"Maybe you can return the favor on both of those counts when I see you next," he said and watched her stumble back with a goofy smile and walk into the cottage fanning herself.

In his studio, Jamie pulled out the sheets and sheets of notebook paper that he'd scrawled out lyrics on while lying next to her on Christmas Eve, watching the gentle rise and fall of her shoulders. He'd written through the night and the melody repeated itself through his head. He picked his favorite guitar, a Takamine acoustic, and picked out the tunes to the words that had driven through his mind that whole night.

He missed her already. But the desire was channeled into the rush of ideas that tore through his fingers and pages. He hadn't written like this since he was young, in the limelight and full of passion. But the lyrics had changed. Instead of parties and sunshine, the songs revolved around her like planets to a star. They delved into the dark of him, the pain of his past, the questions of life and death, and what it really meant to be. It was chaos and beauty, and came out in waves of emotional release, like he'd been storing it up behind a locked door and she was the long-lost key.

He continued on until the wee hours of the morning and showed up on her doorstep exactly one day later.

THIRTEEN

LANEY OPENED THE DOOR, IN HER SOFT LOUNGE SHORTS and a loose shirt that fell over one shoulder. She found Jamie standing there, breathless. He stared hungrily at her. She hadn't expected him for at least another day. She certainly hadn't expected him at her door, past the gate, without even buzzing.

"One of these days, your britches are going to get caught on that fence and I'm just going to let you hang there." She tried not to show how happy she was to see him but failed. He smiled and leaned in towards her.

"How's the writing? Optioned for the Jameson Clark tell-all yet?"

"People are lining up for the juicy details of your sordid love life," she said and let him follow her inside. "I did meet my deadline, in real-world news. How about yours? Bang out another platinum album about the complex advantages of combining tequila and Daisy Dukes?"

Jamie smiled. "They do share an inexplicable bond."

"Inexplicable! Man, my smarts *are* rubbing off!"

He chuckled, and he reached out to grab her by the waist, but before he could, he noticed the short Dominican woman sitting in the living room, with her feet resting on the coffee table. She had on a facemask, cucumbers over her eyes, and freshly painted toes.

"Uh—"

"Oh, Jamie, this is Lupe. She's the caretaker for Marc's cottage. She and I have been talking about raising kids on our own. Her first is going to college next fall thanks to all her hard work. Since I tend to clean up my own messes, I made her join me for a girls' spa day." Then she turned and spoke to Lupe in Spanish, asking her if she needed another cocktail. Jamie looked at Laney with raised eyebrows.

"What?"

"Not sure if I'm more surprised that you do girly things or that you speak Spanish."

"Not very well on either count," Laney said. Lupe smiled and said yes, she would like another cocktail, but only one more. Jamie watched Laney pour the woman a mojito from a pitcher on the kitchen's island, barefoot and smiling.

"The heart in you, woman," he whispered. "I want it."

"Huh?" Laney turned distractedly from the pitcher.

"Uh—I want—I want in," he said.

"Want in?" she asked, setting the drink down. Lupe peeked out from under her cucumber.

"Yeah, do me." He smiled at her and came close enough that his breath caressed her skin. She blushed.

"Really?" she looked sideways at him.

"Yes. Two sisters, remember? I've had my toes painted more times than I care to admit." He jumped into the chair beside Lupe and sunk in comfortably.

"Buenas dias, señora," he said as he wiggled into the couch, folded his arms across his belly, and leaned back. Laney shrugged.

"Okay, Clark. You asked for it." She stirred the bowl of avocado and honey mask she'd made, and began slathering it on his face with her fingertips. He watched her with amused eyes.

"It smells good. Can I eat it?" he said, grabbing her hand. His eyes fell between her bare legs. Laney's fingers trembled, and she felt her body respond.

"Uh—I—I guess," she stammered. His eyes came back to hers. She blushed, and her brain imagined his tongue on her body. She took her hand back and stepped away.

"All right." She took a steadying breath and took off his worn-out sandals before putting his feet into a bucket of warm and sudsy water that smelled like flowers. She washed the mask from his face and spread a green and strong-smelling clay on.

"Oh man!" He made a face. "That one smells terrible!"

"Tea-tree-oil-infused clay. Suck it up, it's good for your pores. And *don't* eat it." She slapped the cucumbers on his eyes and started to massage Lupe's overworked and calloused hands.

He sat still and listened to her and Lupe talking. Laney glanced over and watched his goofy expression turn peaceful. For a guy who had met her at the door, coming on strong, he seemed to be accepting a different kind of afternoon well. Laney went to the bathroom for more towels and came out to study the way his body relaxed into the chair.

"I'm not going to tell you how ridiculous you look," she said, sitting on the coffee table in front of him her legs on either side of his. He smiled as her hands trailed over the tops of his bare thighs seductively.

"I may look like an idiot, but I'm a relaxed idiot. And, I don't probably have to tell the romance writer how erotic it is to be blindfolded and touched," his voice lowered.

"They're cucumbers, Clark, not silk.," she said but her voice was just as husky.

"Close enough. God, your hands..." he whispered as she trailed the pads of them higher up his thighs, unable to stop touching him. Lupe gathered her bag and with a smile and a wave, she thanked Laney again. Laney told her to come back on Friday and they'd play gin rummy if she wanted. Lupe raised her eyebrows suggestively towards Jamie.

"Tienes una *buena* dia," she said suggestively.

"I'd like to give you a *good* day," Jamie chuckled to Laney.

"Just good?" she laughed. He sighed and his whole body relaxed into the cushions. "I think you're enjoying this." She gently tapped one of his knees. "Lift this one out." He did just as he was told and she caught his foot in a towel. When it was dried, she slathered on a fruity-smelling lotion and massaged it in.

"What's not to enjoy? My pores are clear, my feet smell like a fruit salad. I gotta sexy librarian pampering me—"

"Writer—librarians are way cooler than me."

"You could pretend you were a librarian, come around and shush me—"

"Spank you with a book?" she teased.

"Yes, and please." He smiled and his laugh lines cracked through the mask.

"Well, if you're into pain, just wait until I get the hot wax on your legs. You'll be as smooth as the Olympic swim team."

He peeled back one cucumber to check if she was serious. She smiled at him as strong fingers pressed down his arch in such a way that his head lolled back into the cushions.

"Oh, Jesus, that feels nice," he groaned. "Where in the hell'd you learn that? Writing school?"

Laney laughed. "No." Her touch was confident, unrepentant and self-sure. He moaned and Laney pressed her thigh against his. "Katelyn, is an equine massage therapist, she's taught me a few things."

"Equine? As in horses?"

"Yep."

"How does that relate to—" She dug her knuckles into the back of his calf and glided down to his heel. Jamie took in a sharp breath and made a satisfied grunt. "God, I don't care, just don't stop." He pooled into the chair. She continued massaging his feet until not a tight muscle could be felt and then lowered it down to the rug.

"Other one." He obeyed and lifted his other foot from the water. She dried it and massaged it slowly. This time her fingers traveled up a bit more, to his calf and thigh. He sunk into the chair but his hips pressed forward as he let out pleased sighs. Laney watched, her mouth watering, her body wanting. When her fist pressed against his arch, he nearly came out of the chair.

"Marry me, Laney," he groaned then tensed in the quiet moment that settled between them.

"No way, you've got too much baggage." She smiled and rolled her knuckles over his calf causing shivers to tingle in his spine.

While she worked, the thought of coming home to Laney filled Jamie's relaxed mind. He closed his eyes tighter, pictured her curled up in bed with him, drinking coffee and doing the crossword, her ridiculous, thick-rimmed glasses perched on her head. He imagined walking their dog on the beach every morning. Of course, they'd have a dog. She was a dog kind of girl.

They'd laugh and watch the mutt romp in the waves, tongue hanging out the side of its mouth. He thought about flying home to her parents' small ranch, sitting by the fire, fishing with her dad, riding with her girls. Meeting her sisters, looking for acceptance from her mother. Teaching Sylvia and Charlotte to play the guitar. Holding her hand and dancing with her in the kitchen. What would life be like if he had Laney's love? It warmed every cell in his body and felt like home.

He was so caught up in the fantasy that he didn't realize she'd finished. He dozed in the middle of the beautiful daydream. In the slouchy armchair, Jamie was picturing her in a lacy nightgown, coming down to his studio in the middle of the night to coerce him back to bed. He played over the vision of being pressed between her creamy white thighs, pushing up that lacy gown. He imagined her gasping and watched her full lips wetted and parted.

Her long, soft hair spread across his pillow, her breasts in his hands, beneath his tongue. Rosy nipples tight.

Jamie sat up to the reaction his body had. She had gone into the kitchen to dump the water and to get a hot towel for his face. He sighed heavily and tried to slow his heart down. The sexual fantasy was one thing—picturing her as the person he came home to, trusted, and held on to, was a deep canyon he hadn't expected to look into.

He was Jameson Clark; he could have almost any woman in the world. He'd been married before and found it a constant circus of media attention, laced with dramatic and often public fights. His ex-wives were all in the business, and had brought the drama of the spotlight into their bedroom. Laney was different. She didn't belong with someone like him, with his lifestyle. His brain tossed around the fantasy and the reality of their situation.

What if he wasn't Jameson Clark? What if he was just plain, old Jamie from Fox Hill, Tennessee, song writer and part-time musician? Wouldn't Laney be just his perfect match? She came back, and he sat up, took the cucumbers from his eyes, and looked up at her.

———

"Questioning your sexuality?" She grinned but the heated gaze he returned dropped her smile. He narrowed his eyes.

"Not a question in my mind," he said huskily. She swallowed the lump in her throat and tried to calm the butterflies. "Sure is quiet here."

"Sure is," she said.

"No other people around. No mothers or sisters to interrupt. No friends or revelers crowding around us. No house cleaners, no children. No deadlines. No jellyfish," he said. Laney bit her lip. There was nothing between them to stop the need.

"Huh, how 'bout that? You—you probably want to get back

to your friends and revelers. Let's get the mud off and you'll be free to go and do superstar stuff. Sign boobs, destroy hotel rooms... whatever it takes to make you feel like that guy again," she said lightly, but when she came around in front of him, he pulled her down in his lap and held her bottom in his hands. She stared into his eyes as his fingers held her tight against him.

She could feel what his eyes had been telling her as it pressed into her thigh. She took in a deep breath. Her fingers tightened around the hot, wet towel in her hands. Van Morrison played softly in the background.

I can hear her heart beat, for a thousand miles.

"I don't want to be a superstar with you," he whispered, then his brow fell. "Not one for destroying property, I've never signed a boob, and I've only got one girl on my mind. Maybe I don't want to feel like that guy," he rumbled, staring at her lips, her backside in his hands. "Maybe, I just wanna feel like yours."

"Jamie." His name was breathy and soft on her lips. She searched for a joke or insult, anything to hide how much he affected her. But her hard-earned guard was slipping down around the both of them.

"Laney, darlin', you look like a deer in the headlights. 'S okay, we don't have to," he said.

"I'm just—"

"Unsure?"

"I've never been more—" she sighed and settled into his lap with a pleased breath, "sure. I just... want this to be real."

"It's real," he whispered. He raised his hips in a gentle circle, hands gripping her close. "How does it feel? Real enough?" His voice was husky as he closed his eyes with the shiver of pleasure that ran through their bodies.

"G—god, yes." She arched her back and felt her body tighten. "But—"

"But what?"

"But, I'm not gonna kiss you."

His eyes opened, and he scowled. "Well, why'n the hell not?"

"Because." She brought the washcloth up and wiped at his skin. "You look ridiculous and I don't want a tongue-full of clay." He smiled and closed his eyes to her touch. She watched his skin reappear, and when the mud had all been washed away, she followed a small droplet of water running down his neck with her lips, kissed him gently just above his collarbone. Jamie growled and gripped tighter. He rocked his hips. Through the thin cotton shorts, she felt his length and gasped. When she sat back up, she gritted her teeth against the need building up inside her.

"I don't know what you're doing with someone like me," she panted.

Jamie stiffened; his hands went up to frame her face; he made her meet his eyes.

"Goddamn it, Laney. You think you're just some used-up and discarded nobody? Well, you're not! That asshole knocked you off your horse. You believed him when he treated you like you were worthless." Laney's eyes fell, her heart clenched in her chest. Jamie's thumb ran over her bottom lip. "But you aren't worthless, you never were. You've always been beautiful and bright, sexy and smart. Just 'cause that moron couldn't see it— well, that's his loss and my gain. I'm here, with you, because you're the first woman I've ever felt like myself around. Because I wanna work to deserve your company. Because you drive me crazy, and turn me on."

Laney opened her teary eyes.

In the cool morning light, with breezes coming from the open doors caressing her skin, she kissed him. Soft at first, pressing into the hard line of his mouth, then warmly, her tongue teasing those lips apart. He tasted so good, warm and salty. Her hips rolled and her back arched as his hands slipped beneath her t-shirt and traced soft lines up to her shoulders.

He grunted into her mouth; sad and surprised and wholly pained. She broke the kiss to look at him. His hands were still up her shirt, her hands tangled in his hair. Breathing in gasps, she felt lightheaded and dangerous.

"Well, that kiss was just—it was awful," she said, pressing her cheek to his forehead.

"Absolutely terrible," he agreed with a smile.

"Let's never do that again."

"Never." He nodded before taking her lips again. He trailed kisses up her neck, moving her hair aside and pushing her shirt up over her head. His hands were rough and hot and everywhere, touching her arms, her neck, her back. His mouth biting, kissing, eating her alive. His tongue traced just beneath the top of her lace bra. She shivered and moved her hips in need against him.

"Jesus, Laney. Let's get serious," he growled, and stood, with her in his arms. She yelped, and all of her limbs wrapped tightly around him.

"You're gonna throw out your back," she said, but he carried her up the steps to the loft with ease.

"I want you in the treehouse, now."

She clung to his neck and shoulders and tried to read his face. He seemed serious. Not the man who'd filled the last lazy, carefree days with laughter and teasing. But the man in the dark mood of the library. The man who had wondered if anything was worth it. He said she was. He crested the top step and carried her to the properly made bed. He looked around and the seriousness cleared from his face.

"Who in the hell makes their bed on vacation?" he chuckled.

"Uptight schoolmarms. Jamie, I—" But he covered her mouth with a kiss and eased her into the soft mattress. "I—" she gasped again with his lips on her throat, her collarbone. He kissed his way back to her mouth.

"I want to make you feel sexy and amazing, because you are. I'm here to get rid of all that stupid self-doubt you carry around. I want you. So badly, I haven't been able to think straight since you landed on my island. So badly, I may never think straight again because of you." With that, he ran his hands down her stomach and hooked his thumbs into her shorts and panties. He pulled them down and flung them to the side.

"But I—" she sighed as her clothing hit the floor and his lips came back to the smooth skin of her legs. Her body was in such a surge of want, that she didn't care what she looked like, only that he didn't stop.

"God, you're so beautiful. Honestly, Lane—how is it your whole body is like cream? Every curve real and giving." He paused, kneeling between her trembling knees.

Lane, she thought with the sweet notes of love running like an undercurrent to the desire.

He nibbled on her hip bone, kissed her navel, licked his way up between her breasts and bit her collarbone, causing her to gasp and writhe. He smiled down at her. "Ever since the beach, I've been aching to see all of you, have you in my hands." He traced his hands up her torso, unhooked her bra and eased it off. He leaned down with a painful sigh. "God, yes." He smiled into the curve of her breast and traced its fullness with his tongue, stopping to tenderly bite its peak.

Laney threw her head back, her hands running through his hair. She was dizzy, and the delicious way he caressed each breast shot shivers of heat down her body. His kisses met her lips as she slid his shirt up and over his head. He looked down, and a smile quirked on his lips.

"Is that a heart?" he chuckled. She looked down to the forgotten grooming she'd undergone. Laney threw her hands over her face.

"I forgot! Ugh, it's awful!" Her cheeks turned pink, and he traced over the soft brown, freshly waxed patch with his nimble fingers.

"No, it's not!" He was so amused that she nearly screamed when he knelt down and nuzzled. "Why, that's about the cutest thing I've ever seen." He looked up at her, face buried in embarrassment. "Though, let's be honest, you don't need the embellishment." His hands continued, gently sliding the tips of his fingers over her, his eyes turned to watch her face. Her hands had fallen away, and she was flushed.

"Embellishment?" she gasped. "Pretty big word for you." She smiled as his kisses trailed up her neck. He kissed her smile until her tongue met his own and he took her mouth. She moaned as one hand cupped her breast and the other stayed on the core of her desire.

"Jamie—"

"I love the way you say my name," he whispered, one finger slipping inside. She gasped and sat up against the pillows.

"I—" She shook her head. She couldn't say she loved him...that would be ridiculous.

"What is it, Laney?" His fingers gently circled, caressing. Laney couldn't help but shake beneath his hands. Her nails dug into his shoulders where she found the taut muscles straining for control. With his deep and slow strokes, the pressure built up faster than she knew how to stop. She cried out, her eyes closed and teeth clenched. Tears fell down her cheek. Her body tensed into the soft mattress beneath him, she rocked into his hand over and over until she took in a deep, forgotten breath and sighed it out, satisfied.

"Someone *was* tightly wound," he said huskily, and kissed her moistened lips.

"Sorry," she gasped, shakily. He looked into her face. She was confused and torn, and he could read it. She'd never peaked so quickly, or with so little provocation.

"Don't be sorry, Laney," he whispered. "Not for anything, but especially not for that." His face was serious again, and he took her bottom lip in between his teeth and bit her gently. She arched into every move. Desperate and aching for his touch. He was so responsive to her body that it was like he could read her.

"You've gotten me all twisted up. You don't understand what it does to me to be here with you," he said. Her hands ran up his naked torso and her trembling legs wound around his waist. He smiled into her chin, "To have you respond so fast." Laney smiled then.

"Maybe I have been buttoned up too long."

"Well, allow me to loosen your buttons," he growled and grabbed her by the bottom and thrust into her. The shocked pleasure that coursed into her caused her to cry out, and she bit his lip.

Jamie made love to her like a man possessed. As though she was his salvation. His hands found every inch of her skin, caressed it, held it against him, around him. He kissed her, deeply, fully, as if he could open his soul to her in every movement, in every touch. He gasped, groaned her name, felt her velvet warmth tighten around him, take him in. She held on to him as she felt his desperation, the need for a deeper connection. She watched his face, the painful ache that filled his eyes. He was so intense. She'd never felt so completely surrounded and wanted. Never felt so womanly and powerful. She felt her body give in to the complete feeling of abandon, and every nerve ending lit with fire.

He whispered her name over and over, breathless in her ear, against her neck. She was a soft haven, though her hands were strong and sure over his body, holding on, holding close. She kissed and bit at his neck and gasped his name.

"Laney," he growled. "Lord, I might just die and go straight to hell a happy man." Laney felt his body tense with the agonizing need before his whole world exploded. Laney cried his name, as she rode the peak with him.

He stilled their fervent pace and let his head rest against her neck. He inhaled in the space between her neck and shoulder and Laney held him tight to her. He spoke not in words, but through the gentle caress of his lips on her skin. He kissed her all over, softly. *Please, please let's just stay this way...*Laney sighed in her own head.

He groaned, and a small sad sound came from him as he nuzzled into her neck.

"You okay?" she whispered, her hands tugging at his hair. His head rose and exposed the storm in his eyes. "Was it awful?" His dreamy blue gaze hardened, and he sat up, pulling her into his lap.

"Christ on a crutch, Laney, no! No, I'm not okay. I'm never gonna be okay again. Because now all I want to do for the rest of my foreseeable future is stay right here in this bed with you. You completely threw me. I just... I need a minute to get myself together after makin' love to you."

The blush deepened in her cheeks. Making love. Her heart skittered inside of her ribcage and she ignored the nagging voice that warned her. She kissed him.

"Well, I guess we can keep trying until it's old hat and boring," she said, straight-faced.

"Don't go thinking that you're old or boring, and you're definitely not something I'm ever going to get over," he whispered into the curve of her collarbone. She melted beneath his lips, pressed into his tender kisses.

"Jesus, you talk sweet," she whispered, eyes closed and aching. "I think I—"

"What is it, Laney?"

Laney muddled through the emotions as if they could be defined by words alone. "I—" She stopped the absurd idea that she was in love with him.

"You've never held back what you wanted to say to me."

"Some things are harder," she argued, and pulled away. He studied her, his eyes languid, deep and dream like. Her heart pounded.

"What's so hard about it now?" Her hand reached up to caress his cheek. He kissed her and his hands slid up the bare skin of her back. The urge was great. The fear was greater.

"I just—I—I really care about you, Jamie." She faltered and his eyes fell away from hers. Almost like his heart was falling in disappointment. Maybe she'd said too little. She knew she was lying, and she knew he wasn't fooled. But her own scars kept her from saying more.

"I care about you too," he choked.

She pulled the sheet around her and slid off of him. She needed space, she needed to get rational. And fast. He spoke to her retreating back. "What? Isn't that the watered down, safe thing we're saying to one another?" he said as she walked across the room. She turned around, the light from the window fell across the bed, where Jamie sat up, bed-tossed and sexy.

"What in the hell does that mean?"

"Well, shit, I don't know Laney! You tell me!"

"I suppose I should expect a form-letter version of what all the girls get after you toss them in the hay."

"That's not fair!" He rose up and walked over to where she stood. He didn't bother to cover himself, and she couldn't help but stare. In the soft light, his sun kissed skin and well-muscled body made her own body respond in ways that shocked her. She bit her lip. He kept coming.

"You know you mean more to me than that. I just told you in that bed!" He reached out, grabbed the sheet, and pulled her into his arms. He kissed her hard and pulled away, breathless. "We only have a week left, please don't make me spend it fighting with you."

Laney's rational brain offered a small protest before her body and her heart shut it down. "How should we spend it?" she said as he kissed her neck and tore the sheet from her body.

"I think a smart woman like you ought to know that too." His hands found her skin, their callouses scraping the skin of her back. She melted into him. She met his kisses; she pressed her bare breasts into him and backed him up towards the bed.

"Are you sure at your age you can take another round, Clark?" She smiled against his lips. He bit her bottom lip and toppled them over and into the bed.

"The bottle says I have four hours. But after that we should call a doctor." She laughed; a sound that made him smile. He watched as she straddled him. "God, I've never seen a prettier sight," he whispered, his fingers tracing up between her breasts. He cupped them, gently pinched the hardening tips until she gasped. The other hand curved around her ass and brought her closer. Laney felt his hardness press into her, begging, needing. "Come on, Laney," he whispered. He sat up and licked her nipple and bit it as he thrust her down. She cried out and arched her back.

"Jamie," she said, shocked and needy. Her hips moved in deepening strokes and his hands guided her. "You—" She felt it build inside of her, so near the surface.

"Don't stop, Laney," he growled and her thighs shook. "That's it, baby." When she came, his body joined hers coming fast and hard. He sat up, held her close and bit her neck, gasping her name while his hands shook against her skin. Their breaths echoed in the still morning. God, she loved him. There was no way around it. He kissed her collarbone, and she held him close.

What would she do without him? What would she do when it was time to go? He rolled over, snuggled her into the pillows and leaned and looked down at her. She smiled and raised an eyebrow.

"Old hat yet?"

"I don't think it'll ever get there, professor," he said, and she watched his eyes fill with emotion.

"I'm kind of wishing I knew what you were thinking," she said and touched his jawline. "Because when you get serious there's this muscle here that twitches."

He didn't speak. He fell into the pillows beside her. He pulled her against his chest.

"I just want to take all the now I can," he yawned and his body sunk deeper into the bed beside her. "I declare, Laney Sullivan, you wore this old, washed-up, has-been out," he whispered, and she felt the calm weight of satisfaction pulling at her body to sleep. She felt his heart slow beneath her cheek, his breath became even and deep. She reached down, pulled the blankets over them and settled into the crook of his arm and kissed his chest. When he started to snore, she sighed.

"Damn it, Jamie. I do love you." The whisper-light confession slipped out, and she closed her eyes in fear he'd heard.

"I do too," he mumbled and squeezed her. Laney shook her head; how could she have fallen so hard for someone who stood so little chance of having a normal relationship? Maybe she didn't need to have normal. Maybe she'd been too normal her whole life. His hand caressed her arm, and he snorted loudly before snuggling into spoon with her.

"Don't tip the boat, I don't wanna fall," he mumbled into her shoulder. Laney smiled and let the dazed sleepiness take her too.

FOURTEEN

WHEN LANEY WOKE UP, IT WAS SOMETIME IN THE EARLY evening. She could tell by the light that doused the room. The bed was empty, sheets and pillows haphazard. She blew an errant lock of hair from her forehead and cocked her head to listen for him. Odd clanks came from the kitchen below and drove her to pull on her shirt and shorts and take the stairs on wobbly knees. He was there, shirtless in his shorts, hair in disarray and love bites all over his chest and neck. She blushed.

"Hey, Laney," he sang, in a baritone that shivered up through her toes. "That woman makes me so crazy," he crooned, and came towards her with a plate of cut fruit and a sandwich. She smiled so deep that her eyes crinkled.

"What's all this?"

He pulled the plate away and made her pay him with a soft, slow kiss.

"You inspired me to cook," he said, and pinched her chin.

Laney looked at the sandwich and fruit and raised an eyebrow. "Peanut butter and jelly? Fancy. We should chuck it all and start a restaurant."

"You makin' fun of me?" he laughed.

"Oh, I'm not. It looks delicious. Right now, I could probably eat three of them." She snatched the plate from him and sat down at the island.

He stood behind her and ran his fingers through her tangled hair while she ate. "I like this hair of yours. It's soft." She leaned back and put a piece of papaya to his lips. He bit into the sweet fruit and licked the juice from her thumb and palm. She sighed, and her other hand reached back to caress his neck. "You're not going to get a chance to eat if you keep that up." He sighed, brushed the hair from her neck and bit into her skin. She shivered and gasped, her hands seeking him out to pull him closer.

"I don't have to eat," she whispered.

He smiled beneath her ear. "No, you need to eat. I should go. I have to get to my studio and cut another demo."

She turned in her seat and looked at him. Her heart pounded.

"A—another demo?"

"Well, we'll see," he said, and she read the doubt in his features. She stood, threw her arms around his neck and kissed him with papaya juice still on her lips.

"Well, look at that once-washed-up-has-been. Sure is good to see him back up on his horse," she said breathlessly as he continued to kiss her and his hands slipped under her shirt, seeking her flesh.

"I understand," she said, breaking away. "I know what that itch is like, to create something. It's a drive, isn't it? Insatiable," she gasped and his lips found hers again.

"I love when you talk that way. Insatiable..." His hands dipped below to caress her backside. "But I think I'd rather just stay here and scratch a different itch."

Laney pulled away.

"You can't run from it, Jamie. It's hard to put your heart out there when you're not sure anyone's listening, and those who are can be so quick to judge." A crease formed between his brows. "It's hard. And I understand, maybe more than anyone, how hard it can be." He leaned in to kiss her again but she kept just out of reach.

"But it's what you love. And you can't just ignore what you love. You have to strike while the iron is hot."

The words caught in her throat and she tried to keep calm, thinking about what he loved. Jamie pulled her in for a kiss, backing her up against the counter with a hungry grunt. She wriggled out of his arms with a laugh and skipped to the other side of the island. He grunted with frustration.

"What did you tell me? 'The creative process doesn't do well with distraction.'" Her eyebrow lifted over her smile. He threw his head back and made an exasperated sound.

"What about one more time? Just like, a fifteen-minute distraction?" he said, moving around the island. She danced away from him. He stopped and collapsed into the chair in frustration. She came up behind him and kissed his neck. She pressed her curves into his shoulders, he sighed and leaned his head back into her attention. She felt his skin warm as he took her wrist in his hand and pressed kisses up from her palm to the delicate crook of her elbow.

"But if you don't go now, that fifteen-minute distraction will turn into the rest of the hour, maybe—" she nibbled on his ear and he sucked in his breath, guiding her hand down to his lap where he strained for her, "all night. Dishes will get broken, sandwiches will be strewn across the floor. Marc will make me pay for new counters." She smiled against his ear while her strong fingers caressed him. He chuckled.

"I'll buy him a whole new house if I can just have you, now." He stood up, pulled her against him and started to pull her shirt up. She nipped at his bottom lip and pushed him away.

"No."

"No?"

"Go cut your demo," she said, and put her hands on his hips to keep him just far enough away. "Then, when you're done, we'll talk about inappropriate-for-our-age positions." He growled and held her up close against his body to kiss her.

"Can't believe you just told me no."

"Not something you're used to? Oh, wait, I forgot who I'm talking to." She handed him his shirt, and he took it. He sighed, took a deep breath with his eyes closed and she knew he was trying to calm himself down. She felt the same.

"Jesus, Lane. How'm I supposed to do anything when I want you this much?"

She smiled over her shoulder as she picked up his flip-flops from beside the couch and led him to the door.

"For the record, it's not easy for me to let you go," she said.

He leaned in and kissed her cheek.

"Will you come see me tonight?"

"Probably, since you asked so nice." She smiled. "You owe me at least fifteen minutes." He rested his forehead down on hers and sighed.

"Goddamn it, this is going to be a hard afternoon."

"Well, the afternoon isn't the only thing." She smiled.

"One more word, Sullivan and I'll haul you up those stairs again—"

"Get out of here," she laughed, handed him his shoes, and gave him a gentle shove. He turned back to her at the door.

"Eat something." He pointed back to the kitchen. "You're going to need your strength."

Once outside, he leaned on the closed door. It had taken all of his self-control to not say what was in his mind. To tell her he'd fallen. His heart ached, and he wanted to go back in, where she was. He took a deep breath. She was right. He needed to get to the studio while he was in the middle of the fire. He moved to climb the fence when he heard it click open. He looked back and she was standing at the window, sandwich in hand and smiling. Goddamn it, he wanted to stay. He smiled like his heart wasn't breaking for leaving her. The sunlight lit her light brown hair and the memory of her laughter went straight to his brain. His heart thudded, every beat begging him to tell her. *Goddamn it, Laney, I love you so much.*

That afternoon, Laney did her laundry, polished the newest chapter and added another two. In the three weeks she'd been here she'd managed to almost finish a first draft. She hadn't written like this since the girls were babies and she'd used every available naptime to sit down and put words to paper. She felt on fire again and she knew who had helped light her tinder. She'd just gotten out of a much needed shower when her eyes fell on the compass she'd packed with her.

It was heavy for its small size; an antique Gran had given her that had belonged to her grandfather. It was her good luck charm. She thought about Jamie and how he seemed so lost in the world.

When she looked up from her screen, the clock said seven. Her heart pattered in her chest. Was seven too early? She didn't want to wait any longer to see him again. She bit her lip and ran her hands over her still-wet hair.

There was a sundress she hadn't broken out yet. She crossed her arms in front of her chest and walked over to the desk. The cursor flashed on the screen on the last page she'd finished. The breaking point. The point where her characters would either tip towards being together, or be broken from their own flaws. She didn't want to write the ending yet. She closed the screen on her laptop and went to find the dress and put some effort into her make-up.

She walked down the lane, more familiar and unafraid of the strange buzzing of insects and frog songs and bird calls that had stormed her senses. The evening was still warm and still humid. She'd tied her hair back in a braid. In the dry climate of her home state it was normally flat, but the humid heat of the island curled it into golden waves, and made the sun-bleached streaks of it into a beautiful array of highlights. Maybe all she'd needed was more sun. A change of scenery. A lover. She felt her heart hammer as she got closer to his gate. The last weeks they'd spent together played over in her mind. Christmas, the party, the disastrous kayaking trip, even the afternoon they'd spent in the bar insulting one another ran through her head. The morning, the afternoon of the most amazing sex she'd ever had. All of those moments packed into such a short time. Intensity wasn't part of Laney's normal world, and it felt frightening. Like a rollercoaster ride that could end in tragedy at any moment.

Could she really be in love, or was it just the magic of the island? The freedom of not having to be responsible? When she went back home in six days would she still feel the same about him, tucked into her old and safe life again?

"Doesn't really matter, *weirdo*, he's not the hopeless romantic here," she chided under her breath as she reached the gate and buzzed the buzzer. After a few minutes she was convinced he'd forgotten, not remembering that she herself went without answering phones and doors while immersed in her writing. Laney turned to leave, when the lock clicked and his voice came breathless over the rusting speaker.

"Hey, darlin'. Sorry, I was downstairs." She turned back around and her voice stuck in her throat at the endearment.

"O—oh. Is this okay? Am I too early?" She rolled her eyes. No quick comment fired out to disguise her awkwardness.

"You're perfect. I'll be up in a minute." He buzzed her in, but before she could even make it up the stairs to his door, he opened it. "That's some dress," he said after a moment of studying her. She frowned.

"Really?"

"Yeah, it's going to look great on my floor," he said and grabbed her, pulled her into his arms and slammed the door shut with his bare foot. His hands went around her neck to hold her into his kiss, fervent and hot. She shivered. He wasn't easing into anything.

"Jamie, what—" He took her lips. "We—" He stripped off her purse and slid his hands around her back to undo her zipper. "Don't have to jump right into it," she said breathlessly.

"Yes, we do. I do." He slid her straps down. She stilled his hands, pulled her face away. "I've been thinking about you all day, Laney. All day." He nuzzled under her chin. There was something in his demeanor that made her pause. An uncertain pain. A worry and vulnerability.

"Is that all that's going on?"

"Isn't it enough for me to just want to be inside you?" He reached to kiss her again, but she pushed against his chest before her body acted against her reasoning.

"Are you okay? How did the demo go? Did something go wrong?"

"You wanna talk about the demo?" he scowled.

"I want to talk about you. I want to know how *you* are. You seem different." She touched his cheek. He backed her up against the wall, pressing into her curves with his hard body. She gasped and arched into him, even as she asked him for so much more. He held her tighter, sighed into her neck and his hands relaxed.

"Nothing went wrong, actually it all went right. Come here." He took her by the hand and led her down a winding staircase, pocketed with small alcoves full of shells and sculptures, and through a sealed glass door. The studio was calm and quiet with warm woods and dark blue furniture, along with so much technical gear that she couldn't even pretend to know what any of it was for.

He led her to a couch, and when he was sure she was sitting and not likely to bolt, he gave her a signal to wait and ran back to the recording booth. The simple acoustic music poured through the speakers. Jamie walked back into the room and leaned against the wall as his hands hooked into the pockets of his jeans. As his voice warmed the room, soft and deep, Jamie hung his head and closed his eyes. Laney felt goosebumps raise on her flesh at the melodic sound. She closed her eyes too and folded her hands in her lap.

I was out with her last night
Staring at her legs, crossed just right.
I was having those thoughts
making those plots
When fate stepped in
gave me a shot.

Little girl at the table next to us,
Started to cry, started to fuss.
Long curly hair, and big eyes
Daddy fawning over her like stars in the sky.
I looked back and saw her face,
the woman who I'd easily replace.
And lost the wall I'd built so high.

That's somebody's little girl,
She's somebody's great big world.
Tiny hand wrapped around his finger,
big blue eyes always gonna linger
'Fore you take her for a ride,
Remember her daddy's on her side.
Remember her momma's heart'll break
If her little girl comes home too late.
She's everything to someone's heart,
So, think where you're taking her
before you start...

I'm staring at her lips,

those knock-me-down hips,
Thinking of all the ways,
I'll have her tonight.
But before I undo that dress,
before I leave her heart a mess
That's somebody's little girl,
That's somebody's great big world.
She's got her momma's eyes
and her daddy's hair
And all their love to spare.
She's the jewel in their crown
Think of how you're letting her down.

I paid the check, I kissed her cheek.
Told her I'd like to see her next week.
If that girl was mine, at the table next door,
I wouldn't let her date me, for sure.
But I saw the light, I read the signs
I understand there's more to her lines.

She's somebody's great big world.
She's always going to be somebody's little girl.
'Fore you take her for a ride,
Remember her daddy's on her side.
Remember her momma's heart'll break
If her little girl comes home too late.
She's everything to someone's heart,
And someday it might be mine.

Laney's eyes filled as the last strain died away from the speakers.

"Jamie—"

"Campy? Cheesy? It's awful, right?" he asked and drew away,

his eyes pained. "I know you'd be honest with me. So, just tell me you didn't like it, and I'll go back to the drawing board." He barely breathed, let alone gave her a chance to speak. "You don't have to say anything. You don't have to like the song."

"Goddamn it, Jamie, let me get a word in edgewise! You threw me!" He paused to look at her. "That song—" she bit her lip, "was about the sweetest, most beautiful thing I've ever heard..." She ran out of words and her bottom lip trembled. She crossed the room and took his face in her hands. She kissed him slowly with every ounce of love she could. "It had heart, Jamie."

Jamie rained kisses over her mouth and throat.

"I don't know how it happened, Laney. I haven't been able to write in years. But there're pages—hell, practically a whole book since I met you. I don't understand what you've done to me. But you—you unlocked all of this—strange and wonderful stuff." His voice was hoarse. She sniffled into his neck.

"I didn't do anything, you idiot. You've always been able to do it. Don't you understand? You're already amazing."

"I'm not," he shook his head. "I'm not amazing. I've lost so much of myself. I've given so much away." His eyes turned serious. "Will you—stay with me tonight? In my bed?"

She nodded. "Of course."

He held her hand the whole way up the stairs and tugged her gently into the room with its oversized and romantic canopied bed. He untied her hair, ran his fingers through it, pushed it away from her neck as he kissed and bit her. She shivered and tugged at his t-shirt to pull it over his head. Her strong fingers unbuttoned his jeans. Her dress fell in a pool at her feet when he traced it off of her shoulders.

The rest of their clothes followed, and his eyes traced over her skin in the moonlight. He sighed and put his hand to his chest.

"Lord, Laney, I just want to make this night last. Just stay, please just stay—" the words fell away when Laney stopped them with her kisses. She wanted to cry when she put her body in his hands. He pushed her back into the bed, his body so hard for her that he seemed to be in pain from it. She kissed him, traced her fingers down over his back, around his backside, and guided him. When he pushed inside it was slow, and quiet, and deep. She gasped and closed her eyes to the gentle strength that pulsed inside of her.

Jamie held himself above her and locked his eyes to hers. Laney knew he saw every delicate emotion pass through them. His pace quickened, just enough to keep up with the needful rise and fall of her hips. He kissed her, his tongue searching and asking.

"You're so beautiful, Jamie. Everything you are. You're so—" Her breath caught as her body began to crest. "I need—" she said as her nails scratched his shoulders. The darkness just behind his eyes returned. "I—" Her body began to tighten. "Oh!" She shivered, and he held her hands above her head and drove into her, over and over until she climaxed, crying his name with tears in her eyes.

She wanted to love him. She wanted him to love her. But she knew he couldn't make promises to her. She didn't know what kind of future they could have. His life on the road, her life of responsibility. So, for the moment, she stopped the thoughts and only felt what it meant, to lay beneath him, her thighs cradling as his pace quickened.

"I need you. I think I've always needed you, Laney," he whispered, and the soft slowness gave way to a fire that seemed to burn out of control. He drove into her deep and hard, and she gasped with surprise. Until he growled her name again, and she felt his climax snap through him like a whip, just as she peaked again.

Jamie collapsed on top of her, his face wet with tears and sweat. She didn't ask what had brought on the tears, only wrapped her legs around his waist and ran her fingers through his hair. She sighed into his neck.

"I'm here," she said softly. "I'm staying right here," she said. "It's going to be alright." She said, not really knowing if it would be. She didn't know. He probably didn't know what would happen either. She held him close to the beat of her heart.

"You wreck me," he said, subdued against her skin. "And fix me and make me feel like I could do it all again. You make me feel like I could do anything I wanted. Like I could—or should get back up there and start over. Or I could chuck it all and write songs, or—" He snuggled his face between her breasts and sighed. "What in the hell am I gonna do?" His arms slid beneath her and he relaxed his full weight down. Laney ran her fingernails lightly over his back easing him into sleep.

"What do *you* want to do?" she whispered into his hair and pulled at it. He looked up, found her lips, and kissed her.

"I—I just want to stay here with you, for now." The words were quiet and halting. He rolled over and held her body next to his. She was so silent that she thought he'd fallen asleep until he spoke in a quiet, sex-roughed voice.

"My dad died of a heart attack the year I had the breakdown." Laney's fingers touched his chest. "The last thing he said to me was, 'Jameson, find your direction. You've been a boat out to sea too long, and pretty soon they'll be no land left to come back to.' I ignored him. I thought he was trying to tell me to settle down and leave the life I'd worked so hard to build. I thought he was telling me to quit, or that what I was doing wasn't worth enough. I got so mad. I left for the tour and I didn't come back. Then, right before my last show in Atlanta, the last show of the tour, he had a heart attack and died. I couldn't find my voice that night—any night after. It was like my heart broke and nothing else inside of me would work right." He moved, and she sat up to look at him with tears in her eyes. He sat up too and put his head in his hands.

"I couldn't write, I couldn't sing...I couldn't do anything without thinking about him and how he must have died feeling like I'd let him down."

Laney traced her fingers up his bare back.

"I know he didn't. How could he feel like you let him down?"

she said and put her arm around his back. "You spent your life doing what you loved and loving what you did. How could any parent not be happy about that?"

He shook his head. "I don't know, Laney."

"I do. I hate to stroke your ego when there's so many other parts I could be stroking, but you are a pretty damn amazing person. For all my asshole comments and ego bashing, I know how remarkable you are. You've accomplished incredible things. One-of-a-kind things. Once-in-a-lifetime things. And even after such a heart-wrenching loss, you're getting back on your feet. That's not something everyone does. Not everybody stands back up." He turned his head to look at her, he caressed her flushed cheek with his thumb. He opened his mouth as though something important was aching to be let out but he stayed silent.

"So, it doesn't matter what you once did, who you were. It only matters what you want to do now. And there's no wrong in following your heart, and fighting for what you want." Jamie kissed her quickly again and again, and she wasn't sure if he was trying to keep her quiet or himself. When he pulled away, he smiled, in his slow, sexy way, and raised his eyebrow.

"Let's go back a tick—"

"What?"

"Stroke my what exactly?" he asked and Laney smiled wickedly.

"Allow me to instruct you, Mr. Clark," she said with her eyebrow raised. He groaned as her strong and able fingers found him in the dark night.

"You're my favorite teacher...like probably ever," he whispered as her fingers tightened and slid around him. She smiled, bit his chin lovingly, and took away the painful doubt in his mind.

Fifteen

It wasn't that she woke up, every limb heavy and relaxed, in the soft, love-laced sheets of a sexy man. It wasn't that he snored softly beside her, a smile tugged on his cheek, or that the warmth of the morning coastal breeze blew across her skin to wake her. It wasn't only the contentment that filled her heart or the echoed whispers of love that ran through her brain. It was a little bit of all things wonderful that plastered a smile on her face when she heard the muffled tones of her cell phone from across the room.

She threw on his shirt and slipped into her panties, crossed the room, searched for and found her phone and took it outside, away from his soft and pleased snoring. He was completely worn out, and she was rather proud of herself. She was sore, tired, and overwhelmingly elated, as though she'd just run her first marathon. She felt like she deserved a medal. The thought made her giggle as she answered.

"Laney?" Her mother's worried voice came through the other end of the line.

"Hey, Momma!" she said, too exuberantly.

"Are you okay? You sound drunk. Are you drunk?"

"No," she chuckled. "Just having a good morning." She wondered what her mom would say if she knew who was passed out from her lovemaking behind her. Laney bit her tongue wickedly.

"Oh, that's good." Melissa's voice dropped.

"Are you okay? What's going on?" There was a moment's pause and Laney's heart fell with worry. "Mom?"

"It's—everything is just fine, sweetheart. We were just calling to check in with you."

"Mom," Laney sighed. "I can tell when you're lying. What is it?"

"Well, it's—it's nothing you need to worry about right now," Melissa said firmly. "I just wanted to hear about how your trip has been. Are you wearing sunblock? Have you seen any jellyfish?"

Laney blushed.

"Yeah, one. I did see one, I think. It's been—so wonderful. I can't—" Laney stopped and felt at odds. Being happy felt wrong when something was obviously going on at home. "It's been amazing. I'm getting a lot of writing done and haven't felt this relaxed in a long time. Now you go," she said and left the conversation open. "Who died?"

"Laney! No one died!"

"You're calling at 7 a.m. on a Saturday, Mom. Somebody died."

"Oh, Laney don't be dramatic!"

"Are you okay? Is Dad okay? Did something happen?" Laney put the phone on speaker so she could run quickly to grab her purse, looking for her wallet and already planning to look into flights. She took it back on to the balcony.

"No, honey, it's fine, we're all fine here."

"Mom—shit, seriously. Don't lie to me."

"Do not curse at me, young lady," Melissa countered. Laney rolled her eyes. "And don't you roll your pretty, little eyes either!"

"Ha, nobody knows you like your momma. I can't believe you cursed at her, mine would tan my hide." Jamie's voice came from the doorway, sleep-sexy and smiling. Laney spun around and dropped her purse.

"Who's that?" Melissa asked.

"Uh...Hello, Mrs. Sullivan. My name's Jamie. I'm a friend of your daughter's," Jamie said directly at the phone. Laney buried her face in her hands and groaned.

"What are you doing with my daughter so early in the morning, Jamie?" Melissa's voice came over. Jamie smiled and burst out into a laugh, amused that a nearly forty-year-old woman should still be under the propriety of her mother.

"Well, ma'am. Your daughter has graciously taken it upon herself to give me some private tutoring."

"Is that so?" Melissa asked with skepticism dripping from her words.

"She's a very generous teacher. Giving up her personal time and vacation to help me get a better hold on my—writing techniques. I'm working on a how-to manual. As luck would have it, we're both early risers," he said and winked at Laney.

"Oh my God, shut up!" Laney whispered and shoved him. "Mom, tell me what's going on." She reached for the phone to take it off speaker, but Jamie stilled her hand. Laney scowled but before she could protest, her mother spoke.

"It's nothing, really. Just a couple of men, lawyers of Ian Tennyson's I think, came to the ranch while we were gone to Cheyenne yesterday. Blake told them to clear off. Seems they were interested in the property lines and started throwing around threats about back taxes on some of the south property. But it's not worth your worry. I just wanted you to know what was going on in case we end up having to get a lawyer. I don't know what's going to come of this, but I know there's nothing to be worried about right now."

"Are you kidding me? Why wouldn't I worry about this! That

goddamn soulless bastard! I wish I could put his shriveled-up nuts in a vice!"

"Laney!" Jamie and Melissa both said in shock.

"He's just trying to get back at Grant, isn't he? That underhanded, vindictive—"

"Holy thesaurus brain." Jamie tried to lighten the mood.

"Now see, this is why I didn't want to tell you!" Melissa said.

"You just hang tight, okay? Don't you give them a single inch. I'll be home as soon as I can and we'll figure something—"

"Laney June, you'll do no such thing! You take your vacation. You get that book done."

"Mom—"

"I won't ever forgive you if you don't. Your books are my favorite things to curl up with. It's like getting to listen to you in the middle of the chaos, and I need your stories. I need you to be doing what you love. You stay there until you're done." Melissa paused to huff. "Jamie!" He snapped to attention, so enamored with Melissa's heartfelt command, that he wasn't expecting to get an earful himself.

"Yes—uh, yes, ma'am?"

"I don't believe for a minute that you're her student, or that you are even wearing clothes right now, but if you care about her at all, you see that she listens, and you keep her on track."

"Yes, ma'am." Jamie blushed from his bare chest up.

"You stay out of this, Clark!" Laney reprimanded.

"You know how I was raised! I'm not going to tell your mom no!" he argued back and gestured to the phone. Laney rolled her eyes.

"I like him," Melissa chuckled. "It's settled then, you aren't allowed to worry about it until you're back home and have gotten done what you went down there to do." Melissa took a breath. "Now, sounds like you've got things to get to. I've gotta go help your dad vaccinate some new colts at the Spur. I need you to do what I asked. He told me not to tell you at all, but it's your land too."

"Mom, I—" Laney's voice dropped. Jamie came to her, concern on his sleepy face. He gently put his hand around hers. "Okay," was all she could manage.

"I love you Laney June, I'll see you when you get home."

"I love you too," Laney whispered, and the line went dead. Laney's joy crumpled around her feet and Jamie watched the happiness die away in her eyes.

"Who's Ian Tennyson? Why's he threatening you?"

Laney sniffed and shook her head.

"No, it's nothing. Nothing you need to worry about." Jamie's face fell.

"Why wouldn't I worry about it?"

"Because it's just—life. Part of my life that isn't part of this world and this time. It's the other side of the world away."

"Laney," he whispered and tipped her chin up. "When the other side of the world comes calling and rouses my sexy woman out of bed, it becomes part of this time."

"I shouldn't have answered it."

"That's not what I meant," Jamie said. Laney shook her head and looked at her bare feet, back out to the ocean view.

"There's no point worrying, Jamie. My family has always been teetering on the edge of losing the land. But then my little sister fell in love with this wonderful man whose father didn't want them to be together. And—well, he's a heartless tycoon, and he's pissed because Grant disrupted his grand plans for the Tennyson legacy. I'm not blaming Grant. He loves Katelyn so much that he gave up everything to be with her, and I'd rather we all had to shack up in a van down by the river and have him safe, then to have him go back to that monster. But it's—" Her voice broke, and she leaned away, hating the feeling of crying in front of him.

Jamie sighed and ran his hands through his hair. "So, his dad,

Ian, is trying to make your family pay, because he didn't approve of them getting together? What the hell is this? *Dynasty*? No wonder you write romance novels."

"It's nothing like—look, you don't—" She sighed. "I don't want you to worry about me. My life, back there, it's not a part of this, of us, of what little time we have left." She gestured to the brilliant blue sky and the ocean. The lazy rush of waves and soft teasing breezes traced her hair over her neck and cheeks and Jamie watched her with concern in his eyes. "I don't want to ruin what we have here with reality."

Jamie's jaw clenched, and he looked at her strangely.

"So, what we have isn't real?" he asked lowly.

Laney's face flushed. "Well, of course it is! Here, in this moment. But once I go home, and you go back to being you—"

"Then we're done? Is that it? That I have no business being in your life off this island?"

"That's not it at all. *I* don't have any business being in yours!" Laney felt her heart hammering in her throat and a strange feeling filled her chest. Not having felt hope, or elation in so long, it took her a full moment to recognize what it was. "I don't want you to worry about me and I don't want to hold you down or away from what you're meant to be; especially not when you're just starting to get back to being you."

"I—" he began and stopped. "I care about you Laney, and when I see you struggling, hurting, and worrying it makes me hurt. And stop trying not to cry! You can cry around me! I'd rather you cry, than do that strange lip thing you're doing."

"Well, fine!" she yelled and her sniff turned into a small yelp, the gates of her heart and the worry that had built up behind it came rushing out all at once.

"My family has been fighting for as long as I can remember to keep my grandparents' ranch," she paused to sniff and shake her head. "They're all working so hard, and all I do is run away and scramble a few cents together on mommy porn and a below-wage teaching job. I should be doing more! I want to do something but I don't. I'm not good enough at anything." Jamie took her into his arms, pressed her close; warm and safe against his heartbeat. "I don't want you to pity me. I don't want you to see me as someone who—who—can't take care of things." She hiccupped. Jamie's lips smiled before pressing into her temple.

"You silly, crazy woman," he whispered into her hair. "You think I'm a stranger to being scared and feeling helpless?"

"Yes, I do," she said, and tried to pull away, but he held her tighter.

"Come here, don't get mad. You're raising your daughters on your own, you're paying your bills, and doing what you love. Your parents know you love them and would do anything in the world for them. I hear it in your momma's voice. You're a beautiful human, and you wouldn't be nearly so beautiful if you didn't have troubles." He rocked her, and she nuzzled into his chest.

"I was born on that ranch. It's been in my family since my great-grandparents, and now it's going to get taken over by a man who doesn't even care about the land or the community. It's just shitty, and I hate it!" she finished, and felt like stamping her foot like a toddler in the middle of a tantrum. Jamie didn't say anything. "And I didn't want to tell you because I don't want to bother you with my problems."

"I can't figure out if thinking you bother me makes you lovable or annoying," he said into her hair. Laney's tears slowed. His heartbeat calmed her. "There's not much you can do from so far away," he said softly.

"I hardly need reminding."

"I mean that worrying is good—for a bit. It means you care and that you're on the first path to a solution, but there's no sense getting worked up until the battle starts. You're smart, you'll figure something out."

"I know." She nodded, not feeling as sure as she sounded.

"Okay then," he sighed and tucked a strand of hair behind her ear. "Well, get the hell back in my bed, because seeing you cry, just makes me want to take you to bed and make you laugh."

"Is that the reaction you're used to? Women laughing at you in bed?"

Jamie snorted a giggle back. "Not *at* me, Laney! *With* me. Don't laugh at me." His smile and crinkled eyes brought Laney away from the worries back at home that she had no power to change in this moment, anyway.

"Well, I make no promises," she said.

Jamie watched her. You sure you're okay?"

"Don't worry about me, Clark. I'm a tough old hide."

"I'm gonna get that tough old hide all over mine in about two minutes." He brushed her hair away from her tear-lined cheek, and Laney fell into his kiss.

She was lying to save him the worry. She lied because no matter how happy she was, no matter what glow of love she carried in her heart, when her family was suffering, she wasn't whole. Jamie must have understood. He'd run away when his family had suffered. He'd not been able to face his part in their tragedy.

Their time on the island was limited, and despite the new and conflicting feelings in her heart, Laney agreed with her mom. They only had a few more days. Then reality would hit. Life would probably knock her down the minute she flew back to Laramie. Maybe the best thing she could do, the only thing she could do, was take as much happiness as she could before the world reared its ugly head to meet her.

She kissed him again and again. Jamie took her back inside, into the love-laced sheets and made love to her, with all the care and support she wanted to feel, hiding love within each touch and caress until they were spent and breathing heavily.

. . .

"Did you ever write about it?" she asked, later that afternoon. Her feet were propped up on the railing of the veranda, notebook in hand, and she'd paused her scribbling to look at him. Jamie looked up from the worn copy of her first book that Desdemona had lent him. He was just getting into the good, steamy stuff and was making plans to recreate a scene from the shower. Her words cut right through the dropping of clothes and he stared, dazed, into her eyes.

"What?"

"Did you ever write it down? About your dad?"

"Not exactly party song material," he said, distracted.

"I didn't mean that." She shook her head and tucked her pen into her bun. The wind blew through the notebook's pages and rustled them. The same notebook, that not ten pages back, still held her last will and testament to a life she thought she was done living until she'd gotten to know Jamie. "I meant, just write about it. The story. What happened."

"Laney, I don't think—"

"Writing is very cathartic."

"Big words, darlin'. I love when you use big words." He smiled and tried to loosen the knot that threatened to tighten in his chest.

"What if you wrote him a letter?" she asked and turned in her chair to face him.

"What?"

"A letter. Telling him everything you wish you could? I've done it before." Her eyes fell to the notebook. "It's helped." Jamie stared at her, the way she'd sat up on her knees, glasses on and hair in a messy bun. Swimming in one of his t-shirts, biting her lip and holding her breath. His little muse. His beautiful, big-hearted nerd.

"Page 146."

"What?" She sat back; eyebrows drawn in.

"Let me do page 146 to you and then I'll sit down and write a letter."

Laney's eyes shifted to her book and a wicked smile tugged on the corner of her mouth.

"You write the letter, and then you can do 146 and 167 to me —or I guess, I get to do 167 to you."

"I haven't read that far yet!"

"Well, then it'll be a surprise either way. Do you want some paper?"

"You're such an old lady! I have an iPad—"

"Do it by hand," she said softly. "This kind of letter is better written by hand." She stood up, came over to him, and sat in his lap. No qualms about her weight, or self-conscious hesitations. He liked to believe she'd outgrown them in his arms. He wanted her to feel nothing but beautiful and loved. And, in turn she was asking to help him to feel just as safe; just as worthwhile. Jamie smiled as her kisses nudged beneath his ear.

"Page 146 will be better by hand too," he grunted.

"Then you'd better start writing," she chuckled, bit his neck, and handed him her notebook open to a fresh, blank page. It looked so daunting. "Don't stop, no matter what comes out, no matter if you make mistakes, or don't spell something right. Don't stop or try to erase a goddamn thing. Just let it all go. I'm going to give you some space and go make us something to eat. That is, if you have more than frozen margaritas in the fridge. And if that's all you have, I'll have one ready for you when you're done."

He looked up at her as she rose, turned and pulled out the pen from her hair and handed it to him. He watched the graceful lift of his shirt hem above her strong thighs.

"You've got this, Jamie," she said as she leaned in and kissed him. "Just tell him what you need him to know."

Jamie listened to the sound of her bare feet padding out of the room and down the stairs. He'd never thought to write about the loss. He stared out at the ocean for a long minute, her pen, still warm, between his fingers. Jamie took a deep breath, and began.

Dad—

If I had known that night would be the last one I'd ever get to talk to you, if I'd known that last fight would be the last time I'd ever hear your voice—I would have shut my mouth and listened. Really listened. I wouldn't have been proud. I wouldn't have built up walls, just because what you were saying was too close to the truth and I didn't want to see it. I would have listened to you. I would have shaken your hand. I would have hugged you and told you how much I loved you. I wouldn't have run away.

I wouldn't have left.

You were right about me in so many ways. But wrong in others. This life I've built, I'm proud of. I've done a lot of good, lived a lot of good days, made memories and friends I never would have had otherwise. I followed my dream, and I know that you were proud of me chasin' it. But you saw me headed towards the cliff. You saw me throwing nights away in the bottle and breaking hearts. You saw me hurting from being caught in the machine and you tried to stop me, shake me and wake me up. Make me remember why I started. You were trying to stand up for me...for my happiness. I should have listened to you.

Momma is doing fine. She misses you and I don't think she'll ever find another love. Cassie and Jilly Bean are growin' too pretty and obnoxious as shit. They remind me of me when I was that age, so it leads me to believe that it's the fault of the parenting involved. But I won't tell Momma what we're both thinking—it's probably your fault. You loved your kids with every heartbeat and with every breath you took. Right up to the last ones and we love you back, always.

I met a girl, Dad. Well, not a girl. She's a strong, smart-assed, brilliant woman. She's a teacher and a mom and—shit, I think I might love her, Dad. I mean—forty-seven years on this planet and every time I've thought I was in love, it faded out like a season. But I've been trying and I just can't feel this fading. I wish you could meet her, tell me what you think. I would listen this time. I think Momma loves her. She's silly and clumsy, but she can ride a horse and sing decently. She's mean with the truth, but only when she's worried or hurt. Hell, she's the reason I'm writing to you now. She drives me mad and soothes me all in the same breath and I don't know how I ever lived without knowing her.

I like to believe you're out there, somewhere, looking down on me and I hope when you do, you'll read this over my shoulder. And you'll know how much I miss you...every day. How much I love you. How sorry I am.

I love you, Dad.
Jamie

Sixteen

Laney woke to a slamming door from downstairs. And Jamie's voice. She smoothed her hair from her face, looked at the empty sheets. Two days of writing wasted in Jameson Clark's bed, only taking breaks to eat, and sleep, and shower—oh god the shower. Laney lifted one pleased eyebrow. The man was a machine.

"A beautiful, distracting, machine," she mumbled into the pillow. Another voice joined Jamie's. A woman's, followed by his. Neither one of them sounded happy. Laney's smile fell and her heart jolted her the rest of the way awake.

"I don't know if that's what I want yet, Annie!" he yelled, quite clearly. Laney grabbed her dress, slid it on, and tried to contain her bed-messy hair. When she got halfway down the stairs, she stopped to listen.

"This could be your chance, Jameson! Your fans have waited too long for you to get off your ass! These songs are good enough to go back on tour with. They're...*different*. But you've taken so long they'll eat up any shit sandwich you serve."

"Did you just call my work a *shit sandwich*?"

"It's sappy."

"Well, it wasn't yours to listen to."

"Well, you left it in the studio."

"In *my studio*, in *my locked* house, Annie!"

"You haven't changed the codes, Jameson." She shrugged it off. "I had to come and see for myself after I called your mom and she told me that you were working on something. Well, she actually told me to stay away from you, because you were finally getting back to yourself and you didn't need me mucking it up. I don't think that old battle axe ever liked me."

"She didn't. And don't call her that."

Laney leaned against the wall and felt the rabid pace of her heart pounding.

"The world wants you back, Jameson," came the woman's passionate plea. "I want our old life back." Annie's high heels clicked across the floor. Laney heard the light swish of her dress against his jeans and her heart fell into her stomach. Annie Renee Clark. His once-manager and ex-wife. The brutal light of the dawn, and all it demanded, hit Laney like cold water to the face. Jamie in her bed was not the same man that the world knew and expected. Jamie on the beach laughing and crying. Jamie, hands bubble-deep in dirty dishes or in front of the Christmas fire. These were echoes of a man who had no place in his multi-million-dollar image. The one that had models for ex-wives and platinum contracts to sign.

"Annie...I—I don't know." His words, quieter now, as Annie came closer to him, dropped a familiar weight of rejection in Laney's stomach. He was getting a chance to start again, and with a woman who knew how to navigate his super stardom. A tall and leggy model. Laney's fingers clamped down on her skirt as she held her breath. She peered down the stairway at where Annie's hands had wound around Jamie's neck. His hands were loosely on her waist and Laney couldn't tell if he was holding her away or about to draw her closer. Her vulnerable history told her it was most likely the latter.

"Well, you call me when you see what's best." Annie kissed him and Laney looked away. Soon she heard Annie's heels click across the foyer and out the front door with a slam. Laney couldn't swallow the lump in her throat as she climbed back up the stairs. She should have expected this. She should have known that he would move on when his music came back to him. She just didn't know he'd move on while she was still up in his bed, after soul searching their own hearts for two days. If he was conflicted about what he wanted, then she would make it easier on him. She wouldn't be the person holding him back. She ran up to get her shoes and purse. As she came back down the stairs, Jamie stood still beside the door, conflict in his eyes, jaw twitching.

"Hey, professor." He climbed the last three steps to meet her, but she held on to the banister and leaned away. "What is it?" Laney looked at him. She couldn't be mad, she'd known who he really was all along. A superstar playboy, who'd gotten knocked off his horse. She'd given him a boost. And hadn't he done the same for her?

"Nothing."

He turned his head. "Laney, don't lie."

"I heard...I heard it all."

"Laney—"

"It's great. Jamie, it's really great. You'll—" She paused and tried to smile. "You're gonna be fine."

He frowned. "What do you mean I'll be fine?"

"With Annie, with your new start. You've gotten what you wanted."

"I don't want any part of Annie. She's a manipulative b—"

"I know." Laney nodded. "But you still kissed her."

"She kissed me!"

"But you let her." Laney's voice shook, and she stepped away, walling off her heart. "It's okay. I'm not some love-struck twenty-year-old, Jamie. I know how the world works. Remember, this isn't my first two-girl-at-a-time rodeo."

"Laney! That's not what this is!" Laney shook her head.

"I—" She paused as a tear escaped. "I never wanted your forever, I just wanted a little of your time."

He grabbed her by the shoulders.

"Please don't say things like that! I don't want just moments with you. I don't want her."

Laney pushed a small package between them and stopped his words. He looked down at it, wrapped in the crossword of a newspaper.

"I'm—I'm sorry about the wrapping. It was sort of last-minute."

"What's this?"

"Take it. I want you to have it. It means a lot to me, but it really belongs to you." Laney stepped past him and ran down the stairs and out of the house. The sobbing hurt stayed tucked inside until she reached the road and sprinted for home.

When she got back to the cottage, Laney took in a deep breath and dialed the number on the crumpled piece of airplane cocktail napkin. She didn't even know if her fellow passengers were still in town. But it was worth a try. If she knew anything about Jamie, it was that he may try to change her mind. But with her heart so raw, she couldn't take the risk of him succeeding. She needed to tear away the Band-Aid away quick and get off this island as soon as possible and it would give him a little taste of what getting back into the life would mean.

"Ello!" Darla's voice rang loud through the phone.

"Uh, Darla?"

"Yeah? Who is this?"

"Well, this is Laney Sullivan. The nerd from the plane?"

"Oh hello, Laney, darlin'! How's the study abroad program going?" Darla cackled and Laney was torn between annoyance and a strange heartwarming love of being teased.

"Well, Darla, it just so happens it's been a very interesting trip. Hey, listen, are you still on the island?"

"Sure are! We've been to all the clubs downtown and the major beaches and haven't had a lick of luck though." Laney smiled and looked out at the ocean one last time, already missing every single minute of the magic. But it was pumpkin time, and even Cinderella didn't get to keep the fantasy forever.

"Well, Darla, today is your lucky day..."

Jamie was too stunned to move as he watched her turn the corner and disappear into the mangroves. She was fast on her feet. If he had had half a mind he would have run after her. He stared back down at the package. What in the hell had just happened? An hour ago, he'd been awake, watching her sleep in his arms and thinking about the future with her. The next his world had toppled over, handed him a chance to start again, while tearing away the tender starts of his life with Laney. He sank down on the couch, dropped the package to the side, and held his head in his hands.

He'd climbed the stairs, stared at the love-tangled bed, and relived the last few days one agonizing moment at a time. She hadn't been lying about being at her peak. Lord, he thought, exhausted, he'd never met a woman who was so passionate, sweet, unreserved in bed...in the shower. God, the shower. What was he doing? The phone rang a minute later and Jamie rushed to it, hoping it was her, hoping she had changed her mind. Ready and willing to rush down the road to her.

"Jamie, baby, how you doin'?"

"Hey, Momma," his voice dropped.

"Now what's happened?"

"Nothing, just, in the middle of—"

"Oh! Is Laney there? Honey, I can let you go."

"No, Momma, she—she's not here." Jamie didn't have the heart to tell his mom that Laney had left.

"Oh well, good, listen I wanted to talk to you about Cass's graduation this spring if you have a moment." His mom hadn't called, just to talk, in ages. Laney had built that bridge, and Jamie's heart swelled. He was torn between going to talk some sense into her, and spending the long overdue time catching up with his mom. They talked for over half an hour, and Jamie agreed to fly in for the ceremony and after-party, asking his mom what she'd like for a gift.

"I think she just wants her big brother to be there," Desdemona said. Jamie sighed. Family wanting his love, not his fame or his money or his gifts. Just his company. His heart opened even further, and he nearly cried.

"Well, you tell her I wouldn't miss it for the world. She can count on me." Jamie hung up and flopped down on the couch. What was he gonna do? Laney didn't fly out until Saturday, and he didn't want to run over without a plan in his head.

So, what was his plan? Given that she'd seen Annie kissing him and his hands on her, there was a good chance she wouldn't want anything to do with him. Especially after what she'd already lived through with her ex-husband. Especially since she already thought he was moving on. But what she'd seen, and what she thought wasn't exactly the truth. He was moving on, but not towards Annie or his old life. The truth was that he loved her.

Jamie groaned and covered his eyes. He felt hopeless and hopeful all at once. He felt the instant regret of being too guarded in his feelings. Of not kicking Annie out the minute he'd found her in his studio, copying files and scrambling to gather his new material. If only he could convince Laney to give him another chance. But that wasn't going to happen by laying around on his couch, pouting. He rose up, slid into his flip-flops, and ran out the door headed straight to her cottage.

When he got there, the gate was locked, and she wasn't

answering his repeated buzzing. Jamie sighed, he was still spry enough, he just hoped he didn't get his britches caught this time. How unromantic would that be? He smiled as he scrambled up the stone pillars beside the iron fence and hopped over. Their relationship was full of the unromantic and embarrassing. He'd take hanging by his ripped pants if she'd just talk to him. He made it down and to her door, but it was locked and she didn't answer. He yelled at the door.

"Laney! Goddamn it, open the door! Come on, we need to talk about this! I need—" he paused at his own desperation. "I need you to listen."

"Mr. Clark?" came a voice from behind. The slender, black youth on his pedal cart had stopped at the fence. "You looking for Laney?" Jamie came down the stairs quickly.

"Yes! I am. Where is she?"

"I just took her to the airport. She's catching the last flight out for the day."

Jamie groaned and put his hands on his capped head in frustration.

"Son of a bitch," he breathed. "Has that plane left yet?"

"Not sure, sir. Maybe?"

"Hey, uh, could you give me a ride?"

"Sorry! Too busy today!" The young man sped away and Jamie scowled. It was almost as if fate was working against him. He climbed back over the fence, scraping both knees and cutting his hand in the process. She was right, he was gonna hurt himself someday. He picked up a steady jog, and nearly made it to the main street when two women came up the road and approached him in a way he was all too familiar with.

Damn it, not now, Jamie thought. *Not now, not while I have to get to Laney*. He avoided eye contact and beelined to the other side of the road. But they dodged, quicker than he expected. He was taken by surprise by their light and determined steps.

"Mr. Clark!? Jameson Clark! Wait! Can we get an autograph?

Please? We came all this way!" Jamie stopped and slowed his pace. Better to get them on their way than risk getting tackled.

"Why, sure, ladies. I'd love to," he grunted and tried to smile as he stopped and they handed them their pens and scraps of paper from their purses.

"I'm Darla and this is Charlene," one of the women said, and Jamie nodded. "And a picture?"

"Uh—sure, I just gotta make it fast. I need to get to the airport."

"With both of us?"

"I—okay, sure." He looked around them, through their broad-shouldered defense to the empty lane where she'd passed too long ago. He posed quickly for the insanely sharp flashes and blinked to clear his eyes. "Thanks, sweethearts, but I really gotta get going."

He gently patted Charlene on the shoulder and shook Darla's hand quickly.

"Oh! But wait, one more autograph for my momma?" Darla interjected and stepped in front of him as he moved to leave, nearly knocking him over.

"Honey, I'm sorry, I gotta get—"

"She's in the hospital with cancer and it would just mean the world, Mr. Clark," Darla held out the pen. Jamie stopped, closed his eyes with a sigh and nodded.

"Of course, what's her name?"

"It's Jean. Oh, she'll just be so pleased. Can you write her something nice?" Jamie looked down the road where not even a trace of Laney could be seen. His heart fell and his head felt clouded over with regret. He held the envelope with shaking hands and tried to conjure a message of hope, though he felt a dark night settle in his own soul. He flipped over the envelope to sign it and saw Laney's University of Wyoming office address typed across it. His brain slowly ground to life, and he looked up at Darla with a frown.

"Thank you, Mr. Clark!" She smiled and snatched the letter

away. They bustled off towards town, twittering with laughter and excitement, while Jamie stood in awe of the deterring tactics Laney had set up in her wake.

"Clever girl." He smiled and wanted without reserve to find her and drag her back into his bed forever. Into his life forever. "When I catch up to you, Laney June—my God, professor," he whispered and continued on towards the downtown.

The airport was only a few miles from his house and he made it in record time, although his toes were bloodied from the break-neck pace and his scrapes and cuts hurt. He ran up to the chain-link gates and arrived in time to see a small twin engine take flight at the end of the runway. No other flights for the day.

"No! Goddamn it, no!" Jamie sunk to the ground, his back pressed to the fence and head in his hands. He should have stopped her sooner. He should have made her stay. He should have told her that he loved her. That they could have it all as long as they had each other. He watched the sun glint off the retreating plane's rudder. Now he didn't know when or how he'd ever see Laney Sullivan again. Anger and confusion filled his chest. After all they shared, how could she have walked away so easily?

Laney had closed her window shade—otherwise she might have seen the dirty and bloodied man sagging hopelessly against the airport fence. She couldn't bear to watch the island grow smaller in the distance. She simultaneously wanted to forget and feared she would. Her heart was heavy, and she hated herself for getting so attached. She knew better. She had always known it couldn't lead anywhere.

"And that's why you only write them, not try to live them," she whispered to herself and dried her eyes self-consciously. He was probably lounging in the studio, refining the tracks and getting ready to launch the second coming of his career. She would start seeing his face again on the cover of magazines and billboards. His deep voice croon through the radio and streaming services. Singing that song, knowing he'd written it for her, and every time it would ruin her like the first. She took out her computer but couldn't find the stomach to write anything that could give her characters hope.

She tried to focus on anything positive. At least she would be home a few days earlier than the kids. She'd have downtime to get the last chapters to her editor and set her island clothes on fire on the front lawn. Nothing like a burning effigy to let go of a lover. She tried a smile, but it failed. With her heart hurting and the sting of fresh tears in her eyes, she sat back to the constant replay of Jameson Clark in her brain.

SEVENTEEN

"WHY ARE YOU HOME SO EARLY? ARE YOU OUT OF YOUR literary mind?" Marc said before she could even invite him in. He brushed past her and put the scones and coffee on her counter.

"Prolly," Laney said weakly. She traced her finger over the Coal Creek logo and screwed up her mouth to not cry. Marc leveled his eyes on her and watched every small detail of her body language.

"Uh oh, you're doing that weird, don't-cry mouth. Something happened." Marc gasped. "Shake my sugar tree, Laney got laid!" he sang. She threw back her head and groaned.

"It's so much worse than that."

"Honey, if getting laid is a 'worse' for you, you're not doing it right."

Laney sat down and picked at the edge of a scone. She couldn't bring herself to eat one. Her whole body hurt with missing him.

"No, it's so much more, Marc."

"Wait." He sat down next to her and looked into her puffy eyes. "You didn't just get laid; you actually *fell* for somebody down there. Oh, I knew you were a true, hopeless romantic! Tell me how are we going to win the young suitor back? Should we go with a *You've Got Mail* sort of scenario? Or does the quirky best friend step in a la—" When he saw her bottom lip tremble, he stopped.

"I'm not sure I can write a happy ending for this one, Marc."

"What happened?"

"Jameson Clark happened?"

Marc inhaled sharply. "Saints among us, are you serious?" She bit her lip and nodded, tears brimming fresh again. She wiped them away angrily.

"Oh! It's so stupid! How could I have been so stupid! What's wrong with me, Marc?" She closed her frumpy sweater tighter over her body. He sighed and took her in his arms.

"Not a thing, sweetheart. Not a damn thing. The fault is all on him." He held her there for a moment. "Come over to my house tonight, we'll watch movies in our jammies and eat brownies. Alan had to go away for a trip and I hate being alone when there's a Nora Ephron marathon on."

Laney thought of being alone in the house for another night. Just the sound of his voice echoing in her brain, telling her to come to bed. Telling her that he wanted her. There was no point stirring hope where there was none to be stirred.

"Sure," she sniffed. Marc squeezed her shoulders.

"It's going to be okay, Laney. The first time back on that horse is always hard. And you went and chose some wild stallion to start on." Laney thought of Jamie in her bed and blushed. It was a fitting picture. Marc fanned his face dramatically. "Oh my lord, it was good, wasn't it?"

"It was. It was so good. I wish it hadn't been so good. Not just the sex, the well, th—the everything."

"Do I need to go down to St. Croix and beat his ass?"

Laney sniffed and shook her head.

"No. It's not his fault. I'm the one who le—left." Her voice wavered. "I just knew it was ending," she started to sob, "and I didn't want to be the dead weight holding him back."

"If you weren't crying, I would slap you. Dead weight? Are

you insane?" Marc sighed and squeezed her shoulders. "Come on, grab a box of tissues. We'll stop by the liquor store and find the best cheap wine they have and make a good start of it." He gathered her purse and all the popcorn he could find in her cupboard and swept her out the door.

"She knew! She knew what she was gettin' into!"

"What?" Brody startled from the book he'd been reading with Jamie barged into his shop, not knowing that Jamie had been fuming for days. Wobbling between depression and anger, missing her and wondering if she wasn't right about him all along.

"Runnin' out like some character in one of her books, just running away! Then she set up these two ladies to run defense. Like a sneaky little quarterback so she could get away. God, she's so smart. Damn it, I miss her... but that's not the point!" Brody made no argument or assurance as Jamie talked himself into a frenzy while pacing the length of the shop. "She knew this was my life. I never promised her anything!"

"Uh, yeah, I don't think Laney ever thought she and you—"

"She's gotten up under my skin and made me—" Jamie paused the rant to hold in the thought that she'd made him whole again. He walked another length of Brody's shop, willing his heart to unclench. "She knew this was bound to happen. She knew who I was. She kn—"

"Goddamn it, Jameson, stop! Stop saying the same goddamn thing!" Brody yelled. Jamie stilled his pacing and his head swung around to look at Brody, who had jumped off the counter where he'd been sitting since Jameson had blown in like a hurricane off the coast, full of confused anger.

"What?" Jamie demanded.

"Yes, she knew! Laney isn't dumb, Jamie. She knew you'd blow up again. She knew you had it in you and she never pretended

different. She knew you were a man that women loved to be with."
Brody defended. "Look, I know you, man. I've known you for
years and its never your fault. Not. One. Single. Time." Brody
knocked his fist against a shelf. Nautical books tipped over and fell
against each other.

"What in the hell are you talking about?" Jamie rounded, blue
eyes flashing.

"Laney Sullivan knew you'd get back on your horse. Hell, she
put you back up there! She never wanted to ride it with you. She
didn't want to lead it or follow behind. She just wanted you to be
back where you belonged. And now you're mad because she let
you go to do your thing, and went back to her own life? Why *are*
you mad? She knew what you were, and she chose to love you and
let you go. So, what the fuck *are* you complaining about?" Brody
said, his jaw twitching below his beard. "Is it because she broke
your pattern? Because she didn't slap your face and burst into tears
and beg you to stay? Well, guess what, jackass? That's how mature,
worth-it women act," he finished.

Jamie was stunned silent. His breath caught, and he felt his
world spin. Brody's words of reason slowly sunk in. She'd loved
him and let him go. What was he doing? The same thing Jameson
Clark always did. Found a reason that love wouldn't work for him,
and better if it excused him from the responsibility.

"I can see you're starting to get it. But what makes me mad,
Jamie, is that it's too late. You let her walk out of your life then
blamed her for ending it. And most other girls, okay, but Laney?
Jesus, Jamie. Laney Sullivan was a once in a lifetime. She was *your*
once in a lifetime."

Jamie, facing the truth of his emotional failures, felt anger
bubble up in his chest.

"And why do you even care, Brody! Huh? What business is it
of yours?"

"Well, shit dude! You came in here bawlin' to me about how
unfair her leaving was. You want me to tell you that you're in the

right. You want me to reassure you that *she* messed up and you're not at fault, and that you two weren't meant to be. But I'm not going to. I'm tired of watching you make the same mistakes. Big superstar or not, you've failed at being a decent human of late. And I care about you man! I can't tell you how hard it is watching you shut people out. When Laney came around, I thought, man this may be the one. This is her. Then after you puffed up when I tried to kiss her, I knew for sure. She was the one that was gonna get to you."

"I don't know what you're talking—"

"And I was right." Brody stopped him. "She got you. And she stopped your world, and she reminded you of who you are, Jamie. Not who you're trying to be, but *who* you are."

Jamie froze in place. His anger fell away. His eyes stung. Jameson Clark, country superstar on the verge of a brilliant comeback, had just been told what his heart had already tried to tell him the night he'd held Laney Sullivan in his arms and confessed his misdirection in life, his road-weary ache, his need to belong and rest. His face fell, and he sniffed as his eyes filled and his nose ran, torn between what was expected of him and what he wanted. He didn't know how to exist fully in either of the worlds. Brody sighed, righted one of the fallen books and said, softer;

"Look, man, I'm sorry. I didn't mean to be a dick."

"I'll—I'll see you around," Jamie whispered and left. He climbed back into his battered truck and careened out of the secluded bay. Multiple messages waited for him at the house; requests for interviews from various news magazines, producers, collaborators; an explosion of interest for his supposed new album and this new mystery girl. Everyone wanted an exclusive.

How in the hell did they know about Laney? He sifted through the messages, looking for the start of the fire. The first one mentioned that Annie and a former girlfriend had shared some photos of him with Laney. Annie must have been keeping tabs on him for a while.

She'd had done a bang-up job spreading his personal life out for the world to see, he thought, and threw his phone across the living room onto the couch. On every news app and on every social media site, the whole world knew now that he had a single coming out, no doubt from the files Annie had stolen, and that he was in the process of finishing a new album. Maybe even thinking about a tour. All rumor. And all speculated that it was due to his secret new flame. They even had goddamn pictures of Laney and him on their kayaking trip!

He thought back, trying to understand how they'd gotten pictures. Only one other person besides Brody had known they were out there. Meghan. The cosmo-throwing girl from the bar. She must have tipped Annie off when she found out he'd taken another girl. Jamie paced the room and threw his hands around the bill of his cap. What in the hell would he do now?

Everything he'd hoped for since his downfall was coming back into his life. But the horror of exposing Laney to this circus, after she'd been the one to help him, tore at his insides. She wasn't even here anymore, to get mad at him, to talk through it with, to huddle down and think with. The only reason he had for moving on, had gone on herself. He tried calling her cell number from the university's website. But she hadn't answered. She might have her kids back by now, and was probably busy enough without having to worry about him too.

Jesus, she'd be worrying more now. He closed his eyes and pictured the horror on her face. He needed to find out how to warn her. Didn't he? She had to have known there was a risk of getting involved with him. Except—that had never been what they were about. She didn't care about his spotlight, or his ego, or his fans. She just liked him—maybe even loved him. Jamie closed his eyes. How could he have let her go? How could he become just one more burden in her life?

How many times was she balancing her checkbook and coming up short? How many times was she lying awake at night worrying about how she'd afford her kids' college tuition when the time came? Or worrying about her parents and all the wolves at their door? How often would she think about him, back to his old lifestyle? That he'd moved on the minute she'd walked out his door? He slumped down on the couch and something nudged him in the back.

"Ouch!" He sat up and tugged at the sharp-edged paper package, stuck between the cushions. The one she'd handed it to him before she left. He sighed, sat back, and stared at the half-finished crossword paper, her letters. Her voice was in his head. *You could use it, especially now.* She'd folded the paper around it, origami-style, as if those strong fingers were used to making something beautiful from the ordinary. He unwrapped it without tearing through her writing and folded back the delicate sheets of newsprint to find an antique brass compass. It was weighted like something made from a day when things lasted, and it fit into his palm. He looked back to the paper. The words she'd written in the boxes weren't answers for the puzzle.

My grandma gave this to me when I was 10, after I wrote my first story. Every time I read its inscription it seems to steady my feet. I hope it will steady yours too.

Jamie wedged his fingernail into the latch, and it snapped open. The needle still swung when he cupped it in his palm, eventually settling on north. On the inside of the lid Laney's grandmother had inscribed:

When you lose your direction, let love write your course.

His heart staggered. Tears burned in the corners of his eyes when he looked at it. He stood and turned his body to the direction of north. He turned his feet a quarter way between, to the northwest, and the compass paused there, before swinging slowly back.

"Love," he whispered and clutched it to his chest.

"Laney, it's really no big deal," her dad sighed. Laney pressed her phone tighter to her ear as she stood at the snowy intersection of Grand and Third street. Walking across town to her office was a new necessity without her car. It took up time she would have otherwise been pining. It made her colder. And windblown. But it also kept her awake after not sleeping well. Before the girls got back from France, she would have to find an affordable car.

"Mom said that they came to the house. Are you sure it's no big deal?"

"Honey, now, you don't worry about us. We'll be fine. How are the girls? How was their Christmas? How was your trip? Did you fish?" Laney's brow furrowed, she didn't want to talk about her trip, ever again.

"What did they say?"

Warren sighed on the other end and conceded. "Not much after Blake met them on the porch with a shotgun."

Laney found a small smile in the warmth of it. "Good for Blake," she said. "I guess he always did have some hero in him."

Warren cleared his throat and Laney could picture his expression from across the miles.

"Good kid, but I think we can thank Elle for that. I think he needed a woman putting a boot in his ass."

"Don't all you men?" Laney's smile fell off immediately. Jameson's mom had asked her to watch out for him. She had broken a promise to Desdemona.

"Are you okay?" Warren said at her silence.

"Uh, sure. I—" She tried to swallow the thickness in her throat.

"Laney? What is it? Did something happen on the trip?"

"No, it's nothing. It was a good trip; I got a lot done. I didn't catch anything, fish or an STD, if Mom asks."

"Oh, Laney!" her dad laughed.

"I'll be heading up in a couple of weeks and we'll figure something out. I've got a little savings built up, and this next book should bring in a little more."

"Laney, please don't worry."

"Dad, I can't help it." Laney sighed. She navigated across the crowded crosswalk, between the two-lane traffic jam of students coming back to town. "I will find a way to help you. You're my parents. My family. And we'll figure this out."

"Mom said you were getting a lot of writing done. Did you get to finish your book?" he asked, dodging her worry like a pro.

Laney nearly got hit by a large truck rushing to turn into the intersection in front of her. She almost wished it had. Reality nudged her to keep walking.

"Uh, almost. Couple more chapters." She didn't want to talk about the book. She didn't want to talk about the hot and heavy scenes that Jamie had inspired, or the feeling of her heart coming back to life only to be slaughtered again. She couldn't admit to her dad, or anyone else, that her own sadness was keeping her from giving her characters any semblance of hope. She couldn't admit that the new threats to her parents' land and her childhood home and the emptiness she'd carried since leaving the island were weighing like stones on her shoulders.

"Well, I know you'll finish it and it will be wonderful. You've got a big brain, Laney June."

"I can thank you for that problem."

"That's all your mom," he chuckled. Laney melted. To have a love like theirs; her eyes filled with tears.

"Well, I uh...I oughta go," she sniffed.

"Okay, honey. We look forward to seeing you and the girls."

"I can't wait. It will be nice to be home." Her heart hurt with the words. They said their 'I love yous' and hung up. Laney made it to her empty office. Alan had returned from his trip, and he and Marc were now celebrating their survival of the holidays down in Steamboat Springs for the weekend. She stared at the empty walls. Soon, the swing of work would sweep her up again. Same old, drab life, minus a shitty car and plus a few more bills. The brilliance and beauty of her life on the island seemed like a far-away fairytale she'd only read about once.

"What happens when Cinderella comes back from the ball but nothing changes?" she asked the empty room. "Wouldn't she have been better off never knowing magic existed at all, than to spend her whole life missing it?"

Laney collapsed into her chair. She wouldn't have the luxury of self-pity when life started back up, so she took the moment to just cry, letting out all of the stress and hurt. Her old office phone rang its deep and melodic tone, like something from fifty years ago. No one but the landlord, her agent, and a few faculty members including the department head had that number. She wiped her nose on her sleeve and expected an eviction notice to be waiting on the other end. It would round out the whole holiday.

"Hello?" she sniffed.

"Laney?"

She sobbed in surprise at the soft Tennessean drawl.

"Oh, baby," Jamie began, "You aren't cryin', are you? Goddamn it, Laney, don't cry. I can't 146 you from this far away."

"You don't—" she hiccupped. "You don't get to be sweet to

me and you sure as hell don't get to tell me what to do, Jameson Clark," she said firmly.

"Wait, are you mad or sad?" he chuckled.

"I'm both, or maybe...maybe, I'm neither. Maybe, I'm just—I'm fine. I've got a lot on my mind." She wanted to hang up, but her hand disobeyed her mind; tied too closely to her heart and how good it felt to hear his voice.

"Me too, baby," he whispered. "Listen, I've been trying to call—"

"I know," she said.

"Yeah, we can talk about why you haven't answered later. I got this number from information and thought I'd try it. Who has a landline anymore? Prolly, just my delicious, buttoned-up schoolmarm."

"I'm hanging up now."

"No! Wait, please? Listen, I need to tell you before you find out otherwise, Annie talked to—"

"Please, Jamie. I can't listen to this. I mean, I'm happy for—" she hiccupped again. "You know what, I'm not actually happy for you and Annie, but I guess you're getting a new start."

"Laney, there is no me and Annie."

"Your lips said otherwise."

"Is that what you think was happening?"

"It isn't what I think. It's what I know. I know you're getting a chance to start your career again, and with that comes...being with Annie."

"Laney," his voice broke, "please, listen to me about Annie—"

"No," she said more firmly. "I can't." She got up and paced. "The girls come home tonight and my parents are still in trouble and, I just can't pay attention to my broken heart right now. I have people I need to take care of."

"Goddamn it, Laney. What kind of a bullshit thing is that to say?"

"It's called being an adult, Jamie."

"It's not adulting to not even let me explain, And your b—broken heart? Jesus, you know how to cut a guy." His voice caught in a sob.

"Jamie," she steadied her voice. "The state of my heart, isn't your fault. Please, don't call me. It isn't fair. To either of us." She hung up, gathered her notes and spring syllabus plan, and shoved them into her bag. She left, with the sound of the phone trying to call her back into his arms.

Jamie tried calling for the next half hour but got no response. "Damn it, Laney! What in the hell?" He threw his phone across the room and paced. Why was she making it so damn difficult? Why wouldn't she just let him explain? He paused to look at the grey clouds hugging the horizon. It had been dark and rainy since she'd left, like an unseen author was writing the mood of his life over the sky. He thought morosely that she could very well be that author. Her mood, her story, her broken heart.

"God," he whispered and played back her words. Her broken heart. He couldn't bear that Laney's heart was out in the world, broken, because it felt it didn't have a right to love him.

And he didn't even get a chance to tell her about Annie. About the publicity stunt she'd set up after being tipped off by one of his jilted lovers. About the news that was already starting to circulate on the internet. Jesus, she was gonna be pissed. He wasn't going to lie or dispute it. He loved her, and what they'd had was amazing. He didn't like the gut-wrenching feeling that what they'd had together shouldn't have been something that belonged to the public. And yet, that's exactly who was about to own it. Jamie couldn't think straight, Laney's teary voice still in his head, the explosion that was about to hit her life, the hardship she was already under without his 'help'.

He grabbed his jacket and headed out the door. Without

thinking, he drove to the end of the island and found Carlos in his office. The old man was on the verge of retirement. He'd told Jamie he was looking for someone to buy the horses so he could move on to an easier life. Everything kept changing. Jamie sighed and hung his head.

"I'm happy you're gonna take it easy, but I'll sure miss ya," he said softly with a nod. "Can I take Ernest out this afternoon?"

"It's raining," said Carlos with a scowl. "Why you wanna go out in the rain?"

"Please, Carlos. I just need it." Jamie's voice shook. Hearing her voice after days of his heart going back and forth had opened the wound she'd left. And healed it. It tore him apart and gave him hope. He didn't know how he'd fix this mess.

It's called being an adult, Jamie.

He saddled Ernest, while Maria nickered at him from the safety of her dry stall.

"I know darlin'," he whispered. "I wish she were here too." As he rode off down the muddy path between the mangroves, he remembered Laney riding behind him. He remembered her in his bed, soft and patient, cradling him and all of his regret. Her strong heart taking in all of his pain, and her hands pulling him on stage. She knew him. What he loved most. She spoke words of forgiveness and acceptance in the face of his father's death. From the perspective of a parent, a daughter, someone who wouldn't bullshit him. She brought him back to the love of music. She brought him back to love. Not love of the spotlight he stood in, but for the quiet boy from East Tennessee who laughed, and wrote, and sang. He pulled Ernest to a halt and took off his cap. The rain poured over him.

He'd give it all up. He'd give it all up today. Without regret or remorse. He'd happily spend his life on her front porch, watching their children growing on a peaceful spread of land, away from the rush of expectation. Her arms, her world, a safe haven to his world-weary heart. That was his shore. She was his home. His direction.

He looked up and saw a break in the clouds above him, and the bright blue sky shining through. He turned Ernest so quickly that the gelding reared off the ground before setting off towards the stables.

When Jamie finally got back to his house, muddy and wet, he slipped on the marble floor on his way to his phone. He dialed the number he knew by heart.

"Leonard man, listen—"

"Jamie? You okay, man?"

"I owe you, if you can do this for me."

"Name it, man."

"I need to know all you can find out about Sweet Valley, Wyoming, particularly the ranches around the area. Who owns the most land there? Who's buying, who's selling, and if there have been any auctions announced or ranches in trouble in the area."

"Looking to buy up a little vacation spot?" his friend teased.

"Looking for redemption," he said.

Eighteen

Laney was slogging through the laundry at half-speed when her girls came barreling into the room. Charlotte chased Sylvia at a hard sprint, the hatred of a wrongdoing burning in her eyes.

"Give it back! Give it back, you dummy!" she screamed at the top of her lungs. Laney's ears rang from the pitch. The new tension of her post-Jamie world needed no extra provocation to snap.

"Hey!" Laney yelled sharply which stopped them for one instant before they lunged at one another, toppling into the bed and knocking over the piles of laundry. They rolled and wrestled over the stuffed animal until every piece of clothing was haphazardly thrown to the ground.

"Stop it!" Laney shouted, putting her hands on their arms and pulling them apart. "Look at this! All of the work I'm doing and now I have to start over!" They looked up at her with wide eyes, surprised at the tone and firm grip. "I have to start all—over." Laney's voice broke, and she saw the fear that she couldn't take back in her children's eyes. She started to sob. "I'm sorry," she cried and pulled them into her arms as she fell into bed. She thought she'd been holding it together. But a day before school started, a storm that had kept them indoors for too long had worn down her nerves to raw. "Just, please stop fighting," she sniffled. The kids started crying too.

"Don't cry, Momma, we'll be good," Charlotte said and snuggled into her mom's arms. Laney held her warm little body tight and rocked her. With the other arm, she pulled Sylvia in close and smothered her forehead with kisses.

"I'm sorry," she whispered. "I'm so sorry. I shouldn't have yelled. I'm just—tired." She hiccupped. The truth was in there. She was tired. She was tired of missing him. Tired of pretending that she didn't want to answer when he called. She was tired of telling herself that it wasn't meant to be. When she closed her eyes, she saw his, crinkled at the corners as he smiled. She felt the beat of his heart beneath her cheek, smelled his skin, felt the touch of his hands over her body. She saw him walking away along the beach without so much as a shrug, onto his next adventure. It hurt every single time, but she couldn't seem to stop doing it. She dried her eyes with the back of her sweatshirt sleeve and cleared her throat. Charlotte put her hands on either side of Laney's face and stared into her eyes.

"Let's order pizza," she said with the solemnity of the pope giving mass. Laney smiled.

"Capital idea."

"And a movie?" Sylvia asked with an air of cautious excitement.

"Even better," Laney said. Sylvia and Charlotte helped her pick up the laundry and folded it in the disordered and charming way of children. Laney watched them, and a smile spread over the painful hurt that had been brewing inside. Could he have been a man good enough for her children? Her heart warmed. She believed he could be. In a different lifetime.

"Are you *lovelorn*, Momma?" asked Sylvia.

Laney sniffed and looked at her oldest. "What? Where did you hear that word?"

"I read it," Sylvia said in her trademark, eight-year-old, matter-of-fact tone, and started piling up the socks.

"That's a pretty fancy word. Where did you read it?"

"It was on BuzzFeed."

Laney continued to fold and turned her attention away from memories of the island and back to her daughter.

"Wait, you read BuzzFeed? On my phone?"

Sylvia sorted the laundry into separate piles for her sister and herself.

"Yeah, this one was about the island where you stayed, so I wanted to read and see if you were in it." Laney's heart skipped, and she stopped folding.

"Which article?"

"Uncle Marc sent it to your phone while you were in the shower. Oh!" She stopped and looked wide-eyed. "I'm sorry, I shouldn't have checked BuzzFeed, but it lit up while I was playing Pocket God. Oh, and Marc also texted that he wants you to call him as soon as possible." Laney was speechless, her hands frozen on the pair of long underwear in her hands. Sylvia continued on, nonplussed.

"Yeah, so anyway, there was this article about a singer. Uncle Marc said you made friends with him down there. And I read that he is supposed to be making a new album called *Lovelorn*. I thought it was a pretty word. What does it mean?"

Laney swallowed the lump in her throat and dropped the clothes before turning to run downstairs. She sped back up with her phone in hand. She slouched against the bed when she saw the small photo of Jameson Clark. It was from an older photo shoot. She swiped quickly to the page where the article began, and to her horror, saw an aerial photograph of two people in what appeared to be a heated embrace on the coast. Moments before a jellyfish intervened. Thank god they'd made it to the cover of the mangroves before she'd dropped her shorts to pee on him. She didn't think she'd ever be able to explain that to her kids.

"Holy shit."

"Mom!" Charlotte reprimanded.

"Sorry!" Laney reached to her bedside table in search of her glasses. Her fingers patting the empty surface while her eyes looked over the aerial photo. "I can't believe they—when did they take this?" She looked up to see where in the hell her glasses were. Charlotte watched her squint at the words.

"Maybe you left them downstairs, Momma."

"I'll get them!" said Sylvia, speeding down the hall. Laney stood up and folded herself against the pillows in her bed. Charlotte came to snuggle into her arms and picked up her phone, clicking on the link.

"Has hot to trot ba-ck-elor, Jame-son Clark, finally met his forever match?" she read.

"Bachelor," Laney corrected softly as Charlotte continued.

"After two failed marriages, count-ess affairs, and a breakdown from ex-haus-ton—"

"Exhaustion." Laney's lip quivered.

"Exhaustion, have all hampered this aging star's image. Clark was recently seen on his private estate in St. Crocks—"

"Croix," she whispered.

"Croix. With a beautiful and mysterious woman. Sources tell X-Magazine that she may be the inspiration for the new album, due out in the spring of this year."

Laney studied the picture. It did look like he was embracing her; not saving her. It did look like they were in love. Her heart fell.

"Sorry, Momma, I can't find them anywhere," Sylvia came back in, perturbed.

"That's okay. I probably left them at the office." Laney squinted to reread the words again. Sylvia looked over her shoulder and gasped.

"Momma, is that you?" She grabbed the phone and zoomed in on the picture to look closer.

"I'm afraid so."

"But you're in a swimsuit! You never wear a swimsuit! It's so cute on you!"

"Uh huh. Yeah, we were kayaking and I f-fell," she whispered.

"But he caught you! He looks like he's going to snog you!" Sylvia giggled. Laney looked at her daughter in surprise.

"Snog me?"

"You know, kiss!"

"Yeah, I know what it means."

"So, did he?" Sylvia curled up at her feet and looked at her with bright eyes. Lord, but time was going too fast.

"Don't boys still have cooties?" Laney said and pushed a curl away from Sylvia's face.

"That boy looks pretty handsome, Momma. I'd kiss him."

"He is." She swallowed. "And I did. He was—he was amazing." The girls watched as the newly familiar sadness took over their mom's features, and they snuggled closer.

"Doesn't he want to snog you anymore, Momma?" Charlotte asked, looking up at her.

"I—I don't know. It's complicated."

"Why?"

"He has a very busy life; and I've got a job and two amazing girls to look after." She pulled them both closer.

"But Mom! He's so cute! And you should get en-gag-ed too, just like Dad and Tasha," Charlotte burst out.

"Charly!" yelled Sylvia and knocked her on the shoulder.

"Ouch!"

"What?" Laney looked between them. "Your, uh, your dad is en-gag-ed?" Laney's throat closed.

Sylvia hung her head. "Dad was supposed to tell you the next time he picked us up. He didn't want to ruin your holiday by saying anything." Laney's whole body felt tight and she clenched her jaw.

"Why would it ruin my holiday to know they got engaged?"

"Dad says you're lonely, and he doesn't want you to be jealous of his happiness," Sylvia said morosely. Laney scowled.

"Oh, baby. I'm not jealous. And I'm not lonely. I have you guys. And I had a good snogging on the beach. Let's go order that pizza." She boosted them off the bed and followed their wild careening paths down the hall. She scowled. She wasn't jealous, but she was mad. Mad that someone had gotten photos of her and Jamie and took away the tender privacy they'd shared. If she was a betting woman, she would have bet it was Annie or some jilted former girlfriend. She could have cared less about David and Tasha. She dialed Marc while the girls argued toppings.

"What the shit, Marc?" she whispered to him.

"Sorry I couldn't tell you in person. I didn't want to FaceTime you in the shower with the news."

"Do they know my name? I didn't see my name," she whispered.

"I haven't heard it in any of the news online. Even if they do, is that such a bad thing?"

"Marc! I could lose my job with the university!"

"Why? Because you have a healthy adult life? It's not like UW is BYU. There isn't really a moral code here in Wyoming." He paused to gasp. "Think of the publicity for your books!"

"I think it would take more than that to get people to buy *my* books." She turned away from the girls. "What am I going to do?" She rounded the corner and tried to keep her voice low. She picked at a piece of peeling paint from around the window frame and thought back to the phone call. His voice was trapped in her brain, and she didn't have the heart to try to forget.

"Well, I don't know yet, but I do know that a man doesn't name his whole comeback album for a fling, Laney. He names it for a woman who changed him, who moved him to write again. That's fire, girl. That's love," Marc said.

Laney was silent. Her heart thudded in her chest.

"Mom! Charly wants olives, I hate olives."

"Half and half it," she said weakly. "I've got to go, Marc. Thanks."

"Don't pretend like you didn't hear what I just said. I don't think Jameson Clark only wanted a fling with you. I think he fell in love with you."

"Well, if he did, he never said as much."

"And did you tell him how you felt about him?"

"Oh look, the cat's on fire. I gotta go."

"You don't have a cat, Laney!" Marc half laughed and half yelled. "You need to have a serious talking to yourself, young lady, about being honest with your emotions."

"To what end?"

"To the end that you deserve to love and be loved," Marc said quieter.

"I'm not sure I'm in the right place for that, Marc," she said softly and hung up.

The phone played its death-march tone, and Laney pawed at the nightstand. She brought it to her ear but didn't have time to say anything.

"Laney! What the holy fuck?" came Rebecca's voice. Laney looked, through blurry eyes, at the clock: six in the morning.

"Wha? Who's this?" she said and searched for her glasses.

"Your agent? I'm in my office and I just got your last chapter." Laney gave up when she remembered they weren't anywhere to be found, and she couldn't afford new ones. She buried her face in the pillow and covered her head with the blankets.

"Yeah?" she groaned. Rebecca cleared her throat and read the final chapter out loud.

"*'And then, they all died.'*" No response came from under the blanket. "That is not an ending," Rebecca prompted.

"Sure it is. They all died."

"Goddamn it, Laney, it is *not* an ending. Hell, it's not even technically a proper sentence, let alone a whole chapter." Rebecca's voice lowered over the phone. "Seriously, sweetheart, people have been waiting for this book. You have to pull your shit together and give them something amazing."

"Oh, I'm sorry, I'm fresh out of amazing," she muttered from under her covers.

"Bullshit. Start a pot of coffee, down a fifth of gin, go for a run...whatever it is you nutty writers do to get your brains unclogged, but do it fast. I need that chapter by the end of last week. Go find your amazing. I can't possibly feed this shit to the publisher."

"For an agent and editor, you are not very good at self-editing," Laney mumbled.

"Now, Laney!" Rebecca hung up. Laney punched the button and threw her phone to the floor. Monday. School starting. A whole day of have-to's and need-to's just waiting outside of her door. She half expected a save the date card from David for the ostentatious wedding of the year in her mailbox. She was sure it would involve seventeen envelopes, a tissue, a live butterfly, and a tiny cannon filled with glitter to shoot you in the face after seeing glamor shots of Tasha and David smiling from ear to ear with brightly bleached teeth.

Fuck Monday. She pulled the blanket tighter over her face. When she did rise, she roused the kids, fed them, and got their bags ready. She brushed their hair as if she were on autopilot and chucked some sandwiches in bags with an apple each. Never mind that the smell of peanut butter and jelly reminded her of that afternoon in the kitchen with him. Which had led to the amazing night with him. That had ended with the agonizing parting. She clenched her jaw, downed the cold dregs of her coffee and herded the girls to the old Corolla her neighbor had loaned her, until she could afford something else.

On the way to school, she thought of the last chapter she had to write. Rebecca wanted amazing. Laney didn't have any amazing left, least of all to give two star-crossed lovers a chance. The world didn't give real lovers that chance. The world pulled the rug out from under them, just when they were getting on their feet.

What did she really know about happy endings, anyway?

Traffic was bad around the university. It was always bad on the first day back, and with the fresh round of black ice on the roads it was worse. She dropped her girls off at University Prep, a luxury she could afford only because she was a part-time faculty member, and David had offered to make up the difference for the prestige of having his daughters attend a better school.

A new semester for her own classes started today, with new students to ignore her requests, fall asleep in class, and massacre the written word. She was all hope and sunshine on this gray and cloudy day. The radio played a familiar tune as she stopped at the red light two blocks from her office. The well-known strains took her back to that night on stage with the karaoke machine. Only when the voice came in, it wasn't Garth Brooks. It was Jameson Clark. She sat, unable to move a muscle as she heard his voice smoothly nailing every line. Her heart sank and flew. She wanted to laugh, and throw up, and cry all at once.

The car behind her honked.

"All right, all right! Jesus!" She made her turn and continued east to the campus. "The rock keeps rolling, Laney. Just because you're broken up inside, doesn't mean the rest of the world is. And that includes Jameson Clark." She turned the corner and thought about the title of the new album. *Lovelorn*. Had he just used her to get back into the spotlight? Her fingers clenched on the wheel and she wondered if she was any better. The bridge started clear and loud.

Hello, Laney, dear, I hope you're doin' fine...

Her name breezed over the radio and froze her blood. She pulled into the parking lot and stopped the car just before hitting the concrete curb.

"What the hell, Jamie!"

It wasn't going to take long for the rest of the world to put all of the pieces together. She knocked her forehead against the steering wheel. Her mother. Her father. Her students and fellow professors. Even her ex-husband. Everyone was going to know. That down-to-earth, practical-to-a-fault, "Plain Lane" Sullivan had had a passionate affair on an island with the most notable bachelor in country music.

"Ugh," she grumbled. But before she could shut off the engine, the DJ's voice came out fast and excited.

"One of the new singles released from Jameson Clark's creative team. A cover of the popular Garth Brook's song, *Callin' Baton Rouge*. Later we'll be playing *Someone*, a heartfelt ballad that turns Jameson's playboy image on its side. Clark has put out an unprecedented three original songs this week alone, in preparation for the *Lovelorn* album. With me is Annie Renee, wife and manager for the Clark brand."

"Oh, that bitch," Laney breathed and thought back to seeing her in Jamie's arms.

"Well, *ex*-wife," Annie cooed smoothly over the radio. The station was a larger syndicate out of LA, otherwise Laney would have driven to the station herself and decked Annie Renee without hesitation. "I was just in the area and thought y'all would like to hear some of his new work."

"That's certainly convenient, Annie." Laney said.

"Is there a reason Jameson isn't answering these questions himself?" Annie cleared her throat and Laney heard her hesitation.

"Yeah, Annie, how about that?" Laney asked.

"Jameson has a lot on his plate," she offered. Laney stared at the display as if she might be able to see the conniving woman squirm. Did Jamie even know she was spreading his name around? Was this what he had been trying to tell her on the phone?

"What a bottom feeder." Laney wanted a little too much to believe that it wasn't Jameson driving this circus.

"Tell us, Ms. Renee, especially for all of those female fans out there. Who is this Laney?" the DJ's voice needled. Annie sighed, as if that wasn't what she wanted to talk about.

"Yeah, you heartless gold digger, who the hell am I?" Laney sassed to her radio.

"She's, well she's—" Annie paused with an audible squirm in her seat. "She's just some writer he met on St Croix, but it's not really what's important. The thing fans should take away from Jameson's new music is that he's back, baby!"

"Well, I know, as a fan myself, we're all excited by that. The intrigue behind his beachside babe isn't just some ploy to sell us on the record is it?" the DJ joked and Laney lifted an eyebrow.

"Look at you, doing journalism," she said.

"Of course not! I'm not privy to his personal life."

"Like breaking into his house and listening to demos that you had no right to? Throwing your nasty lips all over him?" Laney pointed at the display. The DJ chuckled and began playing one of Jamie's older beach ballads.

"Fair enough! I think it's safe to say, Jameson Clark has turned a corner and will soon be giving us all the new and luscious tracks inspired by his new love."

"Well, I certainly hope they'll go out and download the album when it's complete, and figure out the mystery themselves," Annie's smooth voice chuckled. Laney screamed and shook her fists at the display.

"You're using him!" She turned off the car and grabbed her bag. "Hope you sell lots of records, you harpy," she muttered under her breath and crossed the street to her first class. Laney's brain was torn in two. She tried to focus on the have-to's. Even if she dreaded them, they were also the anchor that kept her brain from imploding. She got her mail from the English office, made it to class on time, and even remembered where to begin freshman English 101.

Halfway through her day, Marc called. "What have you eaten today?"

She looked down at her empty mug. "Coffee and fingernails?"

"Ugh, Laney!"

"I'll get something at the Union," she lied and looked around the English lounge. The tenured professors watched her over their noses. She scowled. She may not have written the great American novel, but she was published. She turned away, not wanting to get into the staring contest. She was only there for a warm-up, anyway.

"Are you coming into the office this week?" Marc asked. Laney swallowed the last of the bitter sludge and coughed.

"Why, there aren't reporters there are there?" She wiped her chin with her sleeve.

"Reporters?"

"Holy Christ, he used my name in one of his songs, and it was all over the radio this morning. It won't take long before someone figures it out. Hell, I think I might have accidentally ratted myself out to two of his biggest fans." She buried her head in her hands as she remembered enlisting Darla and Charlene's help in stalling him.

"Really?"

"Can you not sound so excited?"

"Well, now you're famous!"

"Ugh." She rolled her eyes and tried to lower her voice as two colleagues looked up from their much more important research papers.

"So, knowing that they haven't discovered your dumpy little office yet, are you coming by?"

"Yeah, maybe. I need to rework my last chapter under the wrath of Rebecca. If I have time after I pick up the girls, I'll bring them with me, to do a little writing. Maybe I'll just set my laptop on fire and chuck it all to become a hermit somewhere in Siberia. I'm sure Tasha will be a really excellent mother, and I've always been curious about yak milk. Best of all, they don't have internet or even papers in Siberia."

"God, you're in a mood. Getting some is supposed to make you more relaxed," Marc chuckled.

"Yeah, well, I'm not getting any now."

"Come by. I want to see you and the girls."

"Fine." She hung up and rinsed out her cup. It was always more peaceful writing at the office, anyway. Home was a place where something always needed to be done. Dishes, floors, laundry. The only thing at the office was her writing and grading and the occasional help with schoolwork when Charlotte and Sylvia were with her. If she were going to be able to help her parents fend off the wolves, she'd need the extra money from her book.

If it did sell well, she might even get enough for a ticket to Siberia.

NINETEEN

LANEY LOOKED OUT INTO THE CROWDED LECTURE HALL. Despite living on caffeine and impending doom, she'd survived into the second week of the new semester. Students studied their phones or lazily swiped through TikTok, feet on backs of chairs, unapologetically snapping their gum, and sighing loudly as she unpacked her bag. She couldn't care less how boring English Lit 101 was to them. A month ago, she would have had more patience, but today she was fresh out. She slammed her text of Shakespeare's greatest works down loudly, causing them all to jump.

"Good morning!" she shouted with her teeth clenched. Some students scowled, some looked at her confused through their hungover haze. "Please put your tech away so we can get started."

"Ugh, but whyyyy?" a sorority freshman whined. Someone else groaned, and eyes rolled across the room.

"Look, I get that you're far too important to deal with this old-school bullshit, but I also know that if you don't pass this class then you won't get your degree. Nobody, including myself, wants to be here, up at 8am dealing with the person in front of them, so buck up." The class snapped to attention. A few even smiled. The sorority-pin-wearing blonde rolled her eyes and made a disgusted sound.

"Why are you even still teaching?" she asked.

"Excuse you?" Laney spun on her, pen in hand and scowling.

"Aren't you, like, supposed to be marrying Jameson Clark or something? Why in the hell do you come back here every week? I mean, ugh, seriously," she ended with her appalled valley-girl twang. Laney's brow creased deeper.

"It might surprise you to know this, Miss Carlton, but not every woman, especially those worth the brain they were given, is waiting for some guy to swoop them up and save them. Some of us are perfectly happy on our own. Some of us save ourselves. And on a more personal note, it's none of your goddamn business who I'm dating. If you spent half as much time on *Othello* as with your nose in my affairs you might have pulled more than an F on your first round of English 101 that landed you back in my class. Now shut it and turn to page fifty." Laney's dark and steady voice filled the room and made the rest of the class close their mouths, heads down, diligently studying page fifty. While they took turns reading and stopping to discuss Iago's main objective, Laney's brain ran through traitorous thoughts of Jamie and why she had refused to listen. He seemed to have really tried to warn her and Annie's interview didn't make it sound like they were together.

We don't belong. We never belonged. We aren't meant to be. I was a stepping stone. He was a great adventure. A once-in-a-lifetime. Those don't last. Stepping stones and once-in-a-lifetimes are for romance novels, not real lives.

She redirected the conversation, led them to more in-depth conclusions, deeper meanings about his character flaws, what it said of his own demons, of society, of his views on women. All the while, her mind felt like a multitasking computer. One side exploring the eloquence of a well-developed character, and the other contemplating why Jamie had ever taken her to the magical bay, and why he'd trusted her enough with the pain of his past.

"Stepping stone," she said suddenly in response to her brain's ceaseless rambling.

"Uh, what?" one of the boys said, searching the page as if he'd missed a paramount phrase. Laney closed her eyes, blinked back tears, and shook her head.

"This is a good stepping stone to the next discussion. You guys actually kind of rocked it today. Thanks for restoring my faith." A few shy smiles broke out. "Don't fuck it up by resting on your laurels. You have three chapters to read for Wednesday, and write me at least two pages of your own thoughts about today, and why it's important to build sympathy for the antagonist." The last bit elicited a disappointed groan. "Save your protests for someone who cares," she grumbled, but a small, endearing smile met them as they gathered their books to leave.

The last class, Beginning Creative Writing, had her slogging through on autopilot, giving more prompts and free write time than was really necessary, and she sighed in relief when the bell sounded. She looked forward to seeing her girls, to asking how their days were, to holding them close and remembering that there was still brightness in the world. She was gathering up her notes when the inexplicable sight of her ex-husband standing in the doorway of her classroom stopped her movements.

"David?" she said, and looked around, just in case she'd accidentally fallen into some even more torturous parallel universe. He smiled with his hard-lined lips and ran his hands through his blond hair, thick thanks to follicle surgery. She suddenly thought of Jamie's hair, brown and thinning at the top. A man with means who still didn't try to fight what he was. "What are you doing here? I already saved the date. There's no need to follow up. Especially not in person." She put her notebooks into her satchel.

"Laney," he said and stepped in front of her. "Listen I—well, I've been thinking a lot about us lately." He stared down at the floor when Laney narrowed her gaze.

"There is no 'us'. Unless you mean us as co-parents. Is this about the girls?"

"No." He looked anxious. "I just saw you in that magazine with him." His tone turned husky. "His arms all over you and you in that swimsuit and it just—" He paused and shifted closer with a smile as if he finally got the punch line to a joke they'd shared long ago. "It made me jealous." His voice was a thin whisper now. Laney leaned away.

"What is this?"

"It made me think, Laney. It made me think about you and us, and how before I settle down with Tasha, I should be sure. Really sure, that I didn't make a mistake."

"Be sure *you* didn't make a *mistake*?" she snarled. "Let me ease your mind, David. Because *I'm* sure enough for the both of us. We are *not* getting back together. Ever. Period!"

"Laney," he pleaded. "At least think about—"

"No! You don't get to do this! You don't get to be jealous of who I'm with because you made the choice *to not want me* anymore. You don't get to ask for another chance." She put her finger to his chest. "And what a horrible way to start out a marriage. Seeing if your ex-wife still wants to have a run at it? You're an awful excuse for a human being."

"I'm awful?" David turned defensive and pushed her hand away. "You just spent four weeks sleeping with some shit-kicking playboy, who never had any intention of actually staying with you." The fire in his eyes shot through her and for a moment Laney felt her heart tumble and break. Jamie had asked her to stay. David was wrong. She pulled herself up and met his glare with a withering one of her own.

"*He* never lied to me. Which is a hell of a lot more than you were capable of."

"But, Laney—"

"Go home, David. And if you ever yell at me like that again, I'll call the judge and have your hours with the girls taken away." She shrugged on her coat with a huff and left him in the empty, echoing classroom.

"Don't be ridiculous!" Annie screamed into the phone from her LA office.

"I own what I write, and you stole it. You stole all of the songs I'd recorded and you put them on the air without my consent. The copyright infringement alone is gonna end your career, Annie," Jamie said and held the compass while he walked around his bedroom. There was an odd breeze off the ocean today, and he could see storm clouds gathering in the distance. That Annie had told the radio station the album's name was *Lovelorn* after one of the song titles he'd written in bed next to Laney seemed even more invasive.

"I was doing you a favor!"

"You were doing yourself a favor! You thought that if you put my songs on the air and people started asking for them, you'd get your old job back."

"Well—" she sputtered, "so what if I did? Didn't you kiss me? Don't we have something? Why can't we start again, Jameson?"

"Let me be perfectly clear, Annie, you will never manage my career again. I didn't kiss you, you kissed me and I never even consented to it. You and I are over. Done."

"What about your fans?" Annie's tone turned dark and desperate. "You owe it to them, and they own you just as much as you own what you write. So, what about letting them down?"

Jamie paused in his study of the clouds. While it was true that he wouldn't be anyone without the fans that had loved and supported him through over twenty-five years of his career, no one *owned* him. He deserved to make the best choices for his own life. What was once good for him, now felt binding. What he once needed and loved, had shifted.

"I've given them years, and I love them. But every man should have the chance to change his mind."

"You can't be anything but Jameson Clark."

Jamie's face grew hot, and he resisted the urge to throw the phone off the deck.

"I can be anything I damn well want, and I get to decide what happens from here on out."

"Don't be stupid—"

"And that means no more publicity, not for the album, not for me, and not about Laney Sullivan. I don't want to hear another goddamn word from you. Not in print, not on air."

"But, Jamie—"

"I will press charges for breaking and entering, and theft."

"I'm doing you a huge favor, you idiot!"

"The rest of my work on this is *not* to be publicized. If I find out you leaked it, Annie, so help me God, you and I and a whole mess of lawyers will have words."

"Fine! But I can't guarantee that someone else won't. Eventually everyone is gonna know her. Do you think she's gonna like you hiding out while the rest of the world starts looking for her?"

Jamie's jaw clenched. "I'm not hiding out. And it's none of anyone's goddamn business who I date."

"Baby, you're a superstar, it's everybody's business."

"Well, then maybe I don't want to be a superstar anymore."

"You don't get to decide that, and besides, if you're not Jameson Clark, playboy country superstar, who in the hell else would you be?"

Jamie hung up and threw himself on the bed. Who else could he possibly be? Rather than feel like the words were a noose around his neck, they felt like an open invitation. He looked at the compass, pointing behind him as he looked at the ocean. Who could he possibly be? Annie faded from his mind as he watched the waves roll in and out, and went where it always did when things got quiet.

What would Laney be doing right now? He smirked; probably trying to buy every copy of *X-Magazine* in Laramie and planning a bonfire. Had she heard him on the radio yet? Was she mad? Maybe it was time to tap into his inside source on the matter, gauge the crowd as it were, and see what she was willing to give, if anything at all.

"But the end of May is your two weeks," Laney started.

"Come on, Laney, Tasha has a lot to take care of with the wedding and the guest list and all. She doesn't want to have to take care of the kids too," David said dismissively.

"Is this because you're mad I shot down your booty call?"

"I don't know what you're talking about." His voice was tight.

"Tasha doesn't have to *take care* of our children! They're—" Lancy nearly choked on her anger. "They're your children too and they're amazing. Only an idiot wouldn't want to be a part of their lives."

"Laney—" he stuttered.

"The times when they want to be around you are running out, and soon they won't want anything to do with you. All of that aside, you act like my life isn't full of things that *I* need to take care of."

"Laney, come on, you write smut. It's not like you have to actually work. I mean even your adjunct position barely constitutes a living, and I hear the board might not look at that publicity stunt too kindly."

"You—" She shook her fist at the phone and mouthed that he should go fuck himself. She took a deep breath and measured her next words carefully. "The judge ordered that they would spend time with you during *some* part of the summer." Silence met her.

"You know what? Fine. Even. Better. You and Tasha take care of your ridiculously expensive upcoming nuptials. I will enjoy the extra time with *my* children. I'll make sure they know where your priorities lie." David sputtered indignantly but Laney charged ahead. "In the course of paying for the release of hundreds of white doves, horse-drawn carriages, and whatever other Barbie-princess dream wedding plans she has, if your child support check is even one day late, I will not hesitate to call the judge."

"Now listen—" David's voice faltered on the other end.

"And if Tasha can't handle them during her epic planning process, maybe we don't need to come to that trumped-up lie of a freak show. I'm sure that you and she would barely notice our absence."

Laney hung up and ruffled her hair. She rose from the dining table, abandoned her work in progress, and padded to the kitchen on slippered feet. She'd been pissed off even before she'd answered the phone on account of trying to create a happily-ever-after ending for her novel that she didn't believe in. But she needed to put to rest the book that Jamie had sparked so she could start a new one. A different book, where everyone got their heart broken and no one won. Not in love. Not ever.

"Argh!" The knife she was using cut the foil from her wine bottle slipped and jabbed into her palm, puncturing deep into the flesh.

"Momma? You okay?" Sylvia's voice came from around the corner and she rushed over when she saw the blood dripping down Laney's wrist and across her forearm. "Momma!" Sylvia's voice broke with fear.

"It's fine, it's okay. I just slipped. It's okay."

"It's not okay." Sylvia sobbed and Charlotte sped into the room.

"I'm okay!" Laney tried to reassure, but the sight of the blood, the thought of how miserable she was, and the knowledge that her children weren't immune to her current mood made her realize how the situation may look. Laney wanted to cry. She wrapped her hand in a towel and grabbed her keys.

"Let's go get this sewn up," she said calmly. No matter how amazing Jameson Clark had been, or how horrible her ex was, she wasn't about to let her children believe she'd been beaten by love, or lack of it. She bundled them into their coats, one-handed, and drove to the emergency room in the cold night. By the time they got back it was late. With six shiny new stitches and a sore spot from the recommended tetanus shot, she helped the girls get into bed. Sylvia touched her arm before she turned to leave.

"Momma?" she asked in a whisper above Charlotte's already sound snoring.

"Yeah, baby?"

"Did you—did you mean to cut yourself?" she asked with the honesty that Laney loved her for. She hadn't been giving Sylvia enough credit; she was growing up, and moments like these were pivotal points in the creation of her humanity.

"No, baby. I didn't." Laney sighed and sat down next to her. "I know I've been down lately. Sometimes in life, you're gonna get hit with disappointments, and—" Laney's voice choked back tears, "and you'll get your heart broken. And I wish it wouldn't ever happen to you, because sometimes it's the worst pain in the world." Laney took a breath. "But you know what?"

"What, Momma?"

"Our hearts are the strongest muscle in our body. They're tough and they can survive even the worse breaking. I'm—I'm down right now. But I'm healing. I will always heal. So, please, please don't worry. I will do better," she said, and smoothed a lock of hair off of Sylvia's forehead. "I'll get better."

"I'm sorry Daddy and Jamie broke your heart, Momma."

"Losing your dad was tough, more because it's affected you and your sister. But Jamie," she sighed. "He was, well, actually, he was amazing, and kind, and sweet, and I don't think I ever laughed so much in my life. He didn't break my heart. In a lot of ways, he healed it," she said softly. "I...I just got scared. I saw an opportunity to leave, and I left, before he could leave me. I was the one who decided we couldn't make it work."

"But, Momma, if he made you laugh, and he didn't break your heart, couldn't you be brave enough to tell him that? I know you're brave enough to say I love you. You say it to us all the time."

Laney's heart fell against the reasonable argument.

"I suppose we could. But I'm sure he's already moved on."

"Have you moved on?"

"Sylvia," Laney sighed.

"Because if you haven't, I bet he hasn't either."

"Sometimes you don't—" Laney sighed again. "Sometimes you don't fall in love the same way as the other person. Hearts don't break evenly and usually someone owns a bigger piece, and the other person gets the leftover." She leaned down, kissed her daughter's head, ruffled her hair, and left before she had to face any more questions of hope.

TWENTY

JAMIE CALLED MARC GRAYSON, AT THE END OF HIS ROPE for information, and they had a long discussion about Laney Sullivan and what Jamie's intentions were. Jamie admitted his intentions were to win her back, but he didn't know how to go about it just yet. Then he wheedled information out of Marc.

"How has she been? How did she take the song getting out?"

"Well, I'm willing to bet she cussed up a storm at her radio. She's worried. How it'll affect her job and her family. She also thinks you're using your fling to sell records."

"It wasn't a fling, Marc. Not to me. Not ever. I was so over the moon for her, that I didn't even know someone was taking pictures of us. My ex stole and copied those songs and ran them before I could stop her. I tried telling Laney before it all hit the fan," Jamie said.

"Oh, I'm sure she shut you down. She's a stubborn crank."

"She sure did, n' I probably deserved it. How are her girls? Her family?"

Marc said they were all heading back to Laney's hometown in a couple of weeks. It seemed there was a property line dispute over some adjoining land and the bank had been notified of back taxes the Sullivans hadn't known they were liable for.

"But if they didn't know the land was theirs how could they have known to pay?"

"Seems someone dug down pretty deep to find anything they could on the Sullivans. I even suspect Tennyson had those lines redrawn."

Jamie swallowed. That's what she'd been talking about the morning her mother called. Ian Tennyson, the man angry at her sister for crossing him. She hadn't been exaggerating.

"The girls are fine." Marc brought Jamie back to the present. "They've been researching all about you. Little Charlotte thinks you're about the handsomest man on the planet but Sylvia is a bit more skeptical. They both keep asking me if you're really lovelorn for their momma. And if so, how we can possibly matchmake you back together. I told them big people stuff isn't our business." Jamie's heart melted in his chest.

"But I am. I really am lovelorn over her," he whispered.

"Not matter how hard she's denying it, I know the feeling is mutual, my little buckeroo, but the problem of her pride remains."

That made Jamie ache inside. He thought about what he'd learned from Leonard. Ian Tennyson's vendetta, the Bar Nunn, and the bills Warren and Melissa Sullivan were having a hard time paying. The turmoil already on Laney's heart and how he'd only made it worse. He sniffed.

"So, they're really in trouble? The Sullivans? I thought her dad was a vet, and Katelyn and Grant have the horse breeding and training, and Elle's bakery."

"Look at you listening to her! They have little ways of making things pay the bills, but times are hard when you're starting out behind. And, it seems, as Laney has always told me, that the good doctor Sullivan has been a little too good-hearted, and never charges enough in his practice to make more money than they think they need. I suspect that an auction isn't too far off."

"Damn it," Jamie said. "I want to help but I don't know if she'll let me."

"I know, and she probably wouldn't. You gotta just do it, and she'll either accept it or won't." Jamie was silent for a long moment, thinking. "She's losing weight and always looks tired. Given the lack of paper in her trash bin, I don't think she's been able to write much lately," Marc said.

"Marc—"

"If you really do want her, if you really are in love with Laney, please do something. You don't have to save her, but you should at least be here for her while the world's tumbling down. And if you don't love her, please don't call either of us again. Don't torture her."

Jamie's throat closed. "Thanks for the talk, Marc. I've got— I've got a lot to think about and I'm supposed to be meeting with a collaborator in about five minutes. I appreciate your time." He hung up and went down to his studio.

He needed this album. He needed it out in the world and as closure for all the pain of his father's passing and in honor of the woman who helped him find it. She'd stood by him, in the middle of his world falling down. Jamie's heart hurt and he could barely concentrate.

He made calls and did more creative work in two days than he had in the last two albums. His favorite band members and collaborators had jumped at the chance, and he'd flown them all in the last week to work, mad dash on the tracks. If this album was going to work, he needed to work quickly.

His mom called nonstop. She left embarrassing questions on his machine. What had happened? Why had she gotten a thank you note from Laney so soon after her trip to Tennessee? What had he done? Had he hurt her? Why wasn't she with him now? Had he messed up? He finally called her to end the deluge and tell her he and Laney were in a weird place, and right now she wasn't speaking to him.

"God bless, Jameson. You are thick sometimes."

"I know. I think she got spooked, or I got spooked or...I'm not sure."

"Are you spooked?" Desdemona asked.

"No. I thought I would be. Falling so hard for someone like her."

"Well, then? Get back to her."

"I know! I'm working on it. She's not exactly making it easy on me."

"Well, good. It's about time a woman made you work for her love."

"Mom—" Jamie stared out at the water and sighed.

"When your dad was so worried about you—"

"Momma, do we need to—"

"Hush and listen! He said he was worried that you didn't have direction, but I think part of what he worried about was that you didn't have someone in your life to love you, to hang on to, more than a two-month marriage made out of sex and fame. More than just the fleeting affections of all of those girls who only wanted to change you or get something from you. He wanted you to find someone who could tell you no, once in a while."

"No?" His voice faltered, and he thought about the first morning in Laney's kitchen.

"Someone who kept your head on straight." Desdemona sighed. "Jamie, you know I love you all the way to the moon."

"Love you too, Momma." He hung up and thought about his father. About what Laney meant to him. About what the music meant to him. He grabbed the compass and fell into the couch cushions. He thought about what it meant that she could tell him no. He called her again, just to hear her voice on the message. He paused after the beep and thought about what his mom had said.

"I—" He stopped. What did he want? Nothing he could tell

her over a message. "I wish you hadn't gone," was all he could muster. He hung up and tossed his phone aside.

Laney had to leave town. Reporters had snuck into her class before she'd arrived, hidden amongst the bored freshmen, and started taking photos mid-lecture. It was bad enough that she hadn't showered that day and was dressed in her oldest, frumpiest sweater with jeans, but to have them disrupt her already disrupt-able students was beyond annoying. Laney called them out; told them if they hadn't paid for the class then they could 'mosey their bare, vulture asses out the door.' Campus security was called. Class was cancelled. The dean contacted her, on behalf of concerned parents and students, and recommended that she take a leave of absence.

"But this isn't my fault! I'm not dating him, and even if I was, those assholes were trespassing and taking unsolicited photos!"

"Be that as it may, Ms. Sullivan, we can't have the students disturbed over your new-found fame."

"My new—Christ on a crutch," she grumbled. "Fine." She hung up and spun in her old wooden chair with frustrated fists pushed against her temples.

"Oh lord, one of them just jumped the bushes!" Marc exclaimed from his office, and she didn't have to ask what he was talking about. She pulled her shoddy mini blinds closed to the eruption of a dust cloud, and slumped back in her chair. The phone rang in its 1950s melodic tones and she stared at it for three whole rounds.

"Are you gonna get that?"

"Did you lock the doors?"

"Yes!"

"I feel like we're literally in the middle of a horror movie right now." she grouched back.

"We just can't get separated and thank god neither of us is a virgin," Marc laughed. "You want me to go out and get all 'brute squad' on them."

"No, this is stupid and it will stop if we just pretend like it's not happening," she yelled back.

"Denial never worked for anyone and answer your damn phone!"

"Okay, don't yell at me!" Laney picked up the receiver. "What?"

"Have you seen your numbers?"

"My what? Who is this?"

"Holy shit, Laney, it's Rebecca."

"What numbers? The numbers of pages I still need to get to you? I know, okay? I'm working on it. I sort of have a situation here."

"No, not your page count. Jesus, hang on." The soft sound of keys typing gave Laney pause to peek through a small slit in the blinds. A camera flash went off in her face, blinding her. She stepped back and cursed. "Check your dinosaur email," Rebecca finished with the you're-so-antiquated dig.

Laney hung up and logged into her laptop. She pulled up her email while thoughts of tackling the petite journalists outside and stealing their equipment built a fantastical action sequence in her head. Rebecca had sent a link to Laney's book sales page. Why did she think Laney needed to see that in a time like this? She clicked the link.

"Well, that's not right." She cleared the account number and tried logging on again, certain that Rebecca had her confused with another more prolific writer. Her author picture and account flashed again on the screen. Laney's breath caught.

"Holy shit."

TWENTY-ONE

"LANEY?" ELLE'S VOICE CALLED FROM BEHIND HER. She'd been out on the porch, in the rocking chair, suffering the cold evening breeze, bundled up and tears freezing at the corner of her eyes. She stared across the frozen pasture, her arms tucked around her middle. "Honey, come inside. Dinner's ready." Laney looked behind at the concern on her sister's face and the loving understanding of a woman who'd lived through a fire herself.

"I'm not hungry. Thanks though," Laney said and sniffed. She looked back into the open field. She wasn't ready to sit around a table with her family. She wasn't ready to face the love between them and the normalcy of having someone to come home to. She was here because she'd been put on sabbatical from the university. Because the paparazzi wouldn't leave her alone, not even at her tiny apartment. Because she couldn't think and hurt while the world was shoving cameras in her face or recording every moment for sound bites.

Her home, Sweet Valley, was still a place forgotten by the outside world. With locked gates on the roads and "Trespassers Will Be Shot" signs that were defensible in court. Somewhere journalists didn't know, and internet was spotty, and news traveled slower. She sighed and looked out at a lazy meadowlark swooping through the clear and open sky.

She thought what they had was special. Something just for them, and that he could finally be himself with her, outside of the bright lights. Then he'd started creating again, and his old life had sauntered back in wearing high heels and had kissed him squarely on the mouth.

"Laney June Sullivan, you get off your ass and come in this house. Now!"

Laney startled at the tone and turned around to see Elle with her hands on her hips and a stubborn set jaw.

Blake's voice drifted out from inside, "Uh oh, Laney. You'd better do what she says, she's got her mom voice on."

"Well, I'll be, she's all done grow'd up on us," Laney muttered. Elle's scowl stayed firm. "You're the spittin' image of Gran when you do that, you know?"

"That's what people tell me," Elle said. She put her arm around Laney and brought her into the warm and bright kitchen, where luscious rolls, hot turkey and creamy mashed potatoes were laid out on the old farm table.

"Jesus, I don't need all of this," Laney said.

"Sure you do," Blake said and strapped Emilee into her high chair. Sylvia and Charlotte, who had helped with dinner, fawned over the baby and helped finish putting food on the table for their Aunt Elle. Emilee, the blonde cherub, strained against her belt, eager to be up and moving around. Blake put a plop of mashed potatoes in front of her, which she promptly squished through her fingers and squealed with delight.

"I swear one of these days she'll actually eat instead of playing in it," Elle sighed.

"I imagine she misses breasts," Blake whispered. "Not that I blame her. I miss them every minute I'm away from them too."

"Blake!" Elle blushed.

Laney couldn't be around this. She moved to leave the kitchen.

"I'm going to bed."

"But Momma, I helped with the beans, and Charlotte made the gravy," Sylvia protested.

"It looks amazing, baby. I just don't feel well right now."

"You're going to sit down and eat," Elle said, less a command and more a statement of fact. "Or did you forget all the mother-henning you did to me when I came home? Come on, you aren't leaving this table until you eat something."

"Yeah, but you had—" Laney paused and her eyes filled with tears. "You had Blake here, and a new life to build and I've got..." She paused and didn't finish with 'nothing.' Not when her beautiful girls sat staring at her. Not with a family who loved her and always would, no matter what man came or went in her life. She thought about the conversation with Sylvia. The stitches that were just starting to heal. "I've got a long day tomorrow. I should go to bed early so I can try to work on the online college prep course I said I'd teach, since teaching my usual classes has become too 'disruptive'. We should try to get back to the apartment, maybe tomorrow." Her brain tumbled over itself in anxiety-riddled confusion. "We left in such a hurry that we still need to go back for clothes." Laney tried not to remember the spontaneous trip to Jamie's mother's house, with no clothes at all.

"Momma," Her daughters protested.

"I should—"

"I think you should sit down. The world can wait an hour." Elle stepped in and set a full plate in front of Laney's empty chair.

Laney looked at Elle.

"Look, I get it. You just had your heart broke all to hell, and not for the first time," Elle said, and scooted her chair out for her. Laney plopped down and stared, defeated, as her sister pushed the delicious smelling food closer. "Just because he didn't want to be with you doesn't mean—"

"He did," Laney said suddenly.

"What?" Elle said and all motion at the table stopped.

"He did want to be with me, but I...well, I caught him kissing a woman. Or maybe she was kissing him and, I don't know, I just, freaked out and left. I knew he wasn't going to want me forever."

"Oh, Laney," Elle sighed.

"What?"

"You let your fear decide."

"What? What are you talking about?"

"You just expected Jameson to be like David, and for what you had to end the same way. But Jameson Clark is not David and you aren't the old you. You may think that you were avoiding a mistake, but all you were doing was letting your fear control what you let yourself have. You let your fear decide," Elle huffed and Laney sat back in her chair. She pushed around the potatoes, spreading out the mountain, and watching the gravy drain from the center.

Blake leaned in. "Don't be too hard on her. It's not easy getting over past hurt." Blake said, then he turned to Laney. "I know you don't like to admit it, but Elle is kinda right. You can't blame the man for your ex's mistakes," he said. "Whatever the case; it doesn't matter how your heart got broken, because it's broken all the same, and living without someone you love is like trying to live half a life. They've got so much of you, wherever they are, you can't be yourself without them," he said. Laney looked up from pushing her mashed potatoes around the plate.

"What are you, trying to steal my job or something?" Laney said with a small smile. Elle grabbed Blake's hand from across the table. He leaned over and kissed her.

"Yay!" Emilee broke out with a cheer and raised her hands over her head, dropping big chunks of mashed potatoes into her hair. "Yay, Daddy!" she said and threw her hands out, spraying potatoes behind them on the wall and across the table. The girls watched their mom's face. Laney burst out with a laugh and then promptly cried.

"Damn it, Elle, I'm tryin' to be sad but your baby's so cute she's making it difficult," Laney cried and laughed.

"Oh honey, it's okay." Elle smoothed Laney's stray hair back into her bun. "You're just exhausted. Go up to bed, sleep, and we'll wake up to a different day."

"Can I help you clean up?" Laney sniffed.

"We can get it, you should rest," Sylvia insisted.

"Yeah, you'll wake up better tomorrow." Charlotte smiled and picked a clump of mashed potato out of her hair.

"Okay." Laney nodded and wished that's how easy it worked. She wiped her nose on her napkin and stumbled to her feet. The girls cleared her place and finished their dinners, jumping up to start the dishes in a get-along manner that would have shocked Laney if she hadn't been already passed out, asleep upstairs.

Laney's dreams were haunted with visions of moving back home, living in a bunker while the world shouted and clawed outside for an exclusive. She and her girls had huddled together when her phone rang, and Jamie's voice came through asking if she wanted a peanut butter and jelly sandwich in their treehouse. God did she ever...The dream changed, and she stood in the yard of a small bungalow by the river. Charlotte and Sylvia ran in the large yard and the quiet peace erased the locked-in bunker. She woke sweating through her pajamas and short of breath.

Laney knew then that she wanted to come home, back to Sweet Valley. A place where she and her short-lived romance with Jameson Clark would soon be forgotten, and she could quietly work on her novels, raise her girls, and maybe teach virtually permanently. It would be a complete shift and she wasn't sure, at six-thirty in the morning, if it was the right time to be deciding anything, still, she drafted a letter to the dean and let it sit on her computer. Maybe the craziness that had come from her time with

Jamie was just the thing she needed to start over and reclaim her own life.

Then she offered to do Elle's chores, hoping it would give her sister and Blake a couple more baby-making hours. Someone should be getting some, Laney thought angrily as she lugged a new bag of chicken feed into the coop.

"How you doing, kid?" Laney heard behind her as she spread the chicken feed in the bins. Laney grunted as the fifty-pound sack shifted with each generous pour and looked over her shoulder.

"Who the hell raises chickens?" she grouched to Katelyn. She smiled back at Laney with a crooked grin and crinkled her skewed nose, her features a startling mix of beauty and toughness.

"Some big city girl that read to many issues of *Country Living*, I imagine," Katelyn said in the soft-spoken way of their father.

"She sure did go all out, didn't she?"

"She's got the heavy workload to prove it," Katelyn agreed and bent to help Laney finish filling the troughs on the other side of the coop. Laney shook her head.

"Seems like she's rich in love though, and for that, I can't be too angry." Laney straightened her back with a groan. "Oh, wait. Yes, I can. I can totally hate her for that." She nodded.

"If anyone deserved it, it's Elle. And so do you." Katelyn began. Laney scowled.

"I really don't want to talk about this. Wait! Is that why you're here? Did Elle send you in to pep talk me out of my pajamas?"

"Now why in the hell would I do that?" Katelyn gave a chuckle and glanced over Laney's flannel pants and slippers. "You've got your own look going on there, très chic."

"Shut up, Katie," Laney grumbled and spilled seed across her cat-embroidered slippers and Katelyn's sensible boots.

"Look, everyone knows the youngest can't tell the oldest what to do. Hell, even if I *did* know what you should do and had the balls grow'd to tell you, we all know you wouldn't listen anyway," she finished. Laney continued to scowl. "I just thought that I could hang out and give you some company this morning. Plus, after we help round up our mares, I was hoping you'd be able to take Hugh out for a ride." The added favor was spoken as though it was her original thought in the first place.

"Why in the hell can't you do it? You're the horse whisperer," Laney balked.

"I think he'd benefit from a different set of hands."

"Katelyn, I haven't ridden in—" She stopped before the memory of riding with Jameson Clark pressed against the edges of her brain. "—a while. Why would I start now?"

"He's a bona fide thoroughbred! You have to take him out at least once, it's such a beautiful experience."

"Why are you pushing this?" Laney stopped and studied her, feed bag in midair. Katelyn's eyes hit the floor, and she shuffled her boots.

"I can't ride him today," she said and scowled back up at Laney. "I've gotta go to the doctor."

"What? Why? What in the hell is wrong with you?" Laney's annoyance turned into fear. She dropped the food, causing three of the chickens to spook and flutter madly about the coop, uproaring all the rest. She took Katelyn by the shoulders in the midst of the poultry mayhem and looked her over. "Are you hurt?"

"No! It's nothing. Nothing that needs fussing over. I just don't —" she sighed and looked away. "I don't wanna ride until I'm sure I've got a handle on the situation, that's all."

Laney turned her head and eyed Katelyn suspiciously. "Do you need someone to go with you?"

Katelyn shook her head, "Jeffers is going with me."

"How is the impeccable butler?" Laney said, having met Grant's once caretaker and surrogate father when they'd moved to Wyoming last year, escaping Ian Tennyson's reach. At least they had thought they had.

"He's fine. Impeccable but loosening up. He even talked about getting a dog. Grant is for it of course, since he never was allowed to have one."

Laney sighed. She thought of how little love Grant had had in his life, and how he had found safety and acceptance with their family. Jeffers too. Laney had been partial to the former British serviceman as they were both a little short on height and patience. "Well, you tell Jeffers I miss having my ass handed to me at cribbage."

"I will." Katelyn smiled. "He misses you and your girls."

"He's good with kids," Laney agreed. "I think he would have made an excellent grandpa." Laney looked back at Katelyn just in time to see her eyes fall quickly to the feed-scattered floor. "Wait a minute. You can't ride, Jeffers is taking you to the doctor...Does Grant know you could be pregnant?"

"Psh!" Katelyn began but her cheeks turned red and she looked back at Laney, a scared younger sister. "I—haven't told him. He loves his nieces so much and I know he's sad about not having children. But then, I'm two months late, and my boobs are all big and I—" Katelyn paused to suck in a huge breath and Laney dropped the bag to hug her quickly. Katelyn swallowed, shook her head. "I'm not supposed to even be able to and I don't want to get my hopes up, especially with everything else happening right now. I just... I need someone to take care of Hugh this week, until I know for certain." The wavering plea for help, rarely shown by Katelyn, made Laney's heart race. She wanted to yelp out loud and kiss her baby sister, and scream. For a moment, nothing else had room to be in her heart but the possibility.

"Katie May," Laney whispered and the soft sweet look of concern caused the tough, younger sister to waver. "Of course, I'll take him. Whatever you need."

"Girls?" Elle called from the porch and interrupted.

"Please don't say anything. I don't want anyone to know, until I do," Katelyn said.

"I got you. I'll keep my big, bossy mouth shut."

"Girls!" Elle yelled again more sharply.

"Yeah, Gran?" Katelyn yelled back, happy for the distraction. They heard Elle grumble.

"I'm not that old." She peeked her head into the coop and saw the way they stood together. "What is it? What's wrong?"

"Nothing, Laney was just saying she'd love to take a ride this afternoon. I offered up Hugh, and she's gonna take him. I'm worried he's going to get lazy and overweight with me and Grant being so busy lately."

Elle made a disgusted grunt. "Katie May, no horse of yours has ever been lazy."

"It's settled then, thanks, Laney. I gotta go talk to Blake about his shifts this week." Katelyn nudged Laney's shoulder as a hint to keep her mouth shut, and left the coop as quickly as possible.

"What's gotten into her?" Elle started.

"Hm? I don't know. Nothing. She's fine."

"Laney, I've known you nearly your whole life, and I know when you're lying."

"What could I possibly have to lie about?" Laney grouched and whisked past Elle on her way up to the house.

"Cute pajamas! Isn't it past breakfast?" Elle yelled to her back teasingly. Laney responded by flipping her the bird without even looking back. When Laney got back into the house, barely through her second cup of coffee, her mother and father came through the door, followed by Elle and Blake, Grant and Katelyn. Her parents sat down around the table with the rest of the family. A morose feeling settled heavy around Gran's old wooden table.

"What is this, some kind of intervention?" Laney grouched. But the look on each of their faces said it was much bigger than trying to get her out of her pajamas. Warren cleared his throat.

"Girls, we have to talk."

Twenty-Two

Jamie woke to the sound of his phone going off somewhere in the bed. He patted down the mess of twisted covers and touched something. He put it to his ear, searching with adept fingers for the button before pulling his hand back in confusion to stare at a pair of glasses. The phone continued its muffled ring, as he looked at the glasses and remembered them perched on her head. She was there, always there in his mind, in his bed. Everything was just too much her. He looked at the ridiculously thick, dark rims, the kind an old man might wear, not some hot romance writer. She was thousands of miles away, squinting into her computer screen, wondering where she'd left them. Maybe she wondered where she'd left him too.

His heart sprang to life. He skimmed over the sheets with trembling fingers to find the phone, only to come up with the edges of the tattered notebook she'd perched between her thighs on his veranda when they'd last shared this room. She'd forgotten it too. Her pen was missing, probably stuck in her messy bun when she'd left him. Finally, he felt the phone beneath his thigh and unwedged it. He could barely tear his eyes away from the notebook to look at the number on his screen. It was Leonard. He answered.

"Hey, man."

"Jamie? I just heard from my contact in Sweet Valley." Jamie was half-heartedly listening as Leonard went on to reiterate the property loophole that Ian Tennyson had exposed. Jamie touched the frame of her glasses and slipped them on. It was startling how much clearer things were. He flipped through the first few pages of the notebook.

"Laney June Sullivan's Last Will and Testament," he read the leaning cursive letters.

"What? Jameson, are you listening to me?" Jamie wasn't. He was reading through the thoughts for her girls, her family, the people she loved. As though she might really die on the island. Just in case. It broke Jamie's heart and only made him love her more. The last paragraph, paused and separated by a line from the rest, read:

> I leave to Jameson Clark, the ability to find something greater in life than beer and boobs. I will him the ability to open up, scratch the deep itches and find someone who can handle whatever it is he's hiding in there. May he discover optimism for the future in his life and look beyond the superficial to find a friend in the woman he loves.

"Jamie?" Leonard's voice came through the inscription and roused him. He swallowed back the lump in his throat and felt tears seep beneath the rims of the glasses. He sniffed. That was it. He couldn't be here anymore. He slammed the notebook closed.

"Say that again."

"Which part?"

"All of it."

"The auction of the Sullivan Ranch is happening in a week. Rumor is that Ian Tennyson is plannin' to buy it all and kick them out."

Jamie's heart froze and his hand shook as he took off her glasses.

"Are you sure?"

"As the day's long, Jamie."

"Thanks, I'll call you back." Jamie hung up and speed dialed the familiar number. It was time; past time if he could be honest, that he did something. He'd planned on waiting until the album was finished. But his heart was done waiting. And her family didn't have months to wait. When the line clicked, he didn't wait for a greeting.

"I need a favor, and I need it fast."

Jamie wasn't sure he had the right town. For all the buttering up he'd done of small-town America in the last thirty years, he'd never seen a town as small as Sweet Valley. There wasn't even a stoplight; not a single chain store. In a matter of minutes he'd cruised from one end of its main street to the other, taking in the town that raised her.

It didn't seem to fit her cynical style. It was so ideal. So quaint and sweet. He half-expected a homecoming parade to break out at any minute. At the very least a county fair should be around the corner. He drove up to the high school and sat in the parking lot beside the worn-down football field. The dirt track around it was pitted from the rain and drought cycle. The winter-killed grass had grown in wild patches, and one of the goalposts was listing to the side. It was clear the town wasn't working with a big budget. For all the high-dollar dude ranches surrounding the city limits, very little of their money was going back into the community. If only country songs about tax loopholes sold as well, he could write a platinum album.

He pulled away from the school and went down to the only diner that looked open at the hour. A small place, with big windows all around that offered, if not much else, a peaceful view of the Sweetwater River. The same river, she'd told him beneath midnight and morning afterglows, that she'd learned to fish in, swim in, skate on, think and write down her childhood musings on the banks of. He stared into the rolling gray ripples as they tottered around smoothed river rock and burbled beneath the encroaching icy banks, carrying small branches away to the south.

Where was she now? Could she walk through that door of the diner? Could she be a block away at the bank, trying to convince the loan department that her parents needed an extension? Could she be in the church, praying for a miracle? He shook his head. Laney was too cynical to pray. She'd been hurt too much to believe that you could put your faith in anyone but yourself. When Jamie paid for his coffee to go, the waitress's eyes lingered on his face, and he could see her brain trying to place him. He tipped his cap down and paid in cash, before quickly walking back to the truck.

He sipped the strong coffee and went through the rest of his messages. His lawyers, though befuddled, had called with confirmation of what he'd asked for. Now, he just needed to use all the charm in his arsenal to convince Sweet Valley's most jaded resident that he was worthy of her. The legalities had to be airtight. So that even if she didn't want him, even if she rejected his offer, her parents would still be safe. Her family, her sisters, the people she loved and worried for, would be safe.

Then, maybe with less worry, Laney could find room in her heart for love.

Even as Ian Tennyson had his eyes on the family's land, Jamie had sources scouring the town for information about the family and how best to help them. Katelyn, the youngest, had been working overtime with Grant, Ian's son, to build and manage a therapy center on the back forty acres of Em Sullivan's ranch, which was now owned by Eleanor, the middle sister, and her husband Blake. Katelyn gave riding lessons at a local dude ranch and helped out at her dad's vet clinic with Blake, who was also a vet. Eleanor ran Raising Elle's Bakery and was acclaimed in the state for her baked goods and homemade soaps and lotions. She too, worked to keep the family's collective land maintained and from being bought, but the new burdens were even too much for her successful bakery.

Blake and Elle were working to muddle through the water rights and trust issues with the landowners surrounding them, but their best efforts had been in vain so far, and Jamie worried about Laney's sister putting her business and livelihood on the chopping block to save their parents' land. When he drove out of town to the Sullivan ranch, he wasn't exactly sure what to expect. His stomach was turned with butterflies and worry. What if they hated him? What if they didn't believe him? What if they doubted that he loved their Laney even half as much as they did? What if they rejected the offer and turned him away? He could only give them the truth in his heart. And take some of the weight off their shoulders. For Laney, he hoped it was enough.

TWENTY-THREE

Laramie's main streets, as typical for a game-day weekend, were jam-packed with traffic and slogged Laney's progress. It couldn't have come at a worse possible time. Laney had gone back to gather more clothes from her apartment, settle the details of her online class with her supervisor, and cash out the savings account she'd been carefully building up. She needed to get back to Sweet Valley, and soon. The auction was only a few days away.

Her heart still hurt from the news their parents had relayed. There had been an unforeseen, unmapped portion of land that they hadn't known was theirs. And the back taxes, dating back over forty years, had put the ranch in incomparable debt. But the real kick to the gut had come when news had spread that the Bar Nunn and a "wealthy horse breeder" were rumored to be the top bidders interested. She didn't know what she could do, but she wasn't going to let her family face this alone. Laney sighed as she rested her hands on the wheel while they were stopped yet again on Grand.

"Why's traffic always bad when you wanna get outta town?" Charlotte said from the backseat.

"At least Mom's not cursing," Sylvia whispered to her sister.

Laney put her hand to her forehead and smiled.

"Not yet," Laney sang at them through the rearview mirror. Her cell phone pinged beside her. She looked up at the bumper in front of her as it inched forward slowly and picked up her phone. It was Elle.

> Are you on your way??

Laney looked up at the traffic and responded carefully.

> Trying, but it's game day so we're still in traffic. What's up? Besides the impending doom of everything?

Elle's response was almost instantaneous.

> Katelyn's sick. She's been in bed for two days now, and that's not like her. I told her to see a doctor, and she said it's nothing. Do you know why? Did she say something in the coop? And don't lie to me. I can tell, even by text.

Laney sighed, drove forward another tenth of a mile, and responded.

> She hasn't written. I think it might have something to do with that damn virile Scotsman—

"Mom? What's 'virile' mean?" Sylvia asked from the over her shoulder, leaning in to read the screen.

"Nothing. Don't worry about it. I shouldn't be texting and driving. I'm turning it off. Who can find a Tennessee plate?" She tried to distract them, not knowing why she'd picked Jamie's home state for the boredom-busting game. Probably because he was always in her peripheral. For the rest of her life, he'd always be on the edges of her every waking thought. Her phone pinged.

> Oh my God! Is she pregnant?

Laney scowled. She couldn't get caught telling the secret.

> Driving can't text.

> Liar! Tell me what you know!

> Crashing into a laundry truck. Hope you're happy for cutting our lives short.

> Okay—whatever, we'll have words when you get here.

> Can't wait xoxo

. . .

Laney put down her phone. Katelyn hadn't been sure, but all signs were pointing to the conclusion that she could, in fact, be pregnant. In the middle of all this sadness and chaos, is that what she'd found out at the doctor? Would the stress end it all? Laney's hands clenched on the wheel. After Katelyn's appendix ruptured when she was fifteen, up in the mountains without immediate medical care, she shouldn't have been able to. But Grant was indeed virile, and Elle had told stories about how often they were with one another. Her thoughts went back to Jamie; he'd been inexhaustible too... and they had never used protection. Laney's eye twitched.

"Lord, I can't even—"

"What is it, Momma?" Sylvia asked.

"Nothing." Laney switched on the radio and stayed purposefully away from the country stations, lest she hear his voice filling up the car, and carrying her back to St. Croix and the needling fear that she had acquired a souvenir from Jameson Clark.

When they finally made it out of town, and through the back roads over the mountains, Laney and the girls drove up the old pitted drive to her parents' ranch at half speed. The dirt was covered in pockets of ice and packed snow. Her replacement for the Isuzu, which had been laid to rest in the junkyard of the WyoTech Institute, was terrible for the roads and it felt every divot and rut.

"We're almost there! We're almost there!" Charlotte called from the back seat. "There's Denali and Chase! And Dakota and Lottie! And Goliath—they must be staying at Gramma's!" She pointed to the northern field, where the small herd was standing in the snow, coats bushy from the cold, and their breaths puffing out in front of them.

"Yep," Laney said softly, wondering if they'd have to find new homes after the auction, and how much that would break her sister's heart.

"Sure can't wait for summer," Sylvia said. "Can we come here more after the wedding?" Laney's heart and head argued over which hurt the most. David getting remarried or the auction that meant they wouldn't have a ranch to come to.

"Yeah, baby, let's do that."

When they pulled up to the drive, Laney saw her mom in the window of the old blue farmhouse, waving from the kitchen sink. It made her feel twenty years younger, even though the lines on her mother's face were deeper and the house was showing the weathering of time. Laney's father, Warren, was just walking up from the barn and came to the car first. He opened the girls' door and met them with hugs and smiles.

"Hey, short stack!" he said to Laney as he drew her in for her own hug.

"Hey, Dad." Laney buried her face in the comforting smell of hay and warm flannel.

"How were the roads?" he asked.

"Good." Warren looked over his oldest daughter and turned his head curiously.

"I think that this whole situation is keeping you from taking care of yourself—"

"Well, you're thin as a rail!" Laney's mother, Melissa, said, bustling up and grabbing her into a hug. Though they were the same height, Laney's mom carried a few more curves beneath her clothes.

"I'm fine, Mom," she lied.

"You're not fine." Melissa lowered her voice. "Think I don't know my own baby?"

"Mel, honey. Leave her be. Let them get settled." He turned Laney towards the house, helped the girls with their bags, and led the way inside.

When the girls were set up in Elle's old room and Laney into hers, the girls spread out a board game in front of the fireplace in the cozy living room while Laney and her parents watched them from through the divided wall. Laney sat, hands curled around a cup of coffee, at the kitchen table where she'd written her first stories, gotten her first acceptance letters to literary journals, and made a million memories with her family. It felt so good to be home. Almost like she could remember once being whole. Had Jamie felt that way when they'd been in Knoxville? Whole? Did he feel that way now that he was back in his swanky studio, surrounded by the fawning throng? Her lip quivered. Laney looked up to see her mom watching her.

"How are things?" Laney asked before her mother could interject with more worry, "around here? Any word from the lawyers or if there's anything to be done?"

Warren waved a hand at her and sat back from the table, his own hand around a cup of coffee. "There's no need to worry about it, short stack. We're fine. Your mother and I want to hear about you!"

"Trust me, Dad, you don't," Laney said firmly. "I'm worried about you two. About the ranch. What's going on with Ian Tennyson?" She reached into the back pocket of her jeans and took out a folded piece of paper. "This isn't much, but it turns out that I got a little bump in sales," she grunted the word. "I also have a little extra for signing on for three more books. I think if I can take advantage of this short ride, I can get you a little more by summer." She put the check in front of her father. Warren Sullivan was not a man moved by much in the world, but his bright blue eyes glazed over with tears.

"Honey." Laney's mom shook her head. Her father took the check, unfolded it. He shook his head sadly and pushed it back to her.

"You keep that money."

"But, Dad!"

"That's your money, from your books, and you keep it!"

"Dad! Damn it—"

"It will all be okay," her mother said and searched Warren's face for reassurance.

"How do we know?" Laney said and her head swung from one of them to the other. "If Ian Tennyson wins this auction he's gonna take it all." The volume of their voices had caused Charlotte and Sylvia to look up from their game. Laney composed her worry. "How can we fight him?" she whispered.

"Laney, sometimes in life there are just battles you can't fight."

"That's not true. You always taught me to fight. For what I love. For what I believe in."

"Ian can have the land, as long as Grant stays safe with us." Warren met her furor with calm. As was always his way. "The important thing is that we stay together. Land or not, we have each other. We can move closer to town and be closer to the clinic. We can move in with Elle. We've seen these times and worse. We'll be all right, short stack."

"But Dad..." Tears welled in Laney's eyes and she bit her lip. Melissa grabbed her hand and Warren sat forward.

"Now, Laney—" Melissa began.

"It's okay," Laney stuttered. "It's all right. I mean, you're absolutely right. We have each other and we'll be okay." She paused to wipe away a tear. "It's just—it's just home and, I worry so much about you two. I wish I could have done more, before you had to do this." She wiped her nose with her sleeve and her father pulled out his red handkerchief to offer her. She buried her eyes in it.

"Why does everything have to change?" Laney wept.

"Change can be good," Warren whispered back. "You worry so much, for so many people. But you don't have to worry about us."

"I'm always going to worry about you," Laney said through the veil of sadness. She looked to the old sink and thought of washing dishes with Jamie, four hands better than two, and worried for a lifetime of love that didn't guarantee safety or happiness. The buzzer on the old Kenmore oven rattled.

"Oh! That's the roast. Clean up girls, time for dinner," Melissa said. There was a flurry of movement as the girls put away their game and ran through the kitchen to the bathroom. Melissa paused to look into Laney's teary eyes.

"Is there something else, love?"

"No, it's just been a hard couple of weeks."

"Marc filled us in weeks ago." Melissa nodded and stood on the step stool to reach the plates.

"Jesus," Laney grouched. Marc had always been close to her mother and father, ever since their grad school days.

"Sounds like you got fished outta the ocean by a handsome fella," Melissa teased over her shoulder, and Laney buried her head in her hands.

"Yeah, about that," Warren said with a twinkle in his eyes.

"Let's just—not talk about it. The day's been tragic enough." Laney shook her head and got up to help her mom set the table.

It was a little too close, Jamie thought, watching from behind the barn. He'd just gotten up the nerve to meet her parents and had driven out to the Sullivan's property but was waylaid when he'd seen her and the two girls park and walk with Warren into the house. He'd nearly lost it, seeing her pale in the cold air, circles under her eyes and worn thin with worry. He could have made it easier on them both and just knocked on the door. But he had no guarantees she wanted his help, or even if she needed it. And, Laney didn't deserve just some "hey, how've you been" moment. She needed a romance ending. If he could just stay hidden for a few more days, all the plans would be complete, and the moment of their truth would come.

Still, he had a feeling, with the small town and no doubt a vicious gossip ring, he'd have to be really careful staying out of sight. On his way back into town, he called a local bed and breakfast to hunker down in, using Leonard's name and a private account to book it anonymously.

Laney worked all morning on the ending of the first book, per Rebecca's heated request. Now that more people were blowing up her social media wanting more, having gobbled up her first three books and anxious to see if a character resembling Jameson Clark might be the next steamy hunk in Landry Sullivan's novels, she had a reason to finish. She was already brainstorming her next project, but it all seemed to come back to Jamie.

A book couldn't be built on nothing but heat and laughter, love and inexplicable loss. Could it? It was time to come up for fresh air from the thick of plotting. She was groggy and cranky. While the girls were at their Aunt Elle's, helping with her next round of Bundt cakes, she'd taken a walk to clear her head. Her brain was working through the next series and trying not to think about what he was doing at this very moment. Where he'd be traveling next...who he'd take to bed and tell the story of his father to.

She slogged through the snow of the yard, around the front drive, and pointed her boots towards the stables. She had promised Katelyn she'd take Hugh out, though she didn't know why Grant couldn't take him. Maybe the pompous, ex-racing champ needed a woman's touch. Laney walked sullenly into the stable and found Grant, sitting against the stall on the end, where his transplanted thoroughbred, Hugh, rested comfortably. Grant's legs were long in worn jeans, stretched out on the wooden and dusty floor. He looked up from his book when Laney came in.

"I'm not disturbing you, am I?" she said. Grant smiled, and Laney understood why her baby sister had fallen so hopelessly. "I hate when people interrupt my reading."

"I'm only disturbed by the tears in your eyes, lass." He closed the book and came to stand with a groan.

"Careful, you're in danger of sounding like a flirtatious, old man," she chided.

"Aye, and I am. On both counts," he chuckled.

"Katelyn asked if I could take Hugh out for her this week. That is, if it's okay with you."

"Aye, she mentioned that to me as well. And I would be much obliged. She frets over him like a wee bairn."

"Horses have always been her babies," Laney agreed and came up to Hugh, who recognized not only her Sullivan scent and demeanor, but the calm, sad energy she emitted. He nudged her hand with his nose. "You are a sweetheart, aren't you? I don't know why Katelyn calls you an asshole," she chuckled.

"Aye, well, we have that in common don't we, old man?" Grant chuckled.

"So, big brother Grant," Laney said and looked up at him. It was true that he was older and definitely bigger. She put one hand on her hip while the other scratched behind Hugh's ears.

"Aye?" He quirked an eyebrow. She looked at him pointedly, her sister vibes demanding to know what his feelings were on the matter of Katelyn's condition, he merely studied her back. "Do you need help with his tack?"

Laney scowled. "I get I'm the bookish one around here, but I can still saddle my own damn horse. I want to know what you think about my sister's situation."

"I dinna ken what you mean." Grant crossed his arms and scowled which made Laney think that maybe Katelyn hadn't even talked to him yet.

"Don't you ken?" Laney asked again. "I'm supposed to be riding Hugh for her? She had to go to the doctor? Spending days in bed, sick? Does that sound like the Katelyn we know? Hasn't she talked to you?" Grant looked down at his book, fanning through the well-worn pages while his hands trembled around them. He kept his face down as he spoke quietly.

"No. Recently she just says she's just been feeling off. I dinna ken if it's the stress of the sale or of Ian coming back into our lives," He paused to breathe. "I've brought a real mess to you and your family."

"Bullshit." Laney waved him off. "We're going to be fine. Ian can take land and money, but he can't take love. So, we're gonna be fine. I'm asking you if you know that my sister thinks she might have a little Scottish bun in her oven."

Grant blanched and his eyes widened as if he hadn't even imagined the possibility.

"She told me she couldn't get pregnant."

"That was the consensus, twelve years ago."

"So it's simply not possible, and even if it was, the way I understand it, the damage may be such that she can't carry to term."

"But how would you feel if she *was* pregnant?" Laney asked quietly. Grant stared at her for a long moment. "You know it's ok. You have a family now. People who care about you, who you can talk to. I'm your big sister too," Laney said.

"I— I dinna ken." He wiped at his nose. "Heartbroken and worried for her. Scared I might—" he paused and growled.

"Not be able to handle it?" Laney asked. Grant's head shot up.

"No! I'm scared I might hope for it too much and have," his voice shook, "have my whole world ripped away. What if she is? And she or the baby doesnae—make it?" Tears filled his eyes behind a hundred memories of loss that Laney only knew a few of. What if her sister died, and his whole world with her? Laney came to him, wrapped her arms around his waist and held him tightly.

Her misery was a small thing. She had lost Jamie, but he was still out there, doing what he did, loving his life, and in that she couldn't be completely heartbroken. But losing someone permanently; Laney sighed in his arms and suddenly Grant's embrace felt suffocating. She patted his back awkwardly before stepping away.

"We're not going to let that happen, are we?" She took his hand in hers and promised. "She's going to be just fine and you will too. You're not alone in this family," she smirked, "even when you want to be." Grant looked down at her and the clouds cleared from his features.

"How are you holding up, lass? For the record, I have ways of making a man suffer. My man Jeffers and I can make quick work of wee Jameson Clark."

"Let's not get crazy. Sending in Jeffers alone is overkill," she laughed. "Jamie wouldn't stand a chance against the two of you. I think—I think I actually screwed it up myself," she admitted and frowned. "I thought by letting him go I was doing him a favor."

"Aye, and I've done tha' myself," Grant said. "Thinking they'd be better off without us, so we push them away to protect them." Laney didn't say anything, she picked at a stray string on the cuff of her sweater while Hugh, having grown bored of the conversation, moved back to snuffling around his pen.

"Maybe what we're really doing is just protecting ourselves, huh?" Laney whispered.

"Aye," he said, twinkling in his tawny eyes. She groaned.

"What kind of idiot falls in love with Jameson Clark?" Fresh tears sprang up and she wiped them away with the tattered cuff of the sweater.

"I'm sure there are plenty of that kind around," Grant said and leaned on the wall next to her.

Laney snorted, "Yeah, true."

"The better question would be what kind of man wouldn't follow you?"

"The kind that doesn't love me," she whispered.

"Ach! You're a daft lass to think he doesn't."

"Oh, and how would you know?" she glowered up at him.

"I can't imagine a man not loving you."

"Well, you don't know me, Grant. I'm kind of an asshole," she admitted. "A bossy, pushy, asshole." Grant laughed at this.

"Who loves her whole family so much that she never does for herself the way she deserves. And that makes you loveable, Laney June."

Laney sighed. "Yeah well, maybe, I'm just not loveable to him."

"I dinna ken the inner workings of the man's heart," Grant said. "But sometimes men are thick-skulled and they need time to admit that they're helpless for a lass." He leaned down, kissed her temple, and gave her arm a squeeze. "I'd better go see to the other horses, before my lovely lass comes back to find me snogging another lovely lass." He smiled.

"Thanks, Grant," she said as he walked away. "For the big brother moment." Grant smiled, as though she'd just given him the keys to the world and nodded.

"I'll see you Sunday, at dinner," he said and went to the other end of the stables.

"How thick do you suppose Jamie's skull is?" she asked Hugh. He thrummed with a low nicker and she nodded. "Pretty damn thick. Might never get through to his brain, if it's there at all," she said softly. Hugh snuffled in reply. Jamie wasn't a white-knight type, and even if he was, he wouldn't expend the effort in coming to Sweet Valley just for her. She went to the tack room and found a saddle. Maybe a ride would clear her head.

Jamie watched from the road in his beat-up rental pick up, as Laney walked, head down, into the stables. He tipped his cap down and tried to be as inconspicuous as he could, being the only truck on the snow-covered drive up to the stables. He hunkered down and waited while she saddled her horse and led him from the barn into the cold afternoon. He watched as she lithely swung up into the saddle. She was unfortunately lighter than the last time he'd seen her, and his heart hurt to think of her soft and pliant body being deprived and weak; over him and the unwanted kiss from Annie and the publicity rollercoaster she had put into motion. The horse pranced in anticipation, and she held him with calm and patient hands.

He watched them pass through the paddock gates and into the snowy pasture. The sun lit on her hair and she turned her face into it. God, he'd missed her. Jamie waited until they had disappeared over the hill before he sank back against the seat and allowed himself to breathe.

"That was a wee bit too close, Jameson Clark," a voice chuckled from outside his window. Jamie jumped in his seat and whooped out loud. He'd been so caught up watching her that he hadn't seen the six-foot-plus Scotsman sneak up. "I don't know how long you've been out here, but I do know talking to women is highly preferable to stalking them." Grant's tone was half-teasing, half-threatening.

"I'm working on it. The talking part. Not the stalking part," Jamie stuttered. "I'm working on a plan."

"Oh? What kind of plan exactly?"

"A Hail Mary?" Jamie said without conviction. "I can't get my hopes up until I know it'll work."

"I dinna ken that it'll work at all, lad," Grant said and leaned against the door menacingly. "She's hurt and she's angry. More than usual. She's worried for her family and not in any position to do for herself when they're suffering."

"That I know about her," Jamie whispered. "You're Grant, right? Grant Tennyson?" Jamie sat up.

"Aye," Grant responded with an eagle eye for bullshit.

"You're just the man I need to talk to," Jamie said. "Can I have a moment of your time?"

"If you think I'll take your side over my sister's—" Grant began.

"No. I wouldn't think much of you as a man if you did. But

maybe if I could let you in on my idea, you can help me make sure it works. For the good of all the Sullivans." Jamie looked hopefully at Grant's discerning glare. He was an imposing man in size and countenance. All Jamie had was charm and a heart full of love for Laney. And a large bank account. It was a dangerous, stupid combination.

"Step inside my office, Clark. We dinnae have much time." Grant left his lean on the truck to walk towards the stables. Before Jamie could respond, Grant yelled over his shoulder. "She won't be out long, and I dinnae have to keep my mouth shut when she comes back!"

Jamie smiled crookedly and opened the cab door to follow him.

Laney rode the lines of the property at an even pace and tried to think of nothing but Hugh, the gentle and smooth cadence of his gait, and the cold wind against her face. But the thoughts came along anyway, in this place where there were no deadlines, meddling sisters, or children needing something. It was probably time that she started to think about what she'd do next with her life.

She didn't want to go back to her underpaid, overworked position at the university, hoping that somehow disinterested teenagers would magically come around to the art of writing and literature. She didn't know how long her newfound and unasked-for fame would last, or if it was a flash in the pan, destined to end at the next scandalous affair the media picked up on.

When the rumble of the old two-ton shook through the hard-packed ground along the road to her right, headed towards town, Hugh turned his head and made an interested grunt. Laney looked too. Now that she thought about it, hadn't she seen a similar one at her parents' the night before? Maybe someone was boarding horses or looking to. Hopefully it wasn't someone hired by Ian Tennyson.

The truck passed by and wavered in the icy ruts. Laney shook her head at the tense man at the wheel. He turned his head away as he passed. You'd think, being the middle of winter in Wyoming, whoever was driving would have gotten the hang of driving on packed snow. The truck sped away and the driver didn't wave like a friendly local. She turned Hugh back along the far trail around the property and took him into a nice canter. He was a beautiful horse and she'd missed riding. More than making her think, the joy of it took her mind off all the present worries and opened up heart space.

When she returned, she saw Hugh's stall was cleaned, and she settled him down with a short grooming and a few treats. Katelyn would be back soon from working in the clinic all day; maybe with life-changing news. Laney found the idea a welcome distraction. She walked past the office and saw Grant, feet up on the desk, working on his laptop and remembered the truck.

"Hey, uh, did you see a guy out here?"

"A guy?"

"Yeah, I saw a guy leaving the drive in an old truck." Grant stared back at her blankly, before his brow rose and he stuttered.

"Uh, I dinna ken," he said. "He was lost," he stuttered. "I gave him some direction and sent him on his way."

"Lost? People from town don't get lost out here," Laney said crossly.

"Well, I—are you saying I'm lying?"

"I'm a writer, I deal in details." She crossed her arms and scowled. "What *are* you lying about?"

"What? What are you on about? I swear the lad was lost and I helped him find his way, that's all."

"Men who swear are often liars."

"Weren't you supposed to help Melissa with dinner tonight?"

He swallowed thickly and Laney recognized a man grasping at straws.

"Mmm," she mumbled. "I'm onto you, McDreamy."

"Mc-Who?"

"Never mind." Laney waved and stalked out of the stable. That night, even while her family laughed and talked about Frankie, Elle's three-legged goat's latest antics harassing the horses, Laney's brain was preoccupied. She couldn't put her finger on what was wrong. Except that the sudden calmness of Grant in the midst of their whole world being torn away, and the stranger he was reluctant to talk about unsettled her. When she cornered Katelyn later, to ask how the doctor's appointment had gone, Grant pulled her away quickly with an apology and took Katelyn upstairs to bed.

That night, in her dreams, Laney saw the strange man crossing the field, his gait familiar, his face hidden by his tipped-down cap. Her heart raced to see him and her brain recognized him even though she fought the logical conclusion. When she woke at three in the morning, she grabbed her laptop and typed his name into the search engine. The first article that popped up was topped with their picture on the beach. Was she ever so happy? The article itself was about his latest album, now complete and scheduled for a summer release. It was the last few lines that stopped Laney's breath completely.

```
No details have been released about a tour for
the new album, leaving some to speculate that
it may not happen at all. Sources close to
Clark say he's taking personal time to help
his family.
```

Laney closed her laptop and stared into the darkness while her girls snored softly beside her. Quietly, she snuck downstairs, and started the coffee. She sat down at her parents' table, in the early morning, and waited for her family to wake. Today was the auction. Today could be the last day she had in this kitchen, on this land. Today the Sullivans' world would change. And there was nothing she could do about it but watch.

TWENTY-FOUR

IT WAS THE SADDEST AND MOST HEARTBREAKING moment Laney had ever lived. Through all of the trauma of her husband's infidelity, through their divorce, even in watching her beloved sister Elle come back from the brink of traumatic abuse, watching her parents get ready for the auction of their land made her heart tear itself in two. Warren and Melissa dressed slowly, sat across from one another at the old oak table, and drank their coffee in relative silence. Melissa's hand reached across to caress Warren's fingers. He took her hand in his, looked into her eyes, and smiled.

"For richer or poorer," he sighed, and his shoulders gave a little shrug.

"It's been a beautiful ride," Melissa returned, and gave his hand a squeeze. Laney held her cup between shaking fingers and tried to keep from crying. They didn't need her to break down now. Maybe with her bump in sales, maybe if she could hit a bestseller list, she could afford to get them a little house in town. Her brain made itself dizzy with all the ways she wanted to save them. She turned and looked out at the fields, dusted in snow, and the wind that rattled through the cottonwoods. Her girls came downstairs and sat at the table. They pulled their grandparents back into life with their cuddles and messy curls.

They had raised all three of their girls on this land. And now, all of the places she'd played and daydreamed as a kid were now going to belong to someone else. All her memories were echoes of a past that would never again be. Laney wiped away a tear and sniffed. Charlotte came up behind her and took one of Laney's hands, Sylvia grabbed the other and rested her forehead on her mother's strong shoulder. She squeezed both of them closer. They would survive this. They would find a way to take care of their family.

The auction was going to be held in the stables, so prospective buyers could survey what was being offered. It was a cold morning, and the sky was a dull grey of clouds not wet enough for snow. The wind was bitter and teased through the open doors of the building. The weather didn't dissuade the crowd from showing up in waves, and the dirt drive was quickly filled. Not just with the vultures, intent on acquiring Sweet Valley's most coveted riverfront land, but also with townspeople there to support the Sullivans.

When Laney scanned the crowd, she saw the faces of friends, people she'd known her whole life, as well as a few sharp-dressed lawyer types. Those sent to buy for bigger people. Marc and Alan had come from Laramie the night before and stayed with Elle and Blake. They'd offered to try and bid on the property, but Laney knew that even with their decent living, they couldn't afford to outbid Ian Tennyson. Judy and Ben, and all the Pryms stood in the crowd and nodded up at the Sullivans with tears in their eyes. The Morris family and even Ty Brentwood who'd given a lot of trouble to Elle when she'd first come home, were there in support. Holly, their childhood friend was there with her parents, Blake's mom and aunt, Alice O'Connor, all stood with heads hung. Nearly every person who had helped to raise Elle's barn, every pet owner who ever benefited from Warren's patient and generous care, everybody in the community stood in the crowd, showing their support for their family. Laney knew then, this was the place she wanted her kids to grow up. She knew, without a doubt, that every single one of their friends and neighbors would raise their hands if they had the money to make it work.

Elle arrived, teary-eyed but determined, and brought a whole pickup load of baked goods to set out on tables in the back. Blake stood, lean and strong beside her, holding their baby Emilee, who was almost two now. Katelyn, Grant and Jeffers, who had spent the previous day moving the horses they could keep onto Elle's property, showed up, looking nervous. Grant especially. Laney knew he must be blaming himself. Jeffers hugged her when she came up.

"Miss Laney, how are you?"

"I'm happier now that you're here," she said and gave his wiry arms a squeeze.

"I have every confidence that today will turn out better than expected." Jeffers said and winked at her. Laney leaned back. Jeffers was never one to lie or to be anything but a straight shooter. Perhaps he was simply giving hope to keep them all calm.

"I hope you're right," Laney said.

"Hey big brother," she whispered and saddled up beside Grant. "Don't fret."

"I've been tellin' him that all morning," Katelyn said from his other side. She was looking better this morning, not so gray and tired. Oddly, she didn't look like she'd been crying. In fact, Katelyn's mouth was skewed into that determined frown that meant she was about to cause trouble.

"How are you feeling?" Laney leaned around Grant to whisper. Katelyn looked at her and the corner of her mouth turned up sadly. She shrugged.

"I'll be a whole lot better once we can get through this day and Ian Tennyson is out of our lives forever."

Laney thought it was a weird way to put it. When Ian bought the land, he'd very much be a part of their lives for a long while. They'd never be able to drive past their old home, or have a memory that wasn't scarred by his brutal revenge on Grant. Grant audibly tensed between them.

"Speak of the heartless devil."

Katelyn shifted as if she intended to leap off the platform and take the man by his throat. Grant took her shoulders and pushed her behind him as though to shield her. Laney looked back to the crowd and found the pinched face of a tall man in a suit, staring daggers into both her sister and his son. He resembled Grant in small ways; the intense gaze, the thick hair, but not the warmth.

"Is that him?"

"Yes," Katelyn answered without needing to hear the name.

"We all know that he had the property lines redrawn, right? So that we'd be responsible for back taxes we didn't know about?" Laney asked, eyes never leaving Ian.

Grant seethed. "I'm more than certain that he paid to make sure of it."

Laney's cheeks lit up with anger. "How can he do that?"

"Ah, lass, ye can do anything with money." Grant swallowed. "This is what he's wanted all along. Me to suffer. Katie to suffer. This is all my fault." His voice broke. "He threatened when I left that he'd destroy you—all of you."

"This isn't your fault," Katelyn argued.

"We aren't destroyed," Laney reaffirmed. "All he'd get is a little land. But we'd get you, and that's the only thing worth fighting for."

They all looked to where their parents stood, stoic in the face of their devastating loss. A lifetime of memories wasn't built on the land, but on their daughters, their work, and love, and hardships, the laughter and tears. The people. The Sullivan name. Elle and Blake came up to the front of the auction block to stand with them, Emilee in Blake's arms and Elle's hand on her middle protectively. Grant held Katelyn close, kissed her forehead and she nestled in. Laney sighed and breathed in deeply. She wished she had someone to hold her close right now. She pulled her daughters in.

"Don't worry, we'll get along just fine," she whispered, more to herself, but loud enough the family could hear. "Don't waver. Don't let him see you sweat. Let him have all the damn land he wants."

"He's never gonna own you again," Katelyn whispered lovingly. Grant's jaw relaxed, he broke eye contact with his father and held her close in his arms. Laney watched as Ian's eyes narrowed, his anger poured from his skin in pale and trembling waves, and he raised his paddle.

The bidding began.

Laney's stomach was sick and tumbled with every counter. The Bar Nunn was in the running. They'd always wanted the water rights and the lush pastures of the protected nook of her parents' land. She almost wished they'd take it instead of Ian, and thinking the Bar was the lesser of the two evils was saying a great deal.

They went back and forth, raising each bid by hundreds of thousands of dollars, dizzying amounts into the millions. At three million, the Bar backed off. The silence cut through the cold barn and Laney looked over to her mother, who was glaring at Ian with such ferocity, she wasn't sure he wouldn't be murdered the moment he stepped onto their former land. Someone coughed. Warren, so much the better man, in his quiet way shuffled and looked down at Ian. A scuffling in the back of the crowd spread like a small wave up to the front and a new paddle hit the air.

"Five million."

The call caused an uproar of whispered awe as the crowd turned to the new bidder. The Sullivans' heads moved collectively from Ian to where the crowd had backed away. An unassuming man in a Cruzan Rum t-shirt, a borrowed Carhartt jacket, ratty ball cap, tattered jeans, and little-too-fancy-for-work boots held his paddle aloft. But his familiar-looking face wasn't on the auctioneer or on his competition. He stared at Laney, as if they were the only two people in the whole world.

"Jamie?" she whispered, her heart set to burst out of her chest. Ian swung his head around, shaken and irate.

"Five million and one hundred thousand," Ian barked.

"Careful, Tennyson. I've seen your ledgers, you're gonna let that revenge you're carrying write a check you can't cash," Jamie drawled, not even looking at the old man's face. His eyes were only for Laney. He nodded up to her. "Hey, professor."

"What are you doing here?" she whispered still in shock.

"Five million, one hundred thousand is the current bid," said the auctioneer shakily, trying to buy time. Jamie looked to the auctioneer.

"Six million."

"Jamie, don't do this—"

"Six and one," Ian argued.

"You stubborn old vulture," Jamie growled at Ian. "Who in the hell do you think you are? Trying to buy their land just to get back at your son who'd had enough of your abusive bullshit? Trying to own him? Trying to destroy a family that this whole damn town knows and loves? Don't you have a damn clue who you're dealing with?"

"I don't know you from any other redneck idiot in this town," Ian shot back. The crowd went silent with shocked anger.

"That's Jameson Clark," Katelyn said firmly. "And he's no idiot."

"Well, he's a little bit of an idiot," Laney said and her eyes filled with tears. Some of the people in the crowd, now sure in their first inklings of who he looked like, drew back and stared. The rumors of Laney Sullivan's heated affair weren't just rumors.

"I am an idiot. I let the best thing in my life walk away."

"And who would that be? Annie?" Laney smirked.

"That's my bitter old lady," Jamie smiled back at her.

"Aw, he does know you," Marc laughed from the crowd. Jamie leaned closer to the stage.

"It's you. I should have never let *you* walk away," he whispered conspiratorially.

"The bid stands at $6.1 million," the auctioneer said weakly in the middle of their exchange.

"Eight," Jamie said firmly and turned to Ian. "And don't insult me with another penny. I'll just buy the controlling shares of your stock and get it back anyway."

Ian's face turned grey, and he stumbled back. Grant looked at his father without pity and nodded at Jamie. Jamie nodded back at him.

"Jamie, you don't need to do this; you don't have to save—" Laney started.

"I know what I want, Laney June. It took me awhile to figure it out, and it took me my whole life to find it. But it's you. It's always been you."

"Eight million going once—ah hell, I'm giving it to Clark," the auctioneer said and slammed the gavel into the podium to the eruption of cheers. Ian pushed his way back through the crowd, towards a waiting Town Car. They all watched him go and knew it would be the last time he'd be seen. Jamie came up to the foot of the podium and spoke to the auctioneer.

"My guy Leonard back there, will square everything away. That should cover any of the back taxes, and clear the debt."

"What about the rest? That's a fair bit more than the debt they owed." The auctioneer asked. Warren and Melissa, Grant and Katelyn, Elle and Blake, Laney and the crowd all looked at Jamie. He looked over to Laney.

"I'll talk it over with the family and get back to you on that. For now, I got something important to do."

Leonard, a large and friendly-looking man, sticking out in

cargo shorts and socks with sandals, stepped up and shook hands with the auctioneer.

"Can we talk?" Jamie asked Laney and nodded towards her dad's office in the stable.

Laney shook her head but stepped down to follow him, just the same. Her family watched her go, bated breath and hopeful.

Laney tried to remember the month of heartache. Tried to remember that he had a tour coming up, a life he loved living. That this wasn't going to change anything. She hated that she felt indebted. But she loved him all the more for what he'd done. Confusion kept her from thinking straight until they'd reached her dad's office and he'd closed the door.

"What in the hell are you doing here?" The words burst out ridiculously from her lips as she tried to pull her heart back.

"You forgot your glasses in my bed." He smiled and turned back towards her.

"Wh—what?" she stuttered as he came closer.

"I thought you would want them back." He patted his coat pocket and pulled out the dark-rimmed monstrosities. He held them out to her. Laney stared down at his hands, his beautiful hands, and the fingers she'd dreamed of since she'd left.

"You came all the way here just to return my glasses?" Her eyes shot up to his face. His mouth and the crinkles of his eyes were knotted with desire, and amusement; hope and fear.

"Well, you're old and you can't see well." He shrugged with a smile. "I didn't want you crashing your Buick into the senior center."

Laney stared disbelievingly at him. "Jamie, you can't. You can't do this."

"You can't tell me what to do." He stepped forward and held out her glasses.

"We can't—" she stopped and her eyes filled with tears. She shook her head, hoping to shake away the thoughts of hope and love that flooded her. "I can't—"

"Can't what, Laney?" Jamie said and moved even closer, until the warmth of their bodies commingled and her eyes turned soft.

"I've worked so hard." She swallowed and choked on the tears. "I've worked so hard to try and forget, and to let you go so you can have what you want."

"Laney." He started towards her again, but she backed away around the desk and shook her head and held her hands out to stop him. Jamie sighed in frustration, hung his head, and spoke softly. "I came all this way. After I woke up and found your glasses in my bed. I couldn't just stand back and let that vindictive old bastard hurt you or your family."

"But why?"

"Well," Jamie stopped. He looked nervous. "Because, out of all the women I've been with, all the women I've dated. Out of all the women I've desired—"

"Ugh, please stop."

"They pale in comparison, Laney June. How they faded the minute I met you. I'm doing this because...well—" he shook his head.

"Well, what? And don't say it's because you wanted to keep me from misjudging traffic cones in my Cadillac."

"Buick."

"Same thing!" she bantered back.

"I love you, and they *aren't* the same thing."

"They're owned by the same comp—" Laney's words halted. "What did you say?" she said in a wispy breath. A prayer. The office, in that moment, was suddenly the quietest place she'd ever been in.

"Buicks aren't the same as Cadillacs."

She let out a frustrated grunt and threw up her hands before skirting past him and towards the door.

"I love you!" he laughed at her retreating back.

"Oh, you do not!" she said impatiently, and turned back around.

"I do so! How can you argue about that? You can't argue that!" He threw up his hands and looked light in his whole being, like a huge weight had been taken from his shoulders and he could finally breathe.

"I can so argue, because you don't! You—you just don't know any better, you're confused. It happens to men at your age," she stuttered as he prowled closer to her. She backed slowly up towards the wall.

"It's true, I am an old fool. A bona fide idiot who let the person that meant the most to me walk away."

"Was it Brody?" she said coolly as she looked up at the stubble on his chin.

"I swear to God, Laney, I'm gonna take you over my knee."

"Jamie, think about this. You miss me, okay. I miss you too but—"

"Aw, you miss me?" he said with hopeful joy.

Laney sighed and scowled. "Less every minute you're here."

"Well, you're just gonna have to get used to it," Jamie said and looked her over, bemused desire in his eyes as he traveled over her baggy, oversized sweater, jeans and bright red bog boots. "Though, if Dr. Sullivan could read my thoughts, he'd be within his rights to kick me off the property. Man, did I miss those legs of yours." Jamie's eyes twinkled. Laney crossed her hands over her chest.

"What rights? What are you talking about? You bought their land, you own it."

"Not exactly. Grant and I discussed terms yesterday."

Laney gasped indignantly. "You were the guy in the truck. Grant lied to me! You both did."

"We didn't lie! I just had him and Katelyn withhold some truths. We all knew you wouldn't let me go through with it if I asked. I just had to do it."

"You had no right!" she sputtered, trying to regain her footing.

"To what? Spend my money where I want to? Help my future in-laws?" He winked and stepped forward with a smile.

Laney glared. "How's that supposed to happen? Both the pretty sisters are already taken," she grouched.

"Stop that, or I really will bend you over my knee."

She blushed and her body thought it sounded like a good idea. Jamie took off his hat, scratched his fading hairline, ran his hand over his cold lips, and looked back up at her.

"I love *you*. I need *you*. I want *you*. You're my shore, Laney. My solid ground. It took me too long to realize it. But after you left I finally understood. I was just helpless and floating; I couldn't do anything but miss you." Laney's eyes filled with tears. "Only this time I knew what it felt like to have a safe place and I couldn't go back to the life I had before you. I only want to go forward, and I only want to do that with you."

"Why, in a world full of women clamoring to get into your life, would you settle on me?" She leaned in, inches away and aching.

"I'm not settling. If anything, I'm asking you to settle for a washed-up has-been who's tired of living out his glory days in between the legs of girls named Bambi." He smiled.

She itched to reach out to his stubbled chin, kiss him, and hold on to him for the rest of his life, all the sunshine and dark.

"Jamie," she whispered. "I love you but you can't live here in Sweet Valley. You have to play, and sing, and follow what you love; you don't belong here," she argued, but Jamie pressed in closer.

"Laney, darlin'," he whispered. "I have old ears and they've suffered too much rock n' roll. I need to hear that again." Laney bit her lip and confusion crossed her face.

"You don't belong here."

"Not that part. Start with 'Jamie, I...'" he led and took her hand in his. Tears fell down Laney's cheeks, her other hand loosened on the folds of her sweater, she felt weak and shaken, like the world was tumbling around her. When those words left her lips, it would be all over. Whether he went back to his life on the road, or stayed here with her, admitting she loved him was something she couldn't take back. But who was she kidding? She'd loved him since that dark moment in his library, since washing dishes at his mom's. Since laughing in his bed and listening to the songs he'd written. She'd always been in love with Jamie.

"Jamie, I..."

"Yep—almost there. Two more."

"I love you, you idiot," she laughed.

"Well, that's five words, and it was kinda mean, but I'll take it," he chuckled and she launched into his arms, planting a kiss on his cold lips. He threw his arms around her and they tumbled against the wall, and down into the worn couch together, a fit of legs and arms, lips and tearful giggles.

"Laney Sullivan," he breathed like he hadn't thought to do it since he'd walked into the auction. "Goddamn it, you're going to make me the happiest man in the world."

"I—I missed—I missed you so much!" Her words came in a rush of emotional release. He took her mouth even as she hiccupped and gasped.

"Why are you crying? I'm here now, you silly woman," he whispered and folded her into his arms.

"Because," Laney sniffed. "Because. It was just an island, and a magical bay, and margaritas before noon, and the ocean, and the night, and it was a romance novel and it shouldn't have been real."

"It was real to me. It was real, and it was magical, and it's our story, Laney."

She rolled on top of him, every nerve alight with need. "Are you sure you can leave behind the island?"

"Who says we have to leave it?" he whispered and ran his hands up her thighs.

"But, having to buy my parents' land? You probably had to sell—"

"Lord, Laney," he chuckled. "Sometimes I'm glad you forget who I used to be." He pushed her sweater up with his cold hands.

"Aren't we a little too old for a romp in the stables?"

"As long as there's no jellyfish hiding in here, I think we'll be fine," he chuckled, and took her mouth in a warm, slow kiss. Laney cooed softly, nudged under his chin, and rained kisses along his jawline.

"Jamie, what am I going to do with you?" She shrieked with the shock of his cold hands on her bare torso and laughed as he rolled her over into the couch.

"Well, this seems like a fine start," Jamie looked down at her, love and devotion in the twinkling of his eyes. "Lord, I missed you back. I missed every little thing about you." Laney caressed the back of his neck. She brought him close and kissed him. He sighed as his lips trailed down to kiss the line of her jaw. "I'd like to loosen some buttons on you," he said huskily.

"I don't—" She stopped to gasp as his hand found her breast beneath her shirt and she felt his body respond. "I don't have any buttons."

"I bet I can find *one*," he whispered into her ear, eliciting a delicious plea from her throat. His hand trailed down below her waistline.

"Well, thank god, you two finally figured it out." Katelyn strolled in nonchalantly to the desk to grab a pen and paper. Jamie jumped up, followed by Laney, both red-cheeked and disheveled. "Well, shit, don't stop on my account." Katelyn laughed. "I'll be outta your way in two shakes of a lamb's tail."

"Katie May, you and Grant are in for a talking to," Laney began.

"Psh, you're not so scary. Jamie, are you going to convince her to take a shower today?" Katelyn scoffed. Jamie put his arms around Laney and pulled her back to the warmth of his embrace.

"I have to finish signing some things first."

"Leonard says it's all taken care of," Warren said as he and Melissa came in. He looked discerningly at Jamie. They stood still, trying to overcome their relief and feelings of indebtedness.

"Laney June, do you know this young man?"

Jamie straightened and extended his hand. "Jamie Clark, sir.

From Knoxville, Tennessee. I'm in love with your daughter, something awful."

"Seems to be the way it happens," Warren said in his soft manner. "She make you suffer for it?"

"Yes, sir."

"Good."

"And you, young lady?" Her father turned to Laney. "You torturing this fella?"

"Every chance I get, Dad," she said, unable to stop looking at Jamie's handsome face turned to hers.

"Well, then, I guess I'm greatly in your debt, Mr. Clark." Warren took Jamie's hand in a firm shake. Jamie shook his head.

"No sir, you don't owe me a thing. Once that bill's been paid, the land reverts back to you and the family. And the extra funds will be divided up between your clinic, Katelyn's therapy center, Elle's bakery and the town's budget for the school and community center."

"But, Mr. Clark—" Melissa started.

"Please call me Jamie, Ms. Sullivan," he smiled. "I've spent a lot of my time regretting not being there for my family. And losing my dad," Jamie paused and sniffed. "Made me realize that all the fame and fortune in the world can't buy back time. If my money can buy you some peace of mind and help the woman I love be able to sleep easier at night, well then at least it's good for something. And I want to give back something to the town that raised her. It means a lot to me." Jamie said, and Laney wrapped her arms around him. Charlotte and Sylvia burst into the room suddenly.

"Is that him? He's even cuter than the pictures!"

"Momma, that was just like a romance novel!" Sylvia pushed past her sister. Laney looked at her girls and then up at Jamie. A man deserving.

"Jamie, these are my daughters, Sylvia Jane and Charlotte Elizabeth."

"Lordy, call me Charly!" Charlotte rolled her eyes and Jamie smiled. He knelt down, calmly and looked each one over. He held out his hand to Sylvia first.

"Sylvia is the name of one of my favorite authors," he said. Sylvia gave him a sideways glance; the same one Laney had won his heart with. "Cross my heart."

"What?" Laney gave him the same look. "Do not lie to my children."

"I read!" He chuckled and turned to Charlotte. "Charly, how do you do?"

"Better now you're here. She's been unbearable," Charlotte finished with an impressive eye roll before taking her hand in his.

"To be honest," Jamie whispered back, "I've been pretty unbearable myself. Just ask my mom."

"You have a mom?" she asked with awe.

"I do, and she's gonna love you." Jamie winked and rose up.

"Well? You all gonna just meet and celebrate in that musty old office or get out here?" Elle's voice, an echo of Em Sullivan, rang through the stable. Jamie took Laney's hand in hers. She sighed nervously.

"Are you ready for this?" she asked, and he knew she meant stepping into life as part of her world.

"Darlin' I'm over the moon about it," he whispered back. He smiled and his eyes crinkled, he kissed the back of her hand and they followed her family into the crowd of townspeople waiting to congratulate them.

TWENTY-FIVE

EVEN EARLY SUMMER IN MALIBU WAS TORTURE. THE heavy, warm air felt like a blanket over her skin while she straightened Sylvia's dress and searched her purse for nail clippers. She cut the loose threads from the bouquet's ribbons.

"What else you got in there? Please say snacks." Jamie began foraging through her purse. She slapped his hand away.

"They're for later, after we get through this dog and pony show." Laney fixed Charlotte's hair, and with both girls ready to walk ahead of the bride down the aisle, she stood and admired them. "You both look amazing."

"It's scratchy, and miserable, and I hate it!" Charlotte fumed.

"It's only for a little bit. You can change as soon as it's over," Laney whispered back and shrugged with a sly smile. "I give it three months."

"I don't see why I have to wear this just so Tasha can look like she cares." Sylvia shifted uncomfortably.

"Well, sometimes we have to do things for the people we love." Jamie sighed and strained against his tie.

"I don't love her," Sylvia returned.

"I know. I brought you both jeans and t-shirts to change into as soon as possible," Jamie drawled and Laney smiled up at him.

"And my cowgirl hat?" Charlotte asked with wide blue eyes.

"Yes, ma'am." he nodded.

"You're the best!" Charlotte said and hugged him tight around the waist. "I still don't see why I can't just change now. Nobody's gonna care what we look like, they'll all be looking at the blushin' bride."

Jamie knelt down, in his suit, with complete sympathy for the youngest and her slightly snide twang. Charlotte had captivated Jamie like two old souls that had been apart for too long. She looked back at him, her eyes went suddenly deep like the forest at night and Jamie couldn't look away.

"What is it? Charly? Is something else wrong?" he whispered.

"Your daddy is proud of you. He would tell you that you don't have to be sorry. He loves you forever and for always."

"Charlotte Elizabeth—" Jamie's throat closed.

"He loves Momma too. He knows she's your North Star. He's so proud of you, Jamie." Charlotte's tiny hands framed his face before her eyes lit back up and she kissed him on the cheek and patted his head. "Thanks for bringing my hat!" She danced off, like nothing had happened.

Laney nudged him, where he was still kneeling, chills running through his body, and his heart full to exploding.

"What's wrong, Clark? Arthritis?"

Jamie looked up at her, on one knee.

"He loves you."

"Uh, what?" She leaned back.

"I—I mean, my dad—he would have loved you." He stood and Laney straightened his tie with a smirk.

"I would have loved him too. You okay?"

"You're my North Star, Laney June," he whispered and put his arms around her.

"Listen to you sweet talk! Are you trying to get me alone in the coat check?"

"No! It's not that at all. I just, wait—is that an option?"

"Only if I'm not wearing panties under this dress," she said and waved nonchalantly to the kids now running wild around the expensive fountain, to the dismay of the wedding organizers, who tried to chase them down in their heels and slippery dress shoes. Bare feet and trouble making would always be faster.

"Laney Sullivan, you can't just say things like that to your husband and expect me not to respond."

"I'll page 176 you so hard," she whispered huskily in his ear and Jamie's hand tightened on her backside. He pulled her close to him.

"But where will we find a live chicken at this hour?" he whispered back. Laney burst out with a beautiful laugh.

"You and I aren't on the same page, Clark." Jamie pulled her in and kissed her deep and full.

"Professor, we can write whatever pages we want."

"Yes, we can." She smiled up at him, kissed his jaw, and the world fell away around them. Other people may have stopped, and stared, whispered behind their backs that didn't they know that guy? Wasn't he famous? Jamie held her closer, buried his face in her soft braid and felt her heart beat against his chest.

"By the way—"

"Hmm?" he hummed, sweetly kissing his way down her neck.

"I could have sworn you called yourself my husband."

"Are you really not wearing panties?" he interrupted.

"Are you planning on being my husband?" she countered.

"I wanna be."

"Then, no."

"No? Listen Lane, I think it's time that we at least talk about —"

"No, I'm not wearing panties. I'll see you in the coat check in five minutes, Jamie Sullivan, and don't keep your wife waiting."

"I wouldn't dream of it."

She didn't know what he was doing, but he was sure making a hell of a lot of noise, Laney thought as she scowled into the screen and tried to not lose focus. The three-book contract she'd signed after the media debacle of Jameson Clark's fan base rioting was done, and now she was moving on to a new project, along with a podcast interview about writing and parenting. Late spring was turning into summer and she'd taken the leap into a new life.

After David and Tasha's wedding, she'd left her job at the University and used her book advance to put a down payment on a small bungalow by the river in Sweet Valley. Jamie insisted on the one with the biggest tree in the backyard. He'd converted an old, local radio station into a studio and spent his time writing songs, finishing his album and driving her crazy with laughter and lovemaking. But right now, he was driving her crazy with the off-beat hammering that was coming from the backyard.

Jamie had suggested she work from the kitchen that morning, and avoid her office, before he'd headed out with a tool belt he'd borrowed from Blake. He told her not to worry, he, the girls, Blake, Marc, Jeffers and Grant were gonna do some 'boring man stuff'.

"What the hell is that supposed to mean?"

"Don't worry about it, Mom! He's gonna let us use power tools," Charlotte said and tied back her wayward curls. Marc helped and kissed the top of her head.

"It's going to be fab, but you need to stay in here and get your work done. Leave the manual labor to us manly types," Marc said and squeezed Laney's shoulder as he escorted Charlotte out.

"Now wait a goddamn minute—"

"We have to learn these skills sometime," Sylvia argued with a shrug. "Building an empire takes training," Laney couldn't help but smile. David had never wanted to spend time with them, not the way Jamie did. Since moving to Sweet Valley, he hadn't missed a play, concert, rodeo, or bake sale. So, when Jamie came into the kitchen, kissed her temple, and whispered in her ear "I can keep the tool belt on for later, if you want," she could only shake her head and give in. Every girl *should* know how to use a power tool, and she had work to do, and at least they would all be outside in the sunshine, playing in their big yard, with a man who loved them very much. Truth was, she wanted to be out there with them, until she'd heard the buzzsaw and had to put on her headphones to focus.

Now it was late in the afternoon and she was tired of wondering what was going on. She slid her headphones off and stood up from the tall island chair, stretched, popped her back and walked, barefoot, through the cozy bungalow and its lowkey, comfortable furnishings. When she got to the back of the house, through the living room, she opened the door to her office, once an old porch, and the noise blossomed even louder. Jamie had hung a tarp over the windows facing the backyard so the small room of bookshelves, file cabinets, picture boards, and post-it-note covered walls was bathed in an eerie blue light from the late afternoon sun. She went to the door, yanked it open, and tried to push the tarp away when the sanding suddenly stopped and she heard his voice.

"Well, I think that'll about do it!"

She stepped tentatively through, lifting the tarp at an angle to not be as conspicuous. There, in the large cottonwood tree, overlooking the banks of the river, ten feet up in the branches, was a beautiful, still unstained treehouse. Below, Grant, Blake, and Katelyn, who was rubbing her growing belly, all stared up with hands in pockets and nodded, as if they were the county building inspectors. Marc was piling up the scrap from the project and mopping his forehead with a towel that Jeffers had handed him.

"Jamie, what did you do?" Laney gasped and held her hands to her mouth. All heads swung her way.

"Momma! You're supposed to stay inside!" Charlotte reprimanded.

But Laney's joy overshadowed any other thought, and her eyes filled with tears. Jamie smiled, sawdust covering his cap and his face smeared with dirt. She looked back up to the beautiful octagon, made with sturdy oak and redwood, with its own wrap-around porch, windows, and a ladder. There was even a rope that a kid could swing into the river from one side of the porch. On the other side, he'd hung a swing big enough for three.

"The last thing this house really needed was a treehouse for Laney," he said with a smile.

Katelyn came up to her with a smile even brighter, her skin glowing, and now into the sixth month of a very healthy pregnancy. Though she'd been unable to ride Hugh, she'd been keeping busy in the therapy ring and helping to get their business, which Jamie had funded, off the ground. Laney scowled with worry at her.

"You'd better have not had anything to do with this," she reprimanded.

"Easy, momma hen," Katelyn scoffed. "I was in charge of the little stuff; Marc, your girls and Jamie did the heavy lifting. Jeffers drew up the plans, of course."

"Should have seen the shoddy first draft Jameson brought me," Jeffers shook his head. "Might as well have been done in crayon."

"What did Grant do?" Laney asked.

"Sat around and looked pretty." Katelyn said.

"Hey!" Grant laughed.

Laney stared back up at the treehouse and took Jamie's hand in hers. Never in her life had she thought she'd find this kind of happiness. The day-to-day work, the relationship where they each followed their passions, supported each other, the playful heat of their bedroom, the appreciation they showed one another.

"I love you," she whispered and with tears threatening to spill over, she kissed him, dust, sweat, and all.

"I love you back, Laney June."

She nearly burst with excitement when he led her up the ladder to the rough but well-built little house above the world. He showed her all of the windows, the built-in desk, the space for a bed and hooks for hammocks.

Her laughter and joy spread down to the yard, and Katelyn hugged a sweaty Blake with one arm and Grant with the other.

"I haven't heard her that happy in forever. It's such a pretty sound."

"Aye," Grant whispered and kissed her forehead.

"I'm sure she'll be back to her surly self in no time," Blake teased.

"I hope not anytime soon." Charlotte shook her head.

"Nah, I think she's over that dark, and I reckon if it ever comes again, Jamie will be there to pull her up." Sylvia nodded as Jamie's laugh floated down.

"I hope you're right, short stack." Marc mussed her short hair and pulled her in for a hug. "She's unbearable in self-pity mode."

"I still can't believe he convinced her to get married again," Blake said.

"I think she asked him," Katelyn sighed. "But who knows when it'll happen? They seem to be just fine even if they don't."

"Living in sin is pretty fun," Grant said, arching his eyebrow at Katelyn.

"I told you I'd make an honest man of you any day, down at the courthouse!" Katelyn said.

"And I told you I want a real wedding, with a suit and flowers, and you in a dress," he argued playfully. Katelyn made a gagging motion with her finger down her throat.

"Gonna make me wear seven hundred pounds of tulle with two in the oven?" The circle became quiet. Blake's smile faded; his face went pale.

"Wait—two?" Blake looked down at Katelyn.

Grant shrugged. "She doesn't do anything small, little brother."

"Jesus, does Mom know?" Blake asked.

"I suspect she will now." Katelyn screwed her mouth up teasingly. Jeffers brought over the tray full of iced tea, lemonade, and a pitcher of margaritas. On his heels followed the short floppy white dog, whose hair grew over his eyes. When Jeffers stopped, the dog stopped. When Jeffers turned, the dog turned.

"The Sullivans are going to need a lot of diapers." Blake shook his head, thinking that he and Elle were expecting their second not long after Katelyn.

"Many hands will make light of the work," Jeffers said, "and I do love little ones," he smiled overjoyed with any and all talk of the babies. Katelyn sauntered over and hugged him.

"Elle's gonna shit bricks when she realizes she will have an *au pair*. I hope that your dog likes babies."

"Teddy is the finest ranch dog in town, exceptionally good at herding any crowd, goats or human." Jeffers argued with a smile, and Teddy barked in agreement.

Laney and Jamie both climbed down from the treehouse and met them. Laney handed out hugs and kisses, smiles and happy tears to each and every one of them, including Teddy.

On the banks of a river, where a young girl once dreamed of writing fantastical stories, she finally got to see her own story play out. But not in the way a romance would—just in the way that a life does.

BACK TO THE 80S

We hope that you liked this release from 5 Prince Publishing, LLC. Please enjoy the following excerpt of Back to the 80s by S.E. Reichert and Kerrie Flanagan, available now at 5PrinceBooks.com

BACK TO THE 80S

THE FIRST THING BLAINE REYNOLDS' MOTHER TAUGHT her was that she was named after a main character in an 80s movie. The second thing was that if we don't remember our past, we are doomed to forget the journey of our humanity. Humans were cyclical like that. Advancements and wars, rebuilding and flourishing. Old countries demolished, new ones beginning.

But sometimes you could freeze time and remember when things were simpler. Sometimes you could even find your happiness again, nestled in a shop left to you by your mom that paid homage to the best decade ever—the 80s.

Blaine stared into the eerie eyes of the red-haired Cabbage Patch Kid doll, its chubby cheeks sprinkled with freckles above a freakishly small mouth. This was definitely not part of her happiness. Some of the items from private collectors or donations to the shop were too much, even for her. She shook away the chill that ran up her spine and set down the creepy new tenant before moving on to the next box. How and when her mom had acquired so much, she'd never know. It had been two years since her mother had passed away, and Blaine was finally getting to the last boxes from the old storage unit on the outskirts of town.

She opened each box with a sort of giddy anticipation. Her mother's version of buried treasure. Each box contained remnants from the past: Casio keyboards, Walkman tape players, boxes from cereal no longer made, like Mr. T's Crunchy Corn and Oats. Autographed photos from Don Johnson and movie posters from the Cinema House in Old Town, some of them, like *E.T.*, were tattered around the edges but still sellable.

A lot of the items were still in good shape and could be sold at the store. Blaine couldn't believe she hadn't gone through this stuff sooner, but she never seemed to be at a loss for items. Oddly, for all the items she auctioned, she still managed to find others to buy in the thrift stores around town and bargain sites online to sell in her store. Sometimes people just donated their old toys and tech, because they wanted their childhood treasures to find a home outside of their crawlspace and be loved again. It made the small strip mall store seem crowded with treasures of an era before Blaine was even born. Her mom's favorite decade.

The 80s had become Blaine's favorite too. The music, the movies, the glory days of MTV and music videos. Every day, she went into work surrounded by the neon pink and cool turquoise aura of a time when the world seemed happy. A time when she could imagine her mother in scrunchy socks and big permed hair, dancing to Wham! and Cyndi Lauper Ten years before she'd ever had a child of her own, her mom had been a child of the decade of excess.

Blaine smiled at the photo above the cash register, of her and her mom fifteen years ago at a Mötley Crüe concert, both rocking ripped jeans and Converse. Even though her mom was gone now, being in the shop was like getting to hang out with her every day.

The tinkling of the bells above the door roused her from the memory as she watched JT, purple hair tucked into a Slipknot ball cap, in orange overalls and lime green Converse, scurry in with a blast of the early spring morning air. The way JT came at her with pursed lips could only mean the best gossip had just come from the salon next door.

"You're not going to believe what I just heard," JT said, coming around the back row of mixed cassette tapes and players, some in boxes, some as is.

"Who's sleeping with Deb now?" Blaine laughed and tucked the Cabbage Patch Kid behind the counter. That might be an online special only. She couldn't imagine putting it out on the shelf to stare at her all day.

"No, Blaine, this is bad—"

"Worse than sleeping with Deb?" she asked.

JT shook their head and tried to take a deep gulping breath.

"Oh, God, what is it? Did someone die? Did the sewer back up again?"

JT, in their trademark dramatic fashion, put their hands on the glass counter, leaned into the harrowing news stuck inside, and took a deep breath. Then in a whoosh—

"The Petersons are selling the mall."

Blaine leaned back and shook her head.

"Well, that's not such a big thing. We all knew they were getting ready to retire. I mean, the new people will still have to sign into the rent control addendum, right?"

JT shook their head. "No. Blaine, they didn't sell to another property manager."

"Well? Who did they sell to?"

"Morales Construction."

"Mor—Morales? Like *the* Morales Construction. The ones who've been putting up swanky apartments all over town?" Blaine squeaked. Her heart ticked one beat off. The Morales family weren't landlords. They were demolitionists. Leveling dozens of old buildings in the growing town to make room for larger, more modern amenities.

"That's them—"

"But, they wouldn't. I mean, the mall's been here since, well, forever." Blaine paused, thinking of her mother's shop and how hard she'd worked to build up her clients and establish her business. She thought of JT's salon, The Mane Event, and even Talon Karate; all the little shops and their struggling owners. The Petersons had been kind to let them sign a rent-controlled agreement and keep their costs manageable. The older couple had especially loved Blaine's quirky mother.

Morales Construction only loved neat bottom lines, modern buildings, rising profits, and all things new and shiny.

"I'm sorry Blaine. I think we're all gonna be out of a home in a couple of weeks."

Blaine didn't like getting too emotional, or jumping into drama if it could be avoided. She was level-headed, even if at times a little day-dreamy, so to hear that the foundation of her life was in danger of being pulled out from underneath her brought all her high-flying plans down to the hard ground. Where would she go? She couldn't afford rental space in the booming town of Marshall, Colorado. Rent, mortgage rates, and even just the cost of living had been going up for the last decade.

"I'll figure something out," Blaine said.

"Something?"

"Well, we can't just give up!"

"I'm sorry, maybe you didn't hear me the first time, when I mentioned MORALES CONSTRUCTION," JT enunciated the words slowly.

"I'm sure they can be reasoned with—"

"I heard that John Morales once tore down an orphanage to build a parking garage." JT leaned in for emphasis.

"Well, that's just ridiculous. I'm sure he did not."

"Okay, maybe not, but I could see it happening."

"JT," Blaine sighed, "let's just keep calm."

"Easy for you to say. You have a house and all of this awesome inventory. You'd be fine working out of your home, selling the stuff on eBay. My apartment's sink isn't big enough for half the hair I get!"

"I have no desire to switch to an eBay business and I don't have enough room for all of these things—" she stopped to look out at all the memorabilia. "And Charles Dumar would be traumatized if I moved this next to his cage." She pulled out the creepy Cabbage Patch Kid and its face met JT's. They yelped and jumped back.

"What the hell is that thing?"

"Top selling toy of 1983."

"Unbelievable. Your guinea pig is definitely going to have a heart attack if you show him that. This all makes sense now. I believe that thing is what cursed us for demolition. Or at least caused the downfall of the stock market in '87."

"This?" Blaine looked down at the doll and back to JT's pale face. "Nah, she's sweet."

"In a Chucky had a baby with an actual cabbage kind of way." They both laughed and then fell silent.

"What are we gonna do, JT?" Blaine said and hugged the strange doll to her chest. She looked around the shop that might be gone in a matter of weeks.

"I don't know, Blaine. But if I know you, you'll find some way to make it harder for them to move us."

"I'll try." Blaine sighed, drummed on the top of the doll's plastic head with her fingers and bit her lip. She had to try. They agreed to invite the other shop owners for drinks that Friday, after the Morales' first inspection of the mall. Blaine hoped she'd have something to contribute by that time.

PLEASE REVIEW

We hope you've enjoyed *Composing Laney, book 3 in the Sweet Valley Series*. Please take a moment to rate and review the book, as every review helps our authors. Thank you.

Rate and Review: Composing Laney

Meet The Author

Sarah Reichert (S.E. Reichert) is a writer, novelist, poet and blogger. She is the author of the Southtown Harbor Series and is a member and the Youth Coordinator of the Writing Heights Writers Association. She is also the webmaster for WyoPoets. Her work has been featured in The Fort Collins Coloradoan, Haunted Waters Press, "Sunrise Summits: A Poetry Anthology", "Rise: An Anthology of Change", Poetry Ireland Review, and "We Are the West: A Colorado Anthology" among other journals across the country. Her novella, "Saturn Rising" was produced as a five-part audiocast from Ngano Press Studios, and she recently signed a 3-book contract with 5 Prince Publishing for release in 2023.

She is the head writer of *The Beautiful Stuff*, a blog about writing and fostering a creative and balanced life which aims to help new writers get their start. Reichert lives in Fort Collins with her family. In her non-writing hours, she is a mother to two teenage girls, loves being outdoors preferably hiking up a mountain or sitting next to an ocean, and is a 2nd degree Black Belt in Kenpo Karate JuJitsu.

OTHER TITLES FROM 5 PRINCE PUBLISHING